Australian
Dreams

FIONA McCALLUM

Published in Great Britain 2015
by Mills & Boon, an imprint of Harlequin (UK) Limited,
Eton House, 18-24 Paradise Road, Richmond, Surrey, TW9 1SR

© 2011 Fiona McCallum

(Originally published as *Paycheque* in Australia.)

ISBN: 978-0-263-91548-8

010-0815

Harlequin (UK) Limited's policy is to use papers that are natural, renewable and recyclable products and made from wood grown in sustainable forests. The logging and manufacturing processes conform to the legal environmental regulations of the country of origin.

Printed and bound in Spain
by CPI, Barcelona

Fiona McCallum spent her childhood years on the family cereal and wool farm outside a small town on South Australia's Eyre Peninsula. An avid reader and writer, she decided at the age of nine that she wanted to be the next Enid Blyton! She completed her final years of schooling at a private boarding school in Adelaide.

Having returned to her home town to work in the local council office, Fiona maintained her literary interests by writing poetry and short stories, and studying at TAFE via correspondence. Her ability to put into words her observations of country life saw a number of her articles published in the now defunct newspaper *SA Statewide*.

When her marriage ended, Fiona moved to Adelaide, eventually found romance and followed it to Melbourne. She returned to full-time study at the age of twenty-six and graduated with a Bachelor of Arts (Professional Writing) from Deakin University. While studying, she found herself drawn to writing fiction, where her keen observation of the human condition and everyday situations could be combined with her love of storytelling.

After brief stints in administration, marketing and recruitment, Fiona started Content Solutions, a consultancy providing professional writing and editing services to the corporate sector. Living with a sales and marketing executive and working on high-level business proposals and tenders has given Fiona great insight into vastly different ways of life.

Fiona continued to develop her creative writing skills by reading widely and voraciously and attending short courses. In 2001 she realised her true passion lay in writing full-length fiction and in 2002 completed her first manuscript.

In early 2004 Fiona made the difficult decision to return to Adelaide alone in order to achieve a balanced lifestyle and develop a career as a novelist. She successfully re-established her consultancy and now enjoys the sharp contrast between her corporate work and creative writing.

In memory of my father, Tony McCallum,
to whom I owe my courage and tenacity

Prologue

Claire woke with a jolt and noticed blue and red lights flickering behind the curtains. She checked the time and realised it was after one o'clock. Keith's side of the bed was still empty.

The doorbell chimed. Alarm gripped her as she dragged her pink towelling dressing gown over her pyjamas. She pounded down the hall, heart racing as scenarios filled her head. It had to be urgent to warrant flashing lights—a break-in, an accident, perhaps a missing child. The poor people; she'd help any way she could.

Claire's heart ached for those who had to deliver the bad news. Beginnings of conversations ran through her mind as she unlocked the main door.

The female half of the uniformed couple spoke.

'Claire Louise McIntyre?'

'Yes?'

'I'm Senior Constable Penny Irving. This is Constable Jason Braxton. Can we come in, please?'

Claire swallowed and felt the blood drain from

her face as she nodded, unlocked the screen door and stepped aside. She was dazed, rooted to the floor.

The trio stood awkwardly in the passage, its checked black and white tiles suddenly harsh and busy. The young constable gently closed the heavy wooden door, sending a loud echo reverberating through the hall. Claire pulled the collar of her robe tighter. She knew she should ask what they wanted, why they were there, but also knew she didn't want to know.

The fog of Claire's mind lifted a little as the police-woman suggested they sit. Her arm moved as if uncon-nected to her and she motioned towards the lounge. The trio walked single file with Claire in between. If they were trying to offer comfort, it wasn't working. Instead, she felt like a criminal being prevented from escaping.

Seated, the spacious lounge room felt a third the size. The policewoman sat next to her, gently wringing her hands in her lap. The male officer remained standing, slightly off to the side, shifting his weight.

'Jason, perhaps you could make us some tea, with plenty of sugar,' the policewoman whispered. Silently, the uniformed man moved away. Claire might have laughed if they weren't here doing this in her house. Didn't that only happen on *The Bill*?

After a few moments the policewoman took a slightly deeper breath, looked up at Claire and said, 'I'm afraid I have some terrible news. There's been an accident— a car accident. I'm afraid there was nothing the para-medics could do. Keith…'

Claire frowned, not comprehending when she heard his name. Unable to focus, she suddenly wished she was a child who could go to her room and let the adults deal with this. Whatever *this* was, it was bad.

Her head was fuzzy again. She couldn't grasp exactly what was happening. There had been an accident. Someone had run a red light. *Well, it wouldn't have been Keith, that's for sure. He's such a careful driver.*

'I'm really sorry. They did everything they could.'

Claire nodded and looked up as a mug of steaming tea appeared in front of her. She accepted it with two shaking hands and drew it close to her chest. Her bottom lip quivered and tears began to spill down her cheeks.

Looking down into the milky liquid, she realised that nothing would be the same again—her life had changed forever.

One

Claire rolled onto her stomach and peered at the clock radio on what had been Keith's bedside table. She'd woken early, before dawn, and had managed to doze off again. Now she was surprised to find it was after ten. Anyway, it was Sunday: she'd laze about till lunchtime if she wanted.

Even after four months she still found herself aching for Keith's embrace, his sweet musky scent and...

Snippets of dreams came back to her. In one they'd showered together and then made love in the lounge, on the plush rug in front of the gas log fire. It had been beautiful: him tender, giving; she responding, clinging to him.

She'd woken hot and sweating, despite it being chilly outside, instantly feeling embarrassed at her arousal. But it hadn't been Keith's face at all, had it? No, the face had been blank. Who had it been? She shook her head, trying hard to remember. After a few moments she gave up.

In another dream he'd been lying beside her saying he loved her, that it was okay to move on, that it wouldn't mean she loved him any less. 'I know you have needs,' he'd said with a wink, before drifting from her slumbering memory.

That had definitely been Keith. His face now came to her clearly: the slightly crooked, cheeky grin; the fringe he insisted on keeping too long to cover the scar above his left eye—apparently the result of a silly, drunken escapade at university. She'd never heard the full story— he'd always managed to sidestep her question with a well-timed hug. Now she'd never know. And she'd never have another of his comforting, bear-like hugs.

A tear escaped and her throat caught on the forming lump. She'd give her life for just one more hug with Keith. Would she ever find anything so comfortable again? Did she even want to look?

'Oh, Keith,' she whispered. If only she'd shown him more affection and not taken their contentment so much for granted.

Claire roughly wiped the tears from her cheeks with the back of her hand, pushed aside her mop of unruly hair and sat up.

Claire had a quick shower and stood—towel wrapped around her—studying her reflection in the bathroom mirror. Did her hairstyle make her features appear hard? For years she'd been talking about getting her hair cut like Jennifer Aniston's—chipped into so that it wasn't so full down the back and sides—but had never been brave enough to go through with it. She'd always kept it plain, practical—straight across the bottom and in a ponytail to keep it away from her face. It was the way Keith had liked it. She'd never dyed it, either—always stuck with her natural medium brown shade. Berna-

dette and her hairdresser had both given up trying to
talk her around years ago.

Claire held her hair away from her face and turned
left and right, examining the effect in the mirror. Did
she dare? Keith was no longer there to complain. She
let it down again. Bernie was right: short didn't suit
her. Anyway, she'd feel too self-conscious. But she
could definitely do with less bulk around her face. She
dragged her brush through her hair a couple of times
and put it into a ponytail.

She ran her electric toothbrush around her mouth
while roaming the bedroom—pulling up the quilt and
straightening the pillows. She had her underwear drawer
open, about to pull out socks, knickers and bra, when
her toothbrush buzzed, signalling her two minutes was
up. She turned it off, stood it on the edge of the vanity
beside Keith's and rinsed her mouth. Then she added a
thin layer of foundation to her face and neck with her
fingers, swept the mascara brush once across each set
of lashes, added two layers of deep rose-pink 'God-
dess' lipstick, blotted with toilet paper and returned to
the bedroom to get dressed.

Claire McIntyre was conservative through and
through. Her uniform rarely varied: navy or grey skirt
suit cut just below the knee for work; jeans or tailored
pants and shirt or knit for weekends. Evening wear was
a lolly-pink wrap over a little black dress—if size twelve
was still considered little. It ended four inches above
the knee and showed just the right amount of décolle-
tage to straddle the fine line between tarty and prudish.
Despite the current trend for bare, bottle-tanned legs
and towering stilettos, Claire insisted on sheer, smoky-

coloured pantyhose and sensible plain black shoes with ample room for her toes.

Even her career was conservative. Yes, she'd had different roles, but she'd been with the same company for twelve years when the done thing was to move on every few. But she was happy enough; why go through the stress of looking for something else, just so your CV would show you were progressive? Anyway, there were leave entitlements to think of. Claire wasn't exactly thrilled with her job but enjoyed the security of a regular paycheque.

She'd joined the national advertising firm Rockford and Associates as a marketing graduate. Hard work and long hours had seen her move into a senior role in account management. Three years ago she'd been promoted to Client Relationship Manager for one of the firm's largest clients, AHG Recruitment.

Since losing Keith, she had been all the more grateful for the familiarity of her open-plan cubicle and routine tasks: a welcome—if mundane—source of stability in her life.

But now Claire felt something within her stirring: a strange kind of yearning. But for what? It wasn't Keith. It wasn't a dull sad ache. This was different—more a restlessness.

She focussed on her hair again. Knowing her luck, the Aniston look was now as fashionable as the mullet. Maybe her hairdresser had better ideas—could she offer free rein? Claire felt excited at the prospect, even a little empowered. Yes, she'd definitely phone for an appointment.

Bernadette was right: if grief was like a brick wall, each step towards recovery was the removal of a brick, then a layer. Eventually she'd be able to step over the top and be free. Then she'd look back at the good times without tears and remember the not-so-good times with detachment. But it took time. The trick was to allow the bricks to come away when the mortar loosened— and not to stop their progress with a slap of concrete.

Of course, she wouldn't cut her hair without a second opinion from her best friend. She'd mention it when they next spoke.

Claire and Bernie had known each other since Pony Club and primary school. They'd even studied the same course at university and then started their first jobs at the same company—but in different departments. Twelve months in, Bernadette had been fired for rejecting her boss's advances with a swift slap across his face. Claire had considered protesting by leaving with her, but only for a second; she didn't have the courage to quit without the security of another job to go to. Thankfully Bernie had understood.

The episode had sent Claire into a spin of worrying about what her friend would do, but Bernadette had seen it as a sign she was ready to pursue her dream: opening a nursery specialising in old-fashioned plants, design and accessories. Apparently the Adelaide Hills area was full of people wanting old English-style gardens—God only knew why with the water restrictions.

Regardless, and despite only being in her early twenties, Bernadette had built a successful business on box hedges, white gravel and distressed wrought-iron outdoor furniture.

Claire regularly shook her head in wonder and sometimes felt a twinge—but of what she wasn't sure. Not jealousy; she would never wish her friend anything but all the very best. Seeing Bernadette chasing her dream made her wonder about her own choices. Still, Claire was no different to about ninety-five percent of the population.

Besides, there was no way she'd want to deal with the public every day. She'd spent a lot of time at the nursery, occasionally even manning the till. One virtue Claire McIntyre did not possess was patience, and tolerance with other people's indecision was in pretty short supply as well. She would have strangled someone by now if she was Bernadette and couldn't believe Bernie hadn't.

Bernadette had always been the quintessential redhead. Her uncontrollable curls stood out like a warning, something Claire realised—too late—on the day they met.

It was their first Pony Club rally and they were both eleven. Bernie was on a small cranky grey pony, Claire on a larger bay. Claire had accidently got too close to Bernie's pony and it had darted sideways in fright, almost causing Bernie to fall off. Bernie shouted so loudly that Claire's mother heard the commotion. Grace McIntyre stormed across the arena to tell her daughter off. Mortified, Claire turned her tomato-red face— first to the instructor and then to Bernie—and said she was sorry.

Bernie had smirked, tossing her head in the air before moving her pony away. Claire decided she didn't like this Bernadette girl very much. But later, Bernie had come up to her at the tap while she was filling her water bucket and said it wasn't fair how much Claire's mother had overreacted. They'd been firm friends ever since.

Bernie used to fly off the handle with the slightest

provocation. Once she got started, she wouldn't un-
clamp her teeth from an argument, even if she knew
she was wrong. It was probably the reason she was still
single and most definitely why corporate life hadn't
been for her. You just couldn't scream at your boss that
he was a dickhead one day and ask for a raise the next.
And slapping him was a definite no-no.

But she had mellowed since finding her 'place in the
cosmos', as she called it. Now her fire was being fuelled
with passion, and she was a lot calmer.

Claire bit her bottom lip. No, when it came to Bernadette, if she was envious, it was of her state of mind.
Bernie glowed with contentment and enthusiasm whenever she spoke—and not just about the business. Even
late deliveries weren't enough to unsettle her. She'd just
shrug and say that they'd turn up when they were ready.
According to Bernie, everything would work out in the
end. And for her it usually did.

For the thousandth time, Claire wondered at the rea-
soning behind Keith being taken from her, and then dismissed the thoughts as ridiculous. There was no reason.
He'd had a tragic accident and she just had to get over
it. And what about her father's accident? Why had that
happened?

Whatever the reasons, nothing could alter the fact
that she was having the worst year possible. Things
always happened in threes: she and Bernadette had
pointed out so many instances before. Since Keith's
death and Jack's accident, it had become a taboo subject. Claire wondered what else she was to be faced
with. The doctors had assured her Jack's injuries
weren't life-threatening—he'd come out of his coma

when he was ready. It was just a matter of time. But how much time? It had already been a month.

Claire was relieved she hadn't been the one to find Jack crumpled in a silent heap on the ground. Thank goodness neighbours Bill and Daphne Markson had thought to invite him over for an early dinner—luckier still they had thought to drop in on their way back from town instead of phoning. She knew she should spend more time with her father. She had visited a lot in the months after her mother's death five years ago, but gradually the pace of work and social life in the city had engulfed her again. In the past year, she was lucky to see him every three weeks.

Until the accident, of course. She was now spending a couple of hours each day after work sitting with him—time she didn't really have to spare. She felt guilty every time she turned up because invariably Bill and Daphne were already there—Bill reading the paper and Daphne knitting. It was a jumper for Jack, made from chunky homespun natural grey lamb's wool.

Claire tried to tell herself it was different for them because they were retired, but felt guilty all over again when she remembered that they'd driven nearly forty minutes to be there, not ten as she had. But they didn't have an inbox full of six hundred emails waiting to be read and responded to. Claire had tried to sit and do nothing, but on the third day had given up and started bringing her laptop to make better use of the time. She didn't think you were allowed to use electronic equipment in hospitals, but no one had told her off yet.

Claire checked her watch—visiting hours at the hospital were starting soon. She ran down the stairs, grabbed her laptop bag from the kitchen bench and her keys from the bowl on the hall table. Having punched the code into the security system, she deadlocked the door and pulled it shut behind her.

Claire sat in the vinyl chair beside her father's hospital bed, looking up from her laptop to study his features. Thank God he hadn't needed to be hooked up to a ventilator. She couldn't imagine the agony of deciding when and if to turn it off.

Lying there under the pale blue cotton blanket, he looked peaceful, as though he was just sleeping. Maybe the nurses were right: his body needed the rest and time to heal. When it was ready he'd just wake up.

A week or so ago, one of the nurses had said she thought he needed to be given a reason to wake up. But Claire had nothing to offer. She couldn't chatter with excitement about her life with Keith. There was now no chance of her bringing news she was pregnant with his first grandchild. And the only other important thing in her life—her job—had never interested him much anyway. And it wasn't as if she could tell him what she'd done with the horses.

She hadn't really had a choice. Bill and Daphne had offered to look after them rather than see them got rid of. But they weren't horse people, and there was a lot more to it than just chucking a bale of hay over the fence every few days. Bernie had offered, but Jack McIntyre hated the idea of being a burden as much as Claire did. And she sure as hell couldn't be driving up there every day.

It really had been the only thing to do. She was certain her father would have agreed. So why did she feel so guilty? And why couldn't she get it off her chest, even if she wasn't totally convinced he could hear her?

She felt like a complete idiot—and totally self-conscious doing it—but the nurses were adamant that he could hear everything she said, so while she tapped away on her keyboard she would chatter about the mundane details of her weekend, and about Bernie if she'd caught up with her. Jack McIntyre had had a soft spot for her friend since she'd first visited the farm when they were teenagers. Back then Jack had loved a good debate, no matter what the topic, and didn't care if he lost, which he usually did when it came to the stubborn Bernadette. They'd both mellowed since then, but Bernie and Jack still enjoyed the occasional good-natured verbal tussle.

Sometimes Claire felt her friend was more the kind of daughter he wanted—laid-back and earthy. Bernadette at least had a job he understood, even if he didn't see why people would pay so much for old junk to stick in their gardens. In fact, Bernadette had done very well from the bits of 'old junk' he'd given her.

Claire put her hand over her father's limp, weathered one and squeezed. She was disappointed, but not surprised, to receive no reaction. She took a deep breath. It was so hard to hold a one-way conversation about nothing in particular.

Feeling rejuvenated at home after a Radox bath and quick bowl of pasta, Claire got out her laptop again. She'd been putting it off for a few weeks, but now put 'coma' into the search engine.

She'd heard lots of amazing stories relating to coma patients. Apparently there was a guy in the United States who had woken up after twenty years with no idea there was such a thing as email or the internet.

Having never been in the shoes of a desperate loved one, she'd always been a little sceptical. Now she was beginning to understand the lengths people went to.

She read about Dr Fred Burrows's controversial Stimulation Therapy, where family members undertook a routine of controlled auditory, visual and physical stimulation to encourage the patient to wake up. Apparently some read the newspaper aloud every day, some sang, some had a positive mantra they said over and over. It was fascinating, and it made sense, but there was no way she had the time that was needed— up to six hours a day.

Claire felt as though she'd done nothing constructive so far except talk to Jack. She'd paid the odd bill and made sure the house was secure. Of course, she'd got rid of the horses, but that didn't really count, did it? She was beginning to think she'd been too hasty—maybe she should have at least waited a few weeks to prove to everyone it was the only workable solution. She vowed to make more of an effort trying to get Jack better.

The doctor couldn't tell her whether the kick from the horse had caused the stroke or if the stroke had made him fall under the horse's hooves. Though it didn't actually matter. From what she read, what mattered was getting him awake and out of bed. Apparently four weeks was okay, but much longer and the patient risked contracting pneumonia—the biggest killer of non-vegetative coma patients. It had already been a month. Lucky he was a tough old nut and there was so far no sign of any other problems.

Claire shut down the computer. She needed something Jack would see as worth summoning every ounce of strength to wake up for. But what? There were no home fires burning, no warm bed and wife to return to. His beloved horses had been sold off and he'd recently lost his son-in-law—and with him the chance of grandchildren.

He'd adored Keith—had often referred to him as the son he'd never had. But the loss of the prospect of grandchildren had hurt almost as much as the loss of his 'son' and best mate. Claire tried not to let herself think about the fact that she'd as good as forgotten to have children.

Two

The next day Claire was pleased to be back at her desk, where she could focus on her projects and paperwork and the upcoming Melbourne Cup. It was a struggle to get out of bed and into the shower in the mornings, but she always felt better when she'd escaped the house and its silent, haunting memories of Keith.

Obsessively organised and habitual, Claire started every day with a list. Her job at Rockford was to deliver advertising projects. Some of her larger clients had campaigns covering all media—television, radio and print—so she had a lot to keep track of: ensuring tight deadlines were met, pre-empting any delays and managing everyone's expectations. It was a juggling act that saw much of her time on the phone with creative and graphics staff, and clients' personal assistants. It was a sign of a very, very bad day when the CEO of a client actually called her. The only way she could keep track of everything was with several lists.

Luckily, a lot of projects had been completed in the past few weeks. There was always a short lull while the campaigns were running, then afterwards when their success was being analysed. And then the chaos would start all over. Before that she would make the most of the peace and quiet.

This morning, while she waited for her computer to boot up, she wrote 'Client Phone Calls' and twice underlined the heading at the top of her company-issued A4 pad. Below she added the names of her top five clients. It was no coincidence that they all occupied corporate boxes at the Melbourne Cup. She'd already received a couple of invites, but she wanted to make sure she'd exhausted all options before making her decision.

Years ago, Keith had teased her for only staying in her job for the Cup. She'd taken offence at the suggestion she would be so shallow and calculating and had taken a long time to realise he'd meant it not as a criticism but mere observation.

Anyway, there had to be perks—other than lots of pay that attracted lots of tax.

It wasn't that Claire didn't enjoy her job—aspects of it anyway—but she certainly liked the personal recognition such invites implied.

The first time Keith had accompanied her he'd been blown away by the opulence, finally admitting through a mouthful of lobster that he could see why she spent a whole year waiting for this day.

Rather than being insecure, he'd enjoyed being her handbag for the day—especially being free to ogle all the beautiful tanned, touched-up and terrific women strutting about like the fillies out on the track. Later that night, when they were tucked up in their hotel's five-star sheets, Claire had teased him that it was lucky he wasn't expected to make intelligent conversation and represent a business.

Claire smiled sadly at the memory—this would be her first Cup without him in eight years. This time, when the horses thundered past the mirrored finish line and the nation finally let its breath go, the tears that escaped her eyes would be different. Nothing was the same anymore. That was what she was having so much trouble with—the little things. She even missed his habit of leaving his shoes in the lounge room, having kicked them off while settling into the couch.

But Keith would want her to go, wouldn't he?

She felt guilty even thinking about leaving Jack—even if he was recovering at home by then. But what if he was still in hospital? How could she get all dressed up, sip free champagne, be merry? What would he want her to do? That was an easy one. Jack McIntyre was one of the most humble, gracious men on the planet. Not only would he urge her to go, he'd drive her to the airport himself if he could and offer tips the whole way.

Claire was still lost in her thoughts when Derek Anderson—her boss—appeared beside her.

'Morning, Claire. I like the new haircut—it suits you.'

'Hi, Derek. Thanks,' she said, blushing slightly and putting a hand to her head. She'd completely forgotten that no one had seen her new look. Now she felt self-conscious. He looked as if he'd had a recent haircut as well, but she wasn't about to say anything. His full head of thick, mid-brown hair, dusted with grey, was shorter on the sides and standing up a little more on top than usual.

'Good weekend?'

'Yes, thank you, and you?'

'Good, thanks. My young colt had his first run at Morphettville. Thought we might have to cull him there for a while, difficult sod. My trainer thinks he's not worth the trouble, but something tells me he might do all right once we iron out the kinks. He'd better—he's cost me an arm and a leg.'

'Hmm.' Claire was a little unsettled by the warmth in his blue-grey eyes.

'Owning racehorses outright is an expensive hobby, but a man's gotta have one, right? Maybe I should sell some shares, set up a syndicate to spread the load. What do you think?'

'Sounds good, Derek.' The last thing Claire wanted to hear about was racing, especially Derek's success— he was, after all, a rival to Jack. 'Was there something you wanted?'

'How's your dad doing?'

'Same, but thanks for asking.'

Derek seemed uneasy perched on the corner of her desk. He hadn't casually picked up any of her items and wasn't swinging his leg as he usually did.

'Was there something else, Derek? I have a heap of calls to make and a report due at twelve.'

'Well, um, I…' Derek fumbled with the thick knot of his red-and-gold-striped tie.

'Yes?'

'I was thinking it might be a good time to take some of that leave you're sitting on, since all those campaigns have been wrapped up. You know, spend a bit more time with Jack. Get your head around everything.'

'Thanks, but I'm fine, Derek.'

'Just thought a month or so would be good for you.'

Claire's hackles rose. She eyed Derek coldly, wondering if it was her imagination, or if he really was having trouble looking her in the eye.

'Are you implying my work is not up to scratch? If so, don't be so gutless as to come in here suggesting time off...'

Derek held up his hands in surrender. 'Your work's fine, Claire, as always. I just don't want you regretting your choices later. Family is important. Don't use work as an excuse not to face certain things.'

Claire was almost touched by his words, but couldn't shake the feeling there was something else going on. He was definitely avoiding looking at her.

'I appreciate your concern, Derek, but I've got everything under control.'

'All right, I can't force you to do anything. Just remember, Claire, no one is indispensable. If any one of us got hit by a bus, this place would maybe skip a beat, but the powers that be wouldn't waste any time filling the role and getting things back on track.'

'Jeez, thanks, Derek. Nice to know how valued we are. Now, if there is nothing else...'

'Well, there was just one other thing—sort of more of a personal nature.'

Claire's breath caught.

'That colt, the one Jack registered as Paycheque...'

'Yes?' Her ears pricked up. She straightened in her chair.

'Well, I'm not sure how to tell you this...'

'Don't tell me you've got him,' Claire groaned.

'No. Personally I don't think much of him—too small. But that doesn't excuse what I saw.'

'What? What did you see?'

'I probably shouldn't say anything.'

'So why are you?'

'I honestly don't know—it's really none of my business.'

'Derek, just tell me. I don't have time for games.'

'Al Jacobs had him at the…'

'What? Bill Parsons took him. Dad hates how Al treats his horses. Was he all right? Not that there's anything I can do.'

'Skinny, scared shitless.'

'He wasn't racing, was he?'

'Afraid so. Well, they tried.'

'But he's not ready—Dad said he needed another six months at least.' Claire didn't want to ask the obvious, but had gone too far not to. 'So I guess he didn't do so well?'

'No, wouldn't have a bar of the barriers, poor little thing.'

'Oh God. After all the work Dad put in.'

'I know. Sorry to have to tell you.' Derek shrugged. 'Just thought you should know. I must be going soft.'

'Anything else I should know?'

'Al did mention getting rid of him, but I'm sure it was just his temper talking. You know how hot under the collar he gets.'

'Well, it's a pity, but there's nothing I can do about it.'

'You could take that time off—get him back. I've heard you could have been a half-decent trainer if you'd stuck to it.'

'Jeez, Derek, you are going soft. But seriously, I don't think Dad would want me interfering.' Claire's desk phone started ringing.

'Well, if you change your mind,' Derek said, and left with a wave of his hand.

Claire stared after him for a second before picking up the phone.

* * *

Thoughts of Paycheque niggled at Claire all day. She saw his face in her mind every time she picked up the phone, every time she put it down, while she checked her emails, dealt with her in-tray, and added or scrubbed something from her to-do list.

She'd sold all four of Jack's horses. So why was only Paycheque plaguing her? Storm had much more going for him than Paycheque did—he was the right size for a start. God, she really shouldn't have sold them. *How would Jack react?* He'd be angry, sad and disappointed. Of course he would. She'd known that and gone ahead anyway. Why? *Because I didn't have a choice*, she told herself forcefully and got up to make a cup of tea. It was three o'clock and she was sick of the distraction.

But Paycheque was there again while she filled the kettle, turned it on and put a tea bag in her mug. The small bay colt with the unusual enquiring tilt to his head, large expressive eyes and level-headed willing- ness beyond his age. She thought about what Derek had said. Horses refusing to go into barriers was just part of racing. If they cracked under the pressure, their career was over. Just like any other elite athlete. Only the best horses were worth investing in. And the others... She hated to think about it. But it really was a part of life.

Paycheque was still on her mind when she got back to her desk. Jack had said over and over that he wasn't ready to race. He shouldn't even have been there, shouldn't have been given the chance to fail. But Jack had also said he'd showed the most promise of any of his horses over the years. They were just words, weren't they? Jack had always thought big—bigger than he should, if Claire was being honest. But now that she thought about it, Claire didn't remember him being so vehement about a horse's potential, or so attached to one. Paycheque hadn't been just one of many. He'd held a really special place in Jack's heart. Shit, what had she done? She rubbed a hand across her face.

Maybe it was part of some sick plan of Derek's, some sort of reverse psychology. It could be anything with Derek, you just never knew. Or maybe it was even worse than he'd let on—he hadn't wanted to completely lose his tough-guy, 'racehorses are just a means for making money' attitude and was really concerned. If that was true, after what he'd seen in his time at the track and behind the scenes, it meant things were looking really bad for the little horse. But there was nothing she could do now, was there?

No, she'd kept things together through losing Keith and Jack's illness; now was definitely not the time to go all soft. She had to keep focussed. It was certainly not the time to go gallivanting off on some ridiculous crusade to rescue a racehorse who, for all she knew, had spat the dummy, turned dangerous and was no longer any good. Hell, he'd probably be a dud anyway—Jack had had enough of them over the years. She really had to put Paycheque out of her mind.

Three

Four days later, Bernadette and Claire were curled up on Bernadette's three-seater lounge with glasses of wine and an uncorked bottle on the coffee table in front of them.

'So,' Bernie said. 'Anything in particular you want to do this weekend?'

'Well, I do have a bit of work I need to get done.'

'All work and no play—you know what they say.'

'You'll be at the shop all morning tomorrow.'

'Ah, yes, but that's hardly work—I love it.'

'Well, I could say the same. I…'

'Really?' Bernadette demanded, staring hard at her.

'Actually, no.' Claire sighed wearily. 'But it's something I need to get done.'

'I rest my case.' Bernadette downed the rest of her wine and reached for the bottle.

'So that's tomorrow morning covered. What about afterwards?'

'Well…' Claire fidgeted with the stem of her glass.

'Yes?'

'I think it's time I faced going out to the farm.'

'If you're sure you're ready.'

'I don't even understand what I'm so afraid of.'

'That's the thing about fear—it isn't always rational. So what's the latest with Jack?'

'No change. Stubborn old bugger.' Claire smiled weakly.

'Well, I think he'll be happy you're going out to the farm.'

'Bernadette?'

'Yeah?'

'Do you think people in a coma can hear what's going on around them?'

'Yes, I do. Why?'

'I'd hate him feeling he's a burden.'

'Well, I don't think he'd want you beating yourself up on his account.'

'I just feel so helpless. There's nothing I can do to help him.'

'Except get on with life—make the best of things.'

'I *am* getting on with life.'

'You think so, huh?'

'What? I've got a good job, roof over my head—I'm not exactly a burden on society.'

'But, Claire, are you happy all alone in that big house?'

'Uh-oh, I can feel a lecture coming on. Or worse—a blind date.'

'Damn, why didn't I think of that? Seriously, though, Claire, you do need to get out more. What about that guy Derek—from the office?'

'Derek? Bernie, he's my boss!'

'I thought he was nice at that party you invited me to.'

'Well, you're welcome to him. Anyway, what would

you know, you were pissed, you had your beer goggles on, girly.'

'I wasn't that bad.'

'Ah, how quickly we forget. Do the words "straw" and "champagne" ring any bells?'

'Um, actually, yes, you can stop right there.' Bernadette grinned sheepishly.

The next morning, Claire was restless and couldn't focus on the work she had to do. Bernie's cottage felt cold and too quiet without its effervescent owner banging about. She took a walk around the garden that was a perfect compromise between rambling and tailored, stopping to pat one of Bernie's cats—the big sleek black male—who was curled up under the lemon tree, snoozing in the sun.

Something didn't feel right inside. But what? She'd spent heaps of weekends like this—alone at the house while Bernadette was at the shop.

More than being just bored or restless, Claire realised she felt compelled to go to the farm. And she had to do it alone, without Bernadette's deliberate good-natured chatter keeping her from thoughts too morose.

Claire's heart pounded heavily as she turned into the driveway and the car vibrated over the cattle grid. As she made her way up the corrugated rubble track, she felt an odd sensation that everything had changed yet nothing had changed.

The wild oats wavered in the stiff breeze just as they always did this time of year. Cream-coloured dust rose in a cloud behind her car. The gum trees stood in the same solemn rows, neither bluer nor browner nor even any taller. The only changes were the empty roadside paddocks: the absence of colts and fillies frolicking about, their owner's hopes resting on their withers. A crow scrounged about on the ground, picking through old piles of dung for something edible.

Claire's throat tightened. It was too hard. She should have waited for Bernie after all. She stopped the car, turned in her seat to see how far she'd come, then turned back to look up the track. She was over halfway.

Claire closed her eyes and conjured how it used to be: Jack out there in his trademark Akubra, Yakka work pants, long sleeves, and oilskin coat when it was cold; long-reining a youngster along the fence, teaching it all about the bit, changing direction and balance. It was what he'd been doing when he'd had his accident. Bill and Daphne had found him on the ground and the horse grazing nearby, the long reins trailing behind him. God knew how they'd managed to catch the damn animal and get all the gear off safely—that one had been a snarly beast at the best of times. They'd followed the ambulance to the city and called Claire from the hospital.

Claire opened her eyes and studied the area around her. Thankfully there was no sign of what had happened. She closed her eyes and forced herself to think again about the good times.

When she was younger, Claire had always arrived in jodhpurs and boots, with helmet and gloves in the car. Often when she'd rolled down the window to wave he'd stop and call out, 'Love, would you mind just hopping on him for me?'

Ninety percent of the horses he'd trained had had her on their backs first. She'd loved being included, even

after choosing a career outside racing. She still liked
the idea of it, just liked the regular income more. She'd
seen how much her mother had gone without. But she'd
also seen how much she'd loved her husband. Grace
McIntyre would have lived in a caravan without com-
plaint if she'd had to. There was no way Claire could
have done it.

Claire was glad her father hadn't just given up on
life after her mother had died suddenly of a heart attack five years ago. Though she had noticed much of
the enthusiasm had left him. It was as if he was just
going through the motions. No longer could he run in
the kitchen door, clutching his stopwatch to show his
latest protégé's time, face beaming like a little boy's.
They'd been the perfect team: Jack the passionate one,
prone to getting carried away; Grace the steadying rational force, keeping things real, and keeping the bank
manager at bay.

Claire swallowed hard. She looked behind her, then
back up the driveway to the mass of trees that hid the
shabby, basic weatherboard home she'd grown up in.
Bernadette was the only friend she'd not been too embarrassed to invite out to the run-down, untidy farm.

It was time Jack got real, ended this nonsense. He'd
been slowly winding down anyway, hadn't he? Thirty
years was long enough for chasing rainbows and the
elusive pot of gold. At least he'd be able to say it hadn't
been his decision, and could bow out with his dignity
intact. He'd thank her for that, wouldn't he?

So what was she so afraid of? Was it the guilt of
being the one to end his dreams after all these years?
Even her mother hadn't done that.

When he came out of the coma he was likely to be

incapacitated. Surely he wouldn't want the constant reminder of what he could no longer do. The place really
wasn't the same without the horses. But she hadn't had
a choice, had she?

Her grip was as tight on the steering wheel as sweaty
palms allowed. Her knuckles were beginning to ache.
Claire took a deep breath, put the car in gear and slowly
edged forward. Outside the car, the fence posts and dry
paddocks began to blur as she picked up speed. She
kept her eyes fixed on her destination, forcing herself
not to think about what was missing, or exactly what
had become of the horses that had once provided so
much atmosphere.

Claire pulled into the carport behind the old white
rust-stained ute, just as she had so many times before.
When she turned the key and got out it felt as if nothing had changed; she could have been going in to share
a lunch of steak, chips and eggs with her father before
he put her to work cleaning stables or mixing feeds. But
when she reached the back door, reality hit. She'd had
a new lock fitted a couple of days after her father had
been rushed to hospital. The key was in her glove box.

Claire left it where it was, deciding instead to look
around outside and enjoy the soothing sun on her back.
She walked around the side, past her mother's shade-
house, which was now empty except for a few skeletons
of plants scratching at each other in the gusty breeze.
The unusual orange-and-chocolate leopard-spotted
rock, once a childhood treasure and proud feature of the
corner fernery, was now covered in spiders' webs and
dead leaves. Claire moved on, swallowing thoughts of
how devastated her mother would be if she could see it.

The gates of the day yards in front of each of the

four stables stood open, and the piles of manure dot-
ted around bore evidence of the hasty evacuation. Each
water trough had an unhealthy layer of green slime covering its surface. Claire leapt back in fright as a sudden
gust caused a loose sheet of roof iron to flap and then
settle with a piercing squeal. She was halfway through
a mental note to have someone out to fix it when she
realised how ridiculous she was being. She could fix the
damn thing herself—she'd helped her dad build them
in the first place. Anyway, he'd be disappointed if she
paid someone for something so simple. 'More money
than sense,' he'd say. 'That's the city life for you.' And
of course he'd be right. An only child, she'd been raised
a tomboy and had been more capable with cars and DIY
than most boys her age. But since she'd left the farm
she'd adopted the 'pay someone else to do it, my time
is too important' attitude.

First she'd stopped doing the minor services on her
car. And then the new one was computerised and so
complicated it made sense not to touch it. It was funny
how quickly you lost touch and confidence if you didn't
keep your hand in. There was no way she could ever tell
her father she'd called the RAA out to change a tyre. But
she *was* in her work suit and it *was* beginning to rain—
and get dark—as she made the call. For the whole forty
minutes they took to arrive she scolded herself for becoming a helpless woman. She was almost at the point
of doing it herself when the yellow van turned up. In a
matter of minutes the cheery man was done and beaming while she signed the form.

Claire smiled when she slid the shed door back to
find the ladder leaning nearby, with an old paint tin half
full of roofing nails and a claw hammer sticking out

underneath it. She grabbed the wire handle and tucked the long but relatively light ladder under her arm, relieved that she hadn't had to rummage through the untidy, echoing space.

After banging in the last of the nails, Claire sat back with a sense of pride that she'd been able to do something practical for her father. She'd tell him tomorrow evening. She put her chin on her bent knees and scanned the property stretching out before her.

It seemed a million miles from the responsibilities of a mortgage, a stressful job and her grief. She'd done this often as a child: hidden herself away from it all in her own style of meditation. Now she felt so at peace she was annoyed she'd let herself grow up and get caught up in the web of city life. But everything was a compromise; a quiet farm meant being at the mercy of the seasons and other uncontrollable forces. No, there was no way she could ever live this way again.

Sitting back at Bernadette's kitchen table, Claire looked up from her laptop as her friend made a loud bustling entrance, laden with overflowing calico shopping bags.

'So sorry I'm late. Old Mrs Jericho couldn't make up her mind between the Edwardian or Victorian settings.'

'No worries.'

'I'm starving. Let's eat, then get you over to the farm before you chicken out.' Bernadette tipped a pile of butcher-paper-wrapped parcels and large loaf of crusty bread onto the table.

'I've already been,' Claire said quietly.

Bernadette stopped with the calico bag still aloft. 'Oh,' she said.

Claire shrugged. 'Yeah, it just felt right.'

Bernadette got out plates and cutlery and brought them to the table.

'Was it okay?' Bernadette asked. They'd spent so many hours this year with arms wrapped around each other, Claire sobbing, Bernadette fighting back tears of sympathy. She'd really hoped those clouds were behind them.

'No. Depressing.' Claire laughed, trying to play her mood down.

'I knew it would be—that's why I didn't want you going alone.' Bernadette thought Claire had been a little hasty in getting rid of the horses, as if she'd been waiting for the opportunity. She'd tried to talk her out of it, had even offered to feed them and keep an eye on them herself. But Claire had been adamant.

'It was like those ghost towns you read about—void of life. There was even iron flapping in the wind.'

'Oh, Claire.' Bernadette moved to put her arms around her best friend, but Claire waved her away.

'Don't. I'll become a basket case.' Claire laughed tightly.

'Focus on the positives—he's going to pull through. Remember, where there's life there's hope.'

Unlike with Keith, who was gone forever. The unspoken words hung between them. Bernadette really felt for Claire—the poor thing had had one hell of a year.

Even though Bernadette had no evidence, she wondered if the universe was conspiring to get Claire back up into the Adelaide Hills. Maybe it was just selfishness, wishful thinking on her part. Claire's husband had been cruelly taken—that certainly wouldn't do anything to bring her back. Instead, it had made her focus more on her career in order to outrun the memories. And Jack's accident and confinement to hospital just served to drive her further into the safety of the city's hustle and bustle.

She looked up suddenly at hearing Claire's voice and wondered how long she'd been lost in her musing.

'Sorry?'

'You were miles away. I was just saying I put a couple of nails in some loose iron on the stables.'

'Bit dangerous to do on your own, don't you think?'

'Probably, but it felt good. You know, actually doing something for Dad. For the briefest moment everything was back to normal—before…'

'Did you check inside the house?'

'No. I know I should have, but I just couldn't.'

'There's nothing you should or shouldn't do, Claire. You do it when it feels right and don't when it doesn't. There are no rules.'

'God, I wish I could be like you—not a worry in the world.'

'Hey, I've got plenty I could worry about. I just choose to change what I can and ignore what I can't. And it's taken a lot of practice. Remember, I wasn't always like this.'

Claire remembered, all right. Remembered Bernadette worrying constantly about exam results and subject choices for the best career, while she'd just gone along following the subjects and teachers she liked without giving the future much thought. She'd almost forgotten what a stress-head her best friend had been: the time the ambulance had been called when she'd had a panic attack during the year eleven maths exam; the masses of hives that erupted before opening her HSC results.

Now she thought about it, Claire realised it was bizarre how things had changed—not that *she* could be called a worrywart, she decided firmly.

Four

At work, Claire got herself into a routine blur where she managed to wade through her mass of emails and remove a number of items from her long to-do list. She was feeling a little better—less snowed under and more optimistic regarding Jack's recovery.

She'd been pinching him hard on the arm every so often in the days since reading about Dr Burrows's Stimulation Therapy. She hated doing it and felt terribly guilty afterwards, but on Sunday night she'd got a reaction. It was only a slight change of expression, but it showed a response to pain nonetheless. She was ecstatic and a little reluctant to leave when the nurse told her visiting hours were over.

The next morning Claire went to the office with a slightly lighter step. At her desk, she checked her watch. Derek would be in any second. She looked forward to their ritual Monday morning chats, and especially enjoyed the news from inside the racing fraternity.

She smiled as Derek assumed his customary perch on the edge of her desk.

'How was Murray Bridge?' she asked.

'A couple of winners, couple of losers, you know how it is.'

'Yeah.'

There was an awkward moment when no one spoke. Claire added a note to the bottom of her list.

'Any change with Jack?'

'Actually, there was a little,' she said, beaming up at him.

'I take it by your good mood it was a change for the good.'

Claire gave Derek a brief run-down of Dr Burrows's theory before telling him how she'd pinched her father and got a small reaction.

'That's great. Want to reconsider taking some leave to spend more time with Jack?'

'No, thanks, I'm fine—told you that last week.'

'But if what this Dr Burrows says…'

She gave a tight laugh and waggled a finger at him. 'Anyone would think you were trying to get rid of me.'

'Don't be ridiculous.'

Claire thought he looked embarrassed, caught out, but what she heard next nearly caused her to topple off her chair.

'As you know, I'm off from this Wednesday to next Thursday. I'd like you to come with me—just for a few days,' he blurted.

'What?!' she cried, blushing furiously. But Derek was holding up a silencing hand, an unreadable expression on his face.

'Purely platonic, Claire—separate rooms and all that.'

She was slightly miffed at his apparent lack of interest. Not that she was interested in him. But a little flattery never went astray. Responding to her perplexed expression, Derek began to explain.

'It's just that I really would value your expertise…'

Oh God, Claire thought, *he wants me to give him womanly advice, cast an eye over a potential lady friend or something. Well, no way.*

'…on a couple of horses I'm having some issues with. I know you've got a good eye and thought if you saw them actually racing you'd have more of an idea. I'm heading off to a couple of race meetings in country Victoria.'

It wasn't the sort of flattery Claire was hoping for, but it would do, she decided. Though of course, it was totally out of the question.

'I'm really sorry, Derek, but I can't. I've got mountains of work,' she lied, casting her arm across an almost empty pile of document trays. She wasn't about to admit it to her boss, but she was spending an awful lot of time trying to sort out her corporate box invite for the Melbourne Cup. Apart from that, it would be totally disloyal. Derek was a rival owner to Jack. Even if he did have his own trainer, there was no way she was about to impart her or her father's secrets.

'Please, Claire. You need a break and I need some expert advice.'

'Expert!' Claire snorted. 'I'm a bloody Client Relationship Manager—I deal with people, remember. What about that hotshot team you're always on about?' Claire couldn't resist the dig—she'd put up with his subtle rivalry for long enough.

'They're not naturals like you. They don't understand what goes on in a horse's head the way you do.'

'Look, Derek, I'm flattered. I really am. But not only

do I have a lot of work here, but I have Dad to think of.'
There was no way she could leave him for a week, especially now she could see some progress. According
to Dr Burrows, persistence was the key.

Derek sighed deeply, clearly exasperated. 'Come on,
Claire. You and I both know he won't miss you—he's
in a coma.'

Claire was so struck by the callousness that she could
only stare back with an open mouth.

'Shit, I'm so sorry,' Derek stammered. 'I shouldn't
have said that. It's just I…'

'No, you shouldn't,' Claire snapped. 'Now please
go, I've got work to do,' she growled, and willed herself to stay angry. Her mood only had to waver just a
little and the tears began to show—usually at the most
inappropriate of moments. The last thing she needed
was a 'there, there' and the offer of a shoulder and a
handkerchief.

And there she was thinking the sod had a soft side.
'Pah, bastard,' she scoffed, as she returned to her to-do
list.

But her attention kept going back to Derek. Something didn't feel right. Of course he was just trying to
get her in the sack. But why couldn't he just ask her out
for dinner? Or better still, a movie, so they wouldn't
have to talk?

And what was he doing going on leave at such short
notice anyway? He'd said she knew, but unless she'd
had a complete lapse at some point—which was entirely possible given the shitty year she was having—
she hadn't heard a thing about it. Not unheard of, but
very unusual.

Had Derek really wanted her opinion on his horses?

She wanted to believe it—she needed something positive in her life right now, but the odds weren't really stacked in her favour. Last year, yes. Next year, maybe. So just why was he trying to get her to take time off?

Five

During the following week, Claire spent her spare time trying to rouse Jack from his slumber: with kind words, harsh words and the news of her life in all its dreary black, white and grey detail. One night she'd even tried singing when she'd run out of things to say, but when the nurse came in—perhaps to look for the cat that was apparently being strangled—she took to humming.

Claire just didn't want her father forgetting the sounds of everyday life. She'd have been quite happy if he woke just to say, 'Would you just bloody shut up?' Just as long as he woke up.

But she wished he'd get on with it; all the back and forth between work, home and hospital was very draining. A small part of her wondered whether Derek was right—if maybe she needed a break. Possibly. But an even bigger part was afraid that if she stopped, even paused for just a moment, she might never get going again.

On Thursday afternoon, Claire pulled into the hospital car park and turned the engine off. She laid her head on her arm across the steering wheel to try to gather the strength she needed to chatter to Jack for the next hour or so. She wondered if Bill and Daphne were inside. She hoped so.

A few weeks ago she'd started encouraging them to stay when she arrived, instead of scurrying off as had been their habit. It wasn't fair for them to drive all that way and leave again if Claire happened to be visiting. And they weren't expected to know when that was—Claire just came and went when she had the time.

Often now, the three of them would sit there together as if they were family. They sort of were—Claire had known them her whole life. Bill would sit beside Jack's bed reading the paper to him and Claire would sit beside Daphne as she chattered about the goings-on at the CWA or the Hospital Auxiliary while knitting. Claire was amazed that Daphne could knit a jumper without a pattern. It wasn't just plain, either—it had all sorts of fancy stitches and twisted cables going down the front and back.

'Only the sleeves to go now,' Daphne had said the other day upon Claire's enquiry. Claire had expected the constant *click, click* of knitting needles to be irritating—part of the reason she hadn't insisted they stay early on. But instead, she found the sound strangely soothing.

Claire was startled to find a doctor, stethoscope strung around his shoulders, nose pressed against the window, peering at her full of concern. She must have dozed off in the fading sun. She sat up, rubbed her eyes, mouthed that she was okay, removed the keys and got out.

Her steps were leaden as she made her way across

the car park. As she stared vaguely at the asphalt passing beneath her, she remembered the images that had flashed into her head while she'd dozed.

Paycheque had been screaming, rearing, lashing out, and was eventually manhandled to the ground by a small crowd of men. The images of the panic-stricken young horse—eyes alight with fear and hatred—refused to leave her.

Claire sat down in the visitors' area for a few moments. Her heart was working overtime and her legs were having trouble carrying her. *I'll finish the week and then take the next two off*, she decided. Almost instantly she was rewarded with enough strength to get up and make her way down the long, dark hall to Jack's room. It was empty other than Jack in his bed.

Fifteen minutes later, Claire had run out of topics for conversation. Every time she'd drawn breath or changed tack, thoughts of Paycheque would start taunting her. If only Jack would wake up, she'd confess. He'd know what to do. Claire closed her eyes for a few moments to ponder how she would spend her time off—other than at the hospital. She'd sleep most of the first two days and then she'd visit Bernadette. And look for Paycheque? Maybe. Just to satisfy her curiosity and no more. It was really none of her business. Someone else owned him now.

'Dad, I've decided to take a couple of weeks off. Just hang around, visit Bernie, catch up on some reading. I'll be able to visit you during the day—you won't be so tired then.' Tired! What was she saying? *He's asleep. I'm the one who's tired.*

'Actually, Dad, my boss asked me to take a look at a couple of his horses. Derek Anderson—I think you'll remember the name—he's an owner, not a trainer. Anyway, he wanted me to go interstate with him to see them race. Of course I couldn't go while you're here like this. Not that I'd be much help anyhow—probably been out of the game too long. But I thought maybe I'd go to a couple of race meetings while I'm on leave—see if I've still got any sort of eye. Might be fun.'

Claire had her hand over Jack's and was studying his face, as she usually did, for the slightest sign he was waking up. Even though she wasn't really expecting him to—she'd been doing this too long to still be getting her hopes up at the end of every sentence—it had become a habit to stare at him while she spoke. And part of Claire thought that if anything would get him over the line it was talk of horses.

'Apparently his youngsters are giving his trainer grief. Speaking of which, Paycheque was at Morphettville the other week. He was in a bit of trouble. Apparently Al Jacobs was really piss—'

Claire shut her mouth suddenly. She had become so used to rambling about her bland life that she hadn't realised what she was saying. Shit! Jack would take the news even worse than she had.

Claire bit her lip and looked away. And as she did she noticed the slightest ripple under her hand. She looked back. Were his fingers more bent than two seconds before? Despite looking at her father's hand the whole time, Claire had no idea how it had been lying. Damn it, she should remember.

She rubbed a hand across her face. Why now, of all times, was her memory failing her? She again picked up her father's weather-beaten hand and slid her smooth, soft one underneath.

And then there it was, the slightest contraction and scrape of his thick dry fingertips on the top of hers. Claire's mouth dropped open and she stared. He had actually moved! She was not mistaken. She wanted to shout for joy, grab his shoulders, shake him fully awake. She knew it might just be the muscles readjusting themselves with no consciousness involved. The doctors and nurses had told her over and over.

Claire's gaze travelled up Jack's arm to his face. It was a little contorted, as though he were trying to change the position of his mouth. Was she imagining it? She leant forward and put a hand on his chest.

'It's okay, Dad, take your time.' His eyeballs rolled under his closed lids, and it was then that Claire noticed two tears making their way from the inside corners of his eyes. They became a glistening line, caught in his lashes.

Claire's heart leapt. Tears filled her own eyes and before she could reach for a tissue, there was a hot wet line streaking down her face.

'Oh, Dad,' she croaked, and clutched his hand tightly. A couple of tears had sprung through his lashes and were slowly running down his cheeks as well. Her heart lurched again. Claire had never seen her father cry before and didn't know how to react. Part of her wanted to be happy he was coming around, but another part didn't want him to be anguished, didn't want to be the cause of it, either. She watched the two rows of tears in a slow-motion race down his face, trying to will her own to stop, and for the lump to dissolve and let her speak. Though what was there to say?

Should she get a nurse? Probably. But she couldn't leave him, she might miss something. And without her there, he might give up, slip back to sleep. If she pressed the buzzer they'd all rush in for an emergency, shatter the peace, maybe give him a fright and halt his progress.

Claire could hear the metallic twang of the electric clock above the door. The seconds seemed to pass as slowly as minutes. Should she get a doctor? What if he couldn't breathe, choked, and then died? No, she was being ridiculous, paranoid. *Get a grip*, she told herself. *He's fine. He's just been asleep and is waking up.*

She squeezed his hand harder. Shit, was it too hard? His face was contorting. Was it pain? Claire watched, transfixed, as her father's lips pursed and then turned in on themselves. He was trying to speak. She found her own mouth copying him. What was he trying to say? Claire wished she could do it for him. *What?!* she wanted to shout. *Just spit it out!* She rocked forward in her chair, urging him on, holding her breath. God, she was so frustrated. She wanted to slam her fist into a wall or something—do anything but watch this man who so recently was strong, smart, full of dry wit, and now couldn't even get his tongue around one word. If only she knew what that word was. She checked his lips, which now seemed fused in their pursed position, and tried to work through the possibilities in her head.

Suddenly his lips parted and there was a little pop as some air escaped. 'P,' he'd said. 'P'. Claire frantically searched her memory, her mind whirling like the spinning wheels of a car bogged to the axles. Her mother's name had been Grace, so that hadn't been it. Claire couldn't bear it if he'd lost his memory as well, especially having to break the news again that his wife was dead. It was going to be bad enough confessing what had happened to his horses.

The anguish showed in her father's face. Claire wanted to tell him not to bother, to try again later, not to strain himself. That it didn't matter. But it did matter. What the hell was he trying to say?

And then he was sinking deeper into his pillows, as if giving up. Claire sank right along with him. She wanted to grab him, drag him up, do anything to stop him going back to that state.

Suddenly his eyes opened and he leant forward ever so slightly. He was staring straight ahead, eyes vacant. Claire barely had a chance to react before his mouth opened and the word 'Paycheque' escaped with a cough. He slumped back, eyes closed again. His lips and face relaxed. To Claire it happened in slow motion. He looked just as he had ten minutes before, before she'd mentioned the horse. She frantically patted his arm.

'No, wake up,' she whispered. Her heart began racing as she tried to process what had gone on. Her head whirled. 'Jesus, no!' Her shaking hand reached for the red knob on the wall and she pressed, then pressed a few more times for good measure.

A dishevelled nurse arrived panting in the doorway, paused briefly to assess the situation before striding over to Jack's bed, where she reset the button.

'Has something happened?' she asked.

Claire wanted to slap her, yell at her to do something. Do something to stop her father dying.

But now she was the one who couldn't form her words. 'I, um… He…' But it didn't matter; the nurse was busy checking Jack's pulse, his eyes. And then she was looking from Jack to Claire and back again.

'Is he…?'

'Sorry, no. There's no change.'

No, you don't understand. Finally Claire's mouth was working. There *was* a change. He woke up, spoke. But Claire didn't say any of it. She was now wondering if she'd imagined it.

The nurse was looking a little exasperated.

'He woke up. He spoke,' Claire said.

The nurse smiled at her with sympathy, patted Claire's arm and said, 'Maybe you should go home, get some rest. There's nothing you can do here—we're taking good care of your father.'

But you're not, Claire wanted to yell. *You just check him every so often.* She stared at the nurse, frowning.

'It's all right. Sometimes when we want something so badly…'

'I didn't make it up.' This time she had spoken. It was obviously a fraction of what he would have experienced, but Claire now thought she could understand the frustration Dr Burrows had felt.

'Please keep your voice down,' the young nurse pleaded quietly.

What would she know anyway? She looked like just a kid, was probably barely out of university. Claire felt like slapping some life experience into her.

'I think you really should go. Visiting hours are ending soon anyway.'

Claire took a deep breath, gave Jack's limp hand another squeeze, leant forward to kiss his forehead and got up. She flashed the nurse an icy glare and stalked out.

Still fuming as she marched across the car park, she thought of what might have happened if he'd woken to see what all the commotion was about. That would have shut the smarmy kid up. Except there would have been nothing more humiliating than her father coming out of his coma to tell his thirty-something daughter off.

Claire sat for a few moments, collecting her thoughts and letting her emotions subside. Had she really dreamed he woke up, the tears? No, she hadn't been asleep. Imagined it, then? Anything was possible in the state she was in. Claire sighed wearily. She was beginning to lose all perspective.

Six

The next morning Claire bounded into work full of purpose and energy, her leave form already filled out and awaiting Derek's signature. If she got all her work done, she might even take the last few hours off—get an early start to her break.

After dumping her handbag and laptop, Claire made her way down the corridor to Derek's plush corner office. He had his back to the door and was hunched over something on his desk. Something about his tight, uneasy posture—one hand holding the side of his head in contemplation—stopped Claire at the open door. Her eyes darted across his desk, which was scattered with papers. To his left was a takeaway cardboard coffee cup, the remains of cappuccino froth lining its upper edge, and a half-eaten toasted sandwich lying on a white paper bag. Nothing seemed out of the ordinary. Claire shook the uneasy feeling free. She was just being paranoid. She knocked tentatively on the frosted glass sliding door.

Derek looked up and turned in his chair, startled. His face was clouded in confusion for a split second before reddening. It was as though he'd been caught stuffing company stationery into his briefcase.

He glanced down at a small pile of business-sized envelopes in front of him before roughly shoving them out of sight under some papers. *Definitely caught doing personal business on company time*, Claire thought smugly.

'Claire, please,' he said, sweeping an arm towards a vacant chair.

'Thanks.' Claire went in and sat down at the small round low table, part of the new touchy-feely concept in working environments at Rockford.

'Did you enjoy your time off? Successful week away with the gee-gees?'

'Um, yes, not bad. Something I can help you with, Claire? I'm rather snowed under...'

Claire was annoyed. It was all right for him to stand at her desk fiddling with her bits and pieces, but now when the tables were turned she was getting the royal hurry on. Bloody typical.

But she wasn't going to let it get to her—she was on the cusp of two glorious weeks away. Nothing could ruin that now, not even Derek and his double standards. Claire smiled sweetly at him, got up, flapped her leave form theatrically and laid it on the desk in front of him.

'What's this?'

'Leave form, Derek.'

'Yes, I can see that, but you said...' He ran a hand through his hair.

'I decided you were absolutely right—I need a break. So as of this afternoon, if you agree, of course, you're rid of me for two whole weeks.'

'Great,' Derek groaned, and closed his eyes.

'I'm touched by your concern, Derek, but don't worry, I'll be back before you know it.'

'What a mess,' he murmured, barely audible.

'I don't know what your problem is. It was your idea.'

'This,' he said, reaching over to the small pile of envelopes he'd hidden moments before. He removed the top one and handed it to her.

Claire stared at her full name in bold black type: 'Claire McIntyre'.

'What's this? Party invite?' She laughed. She looked back up at Derek, whose face was now an ashy shade of salmon. His lips were in a grim line. He nodded to the envelope in her hands and she looked back down at it: the words 'Private and Confidential' were in large uppercase print and underlined twice, at the top left. How could she have missed it? Claire had seen similar envelopes before, but had never been handed one with her own name on it. She knew what it was but just couldn't seem to grasp it.

'What is it?' she asked, brow knitted in genuine confusion.

'You'd better open it,' Derek said with a sigh.

Claire knew if she did her life would never be the same again, just like the night she'd opened the door to the police. She didn't want to do it, didn't want to know.

'No, I don't want to,' Claire said, sounding almost childlike. Her hands were already beginning to sweat, her vision blurring.

'Come on, you have to sometime.'

No, I don't, Claire thought. *What are you going to do? Hold me down, jack my eyelids open with toothpicks, have me arrested for not opening a letter?*

'It might not be so bad,' Derek offered.

But Claire disagreed. In her experience, good news came in person or by phone and bad news came by mail. Except, she found herself correcting, when it came to really bad news—like the phone call about Jack's accident. Or *really really* bad news—like the police knocking on her door at one o'clock in the morning to tell her that her husband was dead. There were exceptions to everything.

'You can't fire me. I haven't had any warnings, and my performance...'

'Claire, just open the damn envelope.'

He was right: she was just delaying the inevitable. There was no way it could be the worst news she'd received that year. Claire carefully prised the seal apart and pulled out the folded sheet of Rockford letterhead. She held her breath as she straightened it.

She sighed at seeing 'Redundancy Offer'. *Okay*, she thought with relief, *it's an offer*. She tried to scan the following text but her eyes refused to focus. After a few moments pretending to read, she passed the sheet across to Derek and sat back with arms folded.

'Sorry, no deal.'

'Claire, this is not a game—you don't have a choice.'

'Why not?' Suddenly all Claire's experience of middle management had left her and she was just like any other bewildered employee trying to hold on to her job.

'Claire, you know why not.' Derek was rubbing his face, clearly exasperated.

'No, it says there "redundancy *offer*". And I think you'll find the dictionary meaning of "offer" is "to present for acceptance or rejection".'

Derek blinked twice while he processed what she'd said, and then glared at her.

'Don't be a smart arse, Claire. It doesn't suit you. And being difficult is really not going to help the situation.'

'Difficult, Derek? I'll be as difficult as I bloody well like. I'm about to lose my job, my final shred of security. Kick me while I'm down, why don't you?'

'I know and I'm sorry, I really am.' Derek stared at his fingers in his lap.

'Not sorry enough to stop this.' She jabbed a finger at the piece of paper.

'Please, Claire, don't shoot the messenger,' he said wearily.

'You could have stopped this. I don't know how, but you could have.' Claire's eyes flashed at him.

Derek looked back down at his desk. 'Claire, for the record, I did actually try. If you'd been on leave like I suggested, you couldn't have been made redundant.'

'Oh, so it's my fault now.'

'And if you look at the figures, you'll find the *offer* is well above…'

'This is not about the money, Derek.'

'Of course it is, Claire. It's not personal. The new CEO is just making his mark by changing the organisational structure—it's not about *you*.'

Claire shot him an indignant glare.

'Just sign the bloody letter, take your time off, and then worry about it. You'll have no trouble finding another job—I'll do all I can to help.'

'And if I don't sign it?'

'You will be fired. So that's your choice—twelve months' pay or two weeks.'

'Fine!' Claire snatched the piece of paper back, grabbed a pen from Derek's holder and roughly scrawled her signature. She got up, threw both pen and paper at Derek and stalked towards the door.

'Um, Claire?'

She wanted to keep walking and complete her grand exit, but something in Derek's tone made her stop and turn. He was focussed on the desk in front of him.

'I have to inform management and then you are to be escorted from the building. You have about forty minutes. Go back to your desk and pack your things,' he said, unable to look her in the eye.

Claire sat in her car, panting from the exertion of holding her dignity together while being walked past her colleagues and underlings' workstations flanked by two overweight, middle-aged security men who couldn't have outrun a headless chicken if their jobs depended on it. She hated being the highlight of their day—possibly year—and especially despised the grim, authoritarian expressions that did little to hide their smugness.

Claire barely remembered the faces that had uttered vague messages of hope before bobbing back down, the acceptable length of time between curiosity and nosiness having expired. As she tramped down the hall, forced to keep the slow pace of the Kitchener bun boys beside her, Claire just wished she could disappear.

On the passenger seat beside her was a box of personal items from her desk: clock, phone charger, photo frames, Keith's snow dome. The security staff hadn't stopped her throwing in the stress ball with the company logo—probably figured she'd be needing that.

She knew something major had happened but she didn't understand how. She'd gone into Derek's office to get her leave form signed. She was supposed to be excited about her freedom for the next two weeks, not jobless and terrified of her entire future. Jesus, how was she going to tell her father? Part of her was almost glad he was still unconscious and couldn't say 'I told you so'. He'd told her so many times that these sorts of people couldn't be trusted, that she was just a means to an end, a way to make them more money. They didn't care about her as a person. And as it turned out, he was right.

Claire left the car park for the last time with a sick sensation of going out into the big scary world. All those management texts said to look at redundancy as an opportunity, the potential start of an exciting new chapter—what a crock of shit! Claire felt a little guilty about the times she'd said these same words, and for those who had left her office looking brighter for them.

At the second set of traffic lights, her attention was caught by a billboard advertising an upcoming reality show: 'SMILE, YOU'RE ON CANDID CAMERA!'

'If only,' she moaned.

Claire dropped her box on the kitchen bench, kicked her shoes off and threw herself on the sofa. Now what? She looked around for answers and spied the cordless phone on the tinted glass coffee table.

'Hi, Bernie, it's me, Claire. Look, sorry to disturb you at work, but…' Claire's voice cracked.

'What! What's happened? Are you okay?'

'Um, actually no. I've just lost my job, and…' The lump in Claire's throat exploded and the tears began to flow. 'I don't know what to do,' she sobbed. 'I feel so lost… I was wondering if…well, if…'

'Don't be silly. Come straight up. Are you okay to drive?'

'I think so.'

'Come to the house. I'll shut the shop.'

'I don't want to be a burden—I'm happy to wait. It's just…'

'I know, and don't be ridiculous. What are friends for? Just throw together some clothes and toiletries and get in the car.'

'Thanks, Bern.'

'No worries. And, Claire?'

'Yes?'

'Nothing is ever as bad as it first seems. I'll see you soon—drive carefully.'

'Thanks, I will.'

Claire had been on the phone less than a minute, but just hearing her friend's voice was a big relief. She didn't feel so alone, so out of control. She smiled ever so slightly through her drying tears. Trust Bernadette to take charge. At least now she had a plan for the next forty minutes: she was driving up the freeway to the Adelaide Hills.

Seven

By the time Claire arrived at Bernie's house she was exhausted and dishevelled, as if she'd been physically fighting the goings-on in her head—the war the left and right hemispheres of her brain had been waging the whole way. She was still no more certain. Was the redundancy a good thing, a chance to take a breath and get her life back into order? Or was it the catastrophe she'd initially thought it was?

Bernadette ran down the steps, burgundy curls flying out like a cape behind her. Claire was quietly relieved at the prospect of shedding half her burden. She got out of the car, returned her best friend's hug and burst into tears.

After letting Claire cling to her for a few minutes, sobbing, Bernadette gently turned her to the house. 'Come on in,' she said.

Claire allowed herself to be helped like an invalid up the verandah steps and inside.

Bernie deposited her on the lounge and went out to boil the kettle. Claire listened to her friend pottering about in the kitchen and thought to offer help, but felt fused to her plush surroundings. Her head was fuzzy.

Bernadette brought in a tray with some mugs, a teapot, sugar, milk and a plate of homemade Anzac biscuits, and put it down on the coffee table.

Claire frowned. She could see but wasn't really seeing; she could hear but it was a muffle somewhere in the depths of her brain. Distantly she realised Bernadette was pushing at her arm, almost hitting her. Claire shook her head, trying to shake the cotton wool from her ears and milky film from her eyes. She fought the urge to curl up and go to sleep, pretend this day hadn't happened.

'Here, drink this. I've put some sugar in it to help with the shock.'

Yes, that was what was going on. Shock. How could she have forgotten? Not so long ago she'd been in a similar state after news of Keith, and then, not quite so bad of course, her father.

'Thanks,' she said, accepting the mug. She wrapped her hands around it to try to draw its warmth into her. She took a tentative sip and ran the hot, sweet, milky liquid around her tongue before swallowing. She instantly felt comforted. No wonder tea was the first thing to come out in a crisis. Claire sighed and let herself relax slightly.

Bernadette, who had been watching and waiting for the right moment, spoke. 'Now, starting from the beginning, tell me everything.'

Claire looked down into her cup, searching for the logical order of the day's events.

'Remember how I told you I'd finally decided to take

some time off? Well, I went into Derek's office to get the form signed and instead I got handed my notice.'

'He fired you, just like that?'

Claire took a sip of her tea. 'Not fired, exactly. Made redundant.'

'Oh, well, that's a whole different thing.' Bernadette sighed and took a sip from her mug.

'No, it's not. Either way I'm out of a job with a big fat mortgage to pay. I can't believe the bastard…'

'Derek's not the CEO, is he? Orders are bound to have come from higher up. I doubt Derek's really to blame, as much as you want him to be.'

'Jesus, Bernadette. Whose side are you on?'

'Yours, of course. But, Claire, you really need to get things into perspective. If you've been made redundant, that means you get a payout—and you've been there for ages.'

'Twelve years, eight months, two weeks and three days to be precise—that's what the "offer" says. What's the point of calling it an offer if you don't have a choice? Derek said I'd be fired if I didn't take it. "Your choice— twelve months' pay or two weeks". The smug prick.'

'I hope you took it,' Bernadette said, eyeing Claire suspiciously.

'Of course I bloody took it—I haven't lost all my marbles.'

Bernadette visibly relaxed, sank back into the couch and put her feet on the coffee table. 'Well, I don't know what you're so worked up about, except of course the initial shock.'

'For a start, I'm jobless, Bernadette, with a mortgage I was having trouble paying alone in the first place. "It's not personal," he says. I could lose the roof over my head. How much more personal can you get?'

'Claire, you haven't lost your house.'

'I might.'

'You could always sell, move up here.'

'And move into my parents' house? Great, then I really will end up the old spinster with the house full of cats.'

'You don't have any cats.'

'I'll get some. But seriously, how humiliating.'

'Why? Who would care anyway? Claire, people don't waste as much time thinking about other people as we like to think. And Derek's right, it's not personal. Some bigwigs over in Sydney probably decided to do a shift and shuffle—people you probably haven't even met.'

'Are you sure you haven't been speaking to him?'

'Just because I'm not chained to a desk, doesn't mean I don't remember how these things work. Personally I'd be taking their dough, saying "thank you very much" and looking forward to the opportunities that are about to come your way.'

'What if there are no opportunities?'

'There always are. In a matter of months you'll remember this conversation—actually, you probably won't but don't worry, I'll remind you—and you'll laugh at how paranoid you were because everything will have worked out for the best. It always does.'

'I feel so lost.'

'You just need a plan—a logical way forward.'

'You're right. Do you have Saturday's career section still?'

'Claire!'

'What?'

'Have you not listened to anything I've said?'

'You said I need a plan, and my plan is to find another job so I can pay my mortgage.'

'Would you shut up about your bloody mortgage?! With all the things that have happened to you this year, I would have thought you'd have learnt *something*.'

'I have. That life could be over in a split second.'

'Well, thank Christ you've learnt that much.'

'Which is why I'm going to live comfortably.'

'Claire, forget the fucking money! Life is not just about money.'

'There's no need to swear at me. Just because you decided…'

'This is not about me—I'm not the one who's freaking out because she's lost her job and can't pay the mortgage.'

'I'm not freaking out.'

'Oh, really?' Bernadette looked at Claire with raised eyebrows.

Claire paused for a moment and rewound their conversation in her head. She took a deep breath and pushed some loose strands of hair from her face.

'Sorry, you're right, I am freaking out. But what else am I meant to do?'

'Stop, regroup, have faith in yourself. Let the chips fall where they may.'

Bernadette grabbed a pen and lined pad from the pile of books on the coffee table. 'Now, I'm going to make some notes for you to refer to whenever you start getting freaked. You mentioned twelve months' pay, right?'

'Yeah, about that. Why?'

Bernadette wrote as she continued, 'So, in theory,

you are actually gainfully employed for the next twelve months.'

'I hadn't thought of it like that.'

'No, because you were too busy freaking out.'

'I guess so,' Claire said, looking sheepish.

Bernadette ripped the top sheet from the pad and handed it over.

'What's this?' Claire said, accepting it with a puzzled frown.

'Read it.'

She opened it and couldn't keep the grin from spreading across her face. In Bernadette's large neat script were the words, 'I, Claire McIntyre, agree to take twelve months' paid leave to recuperate from an extremely shitty year. Beginning today, October 7'.

'Do you agree to take said leave and promise not to look for another office job for at least twelve months?'

'Oh, well, um…'

'Do you agree?'

'Yes, all right. I agree.' Claire laughed.

'Right, now sign there at the bottom.' Bernadette handed Claire the pen.

Claire signed the piece of paper and handed back the pen.

'Now, keep that with you at all times.'

Claire nodded and reread the note before folding it and tucking it in the front pocket of her jeans.

'Now, I don't have any jelly beans but I can, however, offer another cup of tea.'

Despite being exhausted and dropping off in front of the television, Bernadette and Claire remained in the lounge room until after midnight. Bernie didn't want to leave her friend alone lest she fall back into being terrified of the future. Claire didn't want to break the spell of feeling that things might just turn out okay after all. Without it being said, both knew this was one of those few occasions when it wasn't safe to 'sleep on it'. So they huddled at their respective ends of the three-seater sofa, pretending the movie was enthralling.

Their silent trance was shattered by the phone. Instinctively, the first thing they did was check their watches. Claire's hand went to her pounding chest. Jesus, no! Not more bad news; not today, not tomorrow, not this year. Bernie's eyes were wide as she untangled her legs and went to get the handset from the small hallstand.

Claire watched her friend's back as she picked up the phone and answered, feeling guilty for bringing her bad karma to Bernadette's home. She felt a strange sense of relief when she heard her say, 'Yes, I'll just get her for you.' Maybe she hadn't cursed her after all.

'It's for you, the hospital. Your mobile must be turned off,' Bernadette said, handing her the phone. Claire's stomach knotted in dreaded anticipation.

'Hello, this is Claire McIntyre.'

'Claire, my name's Abby Lawson. I'm calling from the hospital. It's about your father…'

Claire held her breath and crossed her fingers harder than she ever had before.

'We thought you'd want to know straightaway…'

'Yes?' Claire silently begged her to get it over with.

'He's woken up, just a few minutes ago.'

For a moment, Claire thought her bowels might let go. She took a gasping breath.

'Ms McIntyre? Claire, are you there?'

'Yes, yes, I'm here. Sorry. Oh, that's great. Thank you so much for calling. What happened? Is he okay? What has he said? Should I come in?'

Nurse Lawson waited until Claire's torrent ended. She'd obviously done this before. 'He's fine, calm, lucid. None the worse for wear as far as we can see. Of course, the doctor will have to confirm that in the morning. He seems to know who and where he is, and what year it is. But there was something odd—one of the first things he said after waking. Something about a paycheque. It might be something that's come up from his past. But he was quite adamant that someone needed to find this lost paycheque. Does that make any sense to you?'

'Yes.' Claire sighed, smiling now. 'Paycheque was one of his racehorses.'

'Oh, right, well, I guess that makes sense, then. Look, I'd better get back to my other patients. I just wanted you to know.'

'Thanks so much for calling.'

'It's my pleasure—nice to finally have some good news. Sorry for calling so late.'

'No problem, it was worth it.' Claire was about to hang up when she thought of something. 'Nurse?'

'Yes?'

'Could you please tell him I'll be in to see him in the morning?'

'Doctor will be doing his rounds until about ten, so if you come after that we'll know more.'

'Okay.'

'Goodbye, then.'

'Goodbye, and thanks again.'

Claire put the phone down and looked at Bernadette. They stared at each other in wonder for nearly a full minute before grabbing at each other and whooping with delight as they used to do at the end of exams.

They slumped back onto the lounge, and almost immediately began yawning. Five minutes later they had cleaned their teeth and were saying goodnight and turning off lights.

Claire lay in bed staring into the blackness above, wide-awake. But it wasn't her father's waking that kept her mind ticking over, nor thoughts of the day's events, but Paycheque.

The time was coming when she'd have to tell Jack what she'd done. She couldn't check on the horse and just leave it at that. Not now. No, she had to get him back, give her father something real to come back for. But what if someone had discovered his potential, or perhaps worse, realised his sentimental value? She couldn't afford to pay big bucks for him, but couldn't afford not to. For all she knew she might even be too late. If things had gone as badly at Morphettville as Derek had said, he might have already been sent to the knackers. God, she couldn't bear to think about that.

As the grey light of the new day began to peep under the blinds, Claire decided she'd start by ringing Al Jacobs. And with that thought, she finally drifted off.

Eight

Claire woke to the sound of water rushing through pipes and beating on the bathroom wall next door. She smiled at Bernadette's off-key rendition of 'It Must Be Love'. She lay there until she heard her friend in the kitchen, not wanting to upset her morning ritual and risk her being late opening the shop.

When she thought about the day before, a shiver ran the length of her spine. Twelve months out of work. What if she'd forgotten everything she knew by then?

Claire reached for the folded piece of paper from the bedside cupboard. There it was in black and white: she was having a year off. End of story. Nothing to worry about for ages. She read the note twice more to further convince herself. Anyway, for the next two weeks she was really on holidays—well, that's what she'd keep telling herself. And of course her father.

Claire climbed out of bed and dragged on the worn blue robe that always hung on the back of the guest room door. She breathed in its comforting fresh floral scent. They used the same laundry products—regularly comparing notes on such things—but somehow Bernadette's linen always smelled sweeter, fresher. She pulled on long purple socks and padded out to the kitchen, where Bernie was pouring milk into two mugs.

'Ah, there you are. Good morning,' Bernadette said.

'Morning.'

'Here you go,' she said, passing Claire one of the mugs.

'Thanks.' Claire took a deep whiff of the bitter, earthy aroma of instant coffee, psyching herself up before taking a sip.

'Toast?'

'Yes, thanks.'

'So, other than going down to see Jack, what are your plans for the day?'

'Well, I'm going to wait until after ten, when they think the doctor will have finished his rounds. Are you at the shop?'

'Only until noon. I couldn't find anyone else to cover for me until then—I tried before you arrived yesterday. Otherwise I would have liked to go with you to see Jack.'

'Well, I can hold off a few hours—it's been two months, another few hours won't matter. Bill and Daphne will most likely be there anyway. No doubt she'll be frantically stitching the jumper together now she knows he'll be able to wear it soon.'

'Haven't they been amazing?'

'Hmm. It's been so good to know they were there all the times I got caught up at the office. I'm going to have to get them something to thank them for everything they've done. Any ideas?'

'They really wouldn't expect you to. Just knowing Jack is okay would be enough for them.'

'I know. But their support really has meant a lot.'

'I'll give it some thought.' Bernie glanced at her watch. 'I'd better get going. You're sure you're happy to wait until I finish at the shop?'

'Absolutely. It's always better visiting with company. And he'd love to see you. Anyway, I've got some phone calls to make that will fill in the time.'

'Right. To let people know he's woken up.'

'No, I'm going to wait until I know more before I start doing that.'

'What other calls, then?' Bernadette eyed Claire suspiciously.

'Don't worry, I'm not looking for a job. I'm going to try to track down Paycheque. Remember him? Apparently Dad was asking for him when he woke up. Sign of a true horseman when he asks for a horse before his daughter,' she added, rolling her eyes.

'Well, at least it means his memory's relatively recent.'

'Yeah. So I need to find out where the horse is so I've got something to tell him.'

'Well, the phone's all yours. Cheaper for local calls than your mobile.'

'Bernie?'

'Yes?'

'Thanks for everything.'

'You'd do the same for me—I know that.' Bernie hugged her. 'Well, I'd better skedaddle. Remember, the shop's on speed dial two if you need me.'

'Thanks.'

'Right, I'll see you later. Good luck finding your horse.'

* * *

'Hello, Al Jacobs's stables.'

'Hello, I was wondering if Al is available to speak with?'

'Sorry, he's at Morphettville today.'

'Oh, right.' Claire could have kicked herself.

'Is there something I can help you with?'

'Maybe.' The girl seemed friendly enough. 'Do you have a horse registered under the name Paycheque there—dark bay colour, on the small side?'

'I think I know the one you're talking about. He was here, but only for a few weeks. I got on okay with him but Al and the others didn't. Nearly ate us out of house and home, too.'

'That would be the one.' Claire put on a laugh. 'Any idea where he is now?' She tried to sound nonchalant.

'I could check the journal. Why do you want to know?' the girl asked, suspicion creeping into her voice.

Shit! Claire hadn't thought this far ahead. She took a deep breath. 'Well, my father used to train him and he was sold off when he got sick and now…'

'You mean Jack McIntyre? Why didn't you say? How is he?'

Claire was so taken aback she couldn't speak for a few moments. 'Actually, he woke up from his coma last night.'

'Aw, that's great—you must be so relieved.'

It felt weird sharing something so personal with someone she had never met but who seemed to know so much about her father. One big family—and not necessarily happy—that was the racing fraternity. It was perhaps the thing Claire missed most, but also what she missed least. The fierce rivalry in the industry meant that people were often friends one minute and enemies the next and vice versa. She'd seen it so many times.

'Yeah.' Claire waited in anticipation. Would the girl help her or not? She could hear what sounded like heavy books and folders being moved, and pages being turned. Claire held her breath when the girl finally spoke.

'He went to Todd Newman over at Gawler—a couple of weeks ago now. Al couldn't be bothered with him after he threw a major hissy fit at Morphettville.'

Claire cringed. She didn't want to hear any more. 'You wouldn't have Todd's number by any chance—save me looking it up?'

'It's right here.'

Claire took down the number. 'Well, thanks for your help.'

'No worries.'

'Ta.'

Claire dialled the number, hoping there would be someone at the stables.

'Todd Newman's stables—Graham speaking.'

'Todd's not available, is he?'

'Sorry, no, it's just me—everyone else's at the races. I'm the stable manager.'

'Oh, right. Okay.'

'What can I do for you?'

'Um…' Claire was thrown by his efficient, professional manner. She'd been hoping for another junior to pull the wool over if she had to. 'Well, it's a bit of an odd question, really, but I understand you got a horse registered under the name Paycheque—a small bay—from Al Jacobs.'

'Did have, little monster. Had all sorts of trouble with him ourselves. We heard about his performance at Morphettville and thought maybe it was just Al being Al. But no, he's a dud, all right. Why the interest?'

'Well, my daughter's looking for a new Pony Club mount. She saw him that day and took a bit of a liking to him. Loves a challenge—you know what kids are like…'

'Oh, don't I just—got two myself. Well, that one's certainly a challenge, but I wouldn't let my kids near him. Got a real nasty streak. Anyway, he's gone to the dogs—literally. Truck came three days ago.'

Part of her wanted to scream at this man who didn't care, let him know she'd worked with the horse before, that Paycheque didn't have a nasty bone in his body. The other part of her wanted to curl up and give up. But she couldn't, she wasn't doing this for herself. Maybe it wasn't too late.

'Thanks for the advice.'

'Plenty of other horses around for your daughter. In fact, there's a couple here if you want to bring her over.'

'Right, thanks. I might just do that. Um, just out of curiosity, whose truck did Paycheque go on?'

'Tom Bailey's—we don't use anyone else.'

Claire hated how real lives were traded like this, how someone could make a living—and a good one, from what she'd heard of Tom Bailey—from unwanted horses. They were often healthy creatures in their prime, got rid of because something better had come along. And in the case of Paycheque, simply because nobody had taken the time to figure out what made him tick.

Tears prickled behind Claire's eyes. Her throat was jammed and her stomach a ball of knotted dread.

'Look, I'd better go,' she croaked. 'Thanks for your help.'

'No worries, cheers, then. And remember, bring your daughter up sometime.'

Claire hung up without another word, sat down on the couch and pulled a cushion to her. The poor little horse. What he must have gone through. She had one last phone call but didn't want to make it, didn't want to know any more. What would she tell Jack? Could bad news send him back into a coma?

With trembling fingers, Claire thumbed through the phone book. She stared at the entry: 'Tom Bailey—pick up all unwanted horses anywhere, anytime'. No different from the ads for antique furniture or bric-a-brac.

Claire pressed each number slowly and waited, holding her breath, while the phone connected and started to ring. She let it ring three times, four times... There, she'd tried. She was about to hang up when it was answered.

'Tom Bailey.' He sounded almost cheery. Claire felt the anger welling up inside her.

'Yes, hello.'

'Got an unwanted horse for me, love?'

'Uh, no... Actually, I'm looking for one you picked up three days ago from Todd Newman's.'

'Hey, lady, if you sent the wrong horse it's got nothing to do with me—I only take what's handed to me.'

Claire swallowed hard, building up the courage to say the words. 'You took the right horse—it was someone else's mistake.'

'Well, nothing to do with me,' he said, sounding relieved. 'Anyway, we're way too efficient for people to go changing their minds.'

'Do you remember where he went? Which, uh, facility?'

'There's only one, love. Packers, just outside Williamstown. But you'd be wasting your time. If he went three days ago he'll be long gone—in cans on his way to a supermarket by now.'

'Right, okay, thanks for your help.'

'Bloody women,' he muttered before hanging up.

Claire fought the urge to call him back and give him a piece of her mind. She looked around her friend's cluttered home, searching for some other way to vent her anger and frustration. But nothing would bring Paycheque back. She'd have to find a way to come clean to her father.

Claire buried her head in her hands and began to weep—for Paycheque, for Keith, her mother, her father. But after a few moments, with a force she didn't know she had, she stopped. She couldn't drown in self-pity now. No, she had to do something, get her mind off it. But the distraction that had been there all the other times was gone—her job, her never-ending list of emails.

Maybe Bernadette had been right. Maybe she had been using the corporate world as a smoke screen, as one big fat excuse for everything that had gone wrong—and right—in her life. What had she been doing for the past twelve years? What had she achieved, other than a healthier bank balance and an only slightly smaller mortgage? Claire's tears dried.

At least Bernadette brought joy to people's lives—she'd seen customers arrive at the shop, daunted by the work ahead, only to leave brimming with excitement at improving their surroundings. Bernadette genuinely made a difference, with advice that was about so much more than simply gardening. So what did she have that Claire lacked, apart from a green thumb?

Passion. Bernadette had passion. As she'd said only recently, she felt blessed that she could earn money doing what she loved. Claire looked around at the mishmash of her friend's decor—mostly from op shops. Claire had lived the peasant life—as a kid with her parents—and there was no way she could go back to that.

From somewhere in the depths of her memory she heard the big Texan drawl of Dr Phil. 'And how's it working for you?' Even from the few shows she'd seen over the years, Claire knew there was no pulling the wool over Dr Phil—he was like the air, nowhere but everywhere. She squirmed inside. Her life had taken less than a year to unravel, and she'd have to face up to a few things if she was going to stop the fraying. Claire wasn't yet sure what she had to do, but wondered if just knowing was a start.

Nine

Claire felt less confined in her compact Corolla than Bernadette's lounge room. Sitting behind the wheel she felt more in control. She paused at the end of the driveway with the motor running. She had a choice: left out towards her father's farm at Mount Pleasant, or right towards the regional township of Angaston.

Three days too late. If only she hadn't been so damn stubborn, had taken time off when Derek had suggested it. Bloody Jack—if he'd woken a few days earlier… Claire banged her hand on the steering wheel. There'd be other horses to get her father back on track—there had to be. There was nothing more she could do. He'd have to believe her.

But in the back of Claire's mind she wondered how—when she didn't believe it herself, when she felt so desolate, devoid of hope. *It's only a horse*, she told herself, and began saying it over and over in her head. It didn't help, and she gave up. She couldn't face the farm knowing she'd failed Paycheque, failed her father.

'Retail therapy,' she muttered, putting her right indicator on, then drove carefully out onto the open highway.

Claire had a plan: she'd go shopping in the quaint old town of Tanunda instead of the larger Angaston, buy Bernadette a thankyou gift and some gourmet food for lunch. Then they'd head to the hospital to see Jack. She couldn't wait to see him. Then she could get on with her life, get back to normal—well, her new jobless normal anyway. And she'd forget about Paycheque; enough experts had said he wasn't worth pursuing anyway. Yes, it was probably all for the best. It would save Jack the humiliation and money. There was probably a better opportunity just around the corner. Claire smiled wryly; she was beginning to think like Bernadette. Maybe the redundancy wasn't all bad after all. Maybe a year off was a good idea.

Claire realised just as the big green sign whizzed past that she'd missed the turn-off to Tanunda. Oh, well, she'd take the longer way, via Williamstown. She hadn't been that way for years and it was, after all, the season for change. Claire turned up the radio and began singing along to an ABBA song, hair flying about in the wind through the partially open window.

She was almost past when she noticed the sign with 'PACKERS PTY LTD ABATTOIR' in large plain black letters. She'd completely forgotten it was on this road. Claire checked her rear-vision mirror and pulled onto the gravel edge of the road. With the car idling, she frowned and began tapping nervously on the steering wheel. She turned off the key and wound her window down for more air.

The only sounds were squawking crows and the occasional whoosh of a passing car. When a gust of wind brought the faint aroma of death through her window,

Claire wrinkled her nose and almost gagged—the un-mistakeable sourness of fresh draining blood.

She started the car again. *It's a business just like any other*, she told herself, putting the car in gear. She eased forward slowly along the gravel, but didn't pull out onto the bitumen, even though the road was clear.

Claire felt weird, as if she was on autopilot. She was fully aware of everything around her, but without telling herself to do it, she'd flipped her indicator on, checked her mirrors and was doing a U-turn. She crossed the cattle grid next to the looming sign feeling numb—not sad, hopeful, anxious or even nervous—just a weird sort of numbness.

Around her were a series of small paddocks. Each had a set of high steel yards in the corner closest to the wide white rubble driveway. One paddock held sheep, another held black cattle that Claire decided must be Angus, and in a third, large sleek pink pigs snuffled about. The furthest held about a dozen horses of vary-ing sizes and colours: some shiny and full of life and others with sunken backs and starry coats—obviously at the end of long lives.

Claire looked at the sheep, cattle and pigs. She felt nothing—could imagine them sliced up on black trays wrapped in cling film stacked on supermarket shelves. Looking back at the horses, she tried to think of their meat packed in cans for pet food, hooves boiled down for glue. Tears pricked at her eyes. A couple of horses looked up from their grazing, clearly unaware of the fate that awaited them behind the big corrugated iron door less than two hundred metres away. She sighed deeply. It was part of the cycle. She'd heard it said so many times.

She imagined Paycheque in the paddock in front of her, then closed her eyes and shook her head, not wanting to think about him like these horses, munching their way unawares down the raceway and into the shed. Worse was the thought that he would have put up a fight. He would never have gone willingly into the steel crush that was like the racing barriers but so much darker, more terrifying. He might even have been injured, in agony when the powerful bolt that was supposed to mean instant death connected with his head.

Jesus, why had she come? Why was she putting herself through this? She opened her eyes and looked back at the horses. Four chestnuts, two greys, an Appaloosa, a buckskin and four bays stared back at her. The darkest of the bays reminded her of Paycheque—a small but well-proportioned thoroughbred.

Startled by a tap on her window, Claire turned to find a lad in faded blue overalls and cap. Beside him was a ute with a few bales of hay on the back. Claire wound down her window and attempted a smile.

'Something I can help you with?'

She took in his deep brown eyes and kind features. The lad seemed friendly, not at all the brusque, insensitive type she imagined one would have to be to work in an abattoir.

'Um, no, not really,' she said.

'Well, I'm afraid I'll have to ask you to leave.' He sounded genuinely apologetic. 'The boss doesn't like people hanging around.'

'Okay, I understand,' Claire said, and looked back to the horses.

'Nice looking, some of them—shame to end up here,'

he said, dragging one of the bales off the back of the ute and dropping it on the ground.

'Yeah,' Claire said wistfully. 'Why the hay if they're…?'

The lad shuffled awkwardly. 'We've had a break-down inside—waiting for parts to come from over-seas. Just didn't want them being hungry, you know, for their last…'

Claire looked away, not wanting to think about it.

'My dad runs a feed lot—flogged a couple of bales. I'll be in heaps of shit if he finds out.'

'I won't tell him. It's nice of you to think of the horses.'

The lad shrugged and checked his watch. 'Shit, smoko's nearly over. I've gotta get this out before I get the sack. Hey, wouldn't give me a hand to throw it over the fence, would you?'

'Sure, no worries.' Claire got out of the car.

Side by side they threw hay. Claire was silent while the lad commented on each of the horses that came over. Claire tried to pretend she was feeding ordinary animals—not horses on death row. As she tossed hay, the lad's cheery comments were a dull murmur some-where in her head.

'This one's my favourite,' he said. 'Come on, you big guts.'

She looked up, already smiling at his affection. The furthest horse, the dark bay she'd been admiring ear-lier, wandered over. He looked nice and healthy so she figured he must have had some kind of accident to be here. He certainly didn't look lame. Maybe he had a nasty streak or was too dangerous to ride.

When the horse turned his back to the others to pro-tect his pile of hay, Claire noticed a brand in the soft flesh above his near foreleg. She squinted, trying to decipher the scar. Not all horses were branded—this one must have meant something to someone once. What had gone wrong for him?

On closer inspection, it didn't look unlike Jack's brand. How many people put letters inside a triangle? Probably heaps. Jack McIntyre used a scaled-down version of his grandfather's sheep brand. Claire found herself wondering if there was a tiny white star under the thick forelock. But she was being ridiculous—Paycheque was long gone.

When the horse pawed the ground for a few beats with one front hoof and then changed to the other, Claire began to feel faint. She must be seeing things. She looked away, convinced she was conjuring images with her guilt.

'Funny, isn't he?' the lad said next to her. 'Does it all the time when he eats.'

'Yeah, it's like the puddling some cats do if they are taken away from their mother too early.' She stared at the bay. In all her years spent around horses the only one she'd seen regularly do it like this was Paycheque. But it couldn't be.

'Hey, mate, what's your story?' she called to the horse.

The horse looked up, twisting his head as if contemplating the question. His forelock shifted to reveal a small white star with a jagged scar underneath. Paycheque had one similar from when he'd fallen and got caught under the bottom rail of the cattle crush as a youngster. It was the reason he was so afraid of racing barriers and why Jack had been so careful with him.

Claire's legs felt weak and she grabbed the nearest stable thing—the arm of the lad next to her.

'Are you okay? You look like you've seen a ghost.'

'I think I have,' Claire murmured, and let herself be helped to the side step of the Land Cruiser to sit down. She put her head between her knees. Had she seen what she thought she'd seen? Had it been coincidence or had she imagined the whole thing?

'You know that horse, don't you?' the lad said, becoming excited. 'I thought he was too good to be here—branded and all.'

Claire nodded. 'I think so,' she said, having trouble breathing.

'Hey, don't get upset.' The lad had his arm around her shoulders. It felt nice. It had been so long since she'd had comfort from anyone other than Bernadette. 'You've found him. That's good, right?'

Claire nodded. And slowly it dawned on her that he was right. She'd done it. She'd actually found Paycheque. The relief was so overwhelming she began to hyperventilate.

'You have to breathe—in and out slowly,' the lad coaxed.

Claire tried to focus on controlling her breathing, and after a few moments noticed another pair of human legs standing in front of her. She looked up and took in an older man in an orange safety vest and khakis.

'What the hell's going on here?'

'I was just feeding the horses during…'

'Well, your smoko's over now. Get back to work. May as well bring this lot with you—parts arrived, we'll be ready for them in an hour.'

Claire's breath caught. She looked at the lad through sodden lashes.

'She wants that bay there—right, miss?' he said, pointing at the horse.

Claire nodded, unable to speak.

'Well, she can't have him.'

Her head snapped up, her eyes wide in question.

'Why not?' the lad asked on her behalf.

'I paid good money for him. He's mine now. Not my fault if some horsey chick's got the guilts and changed her mind.'

'But…' Claire stammered.

'You chicks are all the same. It's just a bloody horse that's about to be dog food. Now if you'll excuse me, I've got an abattoir to run.'

'I'll pay you double what you paid,' Claire blurted.

Claire signed the cheque for six hundred and fifty dollars and handed it over. The man was almost salivating at the thought of such easy money. She knew she should have bargained and got the price down a bit—she really couldn't afford to be throwing away good money. And Bernie was going to love the irony of her last paycheque being used to buy a horse of the same name. A strange mix of relief and dread swept through Claire.

The lad with the hay offered her a doubled-over piece of twine, and she led the bewildered horse to the holding yard in the corner of the small paddock. She felt ridiculous dressed in a white linen shirt and dressy three-quarter pants, up on tiptoes so as not to ruin her two-hundred-dollar kitten heels, stepping between the piles of horse poo. She'd wanted to look nice for Jack. If only she'd waited until after lunch to get changed.

The smirk across the face of the bloke with the cheque in his hand suggested he now thought she was one of those totally un-horsey women with too much money, on a crusade because the shops were shut and there was nothing better to do. That horse would end up on her less-than-one-quarter-acre block for sure—that was if she managed to find someone to transport him at such short notice. He shook his head and wandered off.

Claire waited in her car until the other horses had disappeared into the shed, and then another couple of minutes. Part of her wanted to make sure the rest of the horses had gone. Another wasn't really ready to face the contents of the can of worms she was about to open. She savoured the peace before peeling back the lid.

Ten

Speeding along the highway, Claire's head was awash with all she had to do and the short time she had in which to do it. She had to get to the farm, swap the car for the ute—fingers crossed she could get it started—hook on the float and get back to the abattoir. All in an hour and a half—that's when the nice lad finished his shift.

Her hands were tight on the wheel, knuckles white, palms aching. Her eyes darted across to the clock on the radio every few seconds. The needle was nudging 100, but the trip still seemed to be taking forever. *Damn the speed limit*, she cursed. There were hardly any cars on the road. She'd probably get away with speeding. But she continued to check the speedo at regular intervals and ease her accelerator foot.

Two tailgating Commodores rushed past in a roar of V8 aggression and testosterone.

'Bloody idiots!' The vehicles were now taking up both lanes ahead of her. Her heart was racing a little. She took a deep breath and sighed, trying to steady the hammering in her eardrums.

Claire was tempted to pick up her own speed—the cops would be too busy with those two if they were out and about. But deep down she knew it wasn't worth it; cops weren't the real problem, death was.

She shook her head at the splotches of colour already disappearing around a bend a few hundred metres ahead. She really hoped they wouldn't crash—though they deserved to. Nothing too major; just ding up their precious toys and scare a lesson into them.

She really didn't have time to stop. Bernie would be wondering where the hell she was. What would Jack think about her not being at the hospital yet? And the nurses—Jesus, they'd think she was the worst daughter in the world. She really should have rung when they had decided to wait until after lunch.

Claire didn't trust the bloke she'd given the cheque to. There'd been no receipt, no paperwork at all to say she now owned the horse. And he'd insisted the cheque be written out to cash. There was probably nothing to stop him selling the horse to someone else who came along. He certainly hadn't seemed that hung up on morals. If she was late, he'd probably have no qualms about processing the horse anyway. And once Paycheque was gone there'd be no proof, nothing she could do about it. Panic gripped Claire. She had to hurry up.

A few kilometres on, Claire came around a sweeping bend and noticed a large object on the road up ahead. As she got closer she frowned, easing back her speed and trying to decipher what she was really seeing. She was almost at a stop when she realised what was blocking one side of the road. Two cars—one red, one white—fused into a mass of colour against a large gum tree like a child's roughly formed lump of plasticine.

Claire turned the engine off and put her hazard lights on while she tried to figure out where the doors were—where she'd go to attempt to offer some kind of assistance.

She took a deep breath and walked towards the wreckage on jelly legs. A big part of her already wished she hadn't stopped, had continued on her way. But you couldn't, could you? It just wouldn't be right. She stood close enough to the cars to feel their heat, smell the toxic odour of scorched plastic and paint. The stench of burnt rubber hung in the air. Claire coughed and pulled a tissue from her pocket to protect her nose and mouth. The radiators were hissing. Twisted metal groaned and sighed as it settled into its new form. Crows and galahs squawked and flapped away overhead, oblivious.

Claire wondered if perhaps she shouldn't touch anything—it looked too bad for anyone to have made it. She wasn't sure she could cope with blood and guts and death. Somewhere in the depths of the wreckage she heard the faint electronic tone of a mobile phone. Snapping to attention she raced back to her car. Everything was a blur around her—in slow motion—as she grabbed her own mobile from her handbag. Shit, what was the mobile emergency number? She was about to dial triple zero when she realised there were no bars indicating reception.

'Damn it,' she cursed. She must be in a dead spot. Maybe if she climbed on top of her car she'd get a signal. Just as she was taking off her shoes, another vehicle came around the bend. She leapt onto the road and started waving her arms, the sharp bitumen cutting into the delicate skin of her bare feet.

An older style four-wheel drive stopped on the edge

of the road behind her car. Claire hoped the middle-aged couple inside were locals.

'There's been an accident,' she said through their open window. 'Do you have a mobile? I can't get a signal with mine.'

They both got out of the vehicle.

'Bloody hell,' said the bloke, looking ahead at the pile of wreckage. 'Is anyone alive?'

'I...I don't know. I just arrived,' Claire said.

'Shit!' he said, and bolted up the road towards the carnage.

The woman punched numbers into a mobile phone and then calmly told whoever answered that there had been an accident. She proceeded to give precise directions and local road names.

Claire felt helpless, left out and almost miffed because she'd seen it first and here they were taking over.

Short of anything better to do, she made her way to the mangled cars. The man was circling the wreckage, calling to the occupants, trying to pull on what must be handles on doors but didn't look like anything to her.

Claire realised she could smell fuel. Then she noticed a darker patch of gravel. The bitumen was stained and glistening. She remembered hearing somewhere how the battery had to be disconnected to stop sparks igniting spilt fuel. Claire stared at the fused cars, walked around looking for the front ends. She frowned, trying to decipher the mess. Then suddenly, as if she'd adjusted the focus on a camera, the bonnet of the red car became apparent. She walked over, aware of the other Good Samaritan leaning into one window and talking, urging the victim to hold on, telling him that help was on its way. The bonnet was folded back in three, the engine still hissing steam.

Claire didn't want to put her hand in but knew she didn't have a choice. The battery was lying there with fluid of some sort dripping onto it. The car's wiring had already had the plastic coating scorched off. Any second the unprotected wires could short. For all she knew, the scorching had already worked its way through the dash-board and into the cabin. She pulled at the terminals with her only protection: the small wad of tissues she'd been using to shield her nose. They were both stuck fast—she needed a screwdriver. There wasn't one in her own car and she couldn't disturb the man who seemed to be getting some response from someone in the car.

Claire was relieved to hear a siren and, when she looked up, see a white CFS truck and police car pull-ing over, and uniformed people jumping out and run-ning towards her. They pushed past, literally shoving her aside in their haste. Claire didn't mind at all—she was just glad to be off the hook.

'I couldn't get the battery out,' she said, raising a helpless arm in the general direction.

'It's okay, we're here now.' A young male police offi-cer was beside her. He ushered her back to her own car.

She put her hand on the door handle.

'I'm afraid I'll need a statement before I can let you go,' he said, taking a notebook from his top pocket.

Claire checked her watch. 'I really need to get going. I…'

'It'll only take a few moments.'

I don't have a few moments, Claire wanted to tell him. 'I really don't think I'll be much help,' she said, quickly, hoping her tone would hurry him up.

'How about you let me be the judge of that?' he said.

'I don't mean to be rude but there's somewhere I really need to be. Could I just call into a police station later? Or maybe phone you in a couple of hours?'

'I'm afraid not—it's important to get the facts down as quickly as possible.'

Claire took a deep breath and tried to keep her exasperation at bay. But her eyes kept going to the watch on her wrist.

'Right. Full name and address, please.' The pencil he held was poised above a small notepad.

Claire rattled off the details.

'Now, what exactly did you see, Ms McIntyre?'

'Well, I was just driving along, on the speed limit, and they roared past me, definitely speeding. When I came around this bend they were just there, like that,' she said, indicating towards the wreckage.

'You say they were speeding—any idea how fast?'

'No, not really.'

'Significantly faster than you or just a bit?'

'I have no idea. It all happened very fast.'

'But they were definitely speeding?'

'Yes.'

'And you can be sure because…'

'Because I was doing the speed limit—100—and they both went past me. That means they were speeding, right? Look, I really don't have time for this.'

'And you say you came around the bend and there they were?'

'Yes.'

'And then what did you do?'

'I was trying to call emergency but my phone didn't

have a signal. And then the couple in the four-wheel drive turned up.'

'So they were the ones who called the emergency services?'

'Yes—the woman did.'

'So their phone had service, then?'

'I guess it must have done,' she said, a sarcastic tone creeping into her voice. She half expected him to tell her to change her carrier to someone more reliable.

'Right. And then what did you do?'

'Well, I was trying to figure out how to disconnect the batteries. That's what I was doing when the CFS— and you—turned up. Please, can I go now?' She willed herself not to look at her watch.

'If you're sure you've got nothing more to add.'

'Yes, I'm sure. That's all I know.'

'Right, thank you. Yes, you can go. But we might need to contact you at a later date.'

'Fine.'

The police officer opened Claire's door and she got in.

'You okay to drive?' the policeman asked. But it sounded more like a statement than a genuine enquiry.

'Yes, fine, thanks,' she said, nodding. But Claire didn't feel fine at all. She felt shaken and traumatised, not at all as if she should be driving. But she had to sort out Paycheque, and time was running out.

She started her car and looked down the road. She began to feel queasy at the thought of having to drive past the wreckage. Suddenly Keith was in one of those cars, fighting for his life, in immense pain but only able to offer groans as his body failed. She had to get out of here.

'You sure you're okay? You look a bit pale. Maybe you should hang around for a bit longer.'

'I'm fine, really,' she lied. She checked her mirrors, put the car in gear and pulled carefully onto the road. After she'd passed the wreckage she noticed in her rear-vision mirror that the CFS crew were beginning to block the road with witches' hats.

As she drove, Claire debated whether to call in and see if Bernadette was available to lend a hand. She felt wrecked. It had already been a long, difficult day and it was far from over. Claire pulled a sticky hand from the wheel, ran it across her forehead and let out a deep sigh. She'd gone off to clear her head with a bit of shopping before visiting Jack. If only she'd gone for a walk instead.

Claire pulled into the rough driveway and tried to ignore the depressing emptiness that was the absence of horses mooching about in paddocks. She consoled herself that all that was about to change. But would it? She wondered. One horse was a start, but it would hardly bring the old place back to life. Horses were so-cial animals—what if Paycheque was miserable here on his own? She brightened—people were always trying to find homes for unwanted horses and ponies. Berna-dette was bound to know someone who knew someone. That was one of the great things about country life.

Claire was so focussed on summoning the energy to go into the house she almost didn't see Bernadette's car by the front verandah. Her best friend was grinning cheekily at her from the back steps. Claire leapt out of the car and threw her arms around her.

'What are you doing here?'

'Little bird told me you might need a hand picking up a horse.'

Claire's eyes were wide. 'How the hell…? This place is far too small,' she said, and laughed.

'I'll tell you on the way,' she said, clapping her hands. 'Let's get this show on the road.'

'The ute keys are inside,' Claire said. She retrieved the house key from her glove box and then stood in front of the door. She wanted to be strong and just open the door and walk in. But she couldn't. She felt a complete fool—it was so damn childish.

In a split second Bernadette had grabbed the key.

'Pathetic, huh?'

'Not at all. But I say we deal with it another day— we've got a horse to get.'

'Keys are on the shelf above the kettle, just inside the kitchen.'

'Thanks. Now you organise a halter and fill a hay net. I'll meet you at the float.'

Rarely did Claire McIntyre enjoy being told what to do, even by her best friend. But right now she was relieved to have someone else giving the orders.

Twenty minutes later they were heading off.

'I can't believe the ute started first time,' Claire said.

'Obviously I had my tongue held right.' Bernadette grinned and patted the steering wheel, cooing, 'Who's a good girl, then?'

Claire hadn't objected when Bernadette had climbed back into the driver's seat after hooking on the float. Now the adrenaline was starting to subside, she didn't think she'd be able to drive anyway. She stretched her legs out and noticed a pair of work boots on the floor at her feet. She picked them up and turned them over wondering what they were doing there.

Bernadette noticed her quizzical expression. 'I grabbed the smallest from the laundry—I assumed they must be yours.'

'Yes, thanks, but I can't possibly wear them.'

'Why not?'

Claire indicated her attire with raised eyebrows.

'I don't care how you look—safety first. I'm not having a cantankerous horse and you with a broken foot to deal with alone. Anyway, Jack would kill me. Remember the day he caught us without boots and helmets at the quarry?'

'God, yes. And we were doing so well impressing those boys until he turned up. How embarrassing.'

'Yeah, but don't worry, no one will see you today.'

They were bound to bump into the whole damn town if her current track record was anything to go by, but Claire was too tired to argue. She just hoped Paycheque would behave himself. At least they had safety in numbers, if not strength. She and Bernadette had always been a great team—highly competitive at times, but a great team when it counted.

After a few moments, Claire snapped to attention. 'Oh my God! I still haven't rung the hospital,' she blurted. 'Jack'll be wondering where I am.'

'It's okay—I rang them and explained. Well, sort of. They said they'd make up some innocuous story. They're still keeping things simple with him until he's stronger. So don't worry, it's all under control.'

'I can't thank you enough, Bernie—you're the best...'

'I know, I know. Don't go getting all carried away,' Bernadette said quickly. 'We've a mission to complete.'

Claire sat upright. 'So how did you find out about all this anyway?'

'About third-hand I think—you know how the bush telegraph works. Daryl Hannaford came into the shop—you remember him, has the cherry orchard out on Grey's Road. Anyway, he was at the post office and overheard one of the guys from the abattoir telling someone else the hilarious story of some crazy, dolled-up city chick by the name of McIntyre turning up and paying double to save a horse from the knackery.'

'Oh, great,' Claire groaned, 'I'm now my very own urban myth.'

'Country, actually,' Bernadette corrected with a grin.

'But I didn't tell anyone my name.'

'It's stamped on your cheque, silly.'

Eleven

A few hours later they had kicked off their shoes, poured glasses of wine, and were curled up on Bernadette's couch. Paycheque was settled at the farm with plenty of food and water.

The horse had behaved perfectly, loading and unloading like a dream—though Bernadette hadn't given him any choice. She'd marched up to the little horse, put the halter on him, and was leading him up the ramp before he had a chance to object. All the time she spoke in a commanding tone, telling him she didn't have time for any games, and to consider himself very lucky not to have ended up in the shed like his friends. He hadn't stood a chance.

Claire had barely gotten her boots on before it was all over, but she didn't mind at all. She didn't have the energy and patience for a battle of wills, which invariably occurred when it was the last thing one could cope with.

Horses always knew the best time—or worst, depending on how you wanted to look at it—to put up a fight. Often you only had to show you had all day and were prepared to win at all costs and their bravado would crumple like a haystack piled too high. Most people just didn't take the time to understand what made them tick.

The girls were silent, enjoying their wine. Claire was too exhausted for chit-chat, Bernadette too deep in thought.

'Claire?' Bernadette asked after a few minutes.

'Yeah?' Claire said wearily.

'What now?'

'What do you mean, what now? Oh. I've outstayed my welcome, haven't I?'

'Of course not! Don't be ridiculous—you've only been here twenty-four hours. No, I mean, what now for Paycheque?'

'Tomorrow I'll turn him out into the paddock and he'll stay there until Dad's well enough to deal with him.'

'But that could be weeks, maybe months. Meanwhile you'll have to check on him at least every second day. How are you going to do that from the city?'

'So I *have* worn out my welcome.'

'No, but you probably will have in a few weeks. Anyway, you're a city chick now, remember? You hate being up here in the sticks for too long. Ringing a bell?'

'Bloody hell, Bernie. You're the one always saying, "feel it inside, listen to your unconscious, follow your heart, blah blah blah". And what do I do? Take a step in that direction and instantly I've done the wrong thing...'

'I'm not saying you've done the wrong thing at all. Paycheque needed saving—Jack needed him saved. But you know there's a lot more to it than that. What the hell are you going to do with him?'

'I don't know. I need a few days to think things through.'

'If only you'd done that the first time around,' she muttered. Claire's face fell. 'Sorry, that wasn't fair.'

'No, it wasn't. Bernie I feel guilty enough about getting rid of Dad's horses so quickly without you rubbing it in, thank you very much. Anyway, this time it's only Paycheque—it's a totally different situation.'

'So why *were* you in such a rush to get rid of them?'

'Dad wouldn't have wanted anyone to be burdened with looking after them.'

'You could have done it. You're his daughter. I think that's a little different.'

'How was I going to do it while working and living in the city?'

'You could have used some of that leave you never took and moved into the farm for a while.'

'Yeah, and what would I have done all day? I would have been bored out of my brain.'

'I don't know—maybe chilled out, enjoyed the fresh country air and contemplated life? You could have kept Jack's horses fit. It would have been good for you. Instead, you had to bulldoze your way into his life and take charge.'

'I had to. Jack wouldn't want to be a burden.'

'So you keep saying—you're starting to sound like a broken record. Anyway, he was in a coma. He wouldn't have known. It's time you stopped with the bullshit and admitted the truth.'

'What do you mean?' Claire sat up.

'Claire, just bloody admit it—the reason you were so quick to sell his horses was to force him into retirement, regardless of what happened with his health...'

'That's not…'

'So why not just send them out for agistment?'

'Because agistment costs a fortune and I needed the money to pay his bills.'

'Get real, Claire. You know nothing about his finances—you haven't shown an interest in years.'

'Why are you being so horrible all of a sudden?'

'I'm not. I'm your friend, Claire, and I love you. I'm just trying to get you to be honest with yourself so you can start dealing with all the pain you're bottling up inside. It's not healthy.'

'I have dealt with it. I've got Paycheque back, haven't I?'

'So you're going to track the others down and have them back in the paddock when Jack returns—pretend nothing's changed?'

'Don't be ridiculous—I have no idea where the others are. Anyway, we don't even know if he'll be up to training again.'

'You'd like that, wouldn't you?'

'Bernie, that's a horrible thing to say. He'd be miserable without his horses.'

'Why didn't you think about that two months ago? Just admit it, Claire. You've tried to control him, just like you try to control everything else in your life.'

'I did what I thought was best.'

'Yes, but for you, Claire, not for Jack. Can't you see that?'

Claire sighed deeply. Bernie was right, just as she always was. She *had* tried to control Jack, taken the first opportunity to try to change his life to better match her ideals. She sat in silent contemplation for a few minutes.

'Maybe you're right. Oh, Bernie, what have I done? What am I going to do?'

'Well, for a start you need to stop trying to control everything. Things tend to work themselves out okay if you let them.'

'You really do believe that, don't you, no matter how bad things get?'

'Yes, I do—and one day you will, too. You just need to learn to trust your intuition.'

'Which is what you can help with, right?' Claire smiled, despite being hurt and annoyed.

'Exactly! Have I ever let you down before?'

'No.' Claire grinned. She could never stay annoyed at Bernadette for long—her friend's wisdom always managed to penetrate her darkest, most negative moods.

'But first we need food—I'll heat up the leftovers. And get another bottle of wine. No reasonable plan was ever laid without copious amounts of wine. Don't you move,' Bernadette ordered.

Later that night, Claire lay in bed emotionally and physically exhausted but unable to sleep. Her head was still spinning, partially from the wine and partially from the day's events. Tomorrow she would find out exactly what Jack's condition and prognosis was, and establish a rehabilitation strategy for when he could come home. Of course Bernie was right: she couldn't oversee his recovery and Paycheque's well-being based in the city. There was no alternative but to move into the farmhouse. She had known it all along, just hadn't wanted to face it.

At first she'd shuddered at the thought of immersing herself in country life—it was quite another thing to be able to escape back to the city when it all got too much. But as Bernie had been quick to point out, she could always rent her own place nearby if it all got too much living with Jack.

Despite the options, Claire had had a vision of herself as a scary old spinster with a houseful of cats. She realised she'd spoken her fears aloud when Bernadette replied that she'd make sure only two cats were on the premises at any one time. At that moment, Bernadette's three rescued moggies had wandered past. The girls had exchanged glances—Claire raising her eyebrows—before both of them erupted into fits of laughter.

'Okay, you're allowed three,' Bernadette had said after a few moments, clutching her stomach with one hand and brushing away the tears with the other.

Now Claire lay in bed wondering exactly what she was so afraid of. Bernadette was perfectly happy, unmarried in her own cottage with her menagerie. But somehow that wasn't enough. She had no idea of what, but she wanted—needed—more.

She finally fell asleep to the droning purrs of the three cats, which had sprawled out around her on the queen-sized bed.

Twelve

'Dad, it's so good to see you finally awake!' Claire cried, rushing over to the bed.

Claire was surprised and disappointed to find the only improvement in her father's health were his open eyes. He was gaunt: a pale salmony grey. He tried to smile a greeting but his face refused to oblige. The corners of his mouth held small glistening pools of dribble. It was heartbreaking.

Ignoring his appearance and the spasm of pity kicking inside her, Claire smiled brightly, sat down and placed her hand over his. He managed to turn his head a little but his eyes were vacant. Claire couldn't tell whether he was staring past or through her, just that this was not what she'd expected at all.

She started chattering about the events of the past few days, squeezing his hand as she told him that Paycheque was home and waiting. Her father's eyes brightened slightly and he squeezed back. For the umpteenth time Claire wondered if she had done the right thing getting the horse back for him. At this point she couldn't imagine Jack out of bed, let alone out in the paddock battling with half a tonne of feisty horse. She sighed deeply. There was certainly a long way to go.

Claire was rambling about Bernadette's shop, trying to lighten the dreary atmosphere by telling Jack how much a bloke had paid for one of Bernie's water features: 'You'd never believe it. It's a piece of rusty corrugated iron that trickles water into an old concrete laundry trough.

'Apparently it's a sculpture, *installation art*,' she was concluding when there was a knock on the door. Claire looked up to find a handsome middle-aged man peering in at them. He was wearing neatly pressed navy trousers, a crisp pale blue-and-white-checked shirt, and shiny tan dress shoes.

'Hello, Mr McIntyre,' the man called, then in a loud whisper said to Claire, 'Ms McIntyre, I presume?'

Claire nodded.

'Could I see you for a minute?'

Claire nodded, put Jack's hand down with a pat and got up. Her shoulders ached from being hunched over the bed too long.

'I'm Dr Jeffries. Michael,' the man said, holding out his hand.

'Claire McIntyre,' she replied, returning the gentle but firm handshake.

'There's a quiet room down the hall, second on your right,' he said, stepping aside and ushering her forward.

Claire experienced an odd sense of foreboding and hope both at once. On the one hand it was good to see how confident the doctor seemed, but she'd seen the lack of progress her father had made.

The door shut behind Dr Jeffries with a gentle click. He indicated for her to take a seat in one of the three modern vinyl tub chairs while settling himself in another. He opened a manila folder on the small round coffee table between them. Claire's stomach flip-flopped in dreaded anticipation.

'Ms McIntyre…'

'Please, call me Claire. You make me sound old.' She laughed nervously, instantly blushing with embarrassment. God, she sounded as if she was flirting.

'Claire, I'm one of the neurosurgeons here. I've examined your father's scans and notes, and all seems fine…'

'Well, he doesn't look fine to me. He's not much different to when he was in a coma.'

'Well, he *is* awake, and that's a big improvement.'

Hardly. Claire bit her tongue to stop herself uttering the word.

'At this stage there seems nothing *physically* holding him back.'

Claire sighed with relief. So this man had seen what she had felt. 'But he doesn't seem pleased to have come out of his coma at all,' she said.

'No, I think it's his emotional state that needs healing now. I think it best we get him back into familiar surroundings as soon as possible. Will you be available to take care of him—providing, of course, we can at least get him out of bed and walking a little? At this stage he seems disinterested—what he needs is some incentive.'

'Well, he was worried about one of his horses—he trained racehorses, you know—and I've managed to get it back. He seemed to brighten a little when I told him, but he didn't exactly leap out of bed with joy.'

Dr Jeffries looked down at the folder. 'I see in his notes he's a widower.'

'Yes. My mother died five years ago. But I've decided to move back home while he convalesces.'

'Good. He'd like that, would he?'

Claire examined every angle of the question for hidden innuendo. She had no doubt that he'd love having her home again—at least she hoped so. They'd always gotten on well before she'd shunned the farm for a life of sophistication and disposable income. Guilt stabbed at her. Of course in doing so, she'd shunned *him*.

'You and your father do get along okay, don't you?' he prompted.

'Sorry, yes, very well. We get on very well.'

'Excellent,' the doctor said, snapping the manila folder shut. 'I suggest you tell him your plans to move back home and see how he reacts. If it's positive, we'll just have to get him up and well enough to do it.' He stood up.

'Well, I have other patients to see. It's up to you now. All the best.' He shook her hand again, smiled warmly and left.

Claire was left standing on her own in the small room. She didn't know whether to be annoyed at the brush-off or relieved at the news.

There was nothing wrong with her father. He had every chance of making a full recovery, and she was to play a very important part in making that happen. Claire felt the empowerment of an achievable challenge, something she hadn't felt for a long time. The only challenge she'd had at work all year was wrangling an invite to a decent corporate box for the Melbourne Cup. Which meant absolutely nothing now, thanks to her redundancy.

It occurred to her that Derek must have made a significant effort to lighten her workload in response to her series of personal issues this year. She hadn't noticed at the time—a sure sign she'd needed it. Now she made a mental note to thank him when the opportunity arose. She wouldn't make a special call—didn't want him getting the wrong idea—but she was bound to bump into him at the races sometime. There were less than two weeks until the Cup. God, she'd miss all the fun. But then she had an idea: maybe she and Bernie could organise something special and give Jack a date to strive for.

Claire strode back down the hall to Jack's room, rehearsing in her head a speech she hoped would prove motivational.

Before heading back up to the hills, Claire called in to her house, checked the answering machine messages: five hang-ups and three messages from friends wanting to organise get-togethers. She'd call them back later. She was dreading having to reveal that she was now not only single and jobless, she was country-dwelling. She'd become her own worst nightmare.

Claire retrieved the esky from the cupboard under the stairs and emptied the fridge into it—no point eating Bernadette out of house and home while all her stuff went off. She packed a week's worth of casual clothes, reset the alarm and closed the door behind her, slightly surprised to feel no pangs of regret or sadness at leaving the house.

'Right, I think we've got everything,' Bernadette said when she and Claire were strapped into her car awaiting departure. 'We've got enough cleaning products to make the Sydney Opera House sparkle, and plenty of food and coffee to keep us going.'

Claire had been both anticipating and dreading returning to the farmhouse to prepare it for Jack's homecoming.

'Bernie, thanks so much for doing this.'

'No worries,' Bernadette said, waving away her thanks with a flick of her hand.

'No, I mean it. You've even had to give up a day at the shop.'

'It's not a problem, Claire, honestly. It's time Darren took on more of a management role, and anyway, I know you'd do the same for me.'

'Well, I really do appreciate it.'

'I know,' Bernadette said, patting Claire's leg. 'So we're off?'

'Guess so,' Claire winced.

They drove in silence, each left to their own thoughts. Claire gnawed at her lip in worried concentration. She needed to be alone in the house to really face what she'd been avoiding these past few months—years, if she was being totally honest. But how could she tell Bernadette to back off when she had set aside the whole day—not to mention practically the whole year—for her?

After ten minutes they turned into the long drive and then pulled up at the front of the house. Claire took a deep breath and got ready to blurt out her rehearsed excuses for cleaning the inside of the house alone. But Bernie got in first.

'How about I start out here since I'm in the gardening game? Put my money where my mouth is, so to speak.'

Claire let out a sigh of relief that sounded more like a gasp, unaware she'd been holding her breath. 'Thanks, that'd be great. I'll start inside, then—after I've fed the 'cheque.'

'You make it sound like some complex refinancing move,' Bernadette said, laughing.

'Well, he is a pretty big risk.' Claire laughed back. 'See you in a bit,' she added, and disappeared around the side of the house.

When Claire returned, Bernadette had already finished weeding one of the garden beds and was starting on the next. She looked up, wiped her sweating brow and watched as Claire stared at the door for a full minute before taking a deep breath and turning the handle.

Claire stood inside the laundry, the back door shut behind her. Her heart was pounding and her sweating hands clenched around bucket and vacuum handles. What was it about the house that did this to her every time? She looked around her at the small square brown tiles her parents had struggled to decide on all those years ago.

Claire had never liked the tiles, but now saw them as a solid memorial to a life possibly too regimented, and definitely less complicated. Her mother had been right when she'd said their size and particular composition would render them less prone to cracking and chipping. She smiled and sent a mental blessing to the woman who had driven her nuts ninety percent of the time.

She took a deep breath, told herself to be strong for Jack and took a step forward, and then another, and another, gathering comfort as she did. This was her father's house now, no longer her mother's tight ship—it hadn't been for a number of years.

Although she'd spent most of her life there, she felt

like an intruder. Even her old bedroom seemed foreign. Her collection of satin-and-felt show ribbons were still piled on a coat hanger behind the door. Trophies lined the top of her wardrobe under a thick layer of dust. Framed photos of her triumphs and various mounts took up most of the pine dressing table. She was nervous about going through this person's things, this stranger whose life she'd once occupied. The feeling doubled when she realised there was not one photo of her parents, cousins, aunts or uncles. It was all just her and her horses. *Selfish*, she told herself. But she'd been horse-mad, competitive, totally driven. She'd had to be.

So when had all that changed? She stared at the flowery quilt cover and matching curtains that her mother—in some guilt-induced moment—had made in an attempt at balancing her daughter's life.

Of course! The curtains had coincided with her teens, boys and—she now groaned—that time when you didn't want anything to do with your thick, unfashionable, old fogey parents.

She remembered how her father had tried to tell her of her mother's chest pains and how she'd cut him off, saying she had to meet some boy—some boy she no longer even remembered the name of. And could he feed the horses for her?

She smiled now. Jack had been a pushover. He had always been there, quietly tending to her horse's feed and water, rugs and bandages, while her mother had yelled at her from the sidelines for letting the horse refuse at the water jump, getting second place instead of first.

For the first time Claire could see what had happened, the fork in the road where she'd chosen one path over the other. But more important she now saw why. It had been more than simple teenage rebellion. She'd got tired of doing her best and still being seen as a failure. She had needed to walk out from her mother's shadow and be her own person, her own success.

But she also had her mother to thank for the determination to prove she didn't need her parents for anything. And it was all because of her mother's tough love—her frosty, arm's-length approach to parenting. Ah, the irony. While Claire was wise enough to understand the origins of her insecurities, she also knew that as an adult, she alone was responsible for her own decisions, right or wrong. And right now her decision was to stop being a big wuss and get on with getting everything in order.

She wiped away the single tear sitting on her cheek, put down the photo frame and got up with renewed determination. She started removing the cobwebs from the corners of the ceiling. As she worked, she decided that next she'd take down her photos, trophies and ribbons, and pack them away. They belonged with the past.

Thirteen

Claire stretched out in bed, listening and feeling her surroundings. It was her third morning waking up at the farm and it didn't really feel like home yet. Warm, comfortable, reassuring, yes; but home, no. Still, it wasn't as bad as she'd imagined. She hadn't actually felt like the spinster daughter moving home, though that could all change when she began sharing the space with her father.

He'd had five years to rebel against her mother's strict standards of hygiene and tidiness. Whenever she'd visited there had never been any obvious evidence of the place having gone to the dogs. But then, she'd never turned up unannounced. Surely if her father lived like a piggy bachelor she would have seen some signs— especially when she'd done her big spring clean the other day.

Claire was starting to realise that she didn't know Jack McIntyre very well at all. She knew him as her mother's husband and then her widower, someone who did as he was told and avoided rocking the boat. Had he changed as a result of those thirty-odd years together?

They did say couples grew alike, just like pets became like their owners. It might actually be quite exciting to get to know the real Jack McIntyre.

As far as Claire could see, the training of racehorses was the only area that had remained free of her mother's domination. Sometime in the early days—before she'd been born—there must have been some kind of major demarcation dispute, which her father had won. You could just tell. She'd often noticed her mother standing at the window, gnawing at the inside of her cheek. The vein at the edge of her eye would pulse as she watched Jack with his horses, the same as it did when she was issuing Claire criticism.

Their methods and personalities were so different. Her mother was all about making the animal submit, do as it was told at all costs, which often meant working it on the lunge—round and round at the end of a long rope—in heavy sand until it was foaming, quivering, dripping in sweat, literally putty in her hands.

Jack subscribed to a natural horsemanship approach: the animal was *asked* to comply, taught to oblige its master out of respect and not fear. This polarising saw Claire's mother take on the eventers—competition horses—and her father the racehorses. Claire had often wished it had been the other way around, then she might have been spared all the emotional baggage that had taken her so long to work through.

It was wrong to think ill of the dead. Of course she'd loved her mother and sometimes still missed her; love of one's parents was one of those things programmed at birth. But it didn't mean she had to like everything about them.

Grace McIntyre had done what she thought was right

at the time. Just like children, horses didn't come with an operating manual with a solution for every problem, and her mother had liked to win at all costs—had needed to, for some reason.

Claire checked the clock radio, threw back the covers and swapped her pyjamas for farm clothes. It was 5:45 a.m. Ordinarily she would have cursed the ridiculous, uncivilised hour and rolled over. But this morning, the first time for as long as she could remember, Claire felt energised and was keen to face the day. And so, it seemed, was the lonely little horse.

'Coming,' she muttered in response to Paycheque's second bout of whinnying.

Claire grabbed a couple of carrots from the kitchen and bolted out of the house, reminding herself to get a big bag of 'horse' carrots and all the other feed he'd require. She wanted him looking his best—bright, shiny coat and eyes—for when Jack returned.

Two days later, Claire visited her father and was pleased to notice a dramatic improvement. His face had a pale pink tinge. It was a long way from a tan, but healthier nonetheless considering he hadn't had any direct sunlight for over two months. He was sitting up in bed dipping a Scotch Finger biscuit into a cup of tea, and wearing the new lumpy grey jumper Daphne had knitted. He beamed at Claire, put down his cup and saucer, and held out his arms for a hug. Claire let out a deep sigh of relief and held on tight.

After what seemed hours, a voice called from the doorway and they parted with little murmurs of embarrassment and self-consciousness.

'Um, Ms McIntyre? I saw you come in. Would you

like a cuppa and a bickie?' The nervous, pimply-faced girl looked about twelve—hopefully she was only in charge of the tea trolley.

'Yes, please. That'd be great—white, no sugar, thank you.' Claire beamed her most gracious smile, trying to make up for her uncharitable thoughts.

'Another cup, Mr McIntyre?' the kid asked, already fossicking about in the trolley.

'Yes, thanks—and for the hundredth time, my dear, it's Jack.'

The young lass blushed. With shaking hands she placed the two cups, rattling dangerously in their saucers, on the side table. She grabbed Jack's empty one and backed away, mumbling for them to enjoy their tea.

'All this "mister this" and "mister that" makes an old bushie like me a bit uncomfortable,' Jack said, reaching for his cup.

'Probably part of their strategy.' Claire laughed, and picked up her cup. 'To stop you wanting to stay too long.'

'Yes, well, no problem there. You know they wake you up all through the night? All part of their strategy, too, I suppose.'

Claire took a sip, put her cup back on its saucer and said with mock seriousness, 'No, I think they really are checking your vital signs—death isn't too good for business, I hear.'

'Of course, quite right,' Jack said, adopting a formal tone. They both laughed.

Suddenly feeling sentimental, Claire put her hand over her father's. 'Dad, I was worried sick. I'm so glad you're okay.'

'I know—gave myself a bit of a fright, too. Truth be

told, if I hadn't heard your voice so much I might have just given up,' he said, staring into his cup.

'So you heard me?'

'Of course—every last word. Bill was here reading the paper, wasn't he? I had no idea what that bloody clicking was until Daphne showed me the jumper. It's really quite something,' he said, looking down his front.

Claire blushed and drained her cup in an attempt to hide it.

'Yes, and so many times I just wanted to tell you all to just bloody well shut up.' He laughed. 'Especially when you took to singing.'

'Yeah, sorry about that,' Claire said, dipping her head. 'But I'd run out of things to tell you, and then I read about this Dr Burrows and his theories—blame him!'

'Well, I'm glad you did because I think it worked. Though next time, read a book instead of singing. There's a good girl.'

Claire slapped his arm. 'There'd better not be a next time.'

Jack put down his empty cup. 'So,' he said, wringing his hands, 'when can I get out of here?'

'Whenever you're ready and the doctor gives the nod. Are you getting about okay?'

'Yep, walked all the way down to the nurse's station and back yesterday. And lucky I did—they were making their picks for the Caulfield Cup. Needed to be set right.'

Claire was relieved to hear him mention the horses. He hadn't said anything about them since waking and asking after Paycheque. At least now she could stop worrying about whether she'd done the wrong thing finding the horse.

'Speaking of which,' he continued, 'how is the little lad?'

Claire's confused look was genuine. 'Who?'

'Paycheque, of course.'

'Er, he's good.' Claire blushed slightly and looked away.

'What aren't you telling me?'

'Nothing. He's fine. Eating enough for two like he always did. He may be a little lonely on his own, but he's fine.'

'Lonely? What about the others?'

'Well…'

'What, Claire?'

'I sold them,' she blurted. 'All of them. Even Paycheque.'

'Oh. Right.'

'I'm really sorry. I didn't see what else I could do… I didn't know if you were going to wake up, and I had so much to do at work, and I just couldn't take care of them as well. It was all too much. But I acted too hastily. I know that now. I should have…'

'No point worrying about "should haves". It's okay, Claire, I'm sure you thought you were doing the right thing at the time.'

'But at least I got Paycheque back.'

'Well, that's the main thing. If I'm honest, he was the only really serious bet anyway. So who ended up with him, then—Mark Leonard?'

'No.'

'Jason Llewelyn?'

'No, no one you know.'

'Oh, I was sure he'd have been snapped up by one of the establishment—got a lot of potential for a little horse. Probably couldn't see past his size, idiots. Yes, that would be it,' he mused.

Claire was silently inspecting her nails, unable to look her father in the eye.

'Claire, what else aren't you telling me? And don't give me that "nothing" crap again. I want the full version and I want it now, in all its gruesome detail, if that's the way it is.'

'Okay.' Claire sighed, defeated. She proceeded to tell Jack the whole story, including how Derek had seen the horse at Morphettville. She watched her father redden with anger and was relieved at no longer having to keep the secret. When she spoke of how Paycheque had ended up at the abattoir and what a close call it had been, Jack McIntyre's chin took on a determined jut and his eyes a steely glint that Claire knew was a signal of his desire to get even.

But she was unconcerned. Jack had never been confrontational or violent. He chose to hit back in an even more powerful way—by beating people at their own game, and usually as the underdog. Paycheque would be a success. She had no doubt now that Jack was back in charge. It might take a year, maybe more, but that little horse would return to Morphettville and not only pass his barrier trial, but also reign victorious over every trainer who'd dismissed him.

'I'm going to need your help, Claire—I'm not as nimble as I used to be.'

Claire dipped her head again.

'What? What else aren't you telling me?'

Claire took a deep breath. 'That's the other thing. I am, was… I was made redundant. I've got all the time in the world at the moment,' she said with a grim smile.

'Well, of course I'm sorry about you losing you job, but I can't help being happy to have you around full-time. Those bastards didn't appreciate you anyway. Don't worry, we'll be a success in no time and you won't need their lousy job.'

The phrases 'famous last words' and 'if only' ran through Claire's head. As far as she knew, Jack McIntyre had only ever made enough to keep one step ahead of the bank—just. Oh, well, she had a year to see how things panned out. Though the lows in the horseracing game tended to last a lot longer—impatience was a dangerous trait in a trainer.

'Well, come on, Claire Bear. Get me out of here,' Jack suddenly said, throwing the covers back and swinging his legs over the side of the bed.

'What, now?'

'Yes, now. We've got work to do. Go and find a doctor to give me permission to leave, will you?'

'As long as you're okay,' Claire said, eyeing him warily.

'Absolutely. Now off you go,' he said, making shooing gestures at her.

When they got back to him, Jack McIntyre was already dressed and sitting back on the bed, pulling on his R.M. Williams dress boots.

The doctor was almost as surprised as Claire. Only two days before they'd had to cajole him into getting out of bed for some exercise.

'Hi, Doc. Here to give me the all clear, I hope.' He beamed.

'Doesn't look like I have a choice.' He laughed. 'I do have one condition, though.'

'Name it.'

'You call me the instant anything untoward occurs—the slightest twinge, dizziness, anything at all.' He looked from Jack to Claire and back again. 'Agreed?'

'Agreed,' Claire and Jack said in unison. They laughed.

'Well then, if you just sign this discharge form you can be on your way.'

Their forty-minute journey back up into the Adelaide Hills was made mostly in silence, Jack staring intently out the window, as if seeing everything they passed for the first time. Claire was still a little dazed by the apparent speed at which he'd come back to health.

Fourteen

Jack was like a teenager home from school for the holidays. He was barely in the house long enough to appear polite and offer thanks for all the work Claire and Bernadette had put in. Claire, wary of tiring him out, insisted they sit for a cup of tea before heading out to see Paycheque.

Jack was like a tightly wound spring: gulping his tea, then sitting with eyes darting about, fingers fidgeting, while he waited for Claire to finish. After ten minutes, Claire gave up stalling and pushed her cup aside. Jack leapt up from the table with the energy of a man half his age and was at the back door pulling his boots on before Claire was halfway across the kitchen.

Claire followed as he trooped along the worn track between the old pepper trees, past the almond beside the disused chook shed. Every now and then he slowed, struggling in the sand that had come to the surface through years of journeys back and forth to rug, feed and exercise horses. From behind, Claire noticed his shoulders taking on a different shape as he went. He was like a snake shedding its skin—shrugging off the tag of convalescing patient and becoming a proud horse trainer once again.

He seemed to pause for a beat when he rounded the abandoned dog compound and saw his uptight, under-sized racehorse standing in the yard like another over-wound spring. There was instant recognition: the horse neighed and Jack called, 'There you are,' in a voice that threatened to crack.

Claire's throat tightened. She stopped, stayed back a few steps so as not to intrude. The reunion was like something out of *The Horse Whisperer*.

'G'day there,' he said, leaning on the rail and putting a hand out for Paycheque to sniff.

Claire moved to the railing and leant on it.

'Bit of a butterball, don't you think?' Jack said, scratching the horse behind the ears.

Annoyed at the reprimand, Claire scowled under her Akubra and behind her sunglasses.

'Claire, he's meant to be a sleek racehorse, not a heavy hunter.' Jack laughed.

'I decided he needed some pampering after his ordeal,' Claire shot back. Nonetheless, she coloured with shame; Jack was right, she had completely forgotten he was meant to be smooth and lean.

'Well, we'll just have to get you out of here and into some exercise,' Jack said, slapping the horse on the neck.

Claire relaxed, telling herself to lighten up. Her father had always teased her in this manner. She thought she'd developed a thicker skin being a number on someone's payroll.

'Sorry I let you down, little mate,' Jack said quietly.

He cleared his throat. 'Right, teatime. Come on, we'll start fresh in the morning.'

Jack strode off towards the house. Claire followed silently, already starting to formulate a fitness regime for the horse in her mind.

'That was the best meal I've ever had,' Jack McIntyre declared as he laid his knife and fork down on his plate later that same evening. Claire smiled.

'Thanks, Dad,' she said, getting up and clearing the plates. 'Simple fare for simple folk,' she added, and was instantly struck by how like her late mother she sounded.

Jack had noticed it, too. His face clouded for a split second before opening up again. 'Thank God for home-cooked meals. The food in that place was very, um...'

'Healthy!' they cried in unison, and erupted into laughter.

It was a longstanding family joke. Jack's mother—Claire's grandma Betty—had been a boiled cabbage and burnt beef sort of cook. She had never liked cooking, and in almost twenty years of weekly dinners until her instalment into an aged care facility, she had rarely deviated from roast beef. In its shrivelled state it was barely recognisable, but while a variety of euphemisms were used to heartily describe the meal, there was always respect for the tradition and family values it represented.

'You could teach those hospital cooks a thing or two. I'm sorry, but roast pork just isn't the same without crackling.'

'No. It'd probably be soggy anyway by the time they got all those meals out.'

'Don't get me started on soggy,' he said, rolling his eyes.

Suddenly his face clouded again and he looked down at the tablecloth under his hands. It was one of the two her mother had made when things had been tough the first time around. He fingered a small hole gently.

When she couldn't afford a new cloth, Grace McIntyre had shortened all the curtains in the house to be level with the windowsills, and then sewn the scraps together. She had used the fabric, interspersed with budget calico, to create a log-cabin-style patchwork. She had been proud of her creations, and rightly so—everyone who visited marvelled at their beauty and intricacy. But no one knew the origins or reasons—Grace McIntyre had her pride.

They'd never hidden from Claire the fact that money was tight, including the two times the banks were threatening to foreclose: when she was nine and again when she was fifteen. One of the unique things about being an only child was that adults included you in conversations you probably wouldn't be privy to if you had a sibling to remind them you really were still just a kid. But it also meant she couldn't remain blissfully unaware, like other children, when adults had tough times to deal with.

She had understood enough to be worried, but not enough to be able to do anything about it. When it mattered, her parents pretended she was just an ordinary child and chose not to ask her opinion. And both times she'd had a solution to get them out of debt.

When she was nine it was a lemonade stand at the gate; when she was fifteen it was going off and becoming an apprentice jockey. But neither idea had even been aired; it was as if they could read her mind—or someone else could. First the lemon tree died for no apparent reason, and then she broke her arm two weeks before her sixteenth birthday, when she had planned to announce her intention to leave school. She hadn't given much credence to coincidence either time—she'd secretly been thankful for being saved.

Claire continued to stare at Jack's fingers. She knew it was corny, but it was as though the table-cloths were the very fabric that had held everything together. Collectively they had been witness to every event—significant and insignificant, happy and sad—in the McIntyre household. While they existed she was always able to convince herself everything would be okay.

'Ice-cream?' Claire asked, dragging herself away from her sadness and gathering the dishes.

'No, thanks, not getting enough exercise,' Jack said, patting a stomach that looked flatter than those of most men half his age. 'But I could murder a cup of tea.'

'Done,' Claire said.

'Speaking of porky…'

Claire stiffened at the sink. Since Keith's death and everything else that had been happening, she was thinner than she'd ever been. Her reaction was merely another legacy of a life spent mainly with adults—listening first to her mother, and then to her friends' tales of constant dieting and calorie-counting. She'd been on guard for as long as she could remember.

'…I'm going to need you to start riding Paycheque—little lard arse.'

'Oh! But it's… I…'

'I've been kidding myself. I'm too old for serious riding.'

God, Claire thought, *he sounds almost cheerful.* She'd spent years hinting he was getting too long in the tooth and always got the brush-off. Now that he was going quietly she wasn't sure how she felt. The dynamics had all changed. She blinked, and when she looked back at her father it was as if he'd aged twenty years. He was an old man. She'd always managed to keep him young in her mind.

'But I'm...' What she wanted to say was, *I'm too old for this shit*, which was laughable, of course, considering she was nearly half his age.

'Don't worry, it'll all come back to you—it hasn't been that long.'

That night, Claire lay in bed wondering how her first ride of Paycheque would go.

The next morning, Claire stretched and lay listening for a few minutes to the sounds of activity coming from the kitchen. She smiled. Old habits die hard, but some never die at all.

Jack had resumed his ritual of coffee and porridge followed by soft-poached eggs. That was what it sounded like anyway. Claire dragged her legs out of bed, hoping tradition had prevailed.

As a rule, two cups of coffee had served as breakfast for Claire, but she was now looking forward to fuelling up in preparation for dealing with Paycheque and any trouble he might give her.

'Ah, there you are. I've made brekky.' The unspoken words 'just like the old days' hung in the air. 'Might need your strength later,' he added with a wink.

'I'd love some breakfast, thanks, but I don't think we have to worry about Paycheque—he's been a dream since he's been back. Even when we loaded him.' Claire added sugar to her coffee.

'Well, like I always say…'

'Expect the unexpected,' Claire said, finishing the sentence for him.

'Exactly. Now, quickly, eat your porridge before your eggs go hard.'

Claire sat at the table spooning the gluggy mixture into her mouth while Jack moved expertly around the kitchen. She was still surprised to find herself really enjoying sharing the house with him.

I could get used to this, she thought, and began tucking into eggs, fried mushrooms and toast. She looked across at her father and was pleased to see him heartily eating also—he was definitely getting closer to being his old self.

'Damn good, if I do say so myself,' Jack said, pushing his plate away and then his chair back from the table. 'Ready to get to it?'

'You go. I'm just going to put a few things away here and then I'll be over.'

'I'll give him a decent brush while I wait for you.'

'I won't be long—not going to bother with the dishes.'

A couple of minutes later, Claire made her way over to the stables. She paused at the empty dog compound and, hidden by the rusty fencing, stood to observe her father for a few moments. He was tying the horse to the rail. Claire smiled. He looked every bit the expert horseman he'd always been, and almost as nimble, she thought, as he bent down to retrieve a brush from the canvas grooming bag by the post.

Suddenly the horse reared up, pulled back hard against his rope, and then broke free. In two strides Paycheque was at the far side of the outer yard, with his chest hard against the solid timber rail, darting from side to side looking for an escape route. The frayed remains of the lead-rope swayed under his chin.

'Hey, hey. There, there. You're okay,' Jack called in a soothing tone. But he made no move towards the horse. He had to wait for the creature's fight-or-flight instinct to subside.

'What happened?' Claire asked, now at the rail beside her father. Paycheque had his back to them a few metres away. His head, with eyes flashing and nostrils flared, was turned towards them—keeping an eye on the enemy. He was quivering from his mane to his hooves, sweat already breaking out on his sleek neck. His ears were back, twitching and rotating towards every sound, every movement.

'I tied him up, bent down to pick up a brush, and bang, he freaked,' Jack said, holding up his hands in despair.

'Poor thing's terrified,' Claire said.

'Yeah, looks like someone's given him a hard time.' Jack pretended to swipe at a fly but Claire saw the lone tear on his cheek before it was wiped away.

'He didn't seem at all nervy the other day when Bernadette and I picked him up. Did you, boy?' Claire called. 'Come on, what's the problem?'

The horse turned a little more towards them and lowered his head slightly. Claire thought he looked perplexed, as if he'd reacted too quickly and now regretted it.

'It's okay,' she soothed, and took a step towards him.

'Claire, don't. He might lash out,' Jack warned.

'We've gotta do something. You're not going to kick, are you? Good boy.' Claire's heart was racing as she took another step forward. She was now within kicking range. If he decided to double-barrel her she wouldn't stand a chance. The horse tensed. Claire paused and waited for a sign that he was relaxing. She couldn't hear herself think above the pounding of blood in her ears. She knew what she was doing was dangerous, but she didn't have a choice. Here was a creature in distress that needed her reassurance, to be reminded that they weren't the enemy. If they didn't put a stop to this behaviour it would be three times as difficult next time. It was a very fine line to tread, and potentially disastrous.

'Come on, you big baby, you just got a fright.' She was now right alongside the half-tonne of horse, aware that if he chose to he could easily crush her against the solid timber railing. But she wasn't afraid: a little anxious, yes; but afraid, no.

Before she'd left for the bright lights of corporate life, she'd dealt with plenty of difficult horses. Many had been written off as dangerous, but Claire often found they were nothing more than misunderstood. Jack had said she had a special gift, but she'd just shrugged it off. She'd never understood all the hype around *The Horse Whisperer*. That's how she'd always dealt with horses.

Paycheque's head was still turned away so that both she and Jack were in his peripheral vision. His ears flickered like antennae. The next thing was to make contact, put out her hand and place it on his shoulder. But did she dare? It could well send him off again. Timing was everything. Claire was still contemplating her next move when the horse lowered his head and turned fully towards her. The remains of the lead-rope was a stretched reach away. But instead of grabbing it she patted the horse and rubbed his ears.

Claire breathed a deep sigh of relief as her heart rate steadied and her breathing returned to normal. She grasped the rope and applied some pressure. The horse didn't flinch—so far, so good.

'It's okay. Come over here with me,' she urged, giving the rope a slight tug. Paycheque hesitated at first but then slowly followed her over to where Jack stood, arms folded over the top rail.

'Hey there, little mate,' Jack said, rubbing the horse's forehead. 'Got a bit of a fright, eh? You'll be right. Claire, do you mind holding him in case it's a tying-up problem.' The horse was no longer quivering but continued to eye Jack warily.

Claire felt a twinge of guilt at the horse's acceptance of her but not her father. Paycheque seemed fine so she sat on the edge of the water trough while keeping a loose hold on the frayed rope. The sun was on her back and in her wandering mind she remembered her childhood when she'd do exactly this: keep her father company under the pretence her help was needed.

Suddenly there was a sharp tug on the rope. She held on and allowed herself to be pulled from her perch and a couple of steps out into the main yard. She turned to see her father, brush in hand, staring bewildered, lips pursed, shaking his head slowly from side to side.

'Some bastard's definitely beaten him,' he growled. He sat down on the trough Claire had vacated and ran his hands through his thick white pepper-flecked hair. 'He's fine until I bend down.' He frowned.

'Hmm,' Claire said. The horse now stood forlornly by her side.

'It's okay, mate. It's not your fault,' Jack said, getting up carefully and going over to the horse. 'See, Claire, it's not me or the brush he's scared of.'

'No, it was definitely you bending down that did it.'

'God, if I ever find out what they did and who did it,' he growled.

They carefully groomed the horse, which was calm but still exceedingly wary, then put his dust rugs on and turned him out into the smallest of the paddocks behind the stables. Jack and Claire stood shoulder to shoulder at the wire gate for a few moments, each silently chewing over their thoughts of what had gone on and their optimism—or otherwise—for the future.

'Think I need a lie-down after all the excitement,' Jack finally announced with a tight laugh.

'Good idea. I'll just do those few dishes and then head over to see Bernadette—give you some peace.' Paycheque stood a little way off, returning their gaze, but still with a perplexed look about him, as if he felt punished or insulted, rather than rewarded, by his freedom.

'Mmm, better find him a friend,' Jack said. He nodded to himself and turned from the gate. Claire crossed her fingers. The last thing she wanted was a return to the old days when they had paddocks full of has-beens and never-will-bes, horses Jack had felt compelled to give a home to. Most had never come remotely close to making the grade.

The trouble with Jack McIntyre was that he was a softy. Any small prize was a win to Jack. Sometimes the way he reacted you'd think he'd won the Melbourne

Cup instead of a dinner-for-two voucher for a local pub out bush. For Jack, the horse's victory was more important than his own.

Claire's heart swelled with pride as she remembered the most memorable victories: old Duke, partially blind, who couldn't see the finish line but trusted his rider to lead the way.

Back in the eighties, Trigger was both Jack's quickest and laziest horse, which was a major challenge until Jack discovered his motivation was food. A smear of molasses in his nose and he finally won his first race, which just so happened to be a local feed merchant voucher!

Claire felt her heart tug at remembering Tango, a small grey who had initially been so timid he wouldn't put his head down to eat until no one was watching and the stable lights had been turned off.

So what if Jack hadn't won even a Group Two race? *He* was happy, and that was most important. There was a deep niggle of envy inside her. Her father had found his passion in life and had the courage to follow it, whatever the price. It was his 'everything will be okay' attitude that saw him keep going despite all the knockbacks. Claire groaned inwardly. She didn't have that. She was not a 'go with the flow' kind of girl— a trait unfortunately inherited from her mother. Keith had got a lot of mileage from teasing her about it. Was it something that could be changed, or was it one of those fundamental personality traits that could only be tempered a little?

Well, she *had* agreed to take the year off from the corporate world.

Fifteen

Claire was rinsing the last of the cutlery, staring out the kitchen window at nothing in particular and wondering if she would learn to enjoy this relaxed lifestyle long-term or become bored, when she noticed a cloud of dust rising from the driveway. She pulled the plug, dragged her gloves off and lay them over the drainer, realising she was excited at the prospect of a visitor. She checked her watch. It wouldn't be Bernadette; they weren't meeting for another hour. Probably Bill and Daphne Markson for her father. There had been a constant trickle of phone calls, but no visitors since his return from hospital.

A silver BMW rounded the huge lemon-scented gum and pulled up in front of the house. No one in her father's racing circle owned a Beemer, and the only people who used the front door were Jehovah's Witnesses and insurance salesmen—and whoever this was. Who the hell was it? The dark tinted windows made any identification impossible.

Claire made her way up the hall and opened the front door, noting the spiderwebs behind the screen. Why was the person taking so long to get out of the car? Must be a woman checking makeup and applying lipstick, she concluded, instantly feeling territorial and on guard. Finally the car door opened and a man emerged. Claire stifled a snorting laugh at how far off she'd been in her surmising. She took in the solid build and broad shoulders and well-cut, slightly spiky, greying brown hair. Handsome, even at this distance. But her mouth dropped open as the dark sunglasses came off and she recognised the man in the lime-green-and-sky-blue-checked shirt and pale chinos.

'Derek?' She felt weird, almost faint. It was as if she'd entered a parallel universe or something. Derek was someone in a suit, not this laid-back country fellow. And not here. To her, he only really existed in public places—the office, the members' stand at the races. But here he was, looking all country squire in his brogues and Akubra. Claire stifled another laugh—he *so* didn't look country. Well-clipped hedge and shiny picket-fence country, maybe, but definitely not barbed-wire and peeling-paint country. But Jesus, she did. Claire looked down at herself and cringed. She couldn't have looked worse if she'd tried.

The elastic sides of her boots had gone, her jeans bore badly done patches in hot-pink floral in all the wrong places—a joke of Bernie's from years ago—and her once-white T-shirt that was now a pale splotchy pink, thanks to a stray red sock in the wash, had a large dollop of dirt-infused horse snot on the front that only a legally blind person could fail to see.

'Howdy, Claire,' Derek said, touching his fingers to the brim of his hat. She wondered if he'd watched a couple of episodes of *McLeod's Daughters* on DVD in preparation for his foray out bush.

'What are you doing here?' she asked, failing to keep the suspicion from her voice.

'Came to visit an old friend.' He shrugged.

And see what goes on out here, Claire mentally finished his sentence. She had butterflies rising in her stomach. God, what if he was there to ask her out? Or worse, what if he had a problem at work he needed her to sort out? No, he would have phoned. The insects had made a ball and were now leaping as one inside her.

'How did you find me?'

'It's a small town, Claire. And your lovely friend at the garden shop gave me directions.'

Claire felt unnerved—he'd infiltrated her entire world.

'I'm really sorry if I've intruded, but I just wanted to see how you are, you know, after...'

Claire wanted to snap, 'I'm fine, no thanks to you,' but she felt a wave of compassion for him standing there in his crisp clothes, trying to look casual, squinting against the sun, so obviously uncomfortable. She smiled. He was so different to the Derek she'd worked with for so long—and he'd probably driven a long way to see her.

'You'd better come in—sun's a bit fierce,' she said, holding the screen door open. Derek bounded up the three verandah steps.

Claire was glad she'd got rid of the past few days' newspapers—the place was presentable in its rustic, old-fashioned country charm.

'What a lovely spot—I can see why you're here,'

Derek said, sitting at the table as indicated and placing his hat carefully on the chair beside him.

'If you like quiet, it's great. Coffee? Only instant, I'm afraid.'

'Oh. You wouldn't have a tea bag, would you?'

'I would, as a matter of fact,' Claire said, trying not to laugh aloud at his polite rejection of instant coffee. She'd once been the same. When she'd moved back into the farmhouse, she'd brought her coffee machine with her, but found she couldn't really be bothered. After two days she'd put it away under the kitchen bench. The ease of instant coffee somehow just went with the country.

'Great,' he said, clearly relieved. 'Milk, no sugar, thanks.'

Claire plonked an open packet of Scotch Finger biscuits on the table and noted Derek's slight look of disappointment. Unable to resist, Claire said, 'Sorry, I'm not baking until this afternoon.' She flicked her hair and offered her most angelic expression.

'Oh, right, well, no worries,' Derek said, his faith in the country lifestyle seemingly restored. He grabbed a biscuit from the pack and dunked it into his tea.

They chatted easily about the weather, horseracing and the merits of country living. Derek avoided any discussion of the office, but when he realised Claire had little interest beyond news of old work colleagues, he gave in. Claire was surprised to find she didn't really miss anyone from the office, and there was no sense of being on the outer. But most surprising of all, she realised she was actually beginning to enjoy Derek's company.

He'd swapped his persona like a hat. Off was his businesslike formality—which Claire likened to a bowler—and on (literally) was a pastoralist-style Aku-bra, making him appear down-to-earth and genuine. She couldn't help wondering which one was the real Derek, the one he'd reveal with the reality of domes-ticity. Claire mentally kicked herself under the table. Domesticity?! He hadn't even so much as asked her out.

This brought her back to postulating over why he was really there, sitting at the table across from her, drinking his second cup of tea. They lapsed into silence, having done a cursory skim across the surface of their lives. The room seemed to have become starved of oxygen. They were looking into their cups, around the room, the table, the carpet—anything to avoid holding each other's gaze too long.

Claire waited for Derek, who was fidgeting with the tags of the discarded tea bags on the small plate in front of him, to make the first move. His face became slightly red and puffed up. He took a deep breath and made his hands into a steeple in front of him.

She was suddenly struck with fear and a sense of foreboding—he always did this with his hands in meetings when he had tough decisions to make or bad news to give. Like her redundancy. But hang on, Claire checked herself. She was being irrational. He was no longer her boss. She was free. Her full redundancy pay-out was safely in the bank—there was no bad news he could bring her now. She let herself relax.

'Um, Claire?'

'Yes?'

'I was wondering if, er...' Claire was urging him on in her mind as a door banged and Jack appeared. He looked like an oversized child, hair all over the place, rubbing his eyes against the apparent bright light. Claire groaned inwards.

'Oh,' he said, stopping short when he noticed Derek at the table. 'I'm sorry, I didn't realise you had company. I'll leave you to it,' he added, and began turning away.

'No, that's okay, I was just leaving.' Derek stood up and collected his hat from the chair. He moved around the table and offered his hand. 'You must be Jack. Derek Anderson, pleased to meet you.' Claire was in knots of annoyance. What the hell was he about to say before they were interrupted?

'Likewise,' Jack said, shaking the hand.

There was an awkward moment when it seemed Derek wanted to say more. Jack seemed to be wondering how he knew the name Derek Anderson.

A frowning Claire followed Derek out to his car. They stopped on the verandah. 'Derek, why are you really here?'

He shrugged. 'Like I said, wanted to check you were okay.'

'And?'

He sighed deeply and stared into her dark green searching eyes. 'And to offer you your old job back.'

'What?! Why didn't you say?'

Derek shrugged again. 'When I got here I realised I didn't want you to have to choose—you look so relaxed, at least ten years younger.'

'Derek Anderson, flattery will get you nowhere,' she said, unconsciously pushing her hair back from her face with a flirtatious sweep of her hand.

'I know,' he said, and dropped his gaze to the ground.

'I can make my own decisions,' Claire snapped.

'I'm sure you can.'

One thing Claire McIntyre hated was being patronised. 'And why is my position available again after becoming redundant?'

'I had a word to the new manager—he's actually not a bad bloke, as it turns out.'

'And said what, exactly, Derek? Some sob-story about poor Claire McIntyre who's already lost her husband this year…?'

'Jesus, Claire, I tried to bat for you before they let you go. I've gone in again for no reason other than you're damn good at what you do and I like you. Why are you making it so damn hard for me? Is this some kind of feminist hoop I'm meant to jump through? You'd better tell me if it is because I don't have a fucking clue.' He stepped off the verandah and strode over to his car, pressing the remote as he went.

Claire felt like a sulky schoolgirl and had no idea why. 'You could have asked me instead of wasting time…'

He sighed. 'All right. Claire McIntyre, would you like the position of Client Relationship Manager, including managing the AHG Recruitment account?' He paused. 'And it wasn't a waste—I like you, Claire. It was nice to see you.'

'Probably.' Her voice came out as a squeak.

'Probably what?'

'I probably would want my job back if it weren't for…'

'I know, your father.'

'No, not Dad. Well, not *just* Dad.'

'What, you want more money, is that it?'

Claire shrugged.

'God, Claire. Give me a break. Now I *am* wasting my time.' He got in the car and through the open window said, 'I'm not into riddles—you either want the job or you don't, and clearly you don't.'

Suddenly Claire felt a strange feeling of sadness overcome her. She really didn't want him to leave—at least not without understanding. She rummaged in her jeans pocket, pulled out the grubby and tattered folded piece of paper and passed it to Derek.

He stared at her, frowning as he unfolded the paper. His eyebrows rose and his mouth curled into a grin as he read. 'Right, I see. I think,' he said, carefully refolding the note and handing it back. 'Bernadette from the garden shop in town, right?'

Claire nodded. 'She made me sign it to try to stop me worrying about things for a while.' She shrugged. 'Bit silly, really,' she said, shoving the note back into her pocket.

'Not at all. Whatever it takes. You're lucky to have such a good friend looking out for you.'

'I know,' Claire said, looking down. Where Bernadette's note sat felt warm and comforting. The feeling spread through her when she looked back up and noticed Derek's expression.

'Would you think about it if it weren't for that?' he asked, nodding towards the hand still in her pocket.

'Probably,' Claire admitted.

'You never know—if it's meant to be, it'll be there for you in a year.'

'Jesus, you sound like Bernadette.' She glanced at her watch. 'Oh, shit! I'm meant to be meeting her for lunch in twenty minutes.' She still had to have a shower and drive the ten minutes into town.

'I'll leave you to it, then.' He turned the car on. 'See you round,' he called, waving as he drove off.

Sixteen

Claire was red-faced and beginning to sweat when she rushed into the small, cluttered café ten minutes late. Bernadette looked up from a battered women's magazine with a knowing smirk.

'I'm so sorry.'

'No worries, just catching up on two-year-old Hollywood gossip,' Bernadette said, tapping the magazine.

Claire pulled out a chair and sat down with her bag on her lap.

'Claire, put your bloody bag down and relax!'

'Sorry, it's just…'

'I know, you hate being late. But it doesn't matter— what's ten minutes in a lifetime? And I was beginning to think you were slipping back into country life.'

Claire sighed and put her bag on the floor, willing the muscles in her back to loosen.

'So, was it a tête-à-tête with that sexy man who came looking for you that held you up?'

'Sexy! Derek?' Claire snorted. 'Hardly!'

'Oh, I don't know,' Bernadette said, putting on a dreamy expression and fluttering her eyelashes.

'You need to get out more, Bern.'

'I thought it was Derek from the office—I only met him that once. So, what did he want—to ask you out?'

'Are you girls ordering or are you just going to sit there making this place look untidy?' David, the café owner, stood over them smiling, pad and pencil in hand.

'David, hi. Sorry, I haven't even looked at the menu,' Claire said, becoming flustered again.

'Well, it hasn't changed since you two were in last week. Usual, Bernie?'

'Yes, thanks.'

'Tuna, lettuce and mayo baguette coming up,' he said as he made a note on his pad. 'I'll give you a few more minutes, Claire.'

Claire looked up and noticed Bernadette had a strange flushed expression on her face.

'Bernie!'

'What?'

'You *do* realise he's gay, don't you?' Claire hissed. 'Camp as a row of tents, that one.'

'Well, I think he's gorgeous. Anyway, we don't know for sure.'

'You know they don't just switch sides, so there's no point fluttering your eyelashes at him!'

'I wasn't! Anyway, just because he's the only well-turned-out man in town does not mean he bats for the other team. Why don't you worry about ordering? I'm starving—you kept me waiting ten minutes, remember?'

Just as Claire folded her menu, David reappeared at the side of the table very near Bernadette. He smiled warmly at her, or was it sympathy for being kept waiting by her friend? Or had she imagined it? He was the café owner; it was just part of the service.

'I'll have the chicken, lettuce and mayonnaise baguette, thank you,' Claire said.

'Excellent choice. Drinks?'

'Just water, thanks,' Claire said.

'Actually, would you try my homemade lemonade? On the house, of course. I need some honest feedback before adding it to the menu.'

'Sure,' Bernie said, beaming at him. He *was* giving her special treatment—she was not imagining it.

'Great, thanks. I'll just go get some.'

'You two are very buddy-buddy,' Claire said when David had gone.

'Just small business people sticking together. Anyway, don't be jealous, you have Derek chasing you.'

'I am not jealous, and I do not have Derek chasing me!'

'So what brought him all the way up here, then?'

'To offer me my old job back, actually,' Claire said haughtily.

'What did you say?' Bernadette was eyeing her warily.

'No, of course.'

'What? Really! Why?'

'What do you mean, why? I signed your contract, or have you forgotten already?'

'Of course I haven't forgotten. I just didn't think you'd take it that seriously.'

'You've never given me bad advice before, Bernie. Anyway, I'm enjoying being free of office politics and all the other crap.'

'That's great. I'm proud of you.'

They barely noticed when David put a glass of cloudy drink in front of each of them and disappeared without a word.

'Thanks, Bern.'

'So, how's your dad doing? Not bossing him around too much, I hope.'

'No complaints so far.'

'And how's Paycheque—settled in okay?'

'A few problems there.'

'Oh?'

'We think someone's beaten him, Bern—he's a bit of a nervous wreck to work with.'

'That's terrible. What are you going to do?'

'Just persevere—nothing else we can do. He just needs some understanding and a lot of time.' They sipped at their drinks.

'Yum,' Bernie said.

'Yes, very nice,' Claire agreed.

'Now,' Bernadette said, pushing her glass aside and rubbing her hands together. 'What are we going to do for the Cup?'

'I'm not sure I want to do anything.'

'Claire McIntyre, just because you can't swan it up in some swanky corporate box doesn't mean we can't have fun. And I will have no sulking, understood?'

'Yes, Mum.' Claire offered a tight smile. What she wanted to do was just hide under a rock until the fireball that was the Melbourne Spring Racing Carnival had passed.

'Well, we don't have long,' Bernadette said, ignoring her friend's mood. 'We could just go to one of the pubs, but I feel like doing something ourselves.'

'I'm easy.' Claire shrugged.

'Don't give me that.' Bernadette laughed. 'Claire McIntyre, easy you are certainly not.'

'Why not?'

'Oh, I don't know, combination of genes, upbringing— usual reasons,' Bernadette said, waving an arm.

Claire slapped at her hand waving about in the air. 'Not *that* why.'

'Oh, well, let me see. Uptight, way too organised, incapable of spontaneity—shall I go on?'

'Jeez, thanks, best friend.' Genuinely hurt, Claire sat back with her arms folded tightly across her chest.

'I wouldn't be a friend if I couldn't see your faults and love you anyway, now, would I?'

'Well, I'm *learning* to be a "go with the flow" girl.' Claire scowled.

'I know. So we'll have the party at your place, then,' Bernadette said with a mischievous grin.

'Yeah, why not?'

'Really?'

'I provide the venue, you provide everything else— fair enough?'

'Oh, well, I guess so,' Bernadette stammered.

'Only kidding.' Claire laughed. 'But seriously, it'll be better for Dad—he'll be able to wander off for a snooze if it all gets too much. He does that a bit nowadays.'

'Good plan—but do you want to run it past him first?'

'I'm sure he'll be cool with it. Anyway, I'm in charge now.'

Claire and Bernadette were hunched low over the table, trying to be heard over the lunchtime rush of the almost-full café. Claire was making notes on an old envelope she'd found in her handbag when David appeared.

'So, does the lemonade get the thumbs up or thumbs down? Honestly.'

'Absolutely thumbs up,' Bernadette said, smiling up at him. 'It's lovely.'

'Claire—verdict?'

'Yes, two thumbs up—delicious.'

'Brilliant, thanks. Hmm. This looks more like a meeting than a nice girly lunch,' he said, pointing to Claire's note. 'Up to no good, I'm sure.'

'Actually, we're just starting to organise our Melbourne Cup soiree,' Bernadette cooed.

'What fun,' David said, clapping his hands. 'If there's anything I can help you with, just say the word.'

'But you'll be too busy here, surely,' Bernadette said, waving an arm around.

'No way—I'm having the day off. Can't compete with two pubs—no one wants to be civilised on Cup Day, and rightfully so.'

Claire thought if he didn't stop being so damn nice she'd throw up, right on his starched white linen. She drank the last of her lemonade in one large gulp. As she did, Bernadette's next words nearly made her choke.

'Oh, well, why don't you join us, then? It's just a small gathering—a few friends, lots of champagne.' She giggled. 'But of course, if you already have something else…'

Claire mentally crossed her fingers.

'No, I'd love to,' David said, beaming down into Bernadette's face, which had the expectant glow and quivering eyelashes of a love-struck teenager.

Claire's spine prickled with annoyance. David surveyed his café briefly before dragging a nearby chair over and seating himself next to Bernadette. Claire felt her jaw tighten and her hands clench around the pen.

'So, where, when and what can I bring?'

'Well, it's at Claire's—her dad's farm. I'll give you directions later. And we haven't organised anything yet. We've only just decided to do something.'

'And you're sure I wouldn't be intruding?' he asked, looking at Claire.

'Of course not. Don't be silly,' Bernadette cried, slapping his hand playfully.

'Claire?'

'Not at all, more the merrier,' Claire said, faking her enthusiasm.

'Look, I'd better get back to it, but how about I call into the shop later and discuss it some more?'

'Okay, that sounds great—we might have decided on what sort of food to do by then.'

'I'll bring some cookbooks just in case, shall I?'

'Good idea,' Bernie said.

'Thanks for including me, it means a lot. Sorry, gotta go,' he said, and left.

'Isn't he gorgeous?' Bernadette crowed, still gazing after him.

'Yes,' Claire said. And she meant it. Why had she been so harsh on him? She didn't even know him. She really must learn to be less judgmental.

'You don't mind, do you?' Bernadette asked, suddenly aware of Claire's silence.

'No, of course not.' Claire McIntyre wasn't sure how she felt. But one thing was for sure: whatever form the day took, she had to have fun and *not* think about what she was missing in a corporate box in Melbourne.

Claire drove home, her head buzzing with ideas for decorations, menus and guest lists. But behind the excitement there was a dull nag of something else. She realised she was annoyed with Bernadette. But why? So what if she wanted to invite David? David was the perfect guest—he could cook, was charming and, as a respectable business owner, was highly unlikely to get really pissed and make a fool of himself. Was she just jealous?

Claire felt a deep sense of impending loss. Telling herself how much she missed Keith, she channelled her grief in that direction and then swallowed it. Keith was gone and that was that. She and Bernadette had survived men coming and going from each of their lives before.

Claire thought about what Bernadette must have gone through when she'd gotten serious about Keith. She had no right to be such a selfish cow. She should be happy and supportive, the sort of friend Bernadette had always been. And she would be, Claire vowed, giving the steering wheel a slap, and then turning up the radio.

Seventeen

Claire pulled off the bitumen and onto the long dirt driveway. For possibly the first time, she didn't flinch at the pinging of small stones on the metallic paint she'd paid an extra eight hundred dollars for. She realised with a sense of both relief and misgiving that she must be finally settling into the rural way of life again. It was a little scary, but at the same time it felt nice not to have to answer to the bean counters and power-hungry corporate types. Maybe it was true what they said about taking the girl out of the country.

Claire noticed Paycheque off in the paddock, standing to attention with his ears pricked. She followed the direction of his gaze towards the house. Her foot eased off the accelerator as she processed what she was seeing: a battered horse truck, tailgate down; her father leading a bay off towards the stables; another man opening a divider and preparing a chestnut for its exit from the truck. As she rounded the corner to the carport, Claire noticed another head in the window. What the hell was going on? They couldn't afford to feed four horses.

She parked and pulled the handbrake on hard. She turned the key off and counted to eight before taking three deep breaths and stepping out. Maybe Jack had taken on some paid agistment—that wouldn't be a bad move. Yes, that's what was going on. Ignoring her usual routine of changing before venturing near horses and farm, Claire strode over. For the first time she noticed the name on the open driver's door of the truck: 'T.D. Newman'. The bastard who'd almost cost Paycheque his life. She would not be involved with such a man. Why the hell would Jack be?

'Miss,' the twenty-something lad greeted her with a nod, leading the last of the horses off the truck.

Claire opened her mouth but shut it again, the words 'no point shooting the messenger' pounding in her head.

'Hi,' she grunted through a grim smile. She moved in three long strides past the truck to where her father stood, arms folded, appraising the horses in their yards. Jack McIntyre turned at the thud of her R.M. Williams boots on the tightly packed rubble.

He was beaming and had more colour in his face than she'd seen since his accident. Even from under his Akubra, the creases around his eyes showed his smile was genuine. If his face wasn't shaded she knew she'd see the twinkle in his watery, weary, but still bright, blue-grey eyes. Her heart, which had been stone-cold since seeing the name on the truck, warmed a little, and she took a deep breath.

'Dad, can I have a word?'

'Sure, Claire Bear. What is it?'

'This might sound really petty, but I don't want us doing Todd Newman any favours like agisting his horses. Remember, he was the one who...'

'Paycheque. I know.' Jack sighed. 'But it's okay, they're not his.'

Claire was relieved. People borrowed or hired trucks all the time. She looked at the horses and for the first time noticed their starry, unkempt coats, and matted manes and tails. She hoped Jack had negotiated a good rate because this bunch sure needed a decent feed. She bit her lip as she wondered why someone would care enough to pay for agistment, yet not enough to brush a bit of mud off.

'Dad, I'm really not sure if taking on three horses for agistment is a good idea right now,' she said, shaking her head.

'We're not…'

Oh, right, Claire thought, *they're in transit. He's doing a favour for a mate or something.*

'…I've bought them,' Jack said brightly.

'You've what?' Claire was glad she had the yard railing for support.

'Bought them—they're the next McIntyre marvels. What do you think?' Jack said, waving an arm.

Mongrels, more like, Claire wanted to snap, but there were more important things to discuss, like where the money had come from and why the hell she hadn't been consulted. She could feel her blood beginning to boil and her face burn. She opened her mouth and then closed it again, and began trying to picture palm trees on a perfect beach. She could not lose her temper in public and would not—thanks to all those middle-management courses she'd attended. She would wait until the office door was closed and they were in a 'quiet room'—metaphorically speaking, of course. She was vaguely aware of the truck tailgate being wound up.

Claire watched, still in a kind of stunned haze, as Jack handed over a cheque and shook hands with the lad. 'Pass on my best to Todd,' he said, slapping him on the shoulder in a gesture that threatened to be the final straw.

The truck was backing up and then turning around. Claire had abandoned the perfect beach island and was now counting, the numbers rolling in her head faster and faster, louder and louder, her jaw tighter and tighter. Fifty-seven. Finally the truck had started back down the driveway and the driver was out of hearing.

'Dad, what the bloody hell are you thinking?!' Claire exploded.

'It's okay, Claire, just calm down,' Jack urged, holding his hands up.

'Don't bloody "Claire, just calm down" me. You've paid God knows how much for three horses with God knows how many problems. The man's a complete arsehole and just look at them!'

'Claire McIntyre!'

'Well, he is. So how much have you spent?'

'I wasn't aware *my* funds were any of *your* business,' Jack said, folding his arms tightly across his chest.

Claire stared at her father, her face becoming the shade of the brick that she felt had just hit her. Of course it was her bloody business. Who'd been running the place lately: cooking, cleaning, getting groceries, making sure the bills were paid? Unconsciously she adopted her father's defiant stance.

'Look, Claire, I really appreciate you staying to help me get back on my feet, but I'm fine now, fit as a mallee bull...' Jack continued to stand above her with his arms folded.

'You don't even ride anymore. How the hell are you going to work four horses without me?'

'I'll manage.'

'But…' Claire had to make a conscious effort to stop herself stamping her foot.

'There's no corporate ladder here, girly, so don't think you can control me like I'm one of your junior staff.'

'Well, *excuse* me for being concerned about your welfare. But you're absolutely right, it's none of my business.' Claire stalked towards the house.

'Some mail came for you—it's on the kitchen bench,' Jack called after her.

'Me, controlling? Pah,' Claire cursed under her breath. *Jesus, I'm going to have to cancel the Melbourne Cup*, she thought, climbing the two back steps. *Bernadette will have a field day.*

Claire was staring at the envelope on top of the small pile of mail when her mobile began vibrating in her pocket. She fished it out. Bernadette's name was lit up. Claire bit her lip, finger poised over the button to cancel the call and send it off to voice mail. The last thing she needed was to confess and then have Bernie side with Jack. But it was nice to know she had a friend who cared and whom she could tell anything to.

'Hi, Bern.'

'Hey, you okay? You sound a bit down.'

'Am a bit.'

'Why, what's happened? It's not Jack, is it?'

'No. Well, sort of.'

'Shit, has he had a relapse or something?'

'No, nothing like that.'

'Well, what is it? You were fine at lunch.'

'Oh, Bern, we had a fight…'

Bernadette laughed. 'Is that all? Jesus, and here I was worried it was serious.'

'It is serious.'

'Right, were there fisticuffs involved and was there bloodshed?'

'Of course not, but…'

'Well, then it's not serious, is it? Look, it'll be fine. Come over, we'll have a glass of wine and you can tell me all about it. I'll make you see how ridiculous it was—fights nearly always are. You both just need some space and time to cool off.'

'He called me controlling.'

'You are controlling—in the nicest possible way, of course.'

'Bernie!'

'Just get your arse over here and let Auntie Bernadette restore your shattered delusions of self-perfection.'

'I can't.'

'Ah, been into the slops already—there's my girl.'

'No, I just can't.'

'Little Miss Feisty doesn't want to be seen as backing down, leaving the battlefield so to speak, eh?'

'Something like that,' Claire said sheepishly, feeling totally embarrassed at being so transparent. 'I'll be fine, Bern, really.' Her voice quavered. The address on the envelope was becoming a mirage.

'You don't sound fine—is it just the fight or is there something else going on?'

Claire swallowed hard. 'There's a letter here from the insurance company.'

'*The* insurance company?'

'Yes, *the* insurance company.'

'What does it say?'

'I don't know—I haven't opened it yet.'

'You know, it might just be your renewal or something.'

'I don't have any other insurance with them. God, Bern. What if they've rejected my claims? I can't afford to…'

'One step at a time, Claire. Just sit tight, I'll be there as soon as I can.'

'Thanks, Bern. You're the best.'

'And, Claire?'

'Yeah?'

'Put the envelope down and step away slowly. Don't touch it again until I get there.'

Claire let herself laugh. 'It's not a bloody bomb!'

'It could be—in a manner of speaking.'

'Yeah.'

'Well, there's nothing you can do now but open a bottle of wine and start building that silver lining. You know, just in case.'

'Actually, I was thinking this warrants breaking out the sherry.'

'Good girl—be there in a jiffy.'

Claire had downed a large glass of cream sherry and was feeling a lot calmer by the time her best friend arrived.

'You do realise drinking sherry this time of the day is a classic symptom of old fartdom, don't you?' Bernadette said as she dumped her handbag on the floor and flung herself onto the couch. 'Count me in,' she added, grabbing the decanter and filling the spare glass on the coffee table. 'That the offending article?'

'Yep.'

They each took a slug of their drinks, both staring at the envelope on the wood-grain laminex surface.

'Ah, I can see why all the old ducks go for this stuff—makes you feel all warm and fuzzy, right from when it goes down,' Bernadette said after a long silence. 'Couple more of these and we might be able to face opening that letter.'

'That's what I'm hoping,' Claire said with a tight smile.

'Right, what scenarios do we have?'

Claire was now feeling decidedly tipsy. 'Well, it's either a cheque for six figures or a letter saying the policy is null and void, in which case I'm poor *and* owe the bank for Keith's bloody four-wheel drive. You know I never wanted the damn thing—they've no place but out bush. And so much for being safer.'

'Would you rather I opened it?'

'No. I think I can do it.'

As she reached forward, Claire noticed how oddly silent it was. There was no rustling in the trees or squawking of birds outside. It was like the emptiness after a drum roll and before a grand announcement: absolute stillness. The sherry mixing with her nerves was making her feel a little queasy. She picked up the envelope.

'Claire, just remember it's not personal. It's business to them. They don't even know you.'

Claire nodded and with shaking fingers peeled the seal off the envelope, prised out the folded single piece of paper and smoothed it out on her lap.

Bernadette held her breath while silently begging the insurance gods to be kind. She watched as Claire's chest sank and her shoulders slumped.

After a few moments, Claire looked up from the

page twitching in her shaking hand and, with a look of consternation and a weary sigh, handed Bernadette the letter. A few tears began to roll their way down her face. Bernadette accepted it with a sympathetic smile and began to read. Claire refilled their glasses.

'Not personal' was an understatement. Beyond her name being part of the address and reference to the policy number, it could have been from the *Reader's Digest* announcing Claire had made it through to the second round prize draw. In two crisp paragraphs it stated that the claim had been assessed and subsequently rejected as per the terms set out in the policy document. In typical proforma fashion it apologised for any inconvenience caused and informed Claire that her excess had increased by five hundred dollars because the drink driving charge showed an increased insurance risk. It was almost ridiculous—someone had bloody well died. Keith had only been a sniff over point oh five—and he hadn't even caused the accident in the first place.

'Jesus, Claire, where do they get off?'

Claire gave a resigned shrug.

'We can't let them get away with it.'

'Looks like they just have.'

'What about contacting the Insurance Ombudsman?'

'And what would that do? They'd read where it clearly states in the policy that unlawful acts render it null and void, and point out that drink driving is an unlawful act—even the tiniest bit over point oh five. You said it yourself. It's about business, the bottom line. They'll try to wriggle out of a claim any way they can. It's their job.'

'So you're just going to lie down and take it?'

'Pretty much—it's not like I wasn't expecting it. To be honest, it's a bit of a relief to have it over with after all this time.'

'But they haven't even got the facts right. They're making it sound like *you* were the one drink driving— that's slander or defamation, or something, surely. Write to the bloody Ombudsman, Claire! At least do something!' Bernadette was so riled that she could hardly breathe.

'Bernie, you're the one always saying we should learn our lesson and move on. Well, that's what I'm doing. Anyway, I'm too tired to fight. It's been a shit-house year and I just want it to end. Maybe this is the cosmos telling me it's time to sell the house. I sure as hell can't afford to keep it *and* pay for the four-wheel drive.'

'I don't know,' said Bernie. 'But I don't think you should do anything rash. Anyway, you don't have to pay it in one hit—just continue with the monthly payments and buy yourself some time. Selling the house is a huge step—you want to make sure it's what you really want, or that it's really necessary. I don't want you having regrets.'

'You're right. I need to calm down and think things through.'

'But seriously, I do think you should contact the Ombudsman or someone. At least then you'll feel like you've done *something*. And it certainly couldn't hurt.'

Eighteen

Claire was relieved her father was still out with the horses when Bernadette finally left. It had taken a few hours, three cups of tea and a mountain of cheese and crackers to soak up the alcohol. He'd come in and then quickly fled the 'girly' scene, saying he had some errands to run in town. Claire was glad. She really needed to have a talk with him, but wasn't yet ready to discuss the insurance being rejected. Part of her really did feel relieved it was over. But Bernie was right: she would regret not at least trying to get their decision overturned.

She busied herself with making dinner—shepherd's pie, one of her father's favourites—all the time dreading how the evening would play out. Already on edge waiting for Jack to come inside, her stomach flip-flopped when she finally heard him banging the dirt from his heavy boots outside the back door.

'Something smells good,' he said, coming into the kitchen.

Claire felt her tension lift. She held out the steaming casserole dish like a child with her first school report.

'Wow, I'm starving.'

'Well, it's ready when you are.'

'Just wash my hands and I'll be with you.'

Claire dished up the meal, shaking her head at the way men just seemed to get over things while women kept stewing. It was marvellous, but at the same time it was an incredibly frustrating trait. Women had to have things thrashed out, resolved. And she, especially, needed everything discussed, the options and courses of action laid out clearly and chosen, and for both parties to state their agreement, before she could really get over it.

Keith had often teased her about needing the solution metaphorically wrapped up, put in a box and sealed with a nice pink bow. She couldn't help it if she liked things to be just so. Claire remembered the withering look he'd give her whenever she asked him to sit down and discuss something. *Bless him*, she thought. He'd been the most patient, loving man in the world. Tears gathered in the corners of her eyes and in her lashes.

'You okay?' Jack asked, appearing next to her.

'Yep. Copped a bit of steam, that's all,' she said, really hoping he wouldn't put his arm around her. She swallowed hard; Keith was gone and that was that.

Claire was ravenous thanks to the sherry, but began pushing the food around her plate after barely tasting a few forkfuls. She was fretting about how to bring up the argument and apologise without completely belittling herself—she still believed her father should have consulted her before getting the horses. Maybe they could ease into it from a safer angle.

'Dad?'

'Yep?' Jack looked up from his plate.

'I was wondering if it would be okay to have lunch here for the Melbourne Cup—something small, just a few friends. I thought then you could have a lie-down if you needed to.'

'Did you just?'

Claire blinked. This was not how it was meant to go at all. 'Well, yes.'

'Are you *asking* me or *telling* me, Claire?'

'Sorry?'

'Well, it sounds to me you've already decided. You've got plans well underway, have you not?'

Claire coloured. 'Um, well…'

'I know all about it. Steve at the newsagent told me—it's all around town. And didn't I feel a right idiot not knowing I was having a do here.'

Claire cursed the efficiency of the bush telegraph. 'Sorry,' she muttered, feeling like a sixteen-year-old caught coming in late with alcohol on her breath.

'Claire, you went off at me for not discussing Newman's horses with you, but it's okay for you to go behind my back and…'

'Oh, come on, it's hardly the same!'

'I wouldn't dream of telling you what house or car to buy, or job to take. Horses are my business and I haven't done so badly over the years.'

'Dad, you're broke. Look around you, the place is a dump.' Claire cringed when she saw the pained expression that crossed her father's face.

'You know nothing about my financial situation and you don't need to. Suffice to say, what you see is not always what you get. You spend your money on dinners, flashy clothes and new cars to—I don't know—uphold your self-image or something. I don't care what people think—quite frankly, I'd rather save a horse with potential from the knackery.'

Claire looked back down at her plate with the roads of thick potato passing through the stewy tomato and mince. She tried to analyse what she'd just been told. Did her own father really see her as some pretentious cow only concerned with making impressions?

'Claire, I'm not having a go at you—merely pointing out we have different priorities. There's nothing wrong with that. And while we're speaking about horses, I bought them because I thought you needed more to occupy you for the year. But I guess I jumped the gun. I should have consulted you.' He offered her an apologetic smile.

'I'll call it even if we can still have the Cup lunch here,' Claire said with raised eyebrows.

'Claire McIntyre, you drive a hard bargain.'

'Really? I wonder where I learnt that.' They both laughed, the tension gone.

'You really bought the horses for me?'

'Of course. As you rightly pointed out, I'm no longer riding. How else am I going to get them up to standard? I thought we'd make a great team—another assumption, sorry. I want these horses to prove that bastard Todd Newman wrong.'

'And if they don't?'

'They will. I know they don't look much now, but they'll come good.'

'And if they don't?'

'It's a gamble, I'm the first to admit that. But life's a gamble. The challenge is what makes it fun.'

'But what if they can't run?'

'They've each got a brain and four legs. Of course they can run.'

'But...'

'How fast just depends on how much they want to—
that's our job.'

Claire did not share her father's optimism. She was
competitive through and through and did not want to
be on a handicapped team, which was what they would
be with a worn-out old trainer, a bunch of reject horses
and facilities that were basic at best.

No, if she was going to be in the racing game, she
wanted to be involved with a big successful outfit with
the best facilities and staff to do the shit work—one
of those establishments with the glossy white wooden
fences and a brightly painted sign standing proudly out
front.

Claire McIntyre did not want to be the laughing-
stock of the racing fraternity. But she couldn't exactly
leave her father to go and work for someone else. What
was this mental job hunt all about anyway? She thought
about Bernadette's folded contract in her pocket. Surely
she could lend a hand for the year. She wouldn't have
to be seen as Jack's partner, just his daughter. It might
even be fun.

'So, are you in?'

Claire looked up, slightly startled from her thoughts.
'Well…'

'I'll need a full commitment or else I'll have to get
someone in. As I said, I can't train four horses alone.'

'Okay, but I can't make any guarantees beyond
twelve months.'

'Thank you, I really appreciate it. Now we just have
to get you fully infected with the racing bug so you
never want to leave,' he said with a smirk.

Claire gave a deep sigh. She really hoped she wasn't
going to regret this.

Nineteen

When Claire woke on Melbourne Cup Day, the dawn was still grey through the curtains. She heard Jack's footsteps through the house and then the slap of the back screen door. Feeling a little guilty at not getting up to help him feed the horses, she rolled over and pulled the quilt up over her head.

What seemed only minutes later she heard tyres on the gravel outside her window and two excited voices: one male, one female. She poked her head out to check her watch on the bedside cupboard. Damn, it was almost nine. She wasn't ready to face the day. Claire rolled over again and buried her face—if only she could wake up when it was all over.

She could hear the mutter of Bernadette issuing orders and cupboards being opened and shut in the kitchen. 'God, why did I agree to this?' Claire groaned.

'Come on, sleepyhead,' Bernie called from the open doorway. 'Thought you horsey people got up at sparrow fart.'

Claire sat up scowling and pushed her hair from her face.

'Turn that frown upside down.'

'I can't.' Claire pouted.

Bernadette leapt onto the bed as she had countless times as a teenager. 'Come on, it's Cup Day. You've gotta get up!' she cried, pulling the quilt from Claire's grasp.

'I just want it to go away,' Claire moaned.

'No, that's what you say tomorrow morning when you're all hung-over and wanting to throw up.'

'God, don't remind me.'

'If you don't get up now I'll…'

'What? What you gonna do, Bernie?' Claire challenged, suddenly grinning.

'I don't know. I was just hoping you'd get up and help us organise one hell of a rip-roaring party. We need something that will take us all far, far away from the mundane reality of our pathetic lives. Well, yours anyway.'

'Pathetic? Thanks a bloody lot!'

'Or I guess I could try to tickle you to death…'

'Good enough for me,' Claire shrieked, relinquishing the quilt and leaping out of bed.

'Thank Christ for that. I didn't want David catching a glimpse and thinking we were lesbian lovers.'

'Bernadette, you do realise…?'

'He's gay—how could I not? You remind me every time I mention his name.' She gave a little laugh but Claire could see through it—Bernadette did not for a second believe David Balducci was gay, and she was clearly besotted.

'I just don't want you getting hurt.'

'I know.'

'Come on, then, better stop him putting umbrellas in our glasses.'

'Actually, he's probably reorganised the kitchen cupboards. He was tut-tutting at the chaos when I left him.' Bernadette got off Claire's bed.

'I'll just throw jeans on for now.'

'I hope everyone else makes an effort to dress up.'

'If they don't we're going to look pretty bloody silly.'

'Oh, well. At least there'll be three of us in that boat.'

'Thank goodness for small mercies.'

Claire emerged a few minutes later to find the open-plan dining-lounge room adorned in gold. There were massive bunches of balloons draped in curling ribbon in three of the six corners, and streamers zigzagging back and forth across the room.

David, dressed in jeans and a black lightweight knit top, turned slightly from the top of the stepladder. 'Ah, here she is, the lady of the house. Got to sleep in, eh? Lucky thing. Bernadette's a slave driver,' he said, rolling his eyes. 'Had me up at some ungodly hour. Anyway, there's heaps to do if we're to have the champagne cracked and look all relaxed when everyone arrives.'

Claire smiled. 'What can I do?'

'Would you mind taking over here? I'm getting a little light-headed and I have to check on the turkey terrine.' Without waiting for Claire's agreement, he had dismounted the steps and was draping her shoulders with pre-cut ribbons and streamers, and her hands with limp balloons. 'Sorry, we don't have a pump or reversible vacuum, hence the light-headedness.'

Claire stared after him. Was he for real? God only knew what he'd be like half-pissed. She chuckled to herself as she started climbing the steps.

* * *

Two hours later, having lined their stomachs with bacon and eggs, they were in their costumes and sipping their first glasses of champagne. A cooked breakfast had instantly endeared David Balducci to Jack McIntyre, a man not usually prone to giving 'nancy boys' the time of day. But while David was a little too feminine in his mannerisms and unusually well-turned-out, Jack found the fellow very likeable, as he was later overheard explaining to bewildered old friends and neighbours.

Personally, Claire would have liked just a few of their friends—without the butcher, baker and candlestick maker—*but that was the country for you*, she thought with resignation as she cast her eyes around the room. It was no corporate box, but she had to admit she was having fun. Claire slumped into a chair in the corner away from the main crowd. She'd really better slow down on the champagne if she was going to see the race out. David appeared at her shoulder as if he'd slid in on skis.

'You okay, pet?'

'Just a few too many bubbles, I think.'

'I'll get you some water.'

And before Claire could thank him or protest, he was off, his multicoloured, sequined jockey silks shimmering and flickering in the gaps between people. Claire couldn't help admiring his behind in the tights that looked painted on. She sniggered—he really was great fun. It was he who'd insisted they get dressed up—and not in finery and hats.

He'd wanted to come in drag until Bernadette had good-naturedly reminded him it was a sedate affair full of conservative country folk. As ridiculous as she felt dressed in a sack as a bag of chaff, at least all her curves were covered and she could wear sensible shoes. Though she was beginning to itch a little.

Bernie looked great as the finishing post, complete with a strip of mirrored plastic. She had to hand it to David: he certainly did have quite an imagination.

Bernadette plonked herself down on the chair next to Claire. 'Do you know how many times I've bloody well been asked what I'm dressed as?' She scowled. 'Old Mr Ramsey said I looked like the Commonwealth Games torch. Oh, I ask you!'

Claire laughed. 'You're lucky David didn't make you go as a portaloo, though you'd be very popular—second only to the boozer.' They both cracked up.

'Isn't it fun to dress up and be really silly?'

'Honestly, Bern, I'm having a ball. I really didn't think I would—so thanks for insisting.'

'Well, you can blame me for the hangover, but David will be to blame for the hay fever. What are friends for?' she added, giving Claire a hug.

'Come on, you two,' David said, arriving with two large glasses of water. 'Can't have the finish line getting the sack.'

The girls began giggling hysterically and he stared at them with mock consternation while they recovered enough to relieve him of the glasses. He sat down and they continued to erupt into fits of laughter.

'Come on, it wasn't even funny,' he said.

'We know—that's what's so hilarious,' they said, erupting again.

'Women,' he said, rolling his eyes. 'On a more serious note, who did you get for the sweep?'

'Garden Gnome,' Claire groaned, pulling the slip from inside her bra.

'They don't give him much hope with a name like that, do they?' David said.

'At two hundred to one, neither do the bookies.'

'What did you get, Bern?'

'Paperchase. Where do they get these names from? What about you, David?'

'Curtain Call.'

'I really hope he does well,' Claire said. 'He was another one of Todd Newman's rejects.'

'I hope he wins, just to show that bastard. David, I told you about the others Claire and Jack are training now, didn't I?' said Bernie.

'You did. How are they going, Claire?'

'Bloody disaster—bunch of misfits,' Claire said, and laughed.

'I think it's great they're being given another chance— Bernadette told me all about Paycheque. Very sad.' Bernadette sure had been spending a lot of time with David Balducci, Claire thought, a little miffed at apparently being the topic of conversation.

'Yes, well. Dad's always been one to bat for the underdog.'

'So, what's wrong with them? Are they difficult to handle, lazy, or what?' David asked. They obviously hadn't discussed it in too much depth.

'Well, they're all a bit nervous, which is quite reasonable given they've been moved about from pillar to post and most likely beaten. I've worked with Paycheque the most while the others settle in. He's a cranky bugger. I thought it would wear off once he figured out how good he's got it here, but he's still crotchety. Nothing nasty, just a general air about him. I swear, if he was a filly I'd think it was hormones.'

Bernadette laughed.

'Women and their bloody hormones.' David laughed. 'Is he a stallion?'

'Technically speaking, now he's over four. Probably should have been gelded after all.'

'Poor bastard—now that *would* make you cranky.' David winced.

The girls laughed and said, 'Men and their bits,' mimicking him.

'Maybe he doesn't sleep well. I'm cranky when I'm tired,' David said absently.

'Aren't we all,' Bernadette said. Claire wasn't sure if her expression was dreamy or just plain weary.

'Anyway, I'd better make sure our guests are happy,' David said, and got up to mingle.

'I don't think I can stand up,' Bernadette groaned.

'No, me neither—"champagne fatigue", I think they call it.'

Claire stared into nothingness, the movement of mingling guests fuzzy to her unfocussed gaze. There was a slight niggle behind the thick fog of champagne and finger food carbohydrates. Could there be something to what David said about Paycheque not getting enough sleep? No, he was just trying to draw comparisons with horses and people. And when it came to sleep, there were none. Horses slept standing up for a start.

Though, now she thought about it, Paycheque was often to be seen stretched out in his day paddock on his side, all four legs stuck out, not curled up as was usual. Claire cringed as she remembered the first time she'd noticed. She'd thought he was dead and had rushed out to check. The poor horse had got such a fright that in a split second he went from peaceful slumber to standing upright with legs spread and bugging eyes.

He was better when she brought him in at the end of the day—still wary, but not the snappy beast with nostrils twisted into a scowl she was greeted with in the mornings. Claire felt ridiculous even thinking it, but began to wonder whether the major problem with Paycheque was that he just didn't do mornings well.

She was having a chuckle to herself when David began tapping a glass with a fork and calling for everyone to crowd around the television. The race was starting in less than ten minutes.

'Cool, we don't even have to move,' Bernadette said.

'Mmm,' Claire agreed, silently congratulating herself on her inadvertent furniture choreography.

Claire appraised the horses with a critical eye as each one made its way into the mounting yard. Garden Gnome was a plain, wiry, highly strung chestnut. Nothing special—which wasn't surprising, given his poor rating. Though you just never knew. It was widely understood that the favourite rarely won.

Claire only recognised Curtain Call by his number and the commentators announcing him. His coat shimmered like molten chocolate around an ample girth. There was no sign of the half-starved creature she'd seen at a country meet less than six months ago. His head was up, his ears twitching, taking in all the sounds. Absent were the distressed whites of his eyes and flared nostrils; instead he had the calm, determined look of a winner. Claire swelled with excitement and squeezed her hands to her heart.

All the parading horses looked capable of winning—finely tuned athletes in the prime of health. Claire tried to picture Paycheque parading with them and when she couldn't, she returned her attention to the last of the horses streaming out onto the track for their warm-up run to the barrier. Her heart pounded heavily with the excitement.

She looked away and bit down on her lip when the camera panned around the huge crowd at Flemington, and then returned to watch as each horse was led into the barrier, noting the calm attentive lowered head of Curtain Call. Her belly was aflutter with all the emotion of The Race That Stops the Nation—dread, excitement, envy—as the stewards battled with the final few cantankerous beasts.

Claire crossed her fingers and held her breath through the shot of the spinning light signalling all was well, the crash of the gates, the thunder of hooves and the sorting out of horses across the track—a ritual she did every time she watched the great race.

As the seconds ticked by and the race progressed, her heart became a lump in her throat, her breathing shallow. She leant forward and, nodding back and forth, rode every stride. They came around the last turn all in one group spread right across the track.

She ducked and weaved as Curtain Call made his move out and around the pack at the one-fifty-metre mark. Her movements in the chair became more urgent as she, too, tried to ride him to victory.

Claire had forgotten all about Garden Gnome until he came from nowhere to snatch victory by a nostril. Her heart eased as they thundered past the blinking mirror of the finish line, the commentators not holding back on their surprise at the upset, but adding—just like every other year—that upsets were what the Melbourne Cup was all about.

Claire wanted to sneak off for a weep—it was how she always felt in the moments just after the finish.

Bernadette was screeching wildly. 'Wasn't he yours?'

'Yeah, he was.'

'Well, don't get too excited, will you.'

'My head's in a spin. That's all.'

'Can you believe he got out from the rail like that? I thought he was boxed in for sure.'

They paused to watch the replay of the final stages and winner's connections going mad in the stands.

'That'll be you next year,' Bernadette said.

'Yeah, right.' Claire laughed.

'No reason why not. They do say it's the most difficult race to predict.'

'We'd need one hell of a miracle—or three or four.'

'Miracles happen every day,' Bernadette said sagely. ''Nother champers?' she asked, getting up with a wobble.

'Yes, thanks.'

Claire remained sitting, eyes glued to the screen. Why *couldn't* that be them up there talking about what a special horse it was? *Exactly*, there was no reason. Claire McIntyre decided then and there that she had exactly one year to make a miracle happen. She looked around the room and across at Jack, wanting to escape and begin her newfound quest.

This was what her father had described: passion. The feeling right to the depths of your soul that you would give up everything in order to do this one thing, that no matter how many battles you lost along the way you'd win the war because you'd stayed true to yourself. She hadn't felt so fired up in years. Claire wanted to spring to her feet and tell the room all about it. But her bum was glued to the chair and her head was starting to spin. She realised she was more than a little tipsy.

She'd have to wait until tomorrow. She just hoped it wouldn't all seem impossible when she went out in the morning to do the feeds and face the grim reality of what lay ahead. In the meantime, she'd start with something more achievable: the dishes.

A few minutes later, David caught her staring out the kitchen window, rubber-gloved hand stuffed in a mug, biting on her lip in concentration.

'The nation is moving again, you know,' he said with a grin, waving a tea towel in front of her face.

Claire blinked, apologised and returned to her task.

'A few too many bubbles has this one had,' he said theatrically.

'Haven't we all?' Bernadette said, flicking the tea towel at him while keeping one eye on Claire.

She, too, had noticed the vacant look in her best friend's eyes and instantly recognised it for what it was. Claire had turned another corner today.

That night, Claire McIntyre watched every news bulletin, feeling more and more determined. Curtain Call's trainer dropped a poignant comment about the horse's second chance. It went right over the heads of the commentators but sent a knowing ripple through racing's inner circles. Claire felt a surge of respect for the new owners of the horse and wished Todd Newman would hurry up and get what was coming to him.

When she caught a glimpse of him on camera— shrugging and saying the almost-win by a horse he'd discarded was merely luck of the draw—she wanted to punch his lights out. It was no secret that the Newman stables had been inspected by the RSPCA on a number of occasions, but no charges had ever been laid. The mystery was how he kept getting away with it. But then, there was always a stable hand to use as a scapegoat.

Claire lay in bed exhausted but unable to sleep. Whirling around in her head were abstract images of the highs and lows of her year ahead. On the one hand she felt exhilarated—imagine actually being there on television as the trainer of the next Cup winner. On the other she felt terrified—what if it didn't work? What if Todd Newman was right and the horses really were useless and untrainable? Claire felt as if she was on a seesaw that had just crashed to ground.

She'd keep her plans to herself, that's what she'd do. Carry on with Jack's meandering and try to pretend there was no urgency. It would be difficult, but not as difficult as failing and being seen as just another wannabe trainer trying to score in the big league when others had spent decades on a fruitless quest.

But why shouldn't I give it a go, damn it? I'm stuck here for the year anyway. The seesaw went up. *Because I don't believe in my team*, she thought guiltily, and the seesaw crashed back down to the ground with an even heavier thud. It really ate at Claire to have less than total respect for her father, but he just seemed to wander through life dealing with things as they arose. There was no great show of determination—no grand plan beyond having enough money to keep himself and the horses fed.

And speaking of horses—they were the other glitch

in her grand plan. None of them bore any resemblance to the sleek elite athletes filmed at Flemington that day.

But they could, a little voice somewhere behind the seesawing thoughts and champagne haze piped up. Yes, she'd give it a shot—she had nothing to lose. And if it didn't work, at least she'd have tried. And with that last thought, Claire set her morning alarm for five o'clock and rolled over.

Twenty

Claire was just getting back from working three of the horses—riding Paycheque and leading another two—when Jack arrived at the stables.

'How did they go?'

'Okay. I didn't exactly put them through their paces—just trotted them out to the old tank and back. Howie and Bell are happy enough, but God, Paycheque is a real grump. Aren't you?' She laughed and scratched the horse behind the ears.

Jack took the two lead-ropes and moved the other horses away so Claire had room to dismount. She unsaddled Paycheque and put the gear on the railing.

'What about Larry?' she asked. 'Do you want me to take him out?'

'No, I'll do him from the ute.'

'You sure you'll be okay?'

'Positive. He's a dream next to cranky pants here,' he said, slapping Paycheque's damp neck affectionately.

'Tell me about it,' Claire groaned. 'He tried to bite me as I was getting on.'

'Didn't get you, did he?'

'Nope—I was ready for him. I don't know what his problem is. He's been here the longest and settled in the worst.'

'Well, these other guys have been stablemates at one time or another. Maybe he's feeling left out.'

'But he's come *home*. Surely life's good after what he's been through.'

Jack shrugged. 'He'll be all right. Just give him time.'

Claire shrugged and tried to appear nonchalant as she led the horse into his stable yard. If this was how he was now, what would happen when they actually started putting him under pressure? She'd have to have him a bit better before that happened or else risk life and limb.

Claire shuddered with a mixture of dread and excitement. Other than the redundancy, the scariest thing she'd faced in her last few months at work was a paper cut—hardly life-threatening.

She stood with her arms folded across the top railing, enjoying the warm sun on her back as the three horses tucked into their breakfast. Howie's ears still twitched, and he'd stop chewing at the slightest noise or movement, but at least he was eating in her presence. Only a week ago he would wait until completely alone before lowering his head into his feed drum. Claire had persisted with standing at a safe distance. With all the goings-on at Flemington, he'd have to get used to people. You couldn't have a half-starved horse run the Melbourne Cup—not if it was to have any hope of winning.

Next she'd try to give him a brush while he ate. If she could manage that without him freaking, a routine could almost work. She made mental notes while she soaked up the rays and watched the rhythmic sway of the horse's large glistening jaw.

* * *

The weeks after the Melbourne Cup blurred as Claire settled into a routine of working the horses in the mornings, and then bringing them in at night. But as the summer came on and the warm days grew longer, Claire began to feel the void of her empty afternoons and yearned for her own space.

Some days she just wanted to curl up with a good book or DVD but always felt self-conscious when her father came in, despite his cheery calls of 'Sorry, don't mind me'. She began spending more time in her bedroom when she wasn't out with Bernadette or helping in her shop.

One Friday morning, Claire was taking a cup of coffee to her bedroom when she realised with a shock that she had come full circle. She was a teenager all over again—though without the lack of responsibility.

She stopped mid-stride, the coffee slapping dangerously close to the edges of the mug. Or maybe it wasn't adolescence but the future—old fartdom—that she was seeing. She looked down at her large fluffy pink slippers and shuffled quickly to the phone, slamming her coffee down on the bench.

'Bernie.'

'Hey, Claire, how's it going?'

'Bernie, I'm turning into an old fart.'

'What, you've just realised *this minute*?'

'I'm serious—you've got to help me.'

'What do you mean?'

'Tell me what you see when I say, "thirty-five-year-old jobless woman living with her father, wearing fluffy slippers at ten o'clock in the morning, carting a cup of coffee to her bedroom so she won't get caught reading a book".'

'Ah, yes. All the classic symptoms. Two questions—is the coffee instant, and do you actually enjoy drinking it?'

'Yes and yes.' Claire laughed despite herself.

'Well, there's only one cure.'

'What's that?'

'Come over here and I'll tell you. This calls for serious measures—I'll break out the Tim Tams and get us some real coffee.'

Claire knew exactly what had to be done, but it was always so much easier having Bernadette take the lead—not to mention more fun.

'Thanks, Bern, see you soon.'

Just before she left, Claire phoned the city real estate agent she'd chosen for when this day came. She was in luck—a lovely couple had come in only the day before looking for a similar property, and gave the impression they were cashed up and ready to buy. Claire could almost hear the agent wringing his hands in delight at earning such an easy commission. She was glad she'd taken Bernadette's advice a few weeks back and set the ball in motion.

She felt a little guilty at how easily she'd been able to hand over the keys to Keith's pride and joy. When she and Bernadette had gone down for a weekend to get some more clothes and check all was in order, she'd noticed how detached she felt about the place—as if she was checking on the home of a friend, not her own. She'd also noticed the contrast to her father's cottage—

realising it was not just tidier and more orderly, but cold, sparse and almost unwelcoming.

On her way over to Bernadette's shop, Claire decided to get a cat or two for company when she got settled. Then she checked herself—it could take her months to find the right house. December could be a tricky time to buy. She was setting herself up for disappointment if she thought she'd find the perfect thing so easily. And she certainly wasn't going to settle on the first one she saw.

Twenty-One

'Right,' Bernadette said, ushering Claire into her office at the back of the shop. 'Have a Tim Tam or three while we wait for the coffees. Now, I hope you don't mind, but I took the liberty of collecting the brochures from the local real estate agents, though there's not really much around. So, what exactly do you have in mind?'

'Oh, you know, whitewashed stone cottage, picket fence, garden full of roses, a couple of acres...'

'Jeez, don't half want much, do we?'

'"Discerning", I think they call it in the industry.'

'Oh, *industry*, is it? Well, don't go getting all high and mighty on me—the rental accommodation has never been very flash out here—unless you fancy cream brick or falling-down rustic.'

Claire was busy perusing the brochures. 'Here, what about this one?' she said, turning the page around for Bernadette to see. '"Just move in and enjoy the country life", it says.'

'That one's for sale, silly, not lease.'

'And the problem is?' Claire challenged with a gleam in her eye.

'What? You're going to buy! Oh, goody. But are you sure? Have you thought it through? Don't you think you...?'

'Shut up, Bernie, you're rambling like a pessimistic old woman—two things you are definitely not! And yes, I have thought things through. I've done the figures—ballpark, of course—and I've even got a list of requirements, from "absolute musts" to "I wish".'

'Ah, you and your lists. That's my girl. Here, give me a look.'

Claire handed her the piece of lined paper.

'Uh-huh, right, yep, seems okay to me,' Bernadette said, and then handed it back. 'But the real estate agents will tear their hair out.'

They raised their heads at the subtle aroma of milky coffee. Moments later, David appeared in the doorway carrying a takeaway box with three cardboard cups in it.

'And what are you devilish women cooking up this morning? Must be serious to require delivery. It's not secret women's business, is it?'

'No, of course you can join us.'

'Thought you'd never ask.'

'Now, what do we owe you?' Claire asked, fishing in her handbag for her wallet.

'On the house. *If* you'll let me in on your little dalliance. I need a bit of excitement this morning.'

'You might change your mind about that.'

'Try me.'

'House hunting for Claire—she's going to *buy*. Isn't it fantastic?'

'Absolutely. Sure you wouldn't rather rent for a while first? It's a pretty big commitment.'

'God. What is it with you two? You sound like parents.'

'Just want the best for you, that's all,' they said in unison, and burst into laughter.

'So, are you in?' Bernadette asked David.

'Only if it's okay with Claire. I don't want to be the third wheel.'

'It'd be good to have a third opinion, won't it, Claire? You can be the voice of reason, the objective one.'

'Wouldn't bet on it.' David smirked. 'I'm a bit of a "love at first sight" kind of guy, but I'll do my best to curb my enthusiasm.'

Claire tried to ignore the private look that passed between Bernadette and David. What was it with those two?

'Well, we can't have her signing up for the first one she sees,' Bernadette said, her blush subsiding.

'Now, where would the fun be in that? No, she has to experience the full range of emotions house hunting brings—disappointment, disappointment and disappointment.'

'Hey, guys? Excuse me, I'm still here, you know.'

'Voices. Do I hear voices?' David said, pretending to search the room.

Bernadette laughed.

'Very funny. I'll have you both know I've had my share of real estate nightmares. This is not my first purchase.'

'Right, then,' David said. 'Back to being serious— the requirements. I'm guessing whitewashed solid stone, picket fence, roses, cottage garden. Not too untidy, set on a couple of acres. Not too much to manage, but not too close to any neighbours.'

Claire was wide-eyed. 'How did you know?'

'Isn't that what we all want? I keep forgetting you still haven't seen my little place yet. So how about dinner? My place, Sunday night? You'll need taking care of after a day of house hunting. I say we sweet-talk the agents into opening privately for us. Then we won't have to be ushered through like cows with everyone else.'

'Oh, David, you are cheeky.'

'Besides, you're off to the races at Morphettville tomorrow, aren't you?'

'Meanwhile, some of us have to work for a living,' said Bernadette. 'Might as well make the agents do the same.'

'Exactly. They wouldn't know what it's like to have to do the hard sell—this place has been selling itself for years. So, how about you leave it to me? I'll make a couple of calls and pick you girls up around ten from here.

'Oh, and if the weather's good we'll put the top down, so you might both want to put your hair up or wear secure scarves. We don't want any Bridget Jones moments, do we?'

'No.' Claire and Bernadette groaned and then laughed.

'Well, I'd better get back to my customers before they think I don't love them—they're already jealous of you two getting all my attention. So, just be here at ten o'clock Sunday unless you hear otherwise. It'll be such a treat to be out with two gorgeous girls.' David got up, kissed them each on the cheek, grabbed a Tim Tam and left.

'See ya,' he called. Both women watched in silent admiration until David was out of sight.

'So, Bernie, you're spending a lot of time with David these days.'

'Isn't he just the best fun?' she said, and shook away the dreamy expression beginning to creep across her face. But Claire had noticed it—they'd been friends too long, shared too much of the good and bad, for her not to.

'There's more to it than that.'

'Don't be ridiculous, Claire. He's gay, remember? So, are you excited about the races tomorrow?'

'Don't remind me, I'm nervous as hell.'

'Ah, you'll be right.'

'I'm not sure the horses are really ready.'

'But you can withdraw them if they totally freak out or something, can't you?'

'Yeah, but we've paid entry fees. And it wouldn't look good.'

'To whom, Claire? Withdrawing would look a damn sight better than a horse wiping itself and its jockey out on the rail—not to mention all the other horses.'

'Jeez, you really know how to put a girl at ease.'

'Sorry, but you know what I meant. Anyway, who are you taking?'

'Paycheque and Howie.'

'And?'

'And what?'

'Their form—do they have any chance? Should I be putting some money on?'

'Howie, maybe. The rate we're going Paycheque will be withdrawn because of his temper. The son of one of Dad's mates came by the other morning to have a ride—we were hoping he'd be our jockey—but the poor lad nearly lost a chunk out of his skinny little arse and now he won't go anywhere near him.'

'So will you find someone else on the day?'

'Hopefully, but most of the half-decent jockeys are already booked. Whatever happens, it'll be good to judge ourselves by what everyone else is doing. I'm learning to lower my expectations these days—less distance to fall.'

'Though there's a fine line between not having faith and setting the bar too high,' Bernadette warned. 'Remember, Claire, a step forward is a step forward, even if you end up taking two steps back. It's still a learning experience.'

Claire wanted to tell Bernadette there wasn't time in her twelve-month grand plan for any steps back. But she didn't get the chance.

'Want me to come? Be strapper, moral support, coffee carrier?'

'Would you?'

'Yeah, why not?'

'The shop for one—I feel guilty taking you away so much.'

'Now, how am I going to be semi-retired at forty-five if I can't leave my trainee manager in charge a few days a week? Anyway, it'll be a fun day out.'

'If that's what you call dodging teeth, hooves and horseshit, and getting covered in dust, snot and slobber.'

'Actually, that doesn't sound unlike running a nursery. I'll wear my steel caps and wet-weather coat, then, shall I?'

Claire let out a huge sigh, unaware she had that much breath to let out. 'You're a lifesaver.'

'I know, I'll just add it to your IOU.' Bernadette

laughed, got up and made a show of going to the white-board on the wall and picking up a marker. They both chuckled.

Claire drained her cup and got up. 'Well, I'd better get back and get these monsters at least washed and presentable so I can have an early night.'

'Yes, it's going to be a whirlwind weekend, what with the house hunting on Sunday as well. We might like being chauffeured around like ladies.'

Claire was secretly pleased she'd have Bernadette to herself tomorrow at the races. She really did like David, but it was true about three being a crowd.

That afternoon, Paycheque was a completely different horse to the one who'd bared his teeth and tried to grab Claire by the ponytail a few hours earlier. He stood patiently in the sun to be washed, doing nothing more than closing his eyes and putting his ears back to stop them filling with water. He even allowed his mane and tail to be vigorously shampooed.

Claire was stunned when he lowered his head to waist level to be dried and gave a contented sigh. Normally, she had to fight to get a towel anywhere near his face. If she hadn't seen it for herself she would never have believed it.

Jack wandered past and she expressed her surprise, only to be greeted with a shrug. 'Told you he wasn't that bad.'

Claire stood with the horse and soaked up the sun for a few minutes before starting on the big chestnut, Howie—also known as Hazardous Waste—who was never any trouble.

* * *

Back in the house, after packing the ute with tack and feed for the next day, Claire marvelled at how similar and yet how different it felt to the old days when she was competing in Pony Club. She was experiencing a few pangs of apprehension, but nothing like the fear of failure that used to stop her eating for most of the twenty-four hours before an event. And she certainly wouldn't miss the diarrhoea when she woke up, and the urge to vomit that always lasted until she went through the start flags for the cross-country.

She lowered herself onto the lounge, savouring the first long slug of a large sherry.

'Ready for your first big race day?' Jack asked, sitting in the armchair with a beer in hand.

'Dad, it's not my first race day.'

'It is as a trainer.'

'Officially, I'm just your sidekick. I'm not actually qualified, remember?'

'Yes, you are.'

'Dad, that's really sweet, but we both know officially I'm just your daughter who helps out.'

'Not anymore.' He reached down beside his chair and handed her a piece of paper, beaming.

Claire took the paper with a perplexed frown. 'What's this?'

'Your very own trainer's licence.'

'What? How? Oh, Dad, I don't know what to say.'

'Thanks will do, and how about a big hug for your old man?'

Claire jumped up. 'Thank you.' They hugged tightly. Her eyes prickled with tears. 'But how? Don't I need to be examined or something?'

'Well, a friend in the know called and said he'd heard the rules were changing. Soon all newcomers will have to do the course, regardless of family connections. Thought we'd better get in first.'

Twenty-Two

Claire stood in front of Howie's and Paycheque's stalls while Bernadette went in search of a hot caffeine fix. Claire said she wanted to keep the horses company while they settled in, but really it was just to make sure Paycheque didn't try to have a go at passers-by. It was as though he chose to rile people just because he could.

Today the horse seemed relatively relaxed, which was amazing given his last race day experience. He had his head over the gate and was snoozing in the sun as if butter wouldn't melt in his mouth.

There was a gentle nudge to her shoulder, and Claire half turned as Howie nuzzled under her arm, trying to get his nose in her pocket.

'Sorry. Nothing for you, spoilt monster.' She laughed, turning out her pockets as proof. She rubbed the horse on his wide forehead and ruffled his forelock. Howie closed his eyes, long lashes fluttering.

'How about I give you a brush,' Claire said, deciding she needed to stop looking like a bouncer outside a nightclub. She grabbed a brush from the box on the ground, opened the gate and entered the bulky chestnut's stall. He stepped aside to let her past. She undid the straps of his rug and folded it back onto itself. The horse let out a deep sigh as she settled into the rhythm of long strokes along his sleek coat.

Suddenly there was a shout from outside the stall. 'Oi! Bloody menace!'

Claire's heart flip-flopped as Howie snapped to attention, nearly planting a hoof on her foot. In two strides she was at the gate and had to put her hand to her mouth to quell the rising laughter.

Paycheque had something in his teeth and Todd Newman was standing, beetroot-red, trying tug-of-war style to retrieve it. 'Give it back,' the man growled. Claire stayed hidden in the shaded stall, peering out from beside Howie.

At that moment, Bernadette arrived carrying two takeaway cups. 'What do you think you're doing to that horse?' she demanded.

Todd let go of the book and turned to Bernie. 'Bloody menace bit me. I'll sue, I will.'

Paycheque disappeared into his stall.

'I'll give you the details of my insurer, after you've shown me the damage. Hang on a sec. I've got a camera on my phone.'

'Well, there's no mark as such,' he stammered, peering down at his chest.

'Looks like you've been slobbered on, not bitten. Sort of goes with the territory, though, wouldn't you say? I'm happy to pay for the dry-cleaning…'

'Just make the damn horse give my form guide back. It's in his mouth.'

'Ooh, really? What a clever boy.'

Claire nearly erupted as she watched.

'Just go in and get my bloody book, will you!'

'No, thanks. Maybe if we ask nicely. Paycheque? Do you have the nice man's book?' There was a shuffle and Claire saw Paycheque's head reappear in the doorway.

'Doesn't look to me like he's got anything.'

'Well, he took it from my pocket. He must have dropped it in the stall.'

'You're welcome to go in and check,' Bernadette offered with a shrug.

'He's bloody dangerous.'

Bernadette shrugged again, put the second cup down and made a show of engrossing herself in removing the lid from her coffee.

'It's my bloody form guide—I need it.'

'Here's two dollars—buy another one,' Bernadette said, fishing a two-dollar coin from her pocket. 'They're selling them over by the gate.'

Claire cringed. She really should warn Bernadette who she was messing with.

'Not today's form guide, you stupid woman. Anyway, what would you know about form?'

'Diddly-squat apparently, because I happen to think those horses you wrote off are destined for great things.'

Shit, she does know who he is, Claire thought, torn between wanting to cheer her friend on and slapping her to shut her up. She started to gather her wits in preparation for her entry into the firing line.

'You're right about one thing—you know absolutely fuck all about form. Keep the book, you clearly need it.' He let out a cynical laugh and strode off.

Claire breathed a sigh of relief and emerged from Howie's stable.

'Ah, that's where you were hiding. Did you hear that smug bastard?'

'What did you have to antagonise him for?'

'Someone's got to defend those who don't have a voice of their own. Bastard deserves to be brought down a peg or two.'

'No, all you did was set us up for further failure,' Claire groaned.

'Lighten up, you're giving him way too much power.' Bernadette sat heavily on an upturned bucket and handed the second cup to Claire.

'I just so badly want to beat him.' Claire sighed and plonked herself on another bucket.

'I know. And you will. *Many forms can winning take. Many forms.*'

'Thanks, Yoda, but I prefer the old-fashioned way— first past the post.'

'Patience, my dear, patience.'

They were startled when there was a slap and a small booklet appeared on the ground between them. They laughed.

'Had your fun, hey? Cheeky boy,' Bernadette said, reaching up and poking the lips that hung over the door.

'Careful,' Claire warned.

'What? I think he's been significantly cheered by his little victory. He looks like he's ready to take on the world.'

'No, I think he just wants your coffee.'

'Well, you can't have it. Auntie Bernadette needs her caffeine fix—she got up way too early.'

Claire checked her watch. 'Shit, I've gotta have Howie ready in an hour. Where's that bloody jockey anyway?' She drained her lukewarm coffee and got up. 'I'm going to look for him.'

'What can I do?'

'Make sure his lordship here doesn't pick anyone else's pocket. Since you're feeling so game you can brush him if you like.'

When Claire returned—the jockey still nowhere to be seen—she found a small, lean, twenty-something girl in jodhpurs and a loose green knitted jumper leaning on Paycheque's gate. Paycheque seemed to be lapping up the attention—there was not a twisted nostril or flattened ear in sight. The girl stepped aside and Bernadette emerged from the stall with the brush in her hand.

Claire was about to continue on her way when Bernadette turned and spoke to someone out of sight. *Don't tell me David's here as well*, she groaned inwardly, instantly annoyed with her childishness.

As she rounded the corner the person Bernadette was talking to came into view. Claire almost dropped her bundle of tack.

'Derek, what are you doing here?'

'I'm in this game, too, you know.'

'Yes, of course,' Claire said, surprised to find herself blushing violently.

'Great to hear you got your own training ticket,' Derek said with a grin.

Claire opened her mouth. How could he possibly know that?

'What? You're really a trainer—in your own right, not just with Jack? Why didn't you tell me?' Bernadette cried, leaping forward and hugging her friend, startling Paycheque into the darkness of his stall, and causing

Howie to open his eyes and check out the commotion. Over Bernadette's shoulder Claire noticed the young lass was still at Paycheque's gate, speaking to him in soothing tones.

'Oh, just some red tape someone managed to cut through or something,' Claire said, withdrawing from her friend's embrace, but keeping her eye on the girl at the gate.

Paycheque was back, peering out warily as the girl stroked his face. 'See, you big goose? Nothing scary out here, just people doing silly people things.'

Claire stared, perplexed, impressed.

Derek cleared his throat. 'Sorry, Claire, this is my daughter, Madeline. Maddie, this is Claire McIntyre.'

'Hi,' Madeline said, beaming and putting her hand out. 'Nice to meet you.'

Claire shook the hand while appraising Derek's daughter. She could see a slight resemblance. Their eyes were a similar blue-grey and both had long, narrow noses.

'Derek, I didn't know you had a daughter.'

'Hasn't been around much—ran away to join the horsey world, didn't you, sweetheart?' he said, putting his arm around the blushing girl.

'So, are you a jockey?' Bernadette asked.

Madeline didn't get a chance to answer because just at that moment Jack McIntyre sauntered up to the group.

'Derek, great to see you again,' Jack said, thrusting out his hand.

'Likewise, Jack. These two look like they're coming along,' Derek said, nodding at the horses.

A few pieces of jigsaw fell into place for Claire. 'It was you, wasn't it?' she demanded of Derek.

'What? What was me?'

'The one who told Dad about the changes for trainers?'

'I might have mentioned it.'

'Suppose I'm meant to thank you for interfering in my life?'

'Claire, don't be like that. He's done us both a favour,' Jack said.

'Dad, rarely does Derek Anderson do anyone a favour, unless there's something in it for him. So what is it this time?'

Bernadette and Madeline were shifting on their feet, looking about awkwardly. Madeline was blushing violently, obviously totally embarrassed.

'Well, er…' Derek stammered.

'See, you can't just do something nice for someone—there's always a catch.'

Derek had recovered his composure and was now looking Claire in the eye. He had a grin on his face, which annoyed her even more. He grabbed her by the arms and before she had a chance to protest said, 'If you would stop being so bloody prickly, Claire McIntyre, you would know that Jack here rang me to see if Madeline would come by and meet Paycheque. Seeing as he's as prickly as you, we thought a woman rider might be the answer. Female jockeys aren't getting much of a look-in at the moment.'

'It's true, Claire,' Jack said. 'I thought maybe we needed a female jockey, since you can't race him.'

Now it was Claire's turn to burn beetroot-red. 'Oh, right, well then, I'm sorry, especially to you, Madeline. I didn't mean to embarrass you.'

'No worries,' Madeline said. 'Could I have a ride? I know he's not going to race today, but…'

'Well, he hasn't actually been scratched,' Jack cut in. 'Why don't you hop on? There's an hour until his race. If you feel comfortable we'll give him a run—no pressure, mind. What do you think, Claire?'

'Don't see why not. I'd just be happy to get him into the barriers and then onto the track without disaster. But I've got to warn you, Madeline, he can put on a real turn.'

'She knows,' Derek said. 'She saw him last time.'

'I'll take him steady, see how we go.' She shrugged.

'Thanks, Madeline, that'd be great,' Claire said, feeling relief flow through her. If this worked her grand plan might just look doable.

'I'll just go and get my helmet,' she said, starting to walk away. She'd only gone a few steps when she stopped, turned back and said, 'Oh, and my friends call me Maddie.'

'I know she's my daughter and I'm totally biased, but she really does have a way with horses,' Derek said as they watched her leave.

'Wow, isn't this exciting,' Bernadette said, clapping her hands. 'I'm going to go for a wander—does anyone need anything? More coffee?'

'No, thanks,' Claire and Derek said.

'Jack?'

'No, thanks. I'll be too busy getting Howie ready.'

'Okay, I'm going to get myself one. See you later.'

'Sorry about before, Derek.'

Derek kicked at a piece of straw. 'It's okay. You had a right to be suspicious—you worked with me for long enough.'

Claire laughed.

'But I'm changing. I've come to realise a few things these past couple of months.'

They both looked at the ground. Claire fidgeted with her zipper.

'Haven't we all?' Claire laughed, trying to break up the awkwardness.

'So, truce?' Derek said, putting out his hand.

'Truce,' Claire said, shaking it. 'But don't think that means we're going to go easy on you on the track.'

'Ah, yes, but if Maddie's the jockey, it'll still be a win for me.'

Claire laughed. 'All right, you got me there.'

Derek checked his watch. 'I'd better get cracking. Places to go, people to see. I'll catch you later.'

Before Claire had a chance to object, Derek had put his hands on her shoulders, pecked her on the cheek, and was striding down the laneway between the rows of stables. She stared after him frowning, her heart beating slightly faster.

Jack led Howie out of his stall. 'Righto, Claire, can you lead him around, stretch his legs while I go and try to find his jockey?'

Claire snapped back to reality as the reins were thrust into her hands.

'Oh, I couldn't find him before.'

'That's okay, I know exactly where he'll be. You head straight out to the floats.'

'Come on, then,' Claire called to the large chestnut beside her, and began walking.

Claire had only met the jockey once before and wasn't at all impressed, but had to agree with her father that with no other options presenting, they couldn't afford to be picky.

She thought about Howie's gentle nature and hoped they weren't letting a cowboy loose on him. But then, how many times had she heard you had to be tough to succeed in this game?

She walked the horse up to the mounting area where Jack stood with the jockey kitted out in the McIntyre colours. The faded state of their red and gold silks was a little embarrassing, but forking out for a new set was a luxury they really couldn't afford right now. Anyway, Jack probably wouldn't hear of it: Grace had made these not long before her death.

Claire took a new dislike to the jockey when he began aggressively slapping his whip against the palm of his hand.

She had never used whips in training—didn't see the point in belting a horse when it was doing its best. All it served to do was distract the animal and unbalance the rider and, in turn, the horse. She couldn't believe the racing industry's occupational health and safety people hadn't seen the potential danger in jockeys only holding on to the reins with one hand. Not to mention leaning wildly to one side to provide a better angle for connecting the whip with the horse's flesh.

What annoyed her most was that no one seemed to see that if whips were banned no one would be advantaged or disadvantaged. All whips or no whips, what was the bloody difference? She shook her head.

'Yep, got you, you're the boss,' the jockey said, nodding his head. But the look of disdain on his face told her he wasn't listening to a word this old codger said.

Claire put the reins over Howie's head with deep

feelings of misgiving. His ears went up and his nostrils flared as if he, too, felt the mood change.

'Righto, let's see what you've got,' the jockey said, gathering the reins and putting his foot out for a leg-up.

'Just take him easy, it's his first time out for a while,' Claire said.

'Yeah, yeah. I heard your old man. Just leave him to me. You go and settle yourself comfortably in the stands,' he said, waving his whip in the air.

Claire scowled at being patronised. She flinched as Howie got a slap with the whip and instantly became a different horse: up on his toes, darting about, looking fearful and bewildered. She shot Jack a concerned glance.

'They'll be right,' Jack said, but looked as concerned as she. 'It's out of our hands now,' he added. 'He's a sensible horse. He'll be okay.'

Claire glanced back at the horse dancing about and felt sick to her stomach. She wished she hadn't had coffee. Part of her also wished she'd kept her involvement to swanning about in the corporate boxes at Flemington and only occasionally helping out her father.

She chose a spot at the rail halfway down the straight and stood there reminding herself to breathe. Howie went past in his warm-up, head down fighting against the bit, already beginning to sweat.

'Jesus, let go of his mouth,' Claire growled, wanting to climb under the rail and rescue the horse from the pint-sized brute. But as hard as it was, it was business, she told herself. Howie was half a tonne of horseflesh— the punk didn't stand a chance if it came down to it.

Anyway, they had been lucky to get a jockey at all. The best jockeys usually went hand in hand with the best stables—two-bit operations like theirs got the dregs.

Claire gritted her teeth. What they needed was a good name for themselves. Not that what she was seeing would go any way towards that. Howie was now rearing up and refusing to go into the barriers.

'Stop reefing at his mouth!' she pleaded under her breath. 'And, Howie, for God's sake, stop giving him something to pull against.' Claire wasn't sure what she feared more: the humiliation of their horse leaving the track unraced, the commentator's announcement of their withdrawal or the jockey's fury. She closed her eyes and put her head on her arms folded across the rail. *Howie, just let him have his way and I promise you'll never have him on you again.*

The crash of the barrier gates and thunder of hooves brought Claire's head up. She looked around, expecting to see Howie being led away in disgrace, but he was nowhere to be seen. She looked back to the mass of horses flying towards her. Her heart surged. There he was, dead last by a long shot, but there nonetheless. But she could see the defeated, exhausted hang of his head.

Jesus, was that blood at his mouth? Claire thought with a start, but the horse was already too far away.

The race was over before it had begun. Howie struggled all the way around, coming past the post a distant last.

'Oh, well, better luck next time,' Jack said, appearing at her side and putting a hand on her shoulder.

She looked up at him, eyes blazing. 'That was nothing to do with luck and you know it.'

Jack squeezed her shoulder a little too hard. 'Not here, Claire,' he warned.

She wanted to scream. *Why not bloody here?* The poor horse wasn't given a fair run because of some reject, upstart jockey. But looking around she realised Jack was right—this was not the time and this was definitely not the place for raised voices.

At that moment Todd Newman sauntered past, tipping his Akubra towards them. A grin was spread across his face. Jack offered a tight smile back and tipped his own hat. Claire tightened her grip on the cold railing.

'Come on, he's not worth it,' Jack said, pulling her by the shoulder.

He was right, but it didn't stop her wanting to thrust her steel cap into his groin.

'Where did you get to anyway?' she asked as they walked over to wait for the horses to emerge from the track.

'I was behind the barrier—thought I might have to retrieve Howie.'

'That bloody jockey should be banned,' Claire growled through gritted teeth.

'He might be yet.'

'Something you're not telling me?'

'Well, I was asking around and apparently he's had trouble interstate.'

'I'm not surprised, but I just wish it wasn't us who gave him a ride.'

'Anyway, I've officially reported him. Let's just hope Howie isn't too worse for wear for the ordeal.'

They fell silent as an exhausted Howie and red-faced jockey came towards them.

The jockey leapt off and threw the reins aside. 'Here,

take your bloody nag,' he growled, ripping his helmet off and then its silk covering.

Claire caught the small piece of fabric he threw at her. She waited in silence as he struggled out of the silks. She stayed silent, willing them to be still intact when he'd finished. She stumbled backwards slightly at the force with which he shoved them into her chest.

He stomped off and Claire watched as two men in suits carrying notebooks approached him.

Howie stood beside her, heaving and dripping in sweat. Pink-tinged foam clung to his lips. She inspected his mouth and found a tiny patch rubbed raw by the bit in each corner. Thankfully it wasn't too bad, probably only take a couple of days to heal. But the psychological trauma would take much longer.

Twenty-Three

Claire was pleased to be distracted by Bernadette bounding up and screeching about how it was just like being at the Cup.

'You've never even been to the Melbourne Cup, Bernie. And you've been to heaps of race meetings before.'

'I know, but it's just so exciting—you know what I mean.' She took in the troubled look on Claire's face. 'Sorry he didn't win.'

'Where were you anyway? I thought you were here for moral support.'

'Out the back with Maddie and Paycheque. I wanted to keep an eye on them while you were busy with the race.'

'Are they all right?' Maddie had suggested she lead the horse around for a while so they could bond before she got on him. Claire had been instantly impressed—finally, someone else who understood the complex little horse.

'So far, so good. She's on and warming him up. Derek's out there with her as well. He said she rode dressage for years—it certainly shows. Beautiful rider, lovely soft hands—Paycheque seems to be putty in them anyway.' Bernadette laughed.

'Hopefully we're onto a winner there,' Jack said.

Claire felt a twinge of jealousy, but reminded herself the results were what mattered, not who got them. As she wasn't a qualified jockey she had to have outside involvement.

'How about I deal with this great lump and you two go over and take a look for yourselves,' Bernadette offered.

'Sure you don't mind?'

'No, I'll hose him down, dry him off and put his stable rugs on. Oh, and is there something to put on his mouth? Ouch, that looks sore. Poor thing,' she said, patting the horse.

'There's some antiseptic cream in a tube in the box under the pile of rugs. You're a star, thanks. His feed is in the bucket just outside his stable—it's got his name on the lid. Once he's cool and his heart rate settles, mix it with a bit of water and give it to him.'

'Okay, got all that. Leave him to me,' Bernadette said, accepting Howie's reins from Claire.

'Thanks, Bernie—you can come with us anytime you like,' Jack said, and sauntered off.

Claire noticed Howie's sideward glance, but shook off her misgivings—this wasn't like handing him over to that jockey. Given half a chance, Bernie would pamper him until he forgot he was a horse.

She stopped beside a float to watch Maddie and Paycheque unseen. Bernie was right: the horse certainly was behaving well. But more impressive were the in-

structions being issued by Derek standing in the centre
of the circle Maddie was riding in.

'Stretch your legs down a bit more, he's not tracking
true to the circle,' Derek commanded.

She realised Maddie was riding without stirrups. Her
legs, which seemed a lot longer than when she was on
the ground, were stretched down Paycheque's rib cage.

'Okay, now see if he'll do a shoulder-in. That's it, inside leg to outside rein. A little more, put a bit of pressure on—he can handle it. Oh, well done! Give him a
pat, bring him back to walk and let him relax.'

'He looks great,' Claire said, striding across to
Derek. 'We could put him in the hack ring judging
by that.'

Derek reddened a little. 'Hope you don't mind. We
thought it might help if he was focussed on his rider.'

'Mind? Not at all. It's a little unorthodox, but if it
keeps him calm and functioning, then I'm all for it.'

Maddie halted next to them, her reins hanging loose
below Paycheque's relaxed long sleek neck. Claire gave
the horse a pat.

'You two seem to be getting on well,' she said, beaming up at Maddie.

The girl was flushed. 'I think he trusts me now. He
was really listening right at the end. Hope you don't
mind—some trainers get a bit weird seeing racehorses
doing dressage. They think it'll corrupt them or something.'

'Well, I can understand that—the way it's always
been done and all that. But no, I say whatever works.
I ride with my stirrups long, too—too old and stiff to
have my knees up near my ears.' Claire laughed.

'Know how you feel,' Derek groaned and they all enjoyed a brief chuckle. Claire looked at Derek and turned away quickly when he caught her eye.

'So. Do you feel he's up to a proper run?'

'Absolutely. You'll do your best, won't you, mate?' Maddie said, giving the horse's neck a pat.

Claire checked her watch. 'Perfect timing, ten minutes till we have to be mounted up. I'll lead him around while you get ready.'

Maddie dismounted and handed the reins to Claire. 'I think I'll be needing these,' she said, grinning and tugging at the silks in Claire's hand.

Claire looked down. She'd completely forgotten she was still holding them. She handed them over. 'Sorry, they're a bit damp.'

'That's okay. Meet you at the mounting yard, then. Thanks for your help, Dad,' she said, and pecked Derek on the cheek before moving away.

'No worries, see you later—just look after each other,' he called as his daughter bolted across to the car park.

Claire and Derek walked side by side. 'I didn't know you were so hands-on,' Claire said.

'With what? Maddie or the horses?'

'Both, I guess,' Claire said with a laugh.

'Well, you know these horsey girls. I realised early on I'd better join them or feel very left out of it all. So I became an instructor—figured it was safer to stay on the ground. Of course, that was all before work took over.'

'Your wife's horsey as well?' Claire kicked herself for her choice of words, but Derek didn't seem to have noticed.

'Was. She died a few years ago.'

'Oh, I'm sorry. I didn't mean to…'

'It's okay, Claire. It was a long time ago.'

They fell silent.

'It was an accident.'

'Sorry?'

'Amy, my wife. She died in a car accident.'

'I didn't… I don't…' Claire's face flamed.

'Claire, I know you're dying to ask.' He shot her a sympathetic look.

What Claire was really dying to know was how she'd worked with him so long and never known he was a widower with a child. Office gossip had got it so wrong. But Derek continued.

'They were coming back from a Pony Club rally. I was at work. A roo jumped out and Amy braked but the float jackknifed and pushed them into a tree. Sometimes I think Maddie found it harder to deal with the loss of her horse than her mother.' Claire could see the pain in Derek's face. He clearly hadn't shared the story with many people. Claire felt privileged.

'Listen to me going on like a sentimental old fool,' he suddenly said, gathering his emotions and shutting the lid.

'You must have loved her very much,' Claire said, cringing as the cliché left her mouth. Why couldn't she come up with something poignant when it mattered?

'It wasn't a perfect marriage by any stretch but, yes, I loved her. Of course, don't we always love them more when they're gone?'

'Ain't that the truth,' Claire groaned, not intending to say the words aloud.

'Ah, hindsight—it's a dangerous, wonderful thing.'

They arrived at the mounting yard at the same time as Maddie. Claire stepped aside as Derek moved forward to leg his daughter up and give her a quick pep talk, a little miffed at being pushed aside.

Jack wandered over and gave the horse a heavy slap on his neck. 'Just do your best, lad, you've got nothing to prove.'

'I'll look after him, Mr McIntyre. Don't you worry,' Maddie said, beaming.

'Call me Jack, love. Just remember, bail out if he gives you trouble at the barriers. We don't want any accidents.'

Claire was struggling for words. 'Good luck' was all she could manage. She just hoped the kid would have the guts to ride out the rough-and-tumble. Looking at her childlike beaming face, tiny hands and legs that now looked half their length all jacked up, she had her doubts. It was all going to end in tears.

'I'm going to watch from the stands. You coming?' Derek called as they stood staring after Paycheque, who was disappearing out onto the track with the other horses.

'Shouldn't we be on hand in case something happens at the barriers?'

'Claire, it's out of our hands now. Leave him to Maddie—she looks more than capable.'

Claire looked at Derek.

'Really, Claire, I know she looks young, but she's not one to take unnecessary risks.'

'If you're sure.'

The trio made their way up into the small corrugated iron grandstand. From the top plank they could see horses moving around behind the barriers, but not in any great detail. Claire held her breath and crossed her fingers as the commentator named the horses that were set to go. Her heart skipped when he announced that the jockey of number twelve—Paycheque—had dismounted.

'Shit, what's going on? I can't see a thing,' she growled.

'I'm sure it's okay,' Derek said, putting a hand on her knee.

Claire stared at the hand that felt as if it was burning a hole in her jeans, only coming to her senses with a start when the caller cried, 'And they're off and racing.'

She looked from behind the barriers to the track and couldn't see Maddie or Paycheque. She wasn't sure if she should be relieved or more worried.

'Come on, easy,' Jack urged.

'That's my girl. Let him settle,' Derek mumbled.

Her heart skipped. There they were, dead last but gathering speed, catching up. She stood and began shouting, 'Come on, you can do it! Go! Go! Go!' She didn't notice Bernie slip in beside her.

'Look at him go! He's catching up,' Bernie cried.

They watched as the horses rounded the last bend and started making their way up the straight. It was a scrappy race. Horses were all over the track jostling each other. Claire held her breath, hoping Maddie would find a line and get through. Paycheque was in the second pack, right on the heels of the frontrunners.

'Too little, too late,' she groaned. Maddie didn't have anywhere to go. The horses approached the finish line with Paycheque locked in behind. He crossed the line in second last place. Claire scowled and let her binoculars fall to the end of the strap around her neck.

They all slumped back down onto the bench with a collective sigh.

'Damn it!' Claire said, slapping her leg.

'God, Claire, what happened to no pressure?' Bernie said, staring at her friend.

'It *was* a good run, considering,' Jack said. 'Maddie did well to just get him to the line.'

Claire's face burnt from the criticism. 'Sorry, Derek, I didn't mean to imply that Maddie...'

'Hey, I didn't say anything,' Derek said, putting his hands up. 'Out there she's your employee as well as my daughter. But if I were the owner of that horse I'd have to say she rode the race about right. He landed on the track like a rabbit caught in headlights. You'll see what I mean when you see the tape.'

'What tape?'

'Oh, I have a mate tape every race—it's good for keeping an eye on the competition, amongst other things.'

Bernie leapt up. 'Come on. Don't know about you guys but I'm dying to tell Maddie how well she did.'

Claire cringed. These were the things she was supposed to be saying, instead of feeling humiliated for her horse coming almost last.

Back at the stall, Maddie chattered nonstop while they tended to Paycheque.

'You should have seen the bloke at the barriers when I told him not to touch Paycheque if he wanted to see the end of the day. I'll probably be reported. They're meant to be there to help, but they're all rough as guts. And when I got off and led him in... Well, clearly they have a problem with independent women or it's just a control thing.'

They all enjoyed a chuckle.

'I wasn't having them upsetting the poor fellow after we'd done so well to calm him down. He called me a bolshie lesbian.' She laughed. 'I can just imagine what he was thinking. Still, better than having them paw you. Men,' she groaned theatrically as she sat down and put her foot up for Derek to pull off her boot.

Derek and Claire exchanged amused expressions. *No wonder the kid was having trouble getting rides*, Claire thought to herself. She was liking the girl more and more.

'I did try to talk you out of this industry,' Derek said.

'You go, girl,' Bernadette said, offering her hand for a high five.

The sun was a large red fireball not far above the horizon when they all finally said their goodbyes.

Bernadette had cried, 'See you at ten,' at the last minute and Claire had flinched, hoping she wouldn't say any more. She hadn't told her father about her plans to find her own accommodation as yet.

Jack and Claire drove home in silence, Jack focussed on driving the ute, Claire on staring out the window and wondering what sort of evening lay in store for Derek and Maddie.

Part of her wished she'd invited them back for a bite to eat. After all, the kid had done more than just be their jockey. She really should have shown more gratitude— she'd have to remember to phone Derek the next night.

Right now she needed a long, hot bath. After that, it would be a big bowl of pumpkin soup and a quiet night in her pyjamas with a DVD.

Her mother had always made a pot of soup for tea after race days and Pony Club competitions. It had been a tradition for as long as she could remember. No matter the weather, it was always just what Claire felt like after an exhausting day out.

Claire turned back from the window at hearing her father's voice.

'Excellent, at this rate we'll have plenty of time to be all settled before *The Bill*. It's the series final.'

Claire's heart sank as her dream evening shattered around her. 'Is it?' she said, glancing at her father.

'You don't mind, do you?'

'No, not at all.'

She turned back to the window and pictured herself tucked up on her own couch in her own cute cottage with her own picket fence.

Twenty-Four

The next morning, Claire arrived at Bernadette's shop at ten minutes to ten, filled with both excitement and trepidation. David arrived soon after in a Mercedes convertible. Claire stared at the gorgeous gleaming red car.

'Always looks better for this type of excursion to turn up in a Merc rather than a common old Holden,' David called from the window. 'No offence, just a tactic of the game,' he added, getting out.

Claire took in his attire. He looked incredibly fetching in tan dress boots, navy chinos and an open-necked long-sleeved blue-and-white-striped shirt with cuffs folded back twice. The girls exchanged quick grins.

'Thought I should at least look the part of the countryman about town,' he said, twirling around to give the girls the full view. 'Now,' he said, leaning into the car and bringing out a cardboard takeaway tray of coffees, 'I took the liberty of collecting a few goodies along the way.' Claire and Bernadette accepted them with coos of gratitude.

'While you drink those, if you will please peruse the

itinerary,' he said, pulling two folded sheets of paper from his jacket pocket.

'Itinerary, what a good idea!' Bernadette cried, accepting hers and shaking it open with her free hand.

Claire shook her own copy open. She was amazed to see their day allocated to driving time, six house inspections, lunch and afternoon tea breaks. Each property had a thumbnail photo, a list of 'must have' and 'I wish' features with boxes to tick, the agent's details and a few lines for additional comments. She tried very hard to appear unimpressed.

'Thanks, David, you're a star. This will make things so much easier.'

'It's just like being on a school excursion or something,' Bernadette said.

'Just as long as you don't go putting graffiti in the toilets,' David said.

'No,' Claire said, chuckling, 'spit balls were more Bernadette's style.'

'Thanks very much, *friend*.' Bernadette scowled, turning red.

'Well, we'd better get this show on the road if we're to make our 10:30 a.m. "Picture perfect—everything and more". Your chariot awaits,' David said, opening the two passenger doors. 'Unless you'd like to be chauffeured properly,' he added, shutting the front door.

'Oh, yes, let's. What fun!' Bernie cried, leaping into the back of the car.

Claire was momentarily stunned. She thought her friend would have wanted to sit up front with David.

'Come on, Claire, in you hop,' Bernadette cried, slapping the seat beside her.

Claire gave David a shrug, bounded around to the other door and got in.

'I would have got the door for you if you'd given me half a chance,' David said, putting on a pout.

David got in the front and fished about under his seat. 'If we're going to be formal I'll be needing this,' he said, holding up a black cap before putting it on.

The girls packed up laughing.

David made a show of putting on his sunglasses and looking over them at Bernadette and Claire in the rear-vision mirror and saying, 'Right, ladies, are we all ready to go?'

'Yes, yes, get on with it,' they yelled through fits of giggling.

There was a collective gasp as the car rounded the bend in the driveway of the first property. It truly lived up to the headline. David brought the car to a halt on the white gravel turnaround next to a Bermuda-blue BMW four-wheel drive.

'Now wait, you two,' David instructed. 'Let's do this properly—except without the hat. I don't want to look like a complete moron.'

Claire stared at the whitewashed cottage and front garden with its deep purple picket fence and masses of multicoloured roses tumbling over and poking through it. She told herself not to get her hopes up too much, but had to admit she had already fallen in love. It was a struggle to snap out of her daze when David opened her door.

Bernadette giggled like a schoolgirl while she waited for David to come around to her side.

The real estate agent was standing at the front door,

armed with clipboard and brochures and an amused smirk.

As David and Bernadette approached him, Claire hung back, pretending to cast a critical eye over the house, but really taking the time to instruct herself not to fall at the agent's feet and beg for it to be hers. *It's probably awful inside and completely unsuitable*, she told herself, continuing the silent mantra as she made her way up the gorgeous rustic redbrick paved path.

But the house couldn't have been more perfect. Each room was lovelier and more light-filled than the last. Remembering rule number one of buying a house—never look too interested—Claire remained mute, twisting her features into different configurations of scepticism and disinterest. She was aware of David asking questions and making lots of notes. *Thank goodness someone was*, she thought vaguely as she continued wandering through the house.

Back in the car, David and Bernadette chattered around her about this feature and that, the colours of the various rooms.

'How about the size of that bath?' Bernie said. 'The tiles are a little dated, but I could live with that to have a big claw-footed tub to soak in.'

'Hmm. What about the kitchen?' David said, sounding dreamy.

'The ceilings were nice and high, and I didn't notice any rising damp,' Bernie continued.

'I liked that they left the bedrooms carpeted. I love bare floorboards but they're too cold in winter. And decent floor rugs cost a fortune.'

'It's the best of both worlds. I love the deep honey

colour of authentic old pine. It's so much nicer than what you get now.'

'It's all laminated floating floors these days. Ever notice how they sound like hard plastic underfoot?'

'Mmm. I liked the built-in bookshelves either side of the fireplace, too.'

'Except for the fact it'll save a trip to Ikea.' David laughed. Bernie joined in. Suddenly they stopped and looked at Claire.

'Well, Claire, what do *you* think?' Bernadette demanded.

Claire was having trouble remembering the details. All she knew was that she'd liked it from the moment she'd walked in, right to when they'd walked out. It just felt right. 'Well, I…'

'Yes?'

'I know I shouldn't, but I absolutely love it! It's perfect! It's silly, but I don't even want to look at any more. I want this one!'

'I know what you mean,' David said with a sigh. 'And I agree it does seem rather ideal. It's not too big but not too small. The rooms are a good size. The price is even in your ballpark.'

'Well, I think we should be sensible—stick with our plan and if at the end it's still the one, then that'll be that,' Bernadette said.

'If it's meant to be, it will be,' David and Bernadette chanted together, and then laughed at their synchronicity.

'Oh, great, you're both as bad as each other,' Claire groaned. 'Come on, then, let's get going before I leap out and manhandle that agent.' She tried to sound jovial, but as they drove away her heart began to ache.

She forced her attention to the description of the next property on their list: 'Diamond in the rough'.

Claire was relieved when finally their appointed lunch hour arrived and they stopped under a sprawling gum tree at the entrance to a winery. It was clear that the first house was the pick. The next had been mutton dressed as lamb—lovely on the outside, falling down on the inside. The third, advertised as a 'gentleman's residence', was more like an opium den with its putrid hazy atmosphere and red 1970s carpet.

She swallowed a bite of her egg, mayonnaise and lettuce sandwich.

'Are you all right, Claire?' David enquired.

'Yeah, it's great, thanks,' she said, making a desperate effort to sound grateful. David really had gone to a lot of trouble for her.

'David,' Bernadette started, with her mouth half full, 'I don't want to be a pain or anything, but do you think the other three are really worth looking at? Personally, I think the only one that has any hope is the first. I'm sick of making enthusiastic noises about peeling paint and musty odours and agreeing that, yes, everything does come back into fashion eventually. As for red and green laminex bench tops, that should be a hanging offence.'

'I'm really not interested in anything that needs renovation,' Claire said tentatively.

David put down his sandwich, raised his hands and, looking skyward, said, 'Thank God. I thought you'd never ask. If I see another room done in apricot or peach I think I'll puke.'

'So, what do we do?' Bernadette and Claire asked together.

'Do? There's only one thing to do.'

'Yes?' Claire said.

'Well, ring the agent and beg him to sell you the property, of course, silly.'

They all laughed.

'Beg? I'm not sure I'm…'

'Well, I guess that depends on how badly you want the house,' David said, already packing up the lunch things.

They enjoyed an early dinner at David's home, which could only be described as stunning. Claire couldn't understand why, with such clear talent in interior design, he'd be working the unsociable hours of a café, when he could be swanning around spending other people's money doing up their houses.

After half an hour of oohing and ahhing over his carefully placed knick-knacks and exquisite feature walls, David popped the cork on a bottle of champagne.

'Here's to an extremely successful day house hunting,' he said, raising his glass.

'And decisive owners who can negotiate quickly—touch wood,' Bernie said.

They clinked glasses and took their first sips.

'I can't believe it's all happening so quickly,' Claire said.

'That's because it's meant to be,' David said.

'*And* because Claire is so damn organised she'd done all the groundwork.'

'I can't believe you sold the townhouse so easily. I thought the market had slowed in the city,' David said.

'Just lucky, I guess,' Claire said with a shrug, and returned her attention to her glass.

'Well, let's hope your luck covers you for moving day. Mine was an ordeal and a half!' David said.

'I think we should just let Claire enjoy the moment, don't you think?'

'Okay, fair enough.'

Claire, giddy with the euphoria of success and being the centre of attention, reminded herself she had to drive home later. Finally, she could feel the tide turning on her otherwise dreadful year.

They discussed Christmas, which no one seemed to have given much thought to. Claire thought she noticed an odd look pass between David and Bernadette, but dismissed it—Christmas had weird effects on people. It would be another milestone in her first year without Keith. When had she last thought of him? Two days? Three? *Oh my God! How could I forget him after all we meant to each other? But hang on*, she thought. *Just because he's not plaguing your every waking moment doesn't mean you didn't love him.*

But he was gone. And she had a life to live.

With her champagne glass halfway to her lips, staring at her oldest and newest friends, Claire McIntyre decided that quite possibly she would be okay. She snapped back to attention at having her glass clinked again.

'You were miles away,' Bernadette said.

'Just thinking life's pretty good right now,' Claire said truthfully.

'That's my girl,' Bernadette said, and hugged her friend.

As Claire turned into the driveway she did a double take and brought the car to a halt. Something was different. But what? She looked about before dismissing the thought as the lights of the car playing tricks with the shadows.

Claire felt a little apprehensive, suddenly regretting not telling her father about her plan to find her own accommodation. It was silly; here she was a grown woman scared of the same conversation she'd had with her father almost two decades before. She looked back up the driveway at the waving shadows of the trees beside the road. Ahead, the porch light flickered like a beacon. She gritted her teeth and put the car into gear.

Twenty-Five

Jack took the news surprisingly well, even agreeing that, yes, he could understand her wanting time away from him and the horses. He went to great pains to tell her how much he had enjoyed her company, and that he really did appreciate all her assistance in getting him back on his feet.

'Dad, I'll still be here every day working, you know,' she said, suddenly concerned he wasn't quite comprehending.

'Don't worry, Claire Bear. Just closing the book.'

'Sorry?'

'Well, it's business from now on, isn't it? So we'll have less of the bossy-daughter-helpless-father routine, won't we?' He sounded jovial, but Claire still felt the criticism. She forced herself to laugh.

'I suppose you think that means you'll be doing all the ordering around from now on?'

'Too right—we'll make you a top-class trainer yet...'

You'd have to become one first. Claire bit the inside of her cheek, hating herself for the thought. What he said next both stunned and impressed her.

'…not an old bushie like me.'

Claire beamed and, as always, could not help pushing for extra compliments. 'You really think I've got what it takes?'

'You're still here, aren't you?' Jack said.

A few days later, Claire was coming back from lunch with Bernadette when she finally realised what was different about the entrance to the McIntyre farm. Something had been bothering her every time she'd driven in, but she hadn't been able to put her finger on it. Now she saw: the faded tin sign announcing 'J.W. & G.L. McIntyre' that had swung untouched for almost four decades had been taken down. It was now being rehung.

Jack was standing holding the ladder while a younger lad—whom Claire recognised from the local hardware store—checked the alignment with a spirit level. Glossy new paint gleamed in the bright afternoon sun. The red, shadowed lettering stood out boldly from the white background and the gold swirling details in the corners.

She pulled over and wound the window down, ready to tell them how good it looked. But as she studied the lettering she noticed something slightly different about it. The 'G' in the second set of initials was now a 'C'.

She got out of the car and stared up at the sign. She cursed the lump forming in her throat and swallowed it.

Jack came over to her. 'So, what do you think?'

'It's great, but…are you sure?'

'I organised it, didn't I? Of course I'm sure. Thought I may as well make the partnership official. The entrance was looking a bit tired anyway. Randal here's going to repaint the gates as well.'

Claire blinked back a couple of tears. 'Thanks, Dad. It means a lot, it really does.'

'I know. And it means a lot to me having you here.' Jack put an arm around his daughter's shoulders, gave it a quick squeeze and let go.

'Right, so we'll just have to live up to this flash sign, then, won't we?' Claire said, getting back in the car. 'I'm going to give Paycheque a workout in the sand.'

'Good idea. I'll see you later.'

Claire was glad to wake on Christmas Day to find a rare cold, wet morning. The bank of dark, low clouds looming outside her window matched her mood. Here she was, thirty-five years old and living at home with her father. She still hadn't signed the contract on the cottage. Her offer had been as good as accepted, but the vendors were still trying to work out how long they needed for settlement. And, of course, there was no escaping the fact it was her first Christmas without Keith. Claire couldn't wait for it to be over.

They were spending the day with Bill and Daphne Markson. When they'd rung to invite her and Jack it was so obviously a pity call—the assumption that poor Claire was now bound to be at a loose end. The worst part was that they were right.

She'd spent so much time away from the city that she'd pretty much dropped out of her social circle. No one had invited her to have Christmas with them. Usually those who didn't have family in Adelaide took a turn hosting lunch. But they rarely called these days, and when they did there was really nothing to talk about. Probably figured she'd be too busy taking care of her father to get away.

Claire looked out the window again. Bloody Keith. If he hadn't died she wouldn't be hating the thought of Christmas. Life would be so different. She groaned. Wasn't that the understatement of the century? She checked her watch beside the bed. No time for wallowing. She had approximately four hours to drink her coffee, feed the horses and put on a happy face before lunch.

'Morning,' Jack said when she entered the kitchen. 'A fine Australian summer day we have.'

'Hmm.' Thank God he hadn't shouted 'Merry Christmas' at her.

Claire had just made her tea when the phone rang on the table beside her. It was Bernie.

'Happy Christmas!'

Claire scowled at her friend's cheer. 'And to you, too.'

'A little bit of enthusiasm would be nice.'

'Hmm.'

'Claire McIntyre, you have lots to be thankful for, so brighten up.'

Ah, so she was in tough-love mode. 'I know. It's just…' Claire sighed.

'I know. It's your first Christmas without him. You're allowed to miss him, just not dwell on it.'

'It's not that. I'm so sick of everything being about poor Claire who lost her husband.'

'Well, that's good. It's a sign you're moving on.'

'I wish everyone else would, too—I've lost count of the number of people who have stopped me in the street the past couple of weeks to talk about the weather.'

'It's just because Christmas is…'

'…a milestone in the first year. I know, and I'm sick of hearing it. I just want it to be over.'

'Well, it will be soon. You just have to hang in there. Look, I'd better get cracking. Just wanted to say hi. I'll speak to you tomorrow. Have a good day—I'm sure it won't be as bad as you think.'

'I know. Thanks for ringing.'

'Love to Jack.'

'Okay—same from him. See ya.'

Claire hung up. 'Bernie sends her love, Dad.'

'Oh, thanks. And back from me.'

'Did that.' Claire got up from the table.

'What's she up to for Christmas anyway?'

'No idea. She wouldn't tell me.' She'd asked her friend at their past three weekly lunches. But Bernie had replied vaguely and quickly changed the subject. There was no point pushing. When Bernie Armstrong didn't want to tell you something, there was nothing to do but wait until she was ready to spill the beans.

'Probably spending it with that nice David fellow.'

'Probably.' Claire supposed she'd find out soon enough. 'Well, I'd better get these horses sorted.'

'Remember, I've told Daph we'll be over at eleven.'

'Yes. I know,' Claire said with a slight groan.

'Don't roll your eyes like that. One day the wind will change.'

'Yes, Dad,' she said, scrunching her nose at him.

'Now, that wasn't so bad, was it?' Jack said as they drove away from the Marksons' at five o'clock that evening.

'No, it wasn't.' It had actually been quite nice. There'd been no awkward moments, and not once had

anyone asked her 'how she was getting on' without
Keith. She was that bit closer to leaving the 'Poor Claire'
tag behind and being just plain old Claire again.

Claire finally got the call from the real estate agent
on the day before New Year's. The cottage was hers—
or would be in early March. So it was done. Her last ties
with city life were gone and she really was moving back
to the country for good. There was no going back now.

Claire tried to get excited about moving, but couldn't
get past the thoughts of packing up one house, cleaning it, and then cleaning and unpacking again at the
other end.

It was early days, but David and Bernadette were
pushing for a house-warming party the day after moving, insisting that if she didn't do it then she'd never get
around to it. Claire was sitting at Jack's kitchen table
making a half-hearted guest list—just in case she lost
her mind and agreed to the party.

The last thing she wanted to do was stand around
making polite conversation while a herd of people
traipsed through her home, opening all her cupboards
and scrutinising her life, spilling wine and crumbs all
over the place. She just wanted to move in and spend the
next month alone curled up on the couch. She closed her
eyes and indulged in her conjured idea of bliss, smiling
and sighing with contentment.

'Ah, the simple things,' she mused aloud, and realised with a mild shock how truly spinsterish her life
had become.

Claire looked about her and felt an odd sense of emptiness and apprehension at the prospect of leaving her
childhood home for the second time. It was exciting,

so why did she feel uneasy? Claire tried to analyse it in the hope of making it go away. After all that had gone on this year, surely it was a simple task of closing one door and opening another.

She turned her page over, wrote the heading 'What I need in life' and began her list. It was a list she made every New Year's, and it always started the same: 'secure job', followed by 'house', 'reliable car' and so on. She knew it by heart—they were all the things Claire McIntyre felt she needed in order to survive. After writing for a few minutes, she stopped. She stared at the first entry: 'secure job'. There was no way what she was doing was secure. Beyond twelve months she didn't have a clue what she'd do. But she was okay—she hadn't fallen apart yet, had she?

Bernadette had once pointed out that most of the things she listed were *wants* not *needs*. Bernie saw needs as things like food, water and shelter, not all the other 'luxuries' she had written down. They used to argue about it, but eventually they'd agreed to disagree. Claire looked down through her list.

Bernadette might be able to live happily with cats and not men, but she—Claire McIntyre—wanted more.

That was what was missing: the love of a good man. A tear escaped as she thought of Keith—the man who had shared her home and heart for over ten years. She wiped her eyes with the back of her hand. He was also the same man who had driven her nuts with his obsession for all things golf and electronic—she certainly didn't miss that.

Lately she wondered whether it was *Keith* she missed or just having *someone* to come home to. Why did the prospect of living alone seem so daunting? And why now, when she was moving into her own little cottage. She'd lived alone for months in her big city house.

Look what had happened to her in the past year: a loving—if at times totally frustrating—husband taken from her; her father's accident; a so-called secure job taken from her; and houses having to be bought and sold.

Bernie was right: there really was no such thing as security. You had to be responsible for your own happiness. Only when you were truly independent could you live in harmony with someone else. It didn't mean you couldn't enjoy company, you just didn't have to suffocate it. Like cats—now *they* had it all sussed. Claire smiled to herself and added 'kittens' to her list.

Twenty-Six

Claire was mesmerised by the hooves in the heavy sand as the horse circled her at the end of the lunge rein. If someone had told her six months ago that she'd be actually enjoying life—not just living it—she wouldn't have believed them. But a lot had happened since she'd lost her job last October: Jack was almost back to his old self; and she'd settled into her role as co-trainer. Apart from a few bumps, the partnership seemed to be working. And she was loving being able to spend so much time with Bernie again. Not long now and she'd be moving into the cottage.

She hugged her oilskin coat around her as the autumn sun was swallowed by clouds and tucked her gloved hands into her armpits. Winter was closing in fast, and soon she'd be cursing the cold and rain and wishing she was back in the comfort of an office with central heating. The stifling heat of summer had been bearable because, with nothing much to be done with the horses in the middle of the day, she'd been able to retreat indoors when it got too much. But if Jack could tough it out at his age, then she could, too.

The horses were all progressing well, if a little slowly. For the past few weeks Claire had been left in charge of training, having questioned her father's seemingly haphazard 'suck it and see' approach once too often. They hadn't had a fight over it. Jack had just shrugged and walked away. Since then, Claire had often seen his silhouette in the kitchen window, watching her as she worked the horses in the front paddock. She wished she'd kept her mouth shut, because she still didn't really have much strategy beyond getting them fit and looking good. But she was winning there. Even if none of the horses ever won a race, each was a picture of rippling muscles under a gleaming satin coat.

Claire studied Howie's form as he cantered around her, his breath puffing out grey from his lips as the warmth collided with the cold morning air around him. His head was lowered in submission and his hooves dragged, kicking up sand. The poor creature had to be bored out of his brain going round and round in circles—she was.

'Aaaaand walk,' she called. The horse registered her voice with a slight flick of his ears and stumbled into a walk. 'Aaaaand halt.' Howie did as he was told and stood on the outer track, his head turned towards her, brown eyes patiently awaiting her next instructions. 'Come here, there's a good boy.'

Howie lifted his head and ambled towards the centre, where Claire stood like a circus ringmaster.

As she rubbed his head and fed him a carrot from her pocket, she noticed his eyes were dull—gone was the cheekiness. Part of her knew it meant she had control: this was what most trainers strove for. But a bigger part of Claire felt an overwhelming sadness. Howie was losing his individuality, his personality.

She thought back to the days she'd been a state Pony Club eventer with her mother in charge, and the many successes they'd had. Standing there with her hand on this horse's big willing sad face, she realised that her successes were only in the ribbons and trophies she'd acquired. Really, the higher the level of competition and the more schooled the horse, the less fun she'd had.

The early days of Pony Club had been a blast—the times after class when they'd roared around on the ponies bareback, sitting on the ground in fits of laughter after falling off when the animal shied sideways for no reason. So when had it got so serious? But it had to, didn't it? You couldn't be a kid forever.

'If only,' Claire heard herself say. She looked from Howie to the other three horses with heads hung over their stable doors awaiting their turns. What did they think? Were they happy to perform in return for a comfortable stable and food, or did they hate the sight of her striding towards them, lunge rein in hand?

'Come on, then, let's give you a hose down.'

Howie would stand with a stream beating his forehead all day if you let him. The absolute contentment was clear in his half-closed eyes. Every now and then he'd grab the hose with his teeth, fill his mouth with water and squirt and dribble in a playful display of huge flapping lips that saw strings of gooey saliva land on anything within five feet.

She turned the water off just as Jack ambled over.

'How'd he go?'

'Good, but I think he finds the lunge too boring. He's lost his spark.'

'Hmm. Never saw much point in going round and round—it was more your mother's style. And what about you?'

'What about me?'

'Do you find the lunge boring?'

'Yes, but so what?'

'You're a partnership. He's looking to you for leadership. If your heart's not in it, his won't be—same with all of them. What do you enjoy doing?'

'Um, I don't know.'

'Yes, you do, just think. Remember back to when you were first starting out in Pony Club. What was it you loved doing the most?'

Claire flushed slightly and shrugged. 'Games, jumping, formation riding. Oh, and roaring around like an idiot,' she added with a grin.

'What you need, my girl, is to recapture your youth. Put him away and come inside—we're going to find ourselves a new strategy.'

'Okay. I'll be over soon. And, Dad?'

Jack turned around.

'Thanks.'

He batted her thanks away and kept going to the house.

Claire stood at Howie's gate for a while, enjoying his contentment while he ate. As she watched his ears flick back and forth in time with the movement of his jaw, it struck her that her father was right: it really was more about the journey. Why hadn't she seen it before? She wondered if she should say something to Jack, maybe apologise and tell him things would be different from now on. Jack had never been one for soppy discussions; she'd just have to show him.

* * *

Jack already had a stack of books, a lined pad and a pen on the table when she arrived. He pushed the pad and pen towards her as soon as she sat down.

'First, I want you to think about each horse's personality and what that translates to in terms of having fun together as a team.'

'But I…'

'No buts or arguments, Claire, just take your time. Think back to when you were a kid, the various partnerships you had and what made them work. For instance, remember Bennie, and how you loved to chase foxes…?'

'Yeah, the time we ran one down and it was hissing and spitting. Bennie loved it. Remember how he won that endurance ride, sprinting at the end and I'd hardly spent any time getting him fit?'

'Exactly—it just worked. On another horse that strategy might have been a disaster. So what we want to do here is match a strategy to each horse.'

'But what do other trainers do? Shouldn't we be reading about horseracing, not thinking about my old Pony Club days?'

'Claire, we don't give a toss what other trainers do. You've got to be true to yourself, first and foremost. Good and bad horses come and go. When it all boils down, all you have is your soul and self-belief.'

Is everyone thinking like Bernie these days? Claire wondered.

'So let's start with Howie. What are his strongest traits?'

'Okay. Well, he's calm and willing, not easily startled, but has a cheeky, feisty side…'

'So that means…' Jack prompted.

'Well, if he wasn't so big, he'd probably enjoy gymkhana games. I'm too old for that anyway.'

'Nonsense. There's nothing to say you have to be good at it. We're just trying to add some variety.'

'So what do you think makes Larry tick?' Claire asked.

'Open spaces,' Jack said without hesitation. 'He's had too many bad experiences cooped up. I've taken him out a couple of evenings for long rides, checking fences when you've been out with Bernadette and David and…'

'When there's no one around?' Claire gasped.

'Why, because I'm too old?'

'No, because…' Claire flushed. 'No, because if you came off we wouldn't know where you were.'

'I'll be right, Claire.'

'Well, could you at least leave a note saying which paddock you'll be in?'

'Okay, if you insist.'

'I do.'

'Right. Now, Bell, he hates open spaces and being alone—much more suited to the round yard. Be a nice dressage horse or hack if he doesn't make it on the track. And Paycheque, well he needs to learn to focus.'

After an hour, several cups of tea and numerous pages screwed up and flung aside, Claire sat back in the high-backed chair and let her breath out loudly. There in front of them was a plan for each horse and trainer for the next few weeks. Secretly, Claire wondered how Jack would be able to fulfil the physical demands. He hadn't even thought he could ride at all when he'd come home from hospital. He continued to surprise her every day, but she still wished they had another bum to put in the saddle.

Her father had been running this place single-handed all these years, regularly having as many as six horses in work at a time. With the two of them it should be a lot easier.

The key was to be organised—an area Claire was gifted in. She started making mental notes. If she organised meals ahead of time, measured out all the horses' feeds once a week, put out her clothes the night before... Hell, she'd coped for years with the pressures of an advertising firm full of difficult artistic types. Four horses and her father should be a doddle.

'Dad, how about I get a big whiteboard to write this up on and put it in the tack room? That way it'll be right there to refer to.'

'How much are they?'

'Not much. But don't worry, I'll get it.'

'Well, I was just wondering if we could get one for the feeding schedule as well. I'd like to experiment more with individual feeds. I suspect Howie would benefit from more oats, but giving Larry more will turn him into a lunatic.'

'Good idea. Two it is, then.'

Claire studied the menu and decided on the asparagus crêpes—she needed something to warm her up. She was halfway through a glass of water when Bernadette arrived at the café.

'Sorry I'm late,' Bernie said, sitting down and grabbing a menu. Within seconds the waitress had pounced on them, taken their orders and retreated to the kitchen.

'No worries, I was a bit early anyway.' Claire poured her friend a glass of water.

'Have you met someone?' Bernadette said suddenly, staring hard at Claire across the table.

'Sorry?' Claire was genuinely perplexed. 'I meet people every day—just saw Jillian Cooper at the post office, Bill Markson at the newsagent...'

'There's something different about you, but it's not your hair, that's the same... Who is it? It's Derek, isn't it?'

'What is? Bernadette, have you been inhaling too much glyphosate or something? You're not making sense.'

'Look at you. You're positively radiant.'

Claire blushed slightly and brought her hand up instinctively to smooth her hair.

'You've found love. It's the only explanation,' Bernadette said triumphantly, and took a deep slug of water.

'All right, I confess,' Claire said, laughing and holding up her hands in surrender.

'I knew it,' Bernadette cried. 'So, spill—tell me everything.'

'Well, the first one,' Claire began, noting with amusement the startled expression on her friend's face, 'has the biggest brown eyes you've ever seen. He's easygoing, gentle yet big and strong.' Claire paused, wondering how much further she should go. Bernadette was leaning across the table hanging on her every word. Just then David appeared. A subtle waft of aftershave stalked him as he kissed Bernadette and then Claire on the cheek.

'Don't you smell yummy,' Bernadette said.

'It's "CK Contradiction". Do you like it?'

'Lovely,' Claire said, sniffing close to him.

'Thanks. And how are my two favourite girls today?'

'Well, I'm good,' Bernadette said, 'but apparently Claire here is in love.' She rolled her eyes.

'Ah, do tell,' David said, pulling out a chair and sitting down. Claire looked from one to the other, a bubble of laughter rising up in her chest. She felt naughty, but their inquisitive expressions were just too much.

'Bern, it's Howie—the horse—you moron!'

'Sorry? I don't follow,' David said, frowning.

'We've been had, David. Claire's been a deceitful cow.'

'You're the one who insisted I was in love.'

'So you're not?' David said, clearly disappointed.

'No, she's not,' Bernadette snapped.

'Actually, I am—with life,' Claire said in an airy tone, waving her arms around.

'Oh God, here we go,' Bernadette and David groaned in unison, and then laughed at their synchronicity.

'Well, clearly nothing juicy here. I'll get back to my boring café, then,' David said, getting up.

'Thanks a bloody lot, Claire,' Bernadette groaned, putting her head on the table. 'I feel like a complete idiot.'

'Oh, well, you'll get over it. Teach you to jump to conclusions, won't it?'

'Probably not, but you're right. I'll get over it. Okay, so tell me what's making you so happy.'

'Well, everything. I don't know, it's like life is finally falling into place, making a bit more sense.'

'So you're on track for the move, is that what you mean?'

'Yeah, that's all fine, but it's the horses, really.'

'What, finally the McIntyre marvels are showing signs of promise? I didn't know you'd been to another race meeting.'

'We haven't.'

'Then what the hell are you talking about? You are *so* not making sense.'

They were interrupted by the delivery of their meals by David's waitress. Claire picked up her cutlery and began to eat. After a few mouthfuls she paused, fork poised midair.

'I never thought it would be so much fun.'

'What, winning?'

'No. God, Bernadette, we haven't *won* anything. Not yet anyway.'

'And you're okay with that?' Bernadette stared at her friend in disbelief.

'Not that I have a choice but, actually, yes, I am. It's like I kind of get it all now. Dad's right. It's about the journey, not the destination.'

Bernadette shot her friend a doubtful look.

'What is it you find so hard to believe?'

'You. This. It's weird.'

'Haven't you been telling me for years to lighten up and "trust in the cosmos"? Have faith in myself?'

'Yes, but, Claire, now you're actually doing it you're scaring me.' She laughed tightly. 'You're sounding like a New Ager.'

'I don't know—I've been trying to put my finger on it.'

'So, what exactly is it that has you so excited?'

'Promise not to laugh.'

'No. I will promise not to laugh *at* you, though.'

'Okay, I can live with that. Well, it's not one particular thing, more a philosophy…' Claire stopped, suddenly it didn't feel right to tell anyone what they were doing. She couldn't understand it—she and Bernie discussed everything. She could probably count on one hand the number of secrets she'd kept from Bernadette over the years.

'Ah, I won't bore you with the details. It'd be like you telling me what you feed each individual species at the nursery,' Claire said.

'Fair enough.'

'What evil plan are you concocting now?' David said, appearing at the table and sitting down again.

'I was just about to have another go at convincing Claire to have a house-warming since she's in such a good mood. You can help twist her arm now you're here.'

'And what is it that has the lovely Claire so chipper?'

'Well, not love, apparently,' Bernadette said, pouting.

'Just country life in general,' Claire cut in. 'You know? Clean, fresh air, good food, friends—the usual things.'

'Claire, you have to have a party. I've got a few recipes I'm dying to try out. I promise we'll do most of the work and not leave until the place looks better than it did to start with. Right, Bernie?'

'Really?' Claire asked with raised eyebrows.

'Absolutely. Won't we, Bernie?' He nudged Bernadette hard.

'All right, if you say so.'

'Okay. And I'll have that in writing, thanks, signed by both of you.' Claire reached over and pulled David's order book and pencil from his shirt pocket and slapped them on the table. She read what was being written and then waited silently while both signatures were added.

'Thank you,' she said smugly, pocketing the note. Claire then fished in her handbag and brought out a folded piece of paper, which she smoothed out and then pushed across the table.

'Here's the guest list. Invitations only went out yesterday so numbers aren't finalised. But I think we're looking at around twenty.'

David and Bernadette exchanged wide-eyed expressions and then set their stunned gazes on Claire, who was already again fossicking in her handbag. She brought out two envelopes with their names handwritten on them.

'I think we've been conned again, David,' Bernadette said, bringing her head down on the table.

'Yep. Done like a dinner, I'd say.'

'Right, so who's having dessert?' Claire said, looking behind her at the display case of cakes, tarts and pastries. 'I think under the circumstances, it should be on me.'

'Sorry, I'd better get back to the kitchen,' said David, and got up. 'See you soon.' He kissed them both again and, with the most subtle of aftershave breezes, was gone.

'Bernie, how about you?'

Bernadette looked at her watch. 'Shit! I didn't realise how long I've been sitting here. I'm meant to relieve Darren at one-fifteen. Sorry, gotta go.' She leapt up, gathered her handbag and, after pecking the bewildered Claire on the cheek, bolted to the counter to pay.

Claire shrugged and got up as well. She'd have dessert next time. It wasn't as if she didn't have anything better to do. She was looking forward to getting back to the farm and the work that awaited her.

She suddenly remembered that she still hadn't sent Derek's and Maddie's invitations. She hadn't seen them since the race meeting in December, but it would be nice to at least invite them. She'd meant to phone Derek for the address, but something held her back. The thought of calling him after such a long time sent a slight quiver through her.

Twenty-Seven

Claire got changed and, armed with her old Pony Club instructor's manual, made her way behind the stables, where her jumps had been stacked for nearly a decade. Jack had built a simple low lean-to out of recycled corrugated iron, but nothing seemed the worse for wear except the dulling of paint where sunlight had peeped under the iron.

Claire had dragged all the rails and other bits and pieces out into the paddock and was planning her obstacle course layout when she heard the crunch of gravel and quiet purr of an approaching vehicle. She turned, shading her eyes against the glare of afternoon sun. Her heart did a quick double-beat as she recognised the silver BMW. She made her way over to the fence as Derek Anderson emerged. They shook hands a little awkwardly and exchanged greetings.

'Are you back teaching Pony Club?' Derek asked, nodding at the coloured rails and other jump paraphernalia.

'Oh. Just something I'm trying out.' Claire blushed slightly and dropped her gaze to the ground where she was now prodding at the powdery earth with the toe of her boot.

'Would you like a hand setting them up?'

'Thanks, but I'll be fine.'

'Really, it's no problem. I'd be happy to help.' Claire felt torn between wanting to spend time shoulder to shoulder with Derek and not disclosing her plans. He was a rival owner after all.

'Come on, we'll have it done in no time,' he said, striding through the gate and out into the paddock. Claire watched him. He was a little heavier than she remembered, but she found she actually liked his bulk. It was comforting. She laughed to herself when she realised she was appraising him and bounded to catch up.

It took them over an hour to measure, place, remeasure and move the various jumps exactly the right distance apart. The fact that Derek had been an instructor saved a lot of time; he was able to space the jumps out correctly without waiting for further instructions.

'Thanks, Derek, I really appreciate your help,' Claire said when they'd finished and were leaning on a white painted forty-four-gallon drum that was part of one of the obstacles.

'My pleasure. Anytime.'

'Come on inside, I'm parched.'

They sat in the faded Black Watch tartan director's chairs under the back verandah, looking over the lawn at the late-afternoon shadows, each with a large tumbler of Bickford's lime cordial and ice.

'Ahh, that's better. I didn't realise just how thirsty I was,' Derek said after his first long sip. Claire realised he had been there two hours and she still didn't have a clue why.

'Derek—' she started.

'Claire—' he said at exactly the same time. They laughed self-consciously.

'Ladies first,' he said after a brief moment of awkwardness.

'No, you've dragged all those jumps around for me. It's the least I can do.'

'Well, all right.' He paused. 'I've got a favour to ask,' he said, shifting in his chair.

'Ask away.'

'It's a big one, I'm afraid.'

'Right, okay.' Claire smiled and took another sip of her drink.

'I need you to employ Maddie. Here,' Derek blurted.

Claire choked and spluttered as she inhaled her drink. 'What?!'

'I'll pay—it won't cost you anything.'

It took Claire a few moments to recover. She wiped her mouth and nose with the back of her hand and stared at Derek.

'What do you mean? You're going to pay *us* to employ *Maddie*? Are you mad? Or just bloody rich?' The words came out in a torrent. She wished she hadn't said the last bit but it was too late now.

'Not rich, Claire, just worried about my little girl.'

'Why? Has something happened to her? What's going on?'

Derek let out a long weary sigh before speaking. 'Maddie's being bullied at Al Jacobs's place.' He put his glass down at his feet and rubbed his face with both hands. 'Thank God she feels she can talk to me, that's all I can say.'

'Can't you talk to Jacobs? Threaten to report him or something?'

'And risk him or someone else taking it out on her? No, I've just got to get her out of there. Are you going to help me or not?' He suddenly turned to her and grabbed both her hands now lying empty in her lap. 'Please, Claire.'

Claire met his searching gaze. 'Derek, there's no question of me doing whatever I can. Maddie's a great girl. And she's amazing with horses...'

'But?'

Claire bit her lip. 'Well, there's Dad to consider, which shouldn't be a problem...'

'And?'

'Well, let me get this straight—we'd employ Maddie full-time, here in the stables, trackwork, and...'

'Yeah, whatever you need.'

'...and you'd be paying her wages?'

'Exactly.'

'Is this legal, Derek?'

'I'll make sure it's all above board. You won't be in any danger.'

Claire shifted in her chair. 'But it's not fair. It's win-win for us. If we could afford to pay her, fine, I'd have no hesitation. But taking money from you? I don't know.' Claire shook her head, shrugged and frowned. 'And what about Maddie? I'm assuming she doesn't know anything about this. If she did she'd be here with you.'

'No, she doesn't. She's desperate to get out of there but needs somewhere else to go.'

'She's a strong, hardworking, intelligent young woman, Derek. How would she feel if she knew her father had bought her a job? I'd be devastated.'

'She wouldn't have to know.'

'And if she found out, she'd be furious with all of us. Derek, you're playing with fire.'

'So what do I do?' he said, throwing his hands up. 'I can't afford to set up my own facility, and I wouldn't know where to start anyway.'

Claire's head spun for a few moments while she processed Derek's predicament and thought about how she could help and at the same time keep everyone's values intact.

'Right,' she finally said. 'Of course, I'll have to run everything by Dad, but I'm sure he'll agree. It could work, but there would have to be two conditions.'

'Name them.'

'One, we discuss all this with Maddie and she decides if she wants to be involved or not. And two, the money is considered a loan—though it will have to be a long-term one at the rate we're going,' she added with a grimace. 'Oh, and I've just thought of a third condition—we put it all in writing. What do you think?'

'Do I have a choice about telling Maddie?'

'Sorry, but if Maddie, Dad and I are going to be a team, we can't keep a secret like this from her.'

'Okay. You have no idea how much this means to me, Claire. Thank you,' he said, grasping both her hands and squeezing them.

'Well, we're not home and hosed yet. I'll talk to Dad this evening. When do you think you can bring Maddie around?'

'Tomorrow. I think she finishes at four-thirty. I can pick her up after that.'

'Then why don't you both stay for tea? Nothing fancy.'

'Okay, if you're sure.'

'No worries. Oh, and wait, I've got something for you both,' Claire said, leaping up. 'I was going to call you tonight to get your address,' she added as she disappeared. Derek stared after her, looking puzzled.

Claire came back with two envelopes, which she handed to Derek. 'I've been bullied into having a housewarming the Saturday after next—I'm moving on the Wednesday. Here's an invitation for you and one for Maddie. I understand if you already have plans.'

'I'm pretty sure I don't, but I can't speak for Maddie. Do you need a hand on moving day? I'd be more than happy to help.'

'Thanks, but I've booked removalists. And I'm having them pack everything.'

'Well, you can always phone if you need any extra assistance—I'm only ten minutes away.'

'Really? I thought you lived down in the city somewhere.'

'No, I'm on a couple of acres just over at Gumeracha.'

'Wow, I had no idea. Travelling to work must be a nightmare.'

'The freeway has got it down to forty-five minutes. We originally bought so Maddie and Amy could have the horses. Never thought I'd like the peace and quiet so much, but there you go—learn something new every day.'

Tell me about it, Claire thought. She really had Derek

picked as a city type through and through. She couldn't believe she'd worked with him for years without knowing he'd been living just a few towns away from where she'd grown up. Claire found that she quite liked the idea of Derek living so close.

'I'd better get going,' Derek said, standing up.

'Thanks for your help with the jumps and everything.'

'My pleasure. And thank you again for your help with Maddie.'

'Well, it's up to her now. We'll see what happens tomorrow.'

'Hmm.'

They walked close together as they made their way out to Derek's car. Claire felt the weirdest urge to grab his hand.

With his car door open, Derek turned to Claire and kissed her full on the lips: a lingering, not entirely platonic, kiss. Claire closed her eyes and drank in his touch. And then he wrapped his arms around her and pulled her into a tight hug. Claire responded by holding him tightly back.

After a few moments he pulled away and got into his car.

'I'll see you tomorrow, if it works for Maddie. Otherwise I'll call,' he said from the open window of his car.

Claire waved him off and stood watching the dust until well after she'd lost sight of the car. She went inside feeling a little as she had twenty-odd years ago when her first boyfriend, Justin, left after visiting.

Twenty-Eight

Claire was in her bedroom finishing drying her hair when she heard a car coming up the track. She carefully tucked a stray wisp of hair back into place and laughed to herself at the absurdity of life. She'd just spent over an hour making sure she looked casual and carefree—pretty much the way she looked every day without any effort or forethought.

And then there was the dinner itself. She'd chosen braised lamb shanks, rice and an assortment of steamed vegetables—a meal she'd cooked countless times. But this time she'd fussed over every detail, paranoid that everything would go wrong.

But why? It was nothing more than a business meeting. Claire rolled her eyes at her reflection, sighed and left the room, ready to answer the door.

She looked out the dining room window in time to see Jack greet Derek with a handshake, and Maddie with a friendly hand to the shoulder and welcoming grin.

As they were being ushered towards the house, Claire did one final check of the pumpkin soup. She frowned as she stared at the bread rolls warming in the oven. She really hoped Derek had come clean with Maddie and that there wasn't about to be any awkwardness.

At what point should they start discussions? Between soup and main, or before they tucked into their bread-and-butter pudding dessert? And who should bring it up? *Just go with the flow*, she told herself, but cringed as Jack let their guests in through the laundry. Not that it mattered. *This was a business meeting, not a date*, she reminded herself for about the twentieth time.

Claire turned back from the oven as Jack, Maddie and Derek entered the kitchen, and instinctively wiped her hands on a tea towel. She wondered at the sidelong bemused smirk on Derek's face as he was ushered past her into the open-plan dining-lounge room, until she remembered with a flush of embarrassment she still had one of her mother's frilly green gingham aprons on. She probably looked the epitome of a 1950s housewife.

Halfway into their soup, Jack got right down to business.

'So, Maddie, tell me what you've been up to at Al Jacobs's place—any newcomers we need to watch out for?'

'To be honest, Mr McIntyre, there are a couple with some talent, but none that really *want* to win.'

'We're going to get on just great, I can tell,' Jack said. 'But please, I've told you before, it's Jack—none of this formal stuff.'

'Maddie does know why she's here, doesn't she?' Claire asked, fixing a stare on Derek.

'I've been totally up front. There's nothing Maddie doesn't know about our arrangement.'

'Which is?' Claire knew she sounded like a school

matron but didn't care. If the words were actually spoken with everyone involved present there could be no misunderstandings later.

'It's all right. I know Dad's paying you to employ me. And I really am grateful. I promise I won't let you down.' Maddie smiled at each person around the table.

'Well, as long as you don't feel like your independence is compromised.' Claire hoped she didn't sound sarcastic, because she certainly wasn't meaning to.

'Of course it is, but I'm not going to be bitter about it. Yes, I would have liked to go it alone, but in a boys' club such as racing, that doesn't seem possible for me right now.'

Claire was impressed with how grounded Maddie seemed. She really was a credit to her father, she thought, instantly feeling very old.

'Apparently it is one thing to be strong and independent, but quite another to be petulant and stubborn,' Maddie said, looking pointedly at her father. Claire tried to hide her bemusement. She felt a whole new rush of respect for the kid.

'Is it okay if I start tomorrow?' Maddie suddenly asked, looking quickly down at her bowl.

'Okay with me,' Claire said. 'Dad?'

'Great.'

'Why the hurry, Maddie?' Derek asked, staring at his daughter with raised eyebrows.

'Oh, you know. No time like the present,' Maddie said, flipping a hand before returning to her soup.

Good on you, Claire thought, *she's left the Jacobs place with a bang, naughty girl*. She looked forward to hearing the full story. But she'd wait. There were some things a father really didn't need to know.

'Dad, how about you top up our glasses while I serve the main. Maddie, could you collect the plates? You're our slave now, remember,' she said, giving the girl a wink.

The rest of the evening passed in a pleasant haze of conversation, good food and Barossa Valley red. At around ten o'clock, Derek and Maddie bid their fare-wells with the promise of her returning at eight the next morning—she was allowed a sleep-in for her first day at the McIntyres'.

The next morning, Claire introduced Maddie to Larry and Bell and reintroduced her to Paycheque and Howie. Then she showed her through the feed room. She was relieved Maddie didn't seem at all perturbed to be in such a rustic, ramshackle outfit after the rela-tive luxury of her previous post.

The tour ended in the tack room, where, after show-ing Maddie where everything was kept, they sat down on the bench under the small window opposite the whiteboard. This was a crucial moment: what if their concept sounded like some fantastical pipe dream when explained to an outsider? Or worse, to herself, when she said it out loud? She took a deep breath and stared at the whiteboard, deciding where to start. But Mad-die got in first.

'So, is this what the jumps and bending poles are all about?' Maddie asked.

Claire nodded. 'At this stage it's really only a plan. It might not even work,' she said, shrugging.

'Of course it'll work!' Maddie cried. 'It's great. They get so bored going round and round day after day—not to mention their riders,' she said, rolling her eyes. 'I was only asking Al the other day if I could take one of the older stayers out over a couple of hunt fences. He wouldn't hear of it, was worried about injury—not to me, the horse…'

'So you can jump, that's a relief. I forgot to ask your dad.'

'Just Pony Club grade three, and I'm a bit out of practice. I haven't done any since I started my apprenticeship.'

'I was in Pony Club myself about a hundred years ago,' Claire said.

'I know. You won't remember me, but I was at one of your jumping schools at Barossa Park when I was a kid.'

'Really? I hope it was useful.'

'You were great. I was on a real scaredy-cat, a small nutty grey-and-black Appaloosa that everyone at the club told me to get stuck into. I thought you'd say the same, but you didn't. You told me to take him easy and let him learn to trust me.'

'I think I vaguely remember,' Claire said, racking her brain. 'Inky-black face and legs—tossed his head and cat-leapt because he'd been ripped in the mouth by a previous rider?'

'Yep. He had a really tough time before I got him.'

'How did he turn out?'

'He won Adelaide Hills Zone Horse of the Year, but a few months later we had a float accident and he had to be put down. Could have won the state title if he'd had the chance.'

Claire could see tears forming in the girl's eyes. 'I'm sorry, Maddie,' she said, moving to put her arm around her. She was pretty sure Maddie was talking about the accident in which she'd lost her mother.

'It's okay,' she said, gently shrugging Claire off.

'So what do you think of our strategy here? Anything else to add?' Claire nodded at the handwritten notes.

'Well,' Maddie said, recovering her composure, 'I don't think you can go wrong with building a trusting partnership. And jumping them will develop their hindquarters and strengthen their tendons.' She got excited. 'Claire, seriously, this is like a dream come true for me. I know it sounds really naff, but I've wanted to see something like this since I first set foot in a racing stable. I reckon most of them are going about it all wrong.'

'I think having the same person working them and racing them will really help as well,' Claire added.

'So when can we get started?' Maddie cried, leaping up.

'Just one other thing.'

'Yes?'

'Dad and I want to keep this to ourselves for now— are you okay with that?'

'Of course. We all had to sign confidentiality agreements at Jacobs's. I can for you, too, if you want.'

'No, your word's good enough for us.'

'Well, you have that. So, who are we going to start with?'

'Do you have a preference—any one in particular that took your fancy?'

'What's Larry like?'

'Bit of a larrikin—hence his name. Staying focussed is his main problem. Has a tendency to throw his head up and look around—anywhere but where he's going. That's why I've got him down for poles on the ground. I figure if he trips over his feet enough he might learn to concentrate.'

'Good idea. Let's start with him, then.'

Twenty-Nine

Claire was glad she'd had the removalists pack everything and only had to meet them at the cottage. Bernie was right: how hard was it to empty a house? Claire didn't agree with her sentiment that whatever got broken wasn't meant to be in her new life, but it was easier than going back to the townhouse again.

She was nervous as she drove out to the cottage. It was a big step. It was so long since she'd seen it; she hoped she'd still love it as much. It was just after noon when she pulled up on the white gravel turnaround under the stand of tall, lean lemon-scented gums away from the front of the house. The autumn sun struck the car in random streaks and patterns. Claire was early, but still checked her watch and silently urged the removalists to hurry up. They should have finished packing up the townhouse and be on their way by now.

That morning she'd kept herself busy, despite Jack and Maddie trying to insist she take time off. She didn't want to change anything with the horses for fear of jinxing their progress. In just the week since Maddie had come on board the horses had improved markedly. They had decided to give them a run in the Autumn Carnival at Strathalbyn.

Weary from her morning's exercise and comforted by the warmth of the car, Claire fought the urge to curl up and go to sleep, and instead got out to take a stroll around her new property. She smiled at the purple picket fence with deep green rose foliage and multicoloured blooms poking through. The gate opened with a creak. The lawn either side of the redbrick path had browned off over the summer. She paused. *It might be best just to gravel it over*, she thought, before moving on. She climbed up the three concrete steps to the front verandah and stepped onto the traditional pattern of tessellated tiles in terracotta, cream and coffee, with a hint of black in the border.

The key turned easily in the lock, and she entered the narrow hallway. The timber floor creaked a little underfoot, and even the soft soles of her runners beat loudly and echoed through the empty house. She stopped at the expanse of bookshelves flanking the fireplace. She didn't have many books. It would be nice to get into reading again. A large collection of photos in nice frames would look good up on the top few shelves. She'd have to start taking her camera with her to the farm and get some nice shots of Jack, Maddie and the horses.

She roamed through her house and felt more and more pleased with her purchase as she went. It really was lovely, and now that the clutter of the previous owners had gone, it looked even more spacious than she'd first thought. And Bernie was right about the tub. It looked so inviting. She looked forward to testing it out soon.

Claire was also relieved to see that the rugs and furniture hadn't been hiding evidence of white ants or rising damp. She took a deep whiff. *Better to be cold and fresh than stuffy*, she decided, and went back through the rooms, opening all the windows wide.

She went out the back and stood on the stone slabs of the back verandah overlooking the few acres that sloped down and away from the house. The grass was browner and the gums bluer, thanks to the harsh South Australian summer, but the setting was still lovely. The quintessential rural setting—ideal for a tree change. Claire smiled. She was going to love living here.

Sitting on the back verandah with her legs hanging over, Claire unfolded the sheet of paper with her hand-drawn plan of where all her furniture would go. She'd measured and then cut out shapes representing each piece. Then she'd moved them all around until everything had a place. Hopefully all she had to do now was have the removalists follow her plan and all would be well. If only they would hurry up!

Claire began to wish she hadn't paid to have cleaners come through the day before after all. It was nice not to have to worry about doing it herself, but this sitting about twiddling her thumbs was excruciating.

Claire pulled out her pad of paper and began making a new to-do list. She pulled a muesli bar from her handbag, tore open the wrapper and began nibbling mouse-like at the edges. The snack kept her engrossed for another half hour. When she finally checked her watch—after tucking the empty wrapper into her pocket and brushing the crumbs from her lap—it was nearly two o'clock. *Shit! Where were they?*

Claire rummaged in her bag for her mobile. Her heart

sank when she found there were plenty of bars indicating coverage but no missed calls. She got up again
and wandered through the house. But there was really
nothing to be done. She returned to the back verandah
and sat listening for the sound of a vehicle approaching. There was still nothing but the crackle and rustle
of the trees in the strong, warm breeze.

'Hello, anyone here?'

Claire was instantly up and bolting around to the
front.

'Oh! Derek!' she exclaimed, stopping short at the
corner of the house. 'What are you doing here?' Claire
had the urge to throw her arms around him.

'Just passing by, thought I'd check you didn't need
any help after all.'

'I've been too bloody organised. And now I've got
nothing to do but wait. I'm bored out of my brain, actually.' She laughed.

'When are the removalists due?'

'God only knows—I thought they would have been
here by now.'

'So where are they? Have you rung them?'

'No, didn't want the "we're going as fast as we
can" speech. They're packing everything—not just
the furniture—so it'll take a while. I've been itching
to call but don't want to risk pissing them off.'

'Fair enough.'

'Derek, thanks for calling in—it means a lot.'

'My pleasure. Actually, I brought you something.
Stay there,' he ordered, and walked away.

Claire watched as he extracted a large wicker picnic
basket from the boot of his car.

'Moving day survival kit,' Derek said, patting the side of the basket.

'Liar, you were not just passing,' Claire said. Derek paused and looked at her.

'Well, I knew you wouldn't call and ask me to help.'

'So, just what have you got in there?' Claire said, breaking the awkward silence and tugging at the basket.

'All the necessities. Where do you want to sit?' he asked, dragging a red-and-black tartan picnic rug from the top of the basket and looking around.

'Here on the verandah is fine. Hopefully they'll be here soon.' As she said it, Claire found herself hoping the removalists would now take their time. Derek spread the rug and Claire watched in amazement as he laid out crusty bread, barbecue chicken, cheese, crackers, dips and a variety of deli foods.

'This is amazing, Derek. Thank you.'

'But wait, there's more,' he joked, and brought out a green bottle of sparkling mineral water. 'There's champagne in the esky, but that's for when you've actually moved…'

'That's if I ever get moved,' she groaned.

'…and there's Coke, Diet Coke, lemonade—I wasn't sure what you would prefer.'

Claire laughed. 'You're just too much. The water is fine. I probably need the caffeine, but I've already got a headache.'

'Well, why didn't you say so?' Derek fished in the basket and brought out some shrink-wrapped packets.

'I've got paracetamol, ibuprofen, aspirin and codeine for if it gets really bad.'

Claire was wide-eyed. 'Derek, you're amazing. How could you have possibly thought of all this? You're a man, for goodness' sake!' *Shit, did I really say that out loud?* Claire blushed.

Derek blushed. 'Actually, I confess I did have some help…'

He'd discussed her with someone? This was more than just a friendly gesture, wasn't it? She hoped it wasn't his girlfriend he'd sought advice from.

'…from Maddie. I wouldn't have had a clue.'

'Well, thank you, Maddie. And two ibuprofens would be great, thanks.'

Sitting next to Derek, making her way through the delicacies he'd brought, Claire couldn't believe she'd never realised how really nice he was. But then, she hadn't been looking, had she?

'Looks like we've got company,' Derek said suddenly, and started bundling everything back into the basket.

'Derek, you don't have to go.'

'I'm not,' he said, getting up and offering her a hand. 'I'm going to stay, have a look around your new home and see you settled. But only if you're okay with me being here.'

'Of course. But if I get stressed you might want to steer clear—I'm told I can get a bit bossy.'

'Claire, how long did we work together? I think I can cope with you ordering me around a bit—I might like it.'

'Derek!' Claire slapped him playfully on the arm.

'So, are you going to give me the grand tour, or not?' Derek said, looking at her with his hands on his hips.

Thirty

Claire and the house had survived the house-warming with only two broken glasses and the odd spill of wine. It was a lovely warm evening, so traffic through the house was kept mainly to guided tours and bathroom stops. Eight of her city friends had made the effort, but Claire was a little relieved when they made excuses to leave early. They'd seemed so ill at ease and out of place.

Bernie and David had stayed true to their word and done all the work before, during and after. They'd left at three o'clock after cleaning up and restoring everything to order.

It was the perfect way to have a party, Claire thought the next morning. There was no sign there'd even been one, except for a box of empty beer and wine bottles, and a couple of tied-up garbage bags out by her back door.

Since the party, Claire had spent a full week in her cottage and was settling into a comfortable routine of going to the farm in the mornings and relaxing at home in the afternoons. She was getting over the novelty of having moved house and had finally stopped apprais-

ing her furniture and knick-knacks and moving them
around.

She was due to start late at the farm that morning,
but her body clock still woke her at five. Claire thrust
her hands behind her head and stared up at the ceiling,
counting the motes floating around her. Her heart felt
heavy. *I'm just overtired after moving*, she told herself.

Claire rolled over and pulled the extra pillow to her
chest, and was surprised to find a lump forming in her
throat. *Must be hormones*, she thought, calculating the
date of her last period. She was actually mid-cycle so
should be feeling ready to take on the world. Instead,
all she wanted was a decent cry.

But why? Her life was pretty good right at the moment. *What the hell is wrong with me?* Refusing to give
in and cry, Claire dragged herself out of bed and into
the shower. It was her usual fix for feeling glum.

Conscious of conserving water, she stood under only
lightly cascading warm water and tried to figure out
what was making her feel so down.

It wasn't second thoughts about the cottage—she
absolutely loved the place. She certainly wasn't missing city life.

Since selling the townhouse, she hadn't even given
it a second thought. No, her mood had nothing to do
with houses and moving.

Her plan with the horses was working out really well
and she, Jack and Maddie were making a great team.
Preparations for the upcoming Strathalbyn meet were
coming along well, too. So it wasn't about the horses,
either.

She had great friends like Bernie and David— and
now Derek—around her to provide support and to hang

out with whenever she needed a change of scene. Derek seemed to get along well with David and Bernie at the party. They'd all been so good to her. So she definitely wasn't lonely.

None the wiser, she reluctantly got out, dried herself and got dressed. It was while staring at the kettle, waiting for it to boil, that it hit her.

'Keith. Oh my God,' she yelped, and went to the calendar on the fridge, which had been a house-warming gift from Maddie. Today was their wedding anniversary. Jesus, how could she have forgotten? She'd been too busy thinking of her great new life without him. Even worse: she'd been thinking of Derek.

The tears Claire had been holding at bay began to roll steadily down her cheeks as she stood looking out of her kitchen window. She pulled herself away and collapsed into her plush sofa. She buried her face in a large feather pillow and sobbed.

In the depths of her foggy mind she heard her home phone ring, but didn't care. Moments later her mobile, just an arm's length away on the coffee table, began vibrating, and then ringing. She turned away and pulled another pillow over her head to block out the sound.

Claire was in almost that same position when Bernadette and David arrived forty-five minutes later. She ignored their knocking at the door and refused to leave her safe, dark cocoon.

'David, in here.' Bernadette's voice was muffled.

Somewhere deep within her, Claire felt the tiniest glimmer of relief. Someone cared enough. But she didn't deserve it. Keith was dead and she'd forgotten him. He was the one who'd suffered the terrifying accident. All she had to do was go on living, getting up, going to work, paying the bills. Work? What work? Bills! That bloody four-wheel drive—how could he have done that to her? Point oh fucking seven.

'Claire, Claire. Come on, wake up!'

The cushions were being dragged from Claire's clutches. She blinked at the sudden change of light. Her best friend was kneeling in front of her. David was a silhouette over by the door.

'Bloody hell, Claire. You scared the shit out of us. Why didn't you answer your phones?'

Claire's mouth was too dry to speak. Her face felt tight under the salty streaks of dried tears. She stared back at her friend.

'I know it's your anniversary—it was always going to be a tough day for you. But, Claire, you've come so far, don't fall apart on us now.'

'But I forgot...'

'Beating yourself up isn't going to bring him back. It's just going to make you miserable all over again.'

'But even you remembered.'

'No, I didn't—Jack did. He rang me.'

'That's even worse,' she said, her chin quivering.

'It's been a big year, Claire. You've had a lot on your mind. It doesn't mean you loved him any less. Seriously, you've got to pull yourself together.'

Claire straightened up and accepted the glass of milk David held out to her. 'It's got a bit of brandy in it. I promise it'll help.'

'Thanks,' she said, and took a swig. She felt the warmth instantly start to seep through her.

'David, I think it's time for the other remedy,' Bernie said.

'I think you're right.'

Claire looked from one to the other, frowning.

'You'll see soon enough,' they said in unison.

David left.

Bernadette patted her hand and laughed. 'Don't worry, we're not carting you off to the funny farm or anything. We got you a little present to cheer you up.'

David walked back in moments later with two squirming, grey striped kittens clutched to his chest.

Claire stared wide-eyed and held out her arms.

'If you really don't like them they can go back.'

'No way. I love them. Come here, you guys. Ooh, aren't you cute?' She peered at the little balls of fluff with bulging eyes. 'They're so tiny. Oh, they're just wonderful. Thank you.'

David sat on the sofa beside Claire and the three of them watched while the kittens clawed their way up over the upholstery. After ten minutes or so the kittens had exhausted themselves and made their way back to Claire's and Bernie's laps, curled up and gone to sleep.

'I'll get their stuff,' David said.

'Yeah, better have a litter box set up for when they need it,' Bernie said.

'So, where did you get them? And are they boys, girls or both?'

'Both boys. You have to take them back in a couple of months to be desexed—it was included in the price.'

'Take them where? What shop did they come from?'

'Shop! Jesus, Claire, you don't think I'd ever go to a pet shop, do you? You know what I think of those places. No, they came from the RSPCA shelter. I know you would have liked to choose your own, but I'm glad you didn't—it was so depressing having to look at all the dear little faces pleading to be taken, too.'

'Oh, were there heaps there?' Claire asked, stroking the sleeping bundle in her lap.

'Well, let's just say there were enough to choose from. These guys are brothers from a litter of four.'

'Poor things. Shame about having to leave their siblings behind—they won't have to be put down, will they?'

'No, all four found homes while we were there.'

'That's good.' Claire sighed with relief.

David bustled back in, struggling with a cat carry box and two bulging plastic bags.

'Sorry, I should have helped. I didn't realise you were bringing *everything* in,' Bernadette said.

'What, there's more?' Claire said, noticing the dark forms behind the mesh door of the carry box.

'Meet these guys' two brothers. We just couldn't leave them there,' Bernie said. 'David's taking one and the other is for the shop—Darren reckons there are mice in the mulch.'

'Oh, you guys are great. Let me see.'

'Soft in the head, more like,' David said.

'What are we going to call the little monsters? It was going to be hard enough with only two.' Claire laughed.

'Well, mine is Basil—my favourite herb, and because he's got sticky-uppy fur,' Bernie said. 'You never know, maybe I'll start selling a few pet products.'

'Oh God, listen to her—a monster has been unleashed,' David said, and sighed.

'He'll have a ball wandering around, sleeping in pots,' Bernadette added.

'Getting under people's feet,' David and Claire said in unison, and chuckled at their synchronicity.

'I could take these guys to the stables, but I'd be

paranoid about them getting kicked or trodden on,'
Claire said.

'Plenty of cats survive living on busy roads,' David
said. 'But I'm so jealous—I can't take my little guy to
work. The health department would have kittens, so
to speak.'

Bernie and Claire looked at each other, rolled their
eyes and groaned.

'You could drop him in at the shop on your way to
work,' Bernadette said. 'What's another one?'

Claire felt a little disappointed that the offer hadn't
been made to her. There was definitely something going
on between these two.

'So what are you calling yours, David?' Claire asked.

David opened the door of the carry box and brought
the kittens out one in each hand. He turned them around
briefly before handing one to Bernadette.

The kittens did look very similar—both were grey
with dark stripes—but each had at least one distinguish-
ing mark of white on it.

'This one is mine,' David said. 'Meet Boots.'

'Great name,' Bernadette cried.

'Hmm,' Claire agreed.

'I know these white bits on his feet look more like
slippers,' David said, 'but you can't call a cat *that*. Your
turn, Claire, what are you going to call yours?'

Claire smiled down at the kittens sitting on her lap
with their little motors purring. She picked them up and
turned them this way and that, examining their individual markings. 'Don't kittens smell so yummy?' she
said, taking a deep sniff.

'They're not for eating,' David warned.

'I don't know what to call them, but I'm sure I'll
think of something when they wake up and show their

true personalities. But isn't it true what they say about pets being good therapy? I feel much better already. Thank you, guys, they're the best.'

'No, thank *you*,' David said. 'I don't know why I didn't do this years ago—precious little darling.'

'I hope you're still saying that in two weeks when they've peed all over the carpet and torn the couch to bits,' Bernadette said with a laugh.

'Oh, no, look at them, butter wouldn't melt,' David cooed.

'Jekyll and Hyde come to mind, or Henry and Edward,' Claire said with a chuckle.

'Don't you dare be so cruel as to call them that,' David said sternly.

'Shit, is that the time?' Bernadette cried, staring at her watch. 'Sorry, David, but we really have to get going—I've got a shipment of pots coming in. Will you be all right, Claire?'

'I'll be fine, thanks. Might even chuck a sickie for the afternoon to stay home and play with these guys.'

'There's food, litter and a tray in here,' David said, leaning one of the bags against the couch. 'They'll have to share your Wedgwood, though. We couldn't find any nice bowls.'

'We're only leaving if you're sure you're all right, Claire,' Bernadette said, full of concern.

'And you'll be okay if we go now?'

'Yes! Now go, before I insist on keeping *all* the kittens.'

Thirty-One

Claire hated leaving the kittens for a moment, let alone when she went to work at the farm. It took her ages to stop laughing at their naughtiness and finally start to introduce some discipline into her now chaotic home. She struggled with telling them off. They only had to rub themselves on her, purr or look up at her with their big green eyes wide and she'd crumble.

Claire awoke with her nose already wrinkling in protest. She sniffed at the air around her. Not again! She sat up and looked to the end of the bed, where the slightly larger of the kittens was trying to cover two small black turds with the quilt, clearly unaware the fabric bore no resemblance to sand or kitty litter. He paused mid-strike when he realised he was being watched. His expression suggested total humiliation. Claire stared back until she realised the second kitten had awoken, stretched, and was preparing the quilt for a gift of his own. She leapt up, grabbed both kittens, flew into the laundry, dumped them in the litter tray and slammed the door shut. When were they going to learn? She returned to the bedroom to survey the damage to her treasured one-thousand-thread-count quilt cover.

It had been over a week and still toilet training was proving a nightmare. They didn't seem to be grasping the concept at all. She'd plonk them in the litter tray at regular intervals and all they would do was scratch about playfully for a while before hopping out. A couple of times they'd used it properly, but Claire had put it down to coincidence rather than good management. She was starting to be driven a little mad with the frustration of it all. Not to mention the damage they were doing with their claws when left unattended. The fact that both David's and Bernie's kittens had settled in well and were doing all the right things annoyed Claire all the more.

Having remade the bed and got dressed, Claire realised she only had ten minutes before she had to be at work. She put some cat food in a container, then grabbed the kittens from the laundry and, ignoring their pleas, stuffed them in the carry box and left.

All the way to the farm she chatted to the plastic box beside her, making bargains and begging the furry little creatures to be on their best behaviour and not cause trouble, not frighten the horses and not get kicked or trodden on.

An instinctive check of her appearance in the mirror before she got out of the car made her laugh—she looked dishevelled, and she hadn't even started work yet.

Claire carried the carry box over to the stables and found Madeline in the feed room.

'Hi, Maddie. Sorry I'm late. Hell of a morning.'

'No worries. Everything's under control. What's this?' Maddie squatted down to peer into the box. 'Kittens. Oh. Whose are they?'

'Mine. Didn't I tell you?'

Maddie's reaction was a little odd. She was standing there looking at them a little suspiciously, not oohing and ahhing and demanding a cuddle as she had expected.

'Aren't they cute? Bernie and David got them for me.'

'Oh. Right. Yes, lovely. What are their names?'

'Unnamed as yet, poor little things. They're both boys, so if you come up with anything I'd be most grateful. I've just got to go over a couple of things with Dad in the office, so could you mind them for a bit?'

'Well, I'm pretty busy organising the feeds, and then I've got the stables to do.'

'Just leave them in their box, then. They're probably due for a snooze,' Claire said, and left.

On her way over to the house Claire wondered about Maddie's reaction to the kittens. The kid was probably just tired. Early-morning starts would do that. At least she didn't have far to travel. That reminded her—she hadn't seen or heard from Derek since her party. Prior to that, since their moving day picnic, he'd called in or phoned her every day. As she opened the back door into the laundry, Claire realised she missed him.

'Dad, are you here?'

'In here.'

Claire made herself a cup of coffee and sat down at the dining room table opposite her father, letting out a deep sigh.

'What's that all about? I'm the old one around here,' he ribbed.

'The kittens—they're gorgeous, but…'

'Kittens?'

'Oh, didn't I tell you, either? I must be losing the plot. Bernadette and David got me two kittens. They're lovely, but they're driving me a bit nuts with trying to destroy the place when I'm gone and keeping me awake at night. I brought them over in a carry box—they're at the stables with Maddie.' Claire noticed a strange expression cross her father's face. 'What's that look for?' she demanded.

'What look? Oh, I was just thinking… Are David and Bernadette something of an item? Only I thought he was meant to be, you know, a bit on the *cheerful* side, if you know what I mean. Or is that what all young men are like these days?'

'Honestly, Dad, I don't know.'

'Have you ever asked him?'

'Dad, it's not exactly something you ask someone.'

'So, we're just to assume, then?'

'I suppose we do. I don't think it matters what David is.'

'No. He seems a nice enough fellow. It's just that I'd hate to see Bernadette get hurt.'

'Well, she's a big girl, Dad, so I think we should just mind our own business. Speaking of which, I need to go over a couple of bookkeeping things with you before I get stuck into the horses.'

Claire did her work as if she were on autopilot. Her head swirled with wondering why she hadn't heard from Derek, whether David was really gay and if Bernadette knew for certain one way or the other. She also spent a lot of time worrying about the kittens: where they were and whether they were about to be kicked or stepped on. Tomorrow they'd have to stay home—they were too much of a distraction.

That night she sat on the sofa watching television while the kittens ran riot around her. She was still racking her brain over what to call them. Maddie had had a couple of suggestions like Tom and Jerry, Calvin and Hobbes, but nothing had struck a chord with her.

Claire laughed at herself. For God's sake, they were kittens! There was nothing wrong with the traditional—Sooty, Smokey, Fluffy, Blackie—except that both David and Bernadette had been so clever naming theirs.

She picked the kittens up and peered at them, and then turned them around a couple of times. Still nothing came to her. She returned them to her lap and stroked them, but after a few minutes they struggled out from under her hands, leapt off the couch and scurried off towards the kitchen. There was a gentle knock on the door. Claire unfolded her legs and got up to answer it.

'Derek! Hi!' He was standing on her step dressed in jeans, burgundy checked shirt and navy blazer. *Hmm, very handsome.* 'Great to see you. Come in.'

'Only if I'm not intruding.'

'Don't be ridiculous. I'm just watching telly,' she said, indicating her trackpants, T-shirt and bright, multi-coloured striped bedsocks. She was surprised she didn't feel even a hint of embarrassment. She stood back from the door for Derek to pass, but he stayed put and shuffled his feet a bit as if hesitant. 'Well, aren't you coming in?'

'I, er, brought you a present.' He turned to get something that was just out of view. Claire's eyebrows shot up in excitement. But her face fell seconds later when he brought a pet carry box into view. *Uh-oh.*

'Maddie and I went on the weekend, and...' He stopped when he saw her expression. 'What, you're not allergic, are you? I thought you mentioned getting kittens. And Jack said...'

'I love kittens. But look.' She stepped back from the door, grinning. In clear view were her two grey kittens wrestling on the floor. 'Maddie found out today. I wonder why she didn't warn you.'

'She probably tried to call but I had my phone turned off all day—back-to-back meetings. Oops,' Derek said, rubbing a hand across his face. 'How embarrassing.' He put the box down.

'Well, I think it was really sweet—so thank you.' Claire peered through the grill. 'Ooh, ginger. Aren't they gorgeous?'

'Hello, you two,' Derek said to the two kittens who had strode over to check out who was in the box. 'What are your names?'

'No Name One and Two at this stage, I'm afraid.'

'Well, these two come ready-named,' Derek said proudly. 'Maddie insisted. The darker one is Terry, for terracotta, and the pale one is Sandy, as in sandstone.'

'Great names. Must be both boys, right, being ginger?'

'Yep, both male.'

'So, could you take them back? I mean, I've become attached to these little guys and I think four would be overdoing it a bit. I'm so sorry, Derek. It was a lovely thought...'

'Actually, I've become rather attached to them myself. And of course, Maddie would only let them go back over my dead body,' he said, and laughed. 'So I guess I have two kittens now, too.'

'Oh, Derek, that's great,' she yelped, grabbing him in a bear hug. An awkward moment passed before Claire released him. 'So, can I get you a tea or coffee, or maybe a glass of red? I'm starting late tomorrow.'

'Oh, well, in that case a glass of wine would be lovely.'

'Have you eaten? I was going to heat up some left-over pasta. There's enough for two, though it's nothing special.'

'I'm sure it's lovely. Thanks, dinner would be great.'

'How about you let Terry and Sandy out while I get it organised.'

'Are you sure you don't mind?'

'They can't be any worse than these two. And we're getting really used to little accidents around here.'

Derek tactfully eschewed her offer of opening a second bottle of wine. At first Claire was a little disappointed—she was really enjoying his company. But he was right, it was getting late. And they did both have to work in the morning.

At the door, he wrapped his arms around her and gave her a firm lingering kiss on the lips. She drank in his breath, waiting for, hoping for, his tongue to push between her lips and search for hers. But instead he pulled back, held her at arm's length for a moment, and then pecked her on the forehead.

'See you later,' he said, and turned to leave. Claire's heart was a little heavy as she waved him off.

Back inside the house, mesmerised by the frolicking kittens, Claire thought about how she felt. She was glad he had enough respect for her to not be trying to get her into bed. Maybe he wasn't attracted to her in that way. Maybe he just wanted friendship. Did she? No. Claire knew for certain she wanted more from Derek. But what if he didn't?

As she locked the kittens in the laundry for the night,

Claire was still trying to convince herself that an uncomplicated friendship was best.

But lying in bed, enjoying the doughy, woozy haze of two and a half glasses of red wine, she felt the dull ache of wanting to be held, embraced. But was she ready to be intimate again with someone new? 'Oh, I don't know,' she said aloud to the dark empty room.

The next morning when she opened the laundry door, Claire found two sheepish kittens peering from between the foliage of the pot plants on the windowsill, a considerable amount of potting mix spilt on the floor beneath. Scooping them up she realised she finally had their names—Bill (with white chest and front feet) and Ben (with a white tip on his tail), the flowerpot men.

'Uh-huh!' Bernie yelled as she rounded the corner of the post office. Claire snapped the phone shut and felt herself blush a little.

'Jesus, Bernie. You scared me half to death.'

'So, who was on the phone? Judging by your rosy cheeks it must be lover boy, Derek.'

'Derek is not my "lover boy", as you so childishly put it,' Claire said haughtily, tossing her head and shoving her mobile in her handbag.

'But he's ringing you, right? Come on, Claire. That blush is a dead giveaway. Don't waste your innocent pout on me—we both know you'd shag him in a heartbeat.'

Claire opened her mouth to protest.

'You're as frustrated as hell. Just admit it.'

Claire threw her hands up and laughed. 'Maybe just a little.'

'Come on, then,' Bernie said, grabbing her friend's

arm and giving it a tug. 'The only temporary cure for that is chocolate or cheesecake.'

Speaking of frustrated, Claire thought as she was dragged down the street towards the café, she had promised herself she'd ask her friend about David next time she saw her.

'Anyway, I have some news of my own,' Bernadette said, puncturing Claire's thoughts.

After seeing out a pair of stooped old ladies with walking sticks, David held the door open for them to enter, pecking them both on the cheek as they passed. Claire noticed Bernadette whisper something in his ear, probably advising quick service was required for a cheesecake crisis meeting. But instead, he followed them to their table and sat down, then beckoned to the waitress across the room. Claire looked from David to Bernie and back again. David grasped Bernadette's hand lying on the table and, after silently seeking her nodding approval, spoke.

'We have something exciting to tell you. Don't we, darling?'

Claire sucked her breath in sharply and felt the blood drain to her feet.

'We're getting married. We're engaged,' Bernie blurted in a loud whisper.

'You're what?' Claire couldn't help it—the words and expression were there before she could stop them. 'But I thought David was…'

'Well, that's a bit of a funny story actually. Isn't it, darling?' Bernie cooed, stroking her fiancé's hand.

'Long story and all that,' he said, flapping his hand.

Claire stared at them in disbelief.

'Well, aren't you happy for us?' Bernadette demanded.

'Of course I am.' She got up and put her arms around both of them. 'I'm just surprised, that's all. I had no idea you guys were so serious.' She didn't think she'd ever felt so hurt.

'Took us by surprise, too. One minute we're going along as friends. The next, over a single candle and two bottles of wine, we realised there was more going on.' David laughed.

Well, that'd do it, Claire thought. She'd got it—David—so wrong. But how could her best friend, with whom she shared everything, not confide in her? Her thoughts were interrupted by the arrival of two slices of cheesecake.

'Darling, I've got to get back to work. I'll see you later. Enjoy!' David got up and gave Bernadette's lips a long firm kiss. He gave Claire a quick peck and was gone.

'We're going to look at rings on Saturday,' Bernadette said, blushing slightly, noticing Claire searching her fingers.

Claire sank her fork into the blueberry jelly topping. 'Are you sure?'

'David's picking me up at ten. We're going to…'

'No, silly. Are you sure about marrying him?'

Bernadette let out a laugh. 'Sure? Of course I'm sure.' They lapsed into silence.

Bernie was only halfway through her dessert when Claire had finished hers. She got up and put some cash on the table.

'Sorry, gotta run. Uh, mail to get, banking to do,

horses to feed,' she said, tossing the words over her shoulder, and bolted.

Out in her car, Claire paused before turning the key and realised she was sweating. Her heart was pounding and she was having trouble getting enough air into her lungs.

What is the matter with me?

Instead of feeling excited and happy for her friend, she felt sick. As she drove home, Claire realised that her whole world had changed. And she didn't like it.

She took a shower, but it did nothing to ease her despondency. In trackpants and a T-shirt, she sat in front of the television, stroking the kittens absently as they clambered over her. She was still there a couple of hours later, engrossed in *The Bold and the Beautiful*, when the doorbell rang. She opened the door to find her best friend in the world standing there.

'Can I come in?' Bernie asked.

'Huh? Of course,' Claire said, finally roused from her stupor.

'Tea? Coffee?'

'Tea, thanks.'

Claire was thankful to be given leave from the tension-filled lounge room. When she returned, they sat on each end of the couch, sipping tea and pretending to watch the kittens. Claire couldn't remember a moment as awkward between them. She knew she should get all gushy about Bernadette's engagement but she was too hurt at being the last to know and felt too stupid at not having twigged they were so serious.

Bernadette was the first to make the effort. 'Claire, I'm sorry I haven't been around much lately, but work's been really hectic. Everyone's frantically putting in dripper systems before the new water restrictions come into force. And…'

'I can't believe you didn't tell me about you and David,' Claire said quietly.

'I wanted to, I really did.'

'Well, why didn't you? Bloody hell, Bernie…'

'Claire, please don't be angry with me.'

'I'm not angry. I'm hurt. Really hurt.'

'Well, I'm really sorry about that, but I didn't really know how to tell you.'

'Why? We've been best friends for years.'

Bernie looked at Claire with raised eyebrows. 'You told me he was gay at every opportunity. And don't think I didn't notice your look of pity every time I said how nice he was.'

'Was I that bad?'

'Yes, you were. So how was I going to tell you we were an item? You probably would have had me committed for being delusional,' Bernie said, smiling at her friend.

Claire thawed and smiled back despite herself. 'Okay, fair enough. But you still should have told me.'

'I know. So are we just a little bit even? Are you ever going to forgive me?'

'Only if you promise never to do it again,' Claire said, putting on a pout.

'Promise. Seriously, Claire, this is it. I'm going to spend the rest of my life with David.'

'That's great news. I'm very happy for you.'

They hugged tightly for a few moments.

'So,' Bernie said after they had separated, 'I saw in the paper you had a win at Strathalbyn. You must be really pleased, especially with Paycheque after all he's been through.'

Claire grinned. 'Yeah, he ran a course record over twenty-two hundred metres.'

'So, should we be booking a honeymoon in Melbourne around the Cup, then?'

'At the rate he's going, anything's possible,' Claire said, and laughed.

'No, I'm serious.'

'So am I. I never thought I'd say this, but he looks as good as any of Al Jacobs's stayers. Even Howie and Larry would be worth taking if we could afford it. I feel terrible for doubting Dad all these years.'

'Well, maybe he needed your influence. You seem to be making a good team.'

'Don't you dare tell anyone I said this—because I'll deny it—but I couldn't imagine doing anything else now, least of all the rat race, even if it does mean keeping the purse strings closed.'

Bernadette stared at her friend. 'Claire Louise McIntyre, do you realise what you just admitted?'

'Yes, and like I said, if you say anything to anyone, I will deny it.' She laughed.

'Righto, I'll change the subject. What's going on with Derek?'

'Nothing, really. Just good friends.'

'His choice or yours?'

'I don't know. I think I want more but I'm not sure if I'm really ready.'

'You'll know when you are.'

'I hope so.'

'So it's working out well with Maddie at the farm?'

'Actually, she's moving into my old room. Dad adores

her, and it will save her travelling back and forth in the dark in the middle of winter. Anyway, enough about me—you're engaged. Wow! Tell me everything. How did it happen? I really thought David was gay.'

'You and me both.' Bernadette laughed. 'But it's all been a bit of an act.'

'Whatever for?'

'Well, it's pretty complicated, and you probably won't believe it—I didn't at first—but...'

Suddenly both Claire's mobile and home phone began ringing. The girls frowned and exchanged puzzled looks.

'Hold that thought,' Claire said, dragging her mobile from the coffee table. 'It's Dad,' she announced as she answered.

'Hi, Dad...Slow down. What?...When?...I'll be right there.'

Claire snapped the phone shut and grabbed her keys. Her hands were shaking.

'Bernie, something's happened to Paycheque. I've gotta get over there.'

'I'll drive,' Bernie said, leaping up and causing the kittens to dart under the couch.

Thirty-Two

On the drive, Claire constantly fidgeted, wrung her hands and pushed her left foot hard into the floor, trying to make Bernie drive faster. She was doing ninety on the dirt, sliding slightly around corners, but still the ten minutes seemed to take forever. In her mind flashed images of the horse lying flat on the ground in a pool of blood, or standing, head hung, a leg dangling limply. 'Something's happened' was all he'd said. Had she missed something? Shit, was Maddie okay? Was it *that* kind of accident?

They arrived at the stables to find Derek's BMW next to the local vet's white four-wheel drive. Claire felt the blood drain from her. She took in the scene: Jack, Derek and the vet stood in a tight group by the day yard gate. The vet was gesturing in what looked like defeat. Jack McIntyre was shaking his lowered head. Bernadette was still coming to a halt when Claire ripped her seat belt off and leapt out.

'What's happened?' she yelled. It was like a silent movie. They all turned to her, each offering a different gesture of apology, regret. But no one was speaking.

Claire wanted to slap them to attention. There were tear tracks down her father's face. She looked at the vet, and only then did she notice the gun hanging by his side.

'Oh my God. What have you done?'

Derek grabbed her by both arms and held her firmly until she looked into his eyes. 'Claire, listen to me. No decisions have been made.'

'Maddie? Where is she? What happened?'

'Maddie's okay, a bit bruised. She's with Paycheque in the wash-bay. It's bad, Claire. It's his near fore—he can barely put weight on it. Looks like a broken sesamoid bone, torn tendon or ligament.'

She turned to the vet.

'My advice is to put the animal down. He'll never race again.'

'And you know that for sure? Do you even know what's wrong?' Claire barked.

'We won't know for sure without X-rays, ultra-sounds…'

'So what *exactly* do you know? Other than that he can barely stand on his near fore? Is it a bone fracture or a soft tissue injury?'

'Either way, he won't race again—you may as well…'

'Thank you for your diagnosis, *Doctor*—you can piss off.'

'Claire! I'm sure he's doing his best,' Bernie said, touching her arm. Claire shrugged her friend off.

'He's doing fuck all other than standing there like a trigger-happy cowboy.'

Claire stormed around the side of the stables to the wash-bay and found Paycheque standing, near foreleg bent, head hung low. Maddie stroked his neck with one hand and held a gently streaming hose with the other.

Claire's heavy heart lurched. She made her way over, trying to hold back the tears.

Paycheque's ears flickered and he lifted glassy eyes towards her. How much pain was he in? Should they just put him out of his misery?

She put her hand on Maddie's shoulder and drew her away. The girl's tear-stained face was almost too much to bear.

'Claire, I'm so sorry. I...'

'Shh, accidents happen. It's not your fault.'

'But they want to put him down. They can't... It's not right. I couldn't let them, not without...'

'I know. Shh.' Claire forced herself to look at the horse. He was standing still, didn't seem to be in any major pain—maybe it was the shock. But whatever it was, it was better than a thrashing, panicked animal.

'So what happened?'

'It's too wet. I probably shouldn't have... I don't know. He just...' Maddie sobbed, on the verge of hyper-ventilation.

'Maddie, slow deep breaths. I need you to calm down and tell me exactly what happened.'

Maddie spent a few moments catching her breath.

'I was cantering through the raceway. He missed his stride on the second—only just made the third. He landed awkwardly. I came off. He tried so hard not to land on me. Oh, Claire.' She began sobbing again.

'Maddie, you're doing really well. I know this is hard, but I need you to concentrate. What do *you* think he's done? Did you hear anything like a snap?'

'I only heard the rails falling. I'm really sorry. I...'

'There can't be anything broken, he can put some

weight on it. He managed to get from the paddock to here.'

Maddie's lips quivered. 'It took him ages. I wanted to put the hose on it to try to keep the swelling down—it's had two lots of fifteen minutes. I don't know if I did the right thing making him walk...'

'You've done really well, Maddie. What about the vet, what has he done?'

A frown crossed Maddie's tear-stained, grim face. 'Felt around a bit. He's a locum. I don't think he's worked with horses much. Reckons best case a torn tendon. Worst—and more likely—a broken bone. You can't tell with soft tissue. What if he's just pulled a muscle in his back or shoulder or something? I wasn't going to let him, you know, not without you being here. What are we going to do?'

Claire wished she knew. She looked around, searching for inspiration. Jack, Bernadette and the vet had followed her and now stood in a group a few metres away.

'Dad, I'm going to try to get him back to his stall. Can you bring Howie in to keep him company?'

'You're wasting your time. He'll never race again, probably always be lame. You really should put him down now, spare him the pain,' the vet said.

'And you can just fuck off.'

'Sorry if it's not what you want to hear, lady, but you need to be told. Someone needs to be a bit objective here.'

'You heard her! Piss off!' Bernie said. 'And take your fucking gun with you—we won't be needing it.'

The vet shrugged and ambled off to his vehicle.

'What can I do, Claire?' Bernie said, appearing at her friend's side.

'Keep an eye on Maddie,' she whispered. 'Maddie, you need to sit down. You're looking very pale.'

'Here.' Derek appeared, clutching a navy woollen horse rug. 'Thought he might need this.'

Claire let herself get close enough to touch the horse, then gently pulled the blanket over him and secured the strap at his chest. She stroked his face. Her heart was in her mouth, her voice a croak. 'I need you to walk with me, one step at a time. Come on, boy.'

The horse slowly stumbled and shuffled beside her. Claire coaxed him with words of praise, pleaded with him and the universe. Claire thought he wasn't doing too badly for a horse the vet had on death row. Was he really so bad? Only Maddie had seen him walk and she, poor girl, was undoubtedly in shock—hardly a reliable witness. When they arrived in front of the stable, seemingly an hour later but in reality only minutes, Howie offered a low, encouraging nicker. Paycheque lifted his head slightly and returned a deep sigh.

'Derek, can you fill his water bucket? And, Dad, can you get him some lucerne hay? Grain will heat him up too much, upset his system.'

Paycheque greeted the hay net with a nod of his head, which brought a slight smile to Claire's tight, worried face.

They stood around the stable watching Paycheque pick at his food, all silently asking the same question: What now?

It was Derek who finally spoke. 'I'm going to take Maddie and get her checked out at the hospital.'

'Dad, I'm fine. I'd rather stay here.'

'No arguments. Come on. I promise I'll bring you

straight back.' Claire returned Derek's sympathetic smile and watched them walk to the car.

'Claire, if there's nothing I can do, I may as well go,' Bernadette said, looking a little guilty. 'Do you want a ride back to get your car?'

'No, we'll have to try to find another vet. You go. I'll be fine. Thanks for everything.' She gave her friend a hug. 'Say hi to David for me.'

'Will do.'

'I'll go and check the phone book,' Jack said.

Claire was left alone with Paycheque. She went into the stable, stroked his neck and buried her nose in his soft mane, breathing in his sweet woody scent.

'You've gotta be okay,' she pleaded. 'But I don't know what to do.' Paycheque's long dark eyelashes flickered. 'What if the vet's right?' Hot tears trickled down Claire's face. Paycheque turned his head and gave her a nudge square in the chest. 'You reckon the guy was a fool?' She draped her arm over his neck. 'If only you could talk. It's going to be a tough road, but we can do this. You're going to get better. You have to.' Paycheque returned his attention to his food and gave a loud snort, sending bits of hay flying all over Claire. She smiled sadly and gave his neck a gentle pat. 'I'll be back to check on you in a bit.'

As Claire made her way back to the house, she wondered where they would find another vet who was good with horses. She wasn't optimistic; there was only one practice in the Adelaide Hills area.

Jack was sitting at the dining table with his head in his hands, the Yellow Pages open and a portable phone nearby. Claire thought she saw the glisten of new tears on his partially hidden face. She put her hand near the kettle—it was cold. She filled it, pressed the button and stood waiting for it to boil.

'Anything?'

'No. I tried a couple in the city but only got answering machines. Probably no point anyway. I doubt they'll be used to dealing with horses. It's not fair—after all he's been through. The thought of losing him again…' Jack mumbled, shaking his head.

'I know.' Claire swallowed back the lump forming in her throat. 'And I'm to blame.'

'Why would you say that?' Jack said, lifting his head and staring at her.

'Well, if I hadn't got them doing the jumps…'

'It was an accident.'

'And Maddie could have been killed.'

'Claire, enough right there. Maddie knows the risks. We all do. It's part of it. We've got to focus on where to go from here.'

'Tea or coffee?' Claire asked as the kettle clicked off.

'Tea. And I'll have a bit of sugar in it, thanks.'

Claire delivered the steaming mugs to the table and grabbed the phone. She needed something to fiddle with.

'So, what now? Even if we can find another vet, do you reckon they'd say anything different? You've been in this game a lot longer than me, Dad.'

'Honestly, no, I don't.' Jack shook his head sadly. 'But that doesn't mean we should just give up on him.'

Claire felt drained. She didn't want to think, didn't want to make decisions—just wanted to curl up, go to sleep and wake to find it had all been a bad dream. Suddenly the phone she held began to ring.

'Bernie. What? Slow down…What? Oh…And you're

sure? Hang on a sec.' Claire grabbed the nearby pen and turned the phone book towards her. 'Right, go ahead… Yes, I've got that. Thanks, that's great…Yes, I'll do it right now…Of course I'll let you know. Thanks, bye.'

'Has Bernadette found another vet?'

'Yes. I just hope he hasn't left for the day as well.' Claire stabbed the numbers into the phone while wondering where the time had gone. It was getting near six. No wonder they were exhausted.

'Hello, I was wondering if I could speak to Dr Douglas—it's an emergency…Yes, I'll hold. Thanks. He's in a consult,' Claire, hand over the receiver, informed her father. After a few moments she sat down at the table and began doodling abstract geometric shapes around the phone number.

'Dr Douglas? It's Claire McIntyre speaking. My friend David Balducci gave me your number…Yes, he's well. Look, we really need your help. One of our racehorses has had an accident. It could be a torn tendon, or maybe worse… We really need a second opinion. The vet thought he should be put down.' Claire struggled to speak. Jack gently prised the phone from her tight grip.

'Dr Douglas, Jack McIntyre here. The horse is very special to us. We don't care if he never races again. We just want to save him.' Jack paused, listening. 'To be honest, sir, if you can help him, I don't care what method you use. But I'm afraid we're a little way away—in the Adelaide Hills…Thank you very much. We really appreciate it.'

Claire listened as her father gave precise directions.

'Right,' Jack said, putting the phone down. 'He'll be leaving in five minutes, once he's packed his things. We were lucky—he was with his last patient for the day.'

'And he was happy to drive all the way up here?' Claire asked. What she really meant was: *And just how much will this cost?* She got annoyed with herself. What was a life worth? *Forget the money*, she told herself. Losing Paycheque could just destroy her father. *No matter what the cost, we'll find a way to pay it.*

Jack fiddled with the handle of his mug. 'I need another cuppa. Want one?'

'Yes, but I'll get it. You sit there and tell me what the vet had to say.'

'Well, not a lot. But apparently he's a holistic vet.'

'A *what* vet?'

'Holistic, prefers to use natural therapies.' Jack shrugged.

'A quack. You've sent for a quack?'

'Well, he did say there was no need to put a horse down for a torn tendon. He's been successful treating them before, so that's something.'

'What's he going to do?'

'He said he wouldn't know until he did his diagnosis, but he did mention massage, pressure points, herbs. I guess we'll have to wait and see.'

'Sounds dodgy to me. Did he say how much he charges?' Claire wanted to kick herself. She had only been thinking it, hadn't meant to actually say the words.

'I don't know, Claire, and I don't particularly care. Anything is better than the bloke here earlier with the gun.'

'I'm sorry, you're right. Let's just hear what he has to say. I wonder how David knows him. I guess we'll find that out in due course, too.' Claire put the mugs on the table.

There was a crunch of tyres on the gravel outside

the window and the toot of a car horn. Claire looked up and saw Derek's BMW through the window. She got up and went to open the back door.

'That was quick,' Claire said to Derek and Madeline.

'Yep, declared her fit as a fiddle, didn't they, Maddie?'

'They reckon I must have bounced...'

'Thank God you're okay,' Claire said, enveloping the wiry girl in a bear hug.

'...because of all the bruises I have,' Maddie said, wincing and pulling away.

'Sorry, I wasn't thinking.'

'I'll survive. How's Paycheque?'

'We're giving him some peace before the next vet arrives. Can I get you a cuppa, something to eat?'

'Tea for me, thanks,' Derek said.

'Could I have a Milo?'

'Of course.' Claire deposited a large tin of bought fruitcake on the table and busied herself with organising the drinks.

'You've found another vet. That's great news,' Maddie said.

'Yes, in the city, a Dr William Douglas. Apparently he's holistic or something—into natural therapies. Some old friend of David's.'

'Oh, I think I've heard of him,' Derek said. 'ABC Radio interviewed him last year. "The first truly holistic veterinary practice in Australia", I think they said.'

'Claire's worried he's a quack,' Jack said.

'From what I remember of the interview, he's a fully qualified traditional vet who's chosen to use natural remedies. Probably anything's better than that bloke who was here earlier.'

'It'll be interesting to see what he says,' Jack said.

'So, how does he know David?' Derek asked.

'I have no idea,' Claire said.

'I'm going to check on Paycheque,' Maddie said, getting up.

'Finish your Milo and we'll all come with you,' Derek said. 'You need to keep your strength up. He's not going anywhere.'

'Your dad's right, Maddie, and the vet should only be another few minutes,' Jack offered. 'Let's leave him in peace for a little longer.'

'Have some cake,' Claire said, offering Derek the chopping board and knife.

Claire had devoured three thick slices of fruitcake and was feeling energised when she detected the crunch of tyres on gravel outside.

'He's here,' she announced, leaping up from the table.

She was beside the faded orange Volvo station wagon when the driver—a tall, lean fellow with greying blond hair poking from beneath a pork-pie hat—stepped out and offered a large, smooth hand. Claire returned his firm grip. She found his calmness and the warm, concerned smile on his slightly lined face reassuring.

'Dr Douglas? Thank you so much for coming,' Claire said, pumping the proffered hand in a tight double-handed grip. 'You've no idea what it means. The other vet just wanted to put him down, but I just know he's going to be all right. He has to be. He's part of the family. If only you knew what...' She shut her mouth mid-sentence when the vet placed his left hand on her shoulder and quite literally pulled his right from her grasp.

'Well, let's see what we can do for him, then, shall

we?' The voice was quiet and calm, with a thick rolling Scottish lilt.

'Yes, of course. I'm sorry,' Claire said, blushing. 'It's been a very stressful afternoon.'

'I'm sure. Now, where is this wee horse of yours?' Dr Douglas looked about him.

'This way,' Claire said, making to stride off.

'I'll need to bring the car, if possible,' he called, staying put. 'I've rather a lot of paraphernalia.'

'Oh, yes, of course. Straight ahead—stables are just to the right, in front of the large shed—you'll see them. I'll meet you there.' As she strode off, Jack appeared beside the vet.

'Jack McIntyre. Thanks for coming so quickly,' he said, offering his hand.

'No problem. I'll meet you over at the stables, then, shall I?'

Jack, Maddie and Derek stood outside while Claire held Paycheque. The vet poked, prodded and moved the injured leg this way and that, before covering it with gel and running the portable ultrasound machine around the swelling. His deft, professional touch and constant soothing words of encouragement had Claire feeling comforted as well.

It seemed as if an hour had passed when Dr Douglas packed up the machine, gave the horse a pat and left the stable. All around him eyes were blinking expectantly.

'You're going to have your work cut out,' he said to no one in particular, 'but I can say with absolute certainty that there is no need to put this animal down.'

There was a collective exhaling of breath.

'It's definitely a torn tendon, but I anticipate a full recovery.'

'By full, you mean there's a chance he'll even race again?' Claire asked.

'I think expecting him to be back on the track within three or four months is not beyond the realm of possibility.' The vet beamed.

'Hear that, mate? You're going to be all right,' Claire said, throwing her arms around the horse's neck, causing him to throw his head up in surprise.

'What's really important at this early stage is to keep the circulation going. I'm warning you, tonight is going to be especially gruelling—bandaging, unbandaging, massaging every hour. I'll need to show everyone who's going to be involved with his treatment the correct method and pressure points to work with.'

'That'll be me and Claire,' Maddie said, stepping forward.

'Count me in, too.' Claire was surprised and pleased to see Bernadette was back.

'Actually, I'd like to see, too,' Derek said.

'David Balducci, how the hell are you?' Dr Douglas exclaimed, noticing David standing behind. They shook hands and gave each other a back-slapping embrace.

'Will Douglas. It's great to see you. Sorry I haven't been in touch much lately. Time sort of got away from me,' David said.

'Aw, I'm as much to blame. Just let me get this sorted and I'll be with you.'

'I'll go and check on the soup,' Jack said, 'There's a pot of Claire's famous thick beef and veg heating as we speak. Come on, David. I don't know about you, but I could murder a whisky or two.'

Thirty-Three

Claire served steaming bowls of soup accompanied by a loaf of sliced bread in its plastic bag. Her hands ached after the massage she'd given to Paycheque.

After the murmurs of gratitude, everyone became engrossed in conversation, eating or both. Derek and Jack were rattling on about odds, racing form, and the results and track gossip from Saturday's fixture. David and Will were chatting earnestly about mutual friends—catching up, swapping anecdotes to bring Bernadette into the fold. Apparently they had known each other for some time, but lost touch when David moved to the Adelaide Hills. Maddie was silent—poor kid looked almost asleep in her chair, picking her way slowly through her meal. When they had finished, Claire collected the bowls with apologies that there was no more soup to offer.

Maddie looked at her watch and said it was time for Paycheque's next round of massage and bandaging. She offered to do it and got up.

'No, I will,' Claire said. 'You need to rest. You look exhausted.'

'I'm all right, really.'

'Go to bed. You can do the early-morning shifts.'

'If you're sure?'

'You had a fall, remember? Your body needs time to heal. Don't fight it.'

'I'll wake up at five. I always do.'

'Well, that gives you about seven hours. You'll feel better then.

'I'm going to head over,' Claire said when Maddie had left the room. As she got up, she remembered that she didn't have her car. 'Derek, can I ask a favour?'

'Of course.'

'Could you wait and run me home when I've finished?'

'Sure. No problem.'

'We'll head off,' Bernie said.

'See you soon,' David said to Will.

'I'll be along shortly, just going to make sure everything goes okay here,' Will told them. 'I'm staying the night with David. That way I'll be able to check in again on my way back in the morning,' he said in response to Claire's perplexed frown. 'Free of charge,' he added, as if reading her mind. 'Wouldn't have caught up with David if it weren't for you—you know what we men are like!'

'So, do you think this holistic stuff can really work?' Claire asked Derek later when they were settled on her couch with large mugs of steaming, rich hot chocolate.

'Will's explanation made sense, about circulation being so important.' Derek shrugged. 'But you're the one who has to have faith—it doesn't really matter what I think.'

'Maybe I should be ringing another *real* vet.'

'Will is a real vet. Claire, what you need to do is step back and let someone else take care of things for a while. As much as you'd like to, you can't control everything, you know.'

The comment bit into an already tired and vulnerable Claire. She stared at the remains of chocolate in the bottom of her cup, trying to find a witty retort that belied her hurt. But Derek, sensing he'd gone too far, put his arm around her shoulders.

'I'm sorry, I didn't mean to have a go at you. It's just that you need to learn to let go of some of the strings—at least loosen them a little. You're like a puppeteer trying to control every aspect of your life and everyone in it. As your friend, I don't like seeing the pressure you put on yourself. Paycheque's been saved. He might or might not race again, but he doesn't seem to be in any major pain. There's nothing to do for now but treat him.'

'But…'

'But what?'

'Why now, when he was doing so well?'

'Because things happen, Claire. They just do. You can't take it personally.'

'It's just so disappointing,' she said, putting her cup down and rubbing her hands across her face.

'I know.' Derek pulled her to him and held her tight. 'I'm sure it'll be okay. You just need to have faith.'

'In what?'

'Life, the universe. The more you try to control, the more *out* of control you'll feel.'

'So what am I supposed to do? Just give up?'

'Chill, go with the flow—however else you want to describe it.'

'But how?'

'By making a conscious effort to trust yourself, someone else, something else. Take the occasional risk. Follow your heart not your head. Take Bernadette's note for instance—you decided to take a year out and trust it was the right decision.'

'But that was her idea, not mine.'

'Claire McIntyre, since when have you done anything you really didn't want to do?'

He was right. It wasn't really about trusting Bernadette at all; Bernadette hadn't known any more than she whether it would be the right decision, but so far it had proven to be.

'Claire, everything happens for a reason—it's taken me most of my life to figure that out and accept it, but it's true. You might not see it at the time, but later, when the fog lifts, you can usually see it. For me—and I know this is going to sound weird—losing Amy was one of the best learning experiences of my life. I wish she hadn't died, but if she hadn't I would never have the relationship I do with Maddie. She's taught me so much about myself—to take time out to stop and smell the roses, to use an overworn cliché. Listen to me, sounding like I've just stepped out of some hippie commune.' He laughed.

'I think it's great you can see all this, Derek. I really do. I just don't see how I can change. I am who I am.'

'I'm only talking about changing some of your ways of thinking, not *who* you are. I happen to think you're great—well, except for the control-freakishness.'

'Jeez, thanks. I feel so much better,' Claire said, scowling. But something inside her had shifted—she couldn't put her finger on what it was, but she felt a little less burdened.

'I'd better get back soon,' Claire said, checking her watch. She yawned.

'Claire, it's been a big day. Are you sure you're okay to drive?'

'I'll have to be, won't I?'

'Well, I could drive you.'

'I'm going to be there for three hours.'

'I don't mind waiting and driving you back.'

'Then you'll only have a few hours before you have to get up for work.'

'Actually, I've taken the day off—just in case. I rang Carla while I was waiting for Maddie at the hospital.'

'Oh.'

'I don't want you driving when you're this tired and distracted—it's not safe. Please, let me help. I'll sleep in the spare room.'

'All right. But only because I don't have the time or energy to argue.'

'Good. Come on, let's go,' he said, grabbing his keys from the coffee table and getting up.

When they got back, Claire was pleased to see Pay-cheque had his head hung over the stable door and his eyes shut. She called to him from well back so he didn't get too much of a fright. He opened his eyes and watched them approaching. But he didn't lift his head. When she got closer she realised he was leaning on the stable doorjamb. He looked as if he'd been drugged. Maybe there really was something to using herbs and acupressure after all. She would never have believed this was the same horse. Lucky the gates were made of steel tubing, and she could access the stable without having to open them. The flickering of his ears—

keeping track of what they were doing—was the only sign he was actually awake.

Claire unwrapped the injured leg and began the ten-minute massage. As she did, she spoke quietly, soothing the horse. Derek sat nearby on an upturned bucket, with his elbows on his knees and his chin in his cupped hands, watching her. It was a lot warmer inside the stable, away from the brisk southerly breeze blowing outside. Claire turned to smile at Derek a couple of times but he didn't respond. He seemed totally mesmerised by her hands moving deftly up and down Paycheque's leg. She wasn't surprised to look back a few minutes later to see his eyes shut and his head lolling.

Claire finished the massage, rebandaged the injured leg and got to work on the pressure points. Having checked that the bandages on his other legs were still secure, she inserted a syringe between his lips to administer arnica. Some of the liquid herbal supplement dribbled out before Paycheque started licking his lips and swallowing. She stood back and ran through the list of things she'd done, checking them off against what Will had told them was needed every hour for the first day.

'Good boy, we're done for now,' Claire said, giving Paycheque a pat on his neck. He still wasn't putting weight on his leg but at least he was calm.

Derek snapped to attention. 'Right, what now?'

'We have to wait and do two more rounds. Sorry, but I did warn you.'

'Did you hear me complain? So, are we going back to the house to wait?'

'No, I don't want to wake the others up. I'm going to just sit and snooze. There's plenty of room.'

Derek and Claire settled themselves on the floor in the sawdust in the far corner of the stable. Derek sat behind Claire and leant against the wall. He wrapped both arms around her and pulled her close. Claire leant back into him with the back of her head against the soft part of his shoulder.

'As nice as this is,' Derek said after a few minutes, 'it's not really a workable solution for the next few weeks.'

'Hmm,' said Claire, on the verge of slipping into a snooze.

'We could set up the feed room with swags and a heater for whoever is over here. I've got spares at home.'

'Hmm. Good idea.'

They fell silent and snoozed until they felt and heard Derek's mobile phone vibrate. It was in the top pocket of his shirt, right next to Claire's head.

'Righto, sleepyhead, time for the next round,' he said.

'I didn't think to set an alarm,' she said, slowly getting to her feet. 'I was almost asleep.'

'Lucky I'm here, then, huh?'

'Derek, I really do appreciate everything you're doing.'

'I know. Now come on. On the hour every hour, Will said—hop to,' he said, staying put and giving her a playful slap on the back of her leg.

Finally, Claire's third stint was finished and they were able to leave. Aching all over, she longed for a hot bath. But what she needed more was sleep—bed would have to do. They drove in silence until they were almost at her cottage.

'I'm exhausted. Can't wait to just get into bed,' Claire said.

'Me, too.'

They lapsed back into silence.

'God, it's freezing in here,' Claire said when they were inside, dumping their keys on the coffee table. 'I'll just turn my electric blanket on and make up the spare bed.'

She turned to walk out of the room but Derek grabbed her hand and pulled her back so they were face to face. 'I don't mind sharing if you don't—save you the trouble. Promise I'll keep my hands to myself.'

A ripple of electricity ran through Claire. She smiled at him. 'Okay. I'm so tired I probably couldn't even unfold a sheet anyway.'

Thirty-Four

The next morning, Claire was a little startled to wake
to heavy breathing beside her. It took her a few moments to remember that Derek had stayed the night. The
room was softly lit from the morning light seeping in
around the edges of the thick curtains. She leant over
to her bedside table to check her watch, careful not to
move too suddenly and risk waking her sleeping com-
panion. It was just after seven-thirty. She'd had barely
four hours sleep. She had to be at the farm for the nine
o'clock stint. *Just half an hour more*, Claire told herself,
putting her watch back down. She stayed lying on her
side and pulled the quilt back over her shoulder. It was
so nice and warm where she was—much better than
the forecast three degrees outside.

Derek had stayed fully dressed and was only under
the bedclothes because she'd insisted it was too cold to
stay on top with a blanket. When they'd gone to bed,
he'd given her a quick hug and pecked her on the cheek,
told her to sleep well and rolled over. Claire had wondered how she'd get to sleep with all the churning going
on inside her over Paycheque and having someone in

her bed again after so long. But somehow she had slept soundly. Well, she thought she had—couldn't remember waking up or having any dreams.

Now what? How awkward were things about to get? There was movement beside her and the rustling of linen. She flinched slightly as Derek's warm body touched hers.

'Good morning, gorgeous,' he said, kissing her behind the ear. She turned her head slightly.

'Good morning, yourself,' she said, and shuffled herself back into him so they were joined like spoons. It felt good to feel his heat seeping into her.

Derek put his arm over her shoulder and held her tight. Claire responded by kissing his hand and tucking it under her chin amongst the gather of fabric. She closed her eyes, enjoying the comfort flooding through her and the feeling of Derek's soft puffs of breath in her hair.

They must have fallen asleep because Claire woke later in the same position, but with aching muscles and a stiff shoulder. She tried to stretch but was trapped by Derek's arm. She reached for her watch and was surprised to find they'd been asleep for half an hour.

Derek stirred as she was putting her watch back on the table. For the first time she noticed his erection prodding her in the back. Claire held her breath for a moment as she wondered how to avoid the inevitable awkwardness. But before she could do anything, Derek was gently trying to turn her towards him. She complied and within seconds they were in a tight embrace, their open mouths upon each other.

Claire tried to ignore the lump in Derek's pants pressing hard against her. Her body was aching in response.

Their kissing became more urgent, their tongues exploring deeper. And then they were grinding against each other. Both were now gasping.

Derek's left hand was at the first button of Claire's pyjamas, then the second and the third. He stopped kissing her mouth and leant back to take in her exposed chest and breasts. Claire tried to pull the open garment back together again.

'No, don't, you're beautiful,' Derek whispered, putting his face closer to her chest. He kissed her lightly, holding the fabric aside.

Claire shivered slightly. His touch was so light, but also so strong. He kissed down her stomach until he got to the elastic of her pyjama bottoms. She let out a quiet groan. She really should stop him. Derek dragged her hand that was around his neck down beneath them until it was on the bulge in his pants.

'I can't,' she said in a hoarse whisper, removing her hand.

'Yes, you can,' he muttered, grabbing her hand again. He kissed her stomach a few more times before tugging gently at the elastic at her hips. She wanted to lift her bum a little, make it easier for him. But instead she put her arm up and pushed at his chest.

'I'm sorry, I can't,' she said, pulling away. Claire leapt out of bed, dragged her bathrobe from the back of the door and bolted from the room.

In the kitchen her hands shook as she filled the kettle and flicked on the switch. She hugged her robe tightly and stared out the window, waiting. She thought back to how nice it had been being held and kissed by Derek. *Why did I have to ruin it?*

She went to the laundry to where the kittens had

been confined for the night. She picked them up, one in each hand, and held them to her, enjoying the gentle rumble of their purring. She breathed in their slightly sweet, slightly sweaty scents—they smelled a little like stale savoury biscuits. When they started wriggling to be put down, she kissed them on their heads and complied. They scampered off out of sight.

The kettle was bubbling when Claire got back to the kitchen. She got out two mugs, spooned in coffee granules and sugar, and added a slug of milk to each.

She thought about drinking her coffee out there. But how weak was that—hiding in her own house? And he was only there because of her. He hadn't put any pressure on her. And it wasn't as though he'd actually done anything wrong. She'd wanted it as much as he had in the beginning. If only he had just stuck to kissing her and not gone any further.

Derek was sitting up waiting for her when she entered the room and delivered the mugs to the bedside tables.

Claire climbed back into bed and turned to him. 'That wasn't fair—I'm really sorry.'

'Don't be sorry. If you don't want things to go any further, then you don't. It's fine, Claire.'

'But...'

'I'm a big boy—I think I can handle a bit of sexual frustration. But I do think we should at least talk about it. I thought you were enjoying kissing me.'

'I thought I was ready, but I guess I'm not...'

'I'm sorry. I shouldn't have pushed it.' He looked a little crestfallen. 'We're obviously not really on the same page with all of this.'

'Derek, please don't think this means I don't like you. I do, I really do. And I do want to—just…'

'I know, just not yet.'

'I'm really sorry.'

'Don't be. Claire, I like you, too. I *really* like you. And I'll wait. What's another few weeks, or months?'

'Are you sure you're okay?'

'I'm fine—as long as it's not too long. I'm not sure I could resist you for the next six months.' He leant over, gave her a tight hug and kissed her firmly on the lips. 'Thanks for the coffee,' he said, releasing her.

'Thanks for being so understanding. White with one—I hope that's okay.'

'Perfect,' he said, leaning over to pick up his mug.

Claire felt content as she sipped her coffee and tried to ignore the nagging feeling that she really had to get up. She sighed and gulped down the last third. Derek noticed her and started doing the same.

'No, don't you rush. I've got to be there at nine but you don't have to go anywhere—you've got the day off, remember?'

'Are you coming back here or staying at the farm all day?'

'I'm not sure. Depends on how everything is going over there.'

'Maybe we could go out for lunch or something, if everything is okay?'

'Maybe. I'll have to see. How about I call you when I know?'

'No, I need to go via home and get changed, so I'll just drop in on my way through.'

Claire turned into the farm driveway, thinking about how much she liked having Derek in her home. She was looking forward to seeing him again in a couple of hours. She noticed Maddie out in the paddock riding Larry. She stopped the car and wound down her window as Maddie trotted over to the fence.

'I didn't expect to see you riding this morning. Thought you'd be too sore after yesterday.'

'Well, I figured not everything could revolve around Paycheque, as much as he'd like it to.'

'So, how is everything with his lordship this morning?'

'Good, no problems so far. Will's seen him and says he's doing well.'

'Well, I'd better get going—my turn to do the massage.'

'I wouldn't worry too much. There's a cast of thousands hanging around.'

'Oh?'

'Yeah. Jack, Will, David, Bernie—they're all there.'

'Oh? I wonder why,' Claire said.

'Don't know. I'll be back soon to do the feeds for the others.'

'I'm happy to do that when I've finished with Paycheque, if you like.'

'That's okay—it's my job, remember.'

'Well, it's my job to make sure you stay safe and well, and I'm thinking you should be taking it easy for a few days.'

'Seriously, Claire, I'm fine,' Maddie said, gathering up her reins and turning the horse away.

Claire wound her window up, put the car in gear and continued her drive to the stables.

Paycheque lifted his head towards her as she approached.

'Hello, boy. How are you doing?'

'He's pretty good,' Bernie said, popping into view from behind the gate.

Claire peered into the stable and noticed the bandage was off his injured leg. 'What are you doing?'

'When you weren't here, I thought I'd get started.'

Claire looked at her watch. 'Bernie, I'm three minutes late, for goodness' sake. And shouldn't you be at the shop?'

'It's okay, I don't mind,' Bernadette said, sitting down on an upturned bucket beside Paycheque.

Well, I do. Claire set her jaw. 'Where's Jack?'

'Not sure. Will and David went with him to sort out a few things.'

'What things?'

'They've gone to see if they can rig up a mini spa for his leg. Oh, and also to choose the right spot for the herb garden.'

'What herb garden? Don't we have more important things to worry about?'

'Herbs for the horses. Will says it'll be really good for Paycheque when he gets back outside, and also for the general health of the others. Look, I'd better get on to this leg—we're already late. After this Will said to change all the other bandages, give him a good brush and change his rugs.'

Did he now? Claire stepped into the stable. 'Well, I'm here now,' she said, standing beside Bernie with her hands on her hips. She had no idea why she felt so annoyed, but she bloody well did.

'Well, do you want me to do the other bandages while you do that, or maybe the grooming?'

Why don't you go and run your damn shop, Claire

wanted to say. 'Either-or. But seriously, I've got nothing else to do once I've done this. You may as well go.'

Bernie got up and stepped aside to let Claire take over, but stayed standing in the stable beside her. 'So, how's Derek?'

'Fine.' Claire concentrated on getting the massage technique right.

'Anything to tell?'

'Bernie, I'm concentrating here.'

'Well, excuse me for speaking.'

'And I'm tired and cranky because I didn't get enough sleep.'

'Ahh. Didn't get enough sleep because of Derek?'

'No. Because I woke up too early.'

'Oh. So why were you late if you woke up early?'

'Look, Bernie, just leave it. Derek is the last thing on my mind,' she lied.

'Okay, okay. I'll leave you to it, then. See you, mate,' Bernadette said, leaving the stable and giving Paycheque's neck a pat on her way past.

Claire bit her lip and watched as Bernie started walking back towards the house, thinking that she shouldn't have given her the brush-off like that. *She wasn't too upset, was she?*

She returned her attention to Paycheque's injured leg. The swelling didn't look as bad as she thought it would. Maddie had really done the right thing hosing the leg down straightaway. He flinched and tried to pull away when she started the massage. But he didn't seem to be at all agitated or in major pain.

After massaging the leg, Claire gave Paycheque the arnica and then did the first stint of four sessions of acupressure for the day. Thank goodness Will had drawn them up a comprehensive schedule to follow and given them a photocopy of the pressure points they needed to stimulate.

She made two trips to the tack room for another set of rugs and the bucket of grooming stuff. As she came back she checked the sky. Good; even though it was chilly, it looked as if there would be enough sun to sanitise the rugs a bit. She brushed Paycheque, taking care to keep him covered as much as possible so he wouldn't get cold. He turned his head and whinnied to Larry when he came back into sight.

'Don't worry, mate, you'll only be stuck in here for a few days.' *If we're lucky.*

Will had said he needed to be confined for between three and seven days, depending on his progress. He'd be one bored, cranky horse by then. His eyes were already looking a lot brighter than the night before, so it was only a matter of time before he'd be back to his cheeky self. In that state they'd have to watch out for his teeth. Paycheque wasn't keen on being stabled at the best of times. She suspected he only put up with it so graciously because of the reward of food. And if he hadn't already realised, there were some significant changes in that department, too.

Paycheque loved nothing more than to tuck into warm, molasses-sweetened mash full of grains and tasty supplements. But while he was out of work he'd only be on a mixture of lucerne and meadow hay—and not a lot of that, either, given the lack of exercise he'd be getting. They couldn't have him putting on weight and adding extra pressure to his leg. And the grains would heat him up and give him too much energy—they'd never keep him calm then. Yep, he would become a very unhappy camper very quickly.

She looked at him as she ducked under his neck to change sides for grooming. His eyes were almost fully closed in what looked like contentment. The herbs and acupressure must really be working to keep him calm and pain free. Whatever it was, if they could keep him in this state, it would make life a lot easier for all of them.

'Okay, Claire. We're off,' Maddie called from outside.

Claire poked her head out of the stable and saw Maddie leading Howie out of the one next door. 'Are you sure you're okay to do this much riding so soon? Seriously, I can do it later.'

'I'm fine. It'll stop me getting stiff, and anyway, we have such a good routine going it would be a pity to upset it.'

'A couple of days won't matter.'

'I'll just take him on a long stroll, stretch his legs. Walk, trot and a little canter.'

'Okay. But don't overdo it. You might be even stiffer tomorrow if you're not careful.'

'You worry too much,' Maddie said, putting the reins over Howie's head and getting on.

'It's my job to worry—I'm the boss.'

'Righto, I'm off.'

Claire finished brushing Paycheque's tail, changed his rug and hung the one he'd been wearing inside out on the day yard rail in the sun. She checked her watch. Damn, it was time to start the massage again.

She sat down heavily on the bucket, took a deep breath and started pulling at the Velcro securing the bandage on his bad leg. Will certainly hadn't been exaggerating when he'd warned them it would be gruelling. Her hands were still stiff from the last massage and her head ached from concentrating and lack of sleep.

At least the regime of an hourly massage was only for the first twenty-four hours. Then they'd get a bit of respite as it became every couple of hours until the swelling subsided. But they were still looking at two to four times a day for the next three months, until Paycheque was fully recovered and back in training. She just hoped it would all be worth it. What if they did all this for seven days and he was no better? Would they have to contemplate putting him down? No, she really couldn't think like that. Will was adamant it could be done—he'd been successful before with the same injury, even with racehorses.

Claire finished doing up the straps of Paycheque's rug, then went over to Jack and Will, who were standing by the rainwater tank at the far end of the stables. Jack was leaning on a shovel.

'What are you up to?' she called as she got close.

'Will thinks all the horses would benefit from a herb garden to pick at.'

'It works well if there's a variety and they can walk past and choose what they want. They'll crave what they need to stay healthy,' Will said.

It sounded a bit far-fetched, but so far he'd been right with Paycheque, so who was she to argue? 'Okay.'

'So, we've decided here by the tank is the best spot, see. We've marked it out. What do you think? We figure there's enough sun in the morning, and when it gets hot in the heat of summer there'll be shade from the tanks,' Jack said.

'Bernie's better with gardening than me.'

'This spot was her suggestion. She and David have gone off to get the herbs she has in stock and order what she doesn't.'

So why bother even discussing it with me? She told herself off for being so catty and put it down to being tired. 'Bernie said something about a mini spa—what's the story there?'

'Running warm water over the injury as much as you can will also be beneficial,' explained Will.

'We had a look around but couldn't find anything the right size,' Jack said. 'So we might have to scrap that idea.'

'How much would it help?'

'Well, not doing it wouldn't jeopardise his recovery, but I do think it would help.'

'Right.' Claire thought for a few moments. 'What about one of the fountains Bernie sells? They pump the water around and around. We could fill the pond with warm water and have the fountain run it up and onto his leg.'

'Brilliant idea!'

'Yes, I think that could work,' Will said thoughtfully. 'Well, I'll leave that to you to figure out. You've got a few days before Paycheque can leave his stable. I'd better get going. I'll just check in on him on my way past.'

'Thanks for everything, Will,' Jack said, shaking the man's hand.

'My pleasure. I'll see you again soon.'

Jack started digging the soil for the herb garden as Claire and Will walked back towards the stables.

'Paycheque definitely seems better this morning, don't you think?' Will said.

'Yes, there's still some swelling but not nearly as much as I thought there'd be. And he seems calm enough.'

'We'll have the wee thing out and about in no time.'

'And you really think he could be back racing in four months?'

'Absolutely. But, remember, it's important to be gradual. You'll all have to resist the urge to rush things.'

Will peered into Paycheque's eyes before going into the stable. He ran his hands down all of the horse's legs and gave him a general, quick going-over.

'You're doing well, son,' he said, leaving the stable and giving the horse a solid pat on his neck.

'I'll see you in a few days, but feel free to phone if you have any worries,' he called from the old Volvo's open window.

Claire waved him off. She checked her watch—nearly time to start again. It was the last stint she had to do that day. Then she could go home for a snooze before the evening schedule of feeding and rugging all the horses. She was sitting down to begin again when she realised she'd forgotten to ask Derek to shut the kittens in the laundry when he left. God only knew what havoc they'd been up to for the past few hours. Speaking of Derek, he'd said he would drop in on his way past. So where was he?

At that moment Claire heard the crunch of tyres on gravel and the purr of a car engine. She returned her attention to Paycheque's leg.

'Hello there, little mate. I come bearing gifts,' Claire heard Derek say from the gate.

'Hello,' she said from her perch on the bucket.

'Ah, bucket. Good idea,' Derek said, peering in at her.

'Did I hear you say you come bearing gifts?'

'Yes. Sorry—for him, not for you. Carrots. He's allowed, isn't he?'

'Yep. Crawler!'

'Guilty as charged,' Derek said, pulling a carrot from inside his jacket and holding it out to Paycheque.

Claire returned to her massage amid the crunching as the horse devoured a number of carrots, one after the other. When she was finished ten minutes later, she got up from the bucket to see Derek holding his jacket open and Paycheque snuffling around at his chest.

'Sorry, mate, none left.'

Claire smiled at the touching scene and slipped through the bars of the gate.

'Can I now take you away from all of this?' Derek asked.

'Well, for a few hours, yes.'

'Come on, then, we've got plans,' he said.

'I'll have to go home first—to have a shower and check on Bill and Ben.'

'No, you don't. They should be fine—I locked them in the laundry when I left. And where we're going, they won't mind one bit if you're covered in horse snot.'

Thirty-Five

They got into Derek's BMW and drove off down the driveway.

'So, where are we going?'

'You'll see.'

Claire watched the large gum trees and green pastures from the car window. Before long, acres of timber and wire trellising with bare woody grapevines dominated the landscape.

'Remember, I said I have to be back around three.'

'Yes, Claire, I haven't forgotten. So, everything is going okay having Maddie working and living at the farm?'

'Yes, great, thanks to your generosity.'

'Well, it's win-win, so let's just leave it at that.'

'Thanks for shutting up Bill and Ben. I forgot to ask.'

'At least you approve. They weren't very impressed with me.'

'No, I'm sure. Little monsters. They wouldn't have to be locked up if they were better behaved. I hope getting them desexed is going to help. How are Terry and Sandy doing?'

'Pretty cute—a lot more laid-back than your two. They're like little old men.'

'Ah. Are we going to your house, Derek?'

'You'll have to wait and see.'

Claire sat back and folded her arms across her chest.

'Do you think Jack will mind having the two cats for a week? I've got to go to Sydney again.'

'Wouldn't have thought. Jack loves cats. Might be a good idea for the feed shed in case this mouse plague they're forecasting hits. As long as they don't get under the horses' feet.'

'Well, they've got nine lives. Hopefully they'll only need a couple to learn to steer clear.'

'Very funny.'

'I thought so.' They shared a grin.

'Seriously, where are you taking me?'

'Worry not, my dear—you'll see soon.'

They turned off the bitumen road onto a well-maintained dirt road. After a few hundred metres they turned into a driveway marked by a large milk-can mailbox painted in a rich, glossy ruby red, lying on its side atop a post. Underneath it hung a small white sign with 'D.L. & A.T. Anderson' in black.

Claire concentrated on taking in as much of the view outside the window as she could. The driveway ended after a right angle at a large double-fronted stone home set high on a wide verandah. A stand of large gum trees in neat rows flanked the house to the right and ended in miniature against a range of blue-green hills in the distance.

'Welcome,' Derek said, stopping the car in front on the white gravel, and turning off the key.

'It's lovely,' Claire said, staring up at the house.

'Thanks. Come on, I'll give you a quick tour outside before we go in.'

Claire was impressed at how neat and tidy Derek kept his property. As she went through his shed she noticed all the tools were lined up on a shadow board with spanners, screwdrivers and sockets all in graduating sizes. The benches were clear. An old ute and a ride-on lawnmower were neatly lined up at one end of the shed. Not a speck of oil was visible on the concrete floor. She wondered what Derek thought when he visited the run-down, chaotic farm.

They finished the tour at the back of the house, where an expansive sandstone patio overlooked a small running creek. It was one of the loveliest settings she'd ever seen.

'Wow,' Claire said, watching the water making its way over the rocks and around the bends. 'That's just gorgeous.'

'It's what originally sold us on the place. The previous owners were clever enough to sell in autumn, when there was water but it wasn't too cold and wet. Amy was a romantic through and through. So of course she fell in love with the idea of sitting out reading in the sun with the sound of water trickling around her.'

'I'm not surprised. I would have, too.'

'Of course, romantic notions are all well and good until reality hits, aren't they?'

'Oh?'

'We've had a couple of close calls with floods. Maddie's old tack room is now home to a stack of sandbags all ready to go. And I have to pump out the cellar every few months.'

'Cellar? Nice.'

'Well, not quite. But we'll leave that for another tour. It's a homemade job. Not by me—some idiot who just thought digging under the house and pouring a bit of concrete was enough. Didn't think about the watertable or the drainage. One day I'll get someone to deal with it properly. Or not—I've lived with it this long.'

The sun went behind the thick bank of clouds overhead, taking with it the heat Claire was enjoying on her back. Without it, it was a pretty chilly day. She shivered. She'd forgotten to grab her coat from her car before leaving the farm.

Derek put his arm around her shoulders. 'Come on, it's too cold to be standing around out here.' He ushered her along the verandah to the front door. 'Bad feng shui to have a guest enter through the back door.'

He put the key into the lock on the solid four-panelled door painted in the same rich red as the milk-can mailbox. She wiped her feet on the mat and was just about to step over when her attention was caught by an enamel sign on the wall. She did a double take. It looked old and traditional like the coach light above it, but there was something different about it. She reread the wording carefully: 'Friends welcome, family by appointment'.

'Cute, huh?' Derek said.

'Very.'

'Maddie's doing—a present last Father's Day. Who was I to argue?'

Derek stepped aside to let Claire pass into the wide central hall with a red oriental runner stretching its length. Floorboards were visible either side of the carpet. He dropped his keys into a polished brass bowl atop the first of three narrow hallstands. Photo frames stood on the second, halfway down, and a large empty

Japanese porcelain vase in blue and white was on the other at the far end.

'Sorry, but not quite tidy enough to give you the full tour,' he said, nodding at the closed doors either side of them as they made their way down the hall.

'These are lovely, Derek,' Claire said, pausing and looking around at the various watercolours and oil paintings adorning the walls.

'Not my doing, I'm afraid. Amy was a bit of a whiz with decorating. I've left everything pretty much as it was. Because I like it, not out of holding on to the past or anything,' he added, looking Claire in the eye. He opened a door with etched glass panels at the end of the hall and stepped through onto a flagstone floor. To their left was an open-plan kitchen in tasteful but dated timber cabinetry and matching bench tops. To the right was a round rustic pine table and six high-backed chairs. Everything was tidy—nothing out of place. Claire found it hard to believe the rooms off the hall—no doubt bedrooms—were too untidy to be shown.

Derek continued forward, and they stepped down into a sunken living area, with huge modular sofas in worn brown velour taking up two sides. 'And now, let me present the best spot in the whole house in winter,' he said, opening his arms wide.

Claire looked around her. He was absolutely right. They were facing a bank of glass sliding doors overlooking the patio and, beyond it, the creek. Just then the sun came out from behind the clouds and flooded through the windows and across the floor to where they stood. Over to their left was a glass-fronted slow-combustion fire with glowing coals.

'You sit there in the sun,' Derek said, pointing to the position closest to the windows, 'and I'll just put some more wood on the fire.'

Claire did as she was told and sat, both watching Derek and taking in the rest of the space around her. She could see why he'd stayed on and left the decor unchanged after his wife had died.

Finished with the fire, he went to the kitchen. 'Right. Would you prefer red or white wine?'

'I'm not sure I should be drinking at all—I've got to drive later.'

'Not for hours. And so do I. Just a glass or two. But don't feel pressured. I'm having a red myself, but I'm happy to open both.'

'A glass of red would be nice, thanks.'

Derek brought the bottle and two glasses and put them down on the large antique trunk that served as a coffee table. 'Feel free to kick your boots off and stretch out,' he said, offering her a glass of wine. 'I'm just going to rustle us up some lunch.

'We're having frittata and salad. Hope that's okay,' he said, now back in the kitchen.

'Perfect. Have you been baking, Derek?' she teased.

'Now, when would I have had time to do that? No, this is courtesy of David. But I assure you, I can actually cook.'

'I can't believe you've had time to organise lunch and light the fire and everything. You could have just given me directions to make my own way—saved you the trouble.'

'Come on, Claire, you wouldn't have come. You would have gone straight home for a nap. Which you can do here once we've eaten.'

Claire checked her watch.

'Stop looking at your bloody watch—I've got everything under control.'

'I know, but...'

'But what? You don't trust me? Is that it?'

'Well, I've got...'

'Claire, please just let yourself relax for a few hours. Indulge me—and yourself—will you?'

Claire sipped her wine. It was a nice rich Barossa red: thick and syrupy. She guessed it to be a Shiraz, given the peppery finish. She put the wine on the table, took off her boots and tucked her feet underneath her to warm them up. She stared across at the now blazing fire. The sun was still streaming in through the windows. Claire turned slightly so it could warm her back. She closed her eyes and drank in its heavenly heat, seeping through her clothes and into her bones. Moments later she detected movement and opened her eyes to see Derek standing before her holding cutlery and two plates piled high with food. Claire accepted a plate.

'Bon appétit,' he said, sitting down with a plate on his lap.

'Thank you. This looks great.'

'I'm sure it will be, but as I said, I can't take the credit. Maybe next time.'

They exchanged smiles and clinked glasses.

'Cheers.'

'Cheers.'

Derek and Claire ate in silence for a few minutes until two ginger kittens—one pale and one dark—appeared in front of them stretching and yawning.

'Ah, here they are. Where have you guys been?' Derek said. They looked him up and down for a moment, sniffed at the coffee table and went over to the fire and lay down. 'Isn't it amazing how much cats sleep?'

'Apparently around twenty-two hours,' Claire said. 'At least yours don't seem to roar around in destruction mode for the other two hours like mine do.'

'Oh, they do their fair share, let me assure you. They're probably just on their best behaviour because you're here.

Claire laughed at the kittens lying with their backs together in front of the fire. 'Thanks, Derek, that was lovely,' she said, putting her empty plate down on the trunk.

'Have you had enough? There's more there.'

'I've had plenty, thanks.'

'More wine?' he asked, already holding out the bottle to her.

'Thanks. But just half a glass,' she said, holding her glass out. 'It's a nice one. I like it.'

'It's not bad, is it? From just up the road.'

'I think I'm going to take up your offer of a lie-down,' Claire said, suddenly feeling sleepy. 'Just half an hour or so.'

'Good idea. I think I'll join you. On the other couch, I mean.'

Claire lay on her stomach so the sun was still on her back and pulled the blanket draped over the back of the couch over her. Derek went to the couch opposite and, after kicking off his boots, lay down on his back. Claire thought to check the time and to set an alarm, but her arm felt too heavy to lift. The wine coursing through her, her full belly and the sun on her back saw her fall asleep before she could muster the energy.

* * *

Claire woke up. She lay with her eyes closed for a few seconds getting her bearings and remembering where she was. She could hear Derek breathing heavily nearby. But what was that other noise? Ah, the purr of two cats—very close. She lifted her head and found herself staring at the two kittens, who were now curled up on the sofa, almost touching her head. Sensing her movement they opened their eyes, looked at her, and then shut them again.

Claire sat up. Outside the day was very grey. No sun shone through the windows now. The fire was back to being a mass of glowing coals. She rubbed her face, trying to wipe away the grogginess. She wanted to lie back down and return to sleep. Instead, she forced herself to check her watch: six o'clock. Surely she couldn't have been asleep that long.

Shit! They really had to get going. But Derek was still fast asleep. She sat on the edge of the couch and started putting her boots on.

'Where do you think you're going?' Derek said, startling her.

'Sorry to wake you, but I really have to get back.'

'No, you don't.' Derek rolled over on the couch and lay facing her.

'Yes, I do. I'm already late. I've got horses to rug and feed.'

'Someone else will do it.'

'No, it's my turn.' Claire got up and went over and stood by the fire. She hoped Derek would take the cue to make a move to get up also. But he didn't. She was starting to get very annoyed.

'Look, seriously, Derek, I have to get going.'

'And I'm telling you, you don't, Claire. It's all organised.'

'What are you talking about? What's all organised? What have you gone and done?'

'Claire, calm down. The horses are being rugged and fed as we speak.'

'But it's my turn.'

'So you keep saying.'

'Well, who's feeding them? Maddie and Jack were going to get more feed—they weren't going to be back in time.'

'Bernie's doing it. David's helping her.'

'But it's my responsibility. You had no right to interfere.'

'They were happy to help out. Claire, you're too tired. You need a break.'

'Well, now I'm pissed off as well!'

'Claire, don't ruin a nice afternoon. It's done now.' Derek got up and came over to where Claire stood. He tried to put his arm around her shoulders but she shrugged it off.

'You had no right to go behind my back. Bernie and David aren't even horse people.'

'Bernie seems to cope okay at the races and you've got all the feeds listed on the board in the shed. It's not exactly hard.'

'That's not the point! You shouldn't impose on them.'

'Claire, I'm sorry, okay? We were trying to help you out.'

'Well, Bernie should have known better. And I don't need any help.'

'Sometimes, Claire McIntyre, you are your own worst enemy,' Derek said, shaking his head slowly.

'What's that supposed to mean?'

'Doesn't matter.'

'No. You've said it now. Come on.' Claire stood with her back to the fire and her arms folded tight across her chest.

Derek sighed. 'You're fighting everything. People who care about you try to make things easier and you just fight it for no reason. Accepting help every now and then doesn't show you're weak, Claire. It shows you're smart. Stop being so damn stubborn.'

Claire glared at him. 'Is my lecture over now?'

'No. And you're too stuck in the past.'

'What's that supposed to mean?'

'We've been spending time together for a while now. This morning was the perfect opportunity to take things to the next level. But you couldn't or wouldn't because of your dead husband. Claire, he's gone. Don't you think he'd want you to be happy? It's not healthy.'

'And neither is you telling me it's fine, that you're sorry for pushing things, that you'll wait, blah blah blah. So it really *is* all about sex.'

'Don't be ridiculous, Claire, of course it's not. This isn't high school anymore. You need to lighten up.'

'And here I was thinking you were caring and sensitive.'

'I am.'

'Well, it doesn't bloody sound like it!'

'I care about you, Claire. I want you to be happy.'

'Well, you can take me back to my car and stop interfering in my life!' She stormed down the hall and out the front door, slamming it behind her. In his car she boiled with anger. How could they go behind her

back and gang up on her like that? They were meant to
be her friends. Especially Bernie. The cow!

A few minutes later Derek got into the driver's side
and started the car without a word. They travelled in
silence. Claire stared out the side window with the mantra 'Don't cry, don't cry' running through her head.

Suddenly she realised they hadn't taken the turn-off
towards the farm. She turned to look at Derek. 'Now
where are you taking me? I need my car—it's at the
farm.'

'No, it's not,' Derek said quietly, without looking at
her. 'Bernie's taking it to your house.'

Claire rolled her eyes, shook her head at him and
turned back to the side.

When they arrived at Claire's house, her car was out
front along with David's. Bernie was standing on the
porch dangling a set of keys, as if trying to figure out
where to hide them. Claire leapt out of Derek's car while
it was still coming to a halt and bolted up the steps. She
snatched the keys from Bernie, who stood staring at her
with a gaping mouth.

'Claire, what's…?'

'Mind your own bloody business and stop interfering
with my life!' she yelled at the startled Bernie, thrusting
the key into the lock of the front door. She was relieved
she got it first go. She slammed the door behind her,
causing the heavy cast-iron knocker to jump against its
base and continue tapping a few times.

Thirty-Six

Claire stood in her house feeling lost and lonely, listening as the sounds of David's and Derek's cars faded away. The birds outside flapped and squawked and then became silent, signalling that they had settled in the trees for the night. She moved her keys from hand to hand. She should just kick off her boots, let the cats out and relax for the night. But she was too angry and too restless.

Claire went back outside, slamming and relocking the door behind her.

'Thought you were out with Derek,' Jack said as Claire entered the feed room, where he and Maddie were stacking bags of chaff and bales of hay.

'I was.' Claire coloured a little. 'Do you want a hand?'

'No, thanks, we're almost done. And Bernie and David sorted out the horses for the night. Why are you here anyway?'

'Just checking everything got done okay.'

'Well, as you can see, everything is fine. So why aren't you still out with Derek?'

'He had a few things to do,' Claire lied.

'Oh. Right.'

'He's going to be in Sydney again next week so I guess that makes sense,' Maddie said, shrugging.

'Guess so.' Claire was looking down at the concrete floor beneath her feet. 'So, how's Paycheque doing?'

'Thought you would have checked on your way past,' Jack said, hefting a bag of chaff onto the pile.

'I did. But I want to know what you think.'

'Well, I think he's doing pretty well. The spa's up and running for when he comes out of his stall—should only have to wait a few more days.'

'I see the herb garden's all planted.'

'Yeah, but we can't let any of them loose on it until it's bigger, else it'll be gone in one gulp.'

'How did the others do today?'

'Fine. Howie's come up well—reckon he could be a winner at the Bridge next week. But seriously, Claire, I've had a long day. What's with the third degree?'

Jeez, is everyone against me? 'It's not—just interested to know what's gone on while I was away.'

'Claire, you've been gone six hours tops,' Jack replied.

'I'll just go and give Paycheque his hay net,' Maddie said quietly, and walked away.

'So, why aren't you with Derek anyway? I thought that was the whole point,' Jack said when Maddie had left.

'We had a fight.'

'Oh, well, I'm sure you'll work it out—all part of getting to know each other.'

'It was a bit serious.'

'Aw, they're almost never as serious as you first

think. You probably just need to sit down together and nut it out.'

It was on the tip of Claire's tongue to tell him that she wasn't speaking to Bernie, either. But she knew what he'd say. That she was being childish, that someone had to make the first move to reconcile and that it may as well be her. He'd use the word 'stubborn'. And she was sick of everyone calling her that.

'Well, I'm exhausted,' Jack said, taking his gloves off and laying them down. 'I'm going to enjoy a beer and then an early night.'

'What are you having for dinner? Is there enough for me?'

'Sorry, Claire Bear. Maddie and I had chicken from the takeaway in town before we came home.'

'Oh.'

'You've got a lovely home to go to, so just go.' He laughed. 'Seriously, you look wrecked. And there's no point you being here—everything has been done for the day.'

'Okay, if you insist. See you tomorrow, then,' she said, forcing her tone to sound cheery.

On her way back she paused at Paycheque's stall to rub his ears. He had his nose puckered in annoyance and he made to try to bite her. They'd have their work cut out trying to keep him happily confined for a few more days.

'Did you have a fight with Dad?' Maddie asked, emerging from the stall.

'Something like that.'

'I don't know what happened, and it's none of my

business, but he really likes you, Claire. Whatever it is, don't let it ruin things—you're good for him.'

Is there anyone on the planet who doesn't want to tell me how to run my life? She *so* hadn't missed that while she'd been living in the city.

'I think we should start increasing Larry's workload,' she said, deliberately ignoring Maddie.

'Actually, he did pretty well this afternoon. I think he's worth taking to the Bridge on Wednesday with Howie.'

'I'll think about it. I've got to go.'

'If you're seeing Bernie, can you give her this?' Maddie took a hooded blue jacket from the rail of the outer yard and held it out to her.

Claire had no choice but to accept it. She recognised it as one of her friend's favourites. 'Right. Okay.'

'Well, that's me done,' Maddie said, giving Paycheque's neck a solid pat. 'See you in the morning.'

'See you,' Claire said. But Maddie was already disappearing behind the pepper trees on her way to the house.

She stood there a few minutes looking at the blue jumper in her hand. She had half a mind to just leave it on the rail. If Bernie wanted it she could damn well come and get it herself, and bring an apology with her. But she held on to it. Maddie had deliberately given it to her—how would it look if she left it there?

Claire gritted her teeth and made her way back to her car. Why had she even bothered coming? She should have just stayed put. She was annoyed at the brush-off she'd got from both Jack and Maddie. But she was more annoyed that she'd put herself in the position to receive it. What had she expected? All the horses had been fed

and tucked in for the night by Bernie and David. There
was nothing for her to do. And Jack and Maddie didn't
know what else had gone on, that she'd come seeking
friendly faces. Claire cursed at her haste in running to
the farm. Lucky they didn't know. If they did, they'd
just say she was being petulant. Which would be even
more annoying.

Claire drove home with the radio turned off. She occasionally glanced at Bernie's jumper on the seat beside
her. It would be a good excuse to call without having to
apologise. Apologise! Why was she even thinking it?
She hadn't done anything wrong. They'd conspired to
meddle in her life. She was the victim!

She and Bernie had fallen out a couple of times over
the years, but always made up. They couldn't go for
longer than a few days without at least talking on the
phone. There was a tendency to never really acknowl-
edge the fight and make up as such; it just sort of happened that one would ring the other with something
interesting to say and they'd be back to being friends
again. Claire tried to dismiss the nagging feeling that
it might be different this time.

What about Derek? She didn't know him well enough
to know what he'd do, or wouldn't do. Maddie said he
really liked her. Well, if he did, then he'd probably wait
a few days for the dust to settle and call her. She gnawed
on her lip and tried to tell herself she wasn't already
missing him. He'd only been gone an hour, for God's
sake. Claire wondered if the sharp ache deep inside was
trying to tell her things were a lot more serious than
she believed them to be. No, she was just overtired and
paranoid. And hungry.

Claire kept herself busy making pasta for dinner and

putting a load of washing on. She sat down in front of the television stroking Bill and Ben, who were soaking up the attention after being locked in the laundry all day. She stared at the screen, trying to follow the drama being played out, but her mind kept going back to the afternoon with Derek. Why had it had to end like that?

She was surprised to find a lump forming in her throat and a tear appearing in the corner of her eye. There was an ache of emptiness in the pit of her stomach that she couldn't ignore and couldn't pass off as hunger. She'd got used to Derek being part of her life. And now he was gone. She wiped a hand across her now runny nose and sniffed. No. If he liked her that much, he'd be back. Surely he wouldn't let something this small get in the way. Or was it small? He'd called her stubborn. Maybe she was. But, damn it, being stubborn was what had got her to where she was and through all the crap of the past year.

Living in the past. Pah! It was all right for him. He'd lost his wife ages ago. And anyway, who was he to tell her when she was ready to be intimate with someone again? Just because they'd been spending a lot of time together didn't mean they should jump into bed. No. She'd do that when she was ready, thank you very much, and not before.

Her mobile rang and then her home phone. She checked the numbers each time to make sure it wasn't Jack and when she saw it was Derek's mobile number, she walked away and let it go to message bank. When she checked, there were no messages on either phone. Obviously he wasn't that keen to work things out.

Later Claire was having a shower when she heard her mobile ring again. She turned off the water and rushed to it. But she was too late. She was still standing dripping on the tiles in the kitchen when her home phone started ringing beside her. Bernie's number was on the screen. She picked up the phone and stared at it, but couldn't make herself press the button to accept the call.

Claire didn't think she'd be able to sleep with all that was going through her mind. But she woke to the radio beside her, signalling her alarm had gone off. She lay there for a few moments thinking back over the day before and went to let Bill and Ben out while she had breakfast and got ready for her day at the farm. She felt refreshed and keen to get physically busy with the horses.

As she waited for the kettle to boil, Claire congratulated herself for insisting they put their arrangement with Derek about Maddie in writing. A handshake would have been enough for Jack. And now where would they be? Then she remembered her carefully worded letters to her insurance company and the Insurance Ombudsman, stating her case. Even if it came to nothing, at least she'd done something. And she was proud of her effort.

Claire was feeling good when she got into her car, but that changed when she saw Bernadette's jumper still on the passenger seat beside her. She wondered when her friend would call again. Would she? Bernie was definitely the more easygoing of the two of them. Derek she wasn't so sure about. She imagined him calling again and her answering. He'd say he'd just called to say hi and then go on as if nothing had happened. They'd take up where they'd left off. *Which was where, exactly?* Claire groaned. Him wanting sex and her not being ready. Part of her hoped he wouldn't call. Maybe that would be best. But another part of her wished he'd call and stop the torment.

Thirty-Seven

From the second she approached Paycheque, Claire sensed his foul mood. He made a half-hearted effort to bite her as she walked past to get the pooper scooper and rake. No teeth were bared, but it was enough to make her leap out of his way.

Normally she'd operate on autopilot and use the time to think about other things. Today she cleaned his stall with one eye on him, fully aware of where the rake was in case she needed to hold it up in defence. He was now standing quite steadily on all four legs so his back end was a potential source of danger as well. She couldn't really blame the horse. He hated being confined and his injury meant he couldn't lie down and stretch out to sleep, which was his preference. If he did, he wouldn't be able to get up again. Thankfully, he'd had the sense not to try.

'Not long now, mate,' she said. Tomorrow they were planning to take him out for the first time and see how he coped. Will had been adamant that a sound recovery depended on taking it slow. As hard as it was to be patient, they just had to be.

* * *

Jack and Claire held their breath as Maddie opened the gate to lead Paycheque out. Claire crossed her fingers as he peered about, looked down and took his first step into the grey day outside. He stumbled slightly but recovered as he went from the soft sawdust up onto the paving. He walked with a pronounced limp but was stable enough on his legs. He snorted, tossed his head and snatched at his lead-rope. He held his head high and, with his nostrils flared, took in the sights, sounds and smells around him, as if experiencing them for the first time.

'So far, so good,' Jack said.

'Hmm,' Claire agreed absently. She was thinking that she'd like the trigger-happy vet to be here seeing this.

'I'll let him have a bit of a graze,' Maddie said.

'Good idea. Take your time,' Jack said. 'Then we'll see how he goes with the spa.'

Claire hummed as she made dinner. She was excited at Paycheque's progress and couldn't wait for Will to see him at the end of the week. Hopefully he'd be ready for being led on a proper walk rather than just grazing. The gruelling schedule of massage and acupressure, which was now starting to taper off, had really made a difference. Claire felt a little guilty at her suspended friendships with Bernie and David, and Derek. They'd had a hand in it and should really be sharing the joy, too. She was surprised neither Jack nor Maddie had mentioned any of their names at all.

'I declare the wee chappy well on the road to recovery,' Will announced late Friday evening. They all shared grins. They'd done it: they'd saved Paycheque. Now they just had to get him back racing. Claire thought of sending Bernadette a text to tell her, but didn't. They hadn't been in touch for a week.

By the middle of the next week, Paycheque was being led on soft ground for an hour a day, followed by spa treatment. A couple of times he'd got a fright and darted sideways. But he always recovered fine. His limp was becoming less pronounced. The bandages supporting his other legs came off.

He was starting to pull at the lead, jog, try to break into a trot. It was a sign he was ready to get more active. Soon they could reduce the acupressure to once or twice daily.

Maddie was tasked with Paycheque's slow return to training. The following week she planned to start leading him from the ute, and hopefully by the end of the month he'd be strong enough to again have her on his back. It was amazing given the original vet's diagnosis.

Claire really wished she had someone to share the excitement with other than Jack and Maddie. She thought about Bernie a lot when she did Paycheque's massage and acupressure. They hadn't gone this long without speaking since they'd met.

A couple of times at night she'd picked up the phone to call her but found she couldn't do it. She'd gone to David's café for their usual weekly lunch, all set to apologise and beg forgiveness. But someone else had been at their table and she'd left without a word to anyone. She'd driven past the nursery to see if Bernie's car was there. It wasn't. Her heart was heavy as she made her way back home.

She still hadn't heard from Derek, either. Claire decided she was a little old-fashioned when it came to men—would rather he was the one to do the chasing, the contacting, if there was any to be done. Anyway, he was in Sydney. No doubt too busy with meetings and dinners to call.

It made it worse that Derek's cats, Terry and Sandy, were now living permanently at the farm with Maddie and Jack. Every time she saw them she was reminded of the lovely day they'd had sitting in front of the fire, eating frittata and drinking wine. Her heart ached for him more with each passing day.

Claire was standing outside Paycheque's stall, about to leave for the day, when Jack and Maddie approached. They stood side by side. Claire looked from one to the other.

'We need a word,' Jack said.

'About what?'

'This tension, Claire. It's got to end.'

'Tension? What tension?'

'This fight you're having with Bernie and Derek.'

'It's none of your business.'

'It is when it's affecting your work here.'

'What do you mean?'

'You're distracted. You're making mistakes.'

'What mistakes? I haven't made any mistakes.'

'You gave Howie the wrong feed last night,' Maddie said quietly. 'I noticed just in time.'

'You packed the wrong bridle for Larry to go to Strath.'

'I did not!'

'You did. There's no point arguing! This fighting with Bernie and Derek has to stop.'

Or what? Claire wanted to ask. She inspected her boots as they scratched at the pavers.

'Bernie's practically family. I saw her in town the other day and she's as miserable as you. And Derek seemed pretty keen on you.'

'He is,' Maddie said. 'And he's a mess—but you didn't hear that from me.'

'They could call me.'

'They've tried—you didn't take their calls, remember?'

'Or call them back,' Maddie added.

'I would have if they'd left a message. So you've *both* been discussing me behind my back—with both of them? How could you?'

'Because someone has to sort this tiff out and you're clearly not going to.'

'I was going to phone them both tonight as a matter of fact. And anyway, it's a little more than a tiff, Dad.'

'They tried to take the pressure off you—give you a nice day out away from things. It's time to admit that you completely overreacted, Claire. And quite frankly, it's a little late for phone calls.'

'So, what do you propose I do?'

'We're having a barbecue here tomorrow evening. Which you are going to attend.'

'And if I don't?'

'Well, then you're fired.'

'You can't do that!'

'I can and I will.'

Claire stared at her father. The look she saw on his

face she'd never seen before. He was deadly serious. She looked at Maddie, who looked at the ground.

'So, Derek and Bernie and David are coming?'

'And Bill and Daphne.'

'So, I kiss and make up—or else.'

'Yes, because this is not just about you. It's affecting all of us.'

Maddie, who was still staring at the ground, nodded.

'Look, no one's forcing you to be in a romantic relationship with Derek if you don't want one. But you need to be at least civil—we're in business with the man. You're making things very awkward for Maddie here. And have you thought that maybe I miss Bernie, too? As I said, she's practically family.'

Claire sighed. 'Okay.'

Both Maddie and Jack visibly relaxed.

Claire drove home feeling as though a burden had been lifted from her shoulders. They were absolutely right. Things could not go on as they were. She was actually a little relieved that it had been taken off her hands.

That night, after she'd eaten and had her shower, Claire curled up in front of the television with the cats on her lap. But after a few minutes, unable to focus on what she was watching, she reached for her phone sitting on the coffee table.

'Hi. It's me, Claire.'

'Hi.'

'Bernie, I'm so sorry. I know you were just trying to help. And I really did overreact. I don't know why. And I've behaved like a complete dickhead ever since. I'm really, really sorry.'

'Me, too, Claire. I've been such a stubborn idiot.'

'I've missed you so much.'

'Me, too.'

'My life isn't as good without you.'

'Mine, either.'

'So, truce?'

'Truce,' said Bernie.

'Lunch again next week?'

'Absolutely.'

'How's David?'

'He's good—you'll see him tomorrow night.'

'Ah, yes. The intervention barbecue.'

'Claire, I'm so glad you called.'

'Well, least it won't be so awkward now. But we could always pretend—just to mess with Jack and Maddie.'

'No, I think the ice you're standing on is way too thin for that.'

'Bernie?'

'Yes?'

'Did I hear you admit to being stubborn just before?'

'Yes. I can admit to my failings, unlike some of us.'

'Touché. I deserved that.'

'Yes, you did. Have you spoken to Derek yet?'

'No, I'm going to call him now.'

'Promise?'

'I promise.'

'Okay, I'm going now. See you tomorrow night.'

'Bye. And thanks, Bernie.'

'Thanks, yourself. Now go and call Derek!'

Claire's fingers shook as she dialled Derek's number. What if he didn't want to talk to her? But he'd agreed to come to the barbecue, hadn't he? So he couldn't totally hate her.

'Claire.'

'Hi, Derek.'

'How are you?'

'Okay. And you?'

'Well, I've been better.'

'Me, too.'

There was a brief silence.

'Claire, I'm so glad you called. I miss you—I really miss you.'

'Me, too, Derek. I'm so sorry.'

'Me, too. Claire?'

'Yes?'

'Can I ask a favour?'

'I suppose so, what?'

'Can we do this in person? Can I come over?'

'Oh. Okay.'

'I'll be ten minutes, just hold that thought.'

'Right. Okay. See you then.'

Claire was in a flutter of excitement and nerves when Derek knocked on her door. He stood on the step holding a bunch of red roses. She accepted them with a frown, wondering where he'd managed to find flowers this late.

'Bit the worse for wear, I'm afraid,' he said apologetically. 'I bought them a couple of days ago but chickened out.'

'Oh, no. I was wondering where you'd got roses from around here this time of night. They're lovely. Thank you.'

'Well, they *were* lovely.'

'It's the thought that counts,' she said, beaming at him. 'Let me just put them in some water.'

In the kitchen, Claire was pleased to have the distraction of selecting a suitable vase and filling it with water. It wasn't going how she'd imagined at all. There'd been no falling into arms, apologising and begging forgiveness. Derek had barely moved from the doorway, just stepped inside and closed the door behind him.

'There we are,' she said, putting the heavy cut-crystal vase on the sideboard at the edge of the room. She went over to him. 'Derek. I'm really so very sorry.'

'I know. It's already been said.'

'Yes. But…'

'So, where's my hug, then? Apologies I can get over the phone. What I need is to feel you.'

Claire put her arms around him and they embraced tightly. Derek kissed her hair.

'Being away from you has been hell, Claire. I never thought it would hurt so much.'

'Hmm. Me, too.'

He held her away from him and stared into her face. 'Claire. I love you. I don't want to live without you in my life.'

'Me, too, Derek.' Claire smiled back at him.

They hugged again. As they did, Claire wondered when she'd be able to utter those three little words again. But right now she knew it didn't matter. What mattered was that she had Bernie and Derek back, and that she wasn't going to stuff up like that again.

They sat entwined on Claire's couch catching up on each other's lives. After a while Claire was stopped mid-sentence while telling of Paycheque's progress by Derek's mouth upon hers. They kissed passionately, drinking in each other's souls. After what seemed hours, Claire eased herself out of his clutches and stood up.

Avoiding looking him in the eye, she gently grasped his hand and led him down the hall towards the bedroom.

They slowly peeled each other's clothes off and got beneath the covers. Claire trembled at Derek's touch and he murmured at hers as they explored each other for the first time.

'Thank you. That was lovely,' Derek said later, raising himself on an elbow and kissing her gently on the lips.

'Mmm. It was. Thank *you*.'

'So. No regrets?'

'No. You?'

'Are you kidding? You're lovely.'

They smiled at each other and then fell into a tight hug. Claire liked the feel of their bare skin.

'I love you, Derek Anderson,' Claire said into his chest.

'And I love you, Claire McIntyre.'

The next evening, Claire was at the farmhouse helping Maddie and Jack get ready for the barbecue when they heard a car pull up out front. She hadn't mentioned reconciling with her friends to them.

'That's Dad,' Maddie said, looking out the dining room window.

'I'll go,' Claire said, and started wiping her hands on a tea towel.

'Are you sure?' Jack and Maddie asked at the same time.

'Yep.' As she turned and practically ran to the back door she noticed an exchange of worried glances between them.

'Hello, sexy,' she said to Derek, just loud enough to be heard in the kitchen.

'Hello, yourself.' They hugged and kissed briefly.

'Come in. We're just doing a few last-minute things. You're the first to arrive.'

In the kitchen, Jack and Maddie were staring at each other in disbelief. Claire grinned at them and wound her arm through Derek's.

'Think we've been had, young Maddie,' Jack said.

'Looks like it, Jack.'

When Bernie and David arrived half an hour later, Claire hugged her friend long and tight. This time Jack and Maddie weren't so surprised. David hugged her and whispered that he was so glad they'd sorted things out.

'Bernie has been miserable and I've missed you terribly. And the café is missing the revenue from your weekly lunches and random cheesecake crisis meetings.'

They enjoyed a chuckle and another hug before moving through to the dining room.

Bill and Daphne arrived soon after, and Daphne puffed up with pride at seeing Jack wearing her hand-knitted jumper and fairly glowed when he insisted it was his favourite.

When they were seated, Jack held up his glass of wine and proposed a toast: 'To good family, friends and neighbours.'

'To good family, friends and neighbours,' they all responded, and clinked glasses.

Claire glanced around the table. They were indeed very lucky. With Paycheque's recovery going so well, and the other horses coming along nicely, life was looking pretty good again.

Thirty-Eight

Claire had spent ages dreading her birthday. Not because she was scared of getting old, but because her life was finally going really well and she didn't want to jinx it. The last thing she needed was to get all sad about Keith again. It wasn't fair on Derek and it wasn't fair on her. She'd been doing so well focussing on the present and the future and leaving all the bad that had happened behind.

Claire rolled over and faced Derek's empty side of the bed. Things were now working well between them. They had shared interests, separate interests, were best friends and made the best love. It was early days, but daydreaming while out riding, Claire often got mental images of them old and shuffling around the house in their slippers, looking over bifocals to discuss something or other in the paper. The fact that it *didn't* scare her was what scared her!

Claire loved how considerate Derek was. She knew he would do almost anything for her. Looking back, she was sure she'd never felt that about Keith, or any relationship before him. Whenever they had time during the week or on weekends, whoever woke first got them both coffee in bed. It was a tradition Claire loved, especially because she was usually the last to wake. She knew that Derek knew she sometimes pretended to be asleep, but he didn't seem to mind. He often said he liked to make his girl happy. It was like having the best of both worlds. They had the passion of lovesick teenagers and the care and consideration of a couple who had been married forever.

The other light in Claire's life was the horses—especially Paycheque. She saw his recovery as miraculous, despite Will saying that there'd never been any doubt. The horse had slowly returned to training and would soon have his first proper gallop. They'd do it when Will could be there. He now spent a lot of his spare time in the Adelaide Hills visiting David and Bernadette, regularly dropping in to check on his star patient. Jack had practically accepted him as another member of the family.

Claire smiled at Derek as he sat on the side of the bed, pulled his socks off and took a long sip of coffee before sliding his feet beneath the sheets and snuggling down. She turned and picked up her cup, and noticed a wrapped parcel the size of a tissue box beside it. She grinned at Derek, who raised his eyebrows before returning to sipping his coffee.

'Oh, thank you,' she cried, leaning over to hug and kiss him.

'You'd better open it first. You might not like it.'

With Keith and every boyfriend before him, she'd opened presents while focussing on the mantra 'It's the thought that counts, it's the thought that counts'. Gifts always seemed to be one extreme or the other: totally practical and boring, or jewellery she had to pretend to love. She cringed at the memory of the last gift Keith had given her: a leaf blower for the garden. She ignored the twinge of guilt and returned her attention to the package on her lap.

This was the first major gift-giving occasion for her and Derek, but she just knew it would be perfect. He was a true romantic. Since their blow-up, she'd come to realise that Derek really did understand her as no one else ever had. He would often turn up with flowers or chocolates for no other reason than that he loved her.

Claire picked up the parcel and curbed her instinct to shake the box. Wrapped so beautifully, it was a shame to untie the mass of pink, purple and silver entwined bows.

'It's too pretty to destroy,' she said.

Derek shrugged. 'There are no rules to say you have to open it, but I did put a bit of thought into choosing the contents.' He took another sip of coffee.

'Oh, well, I'd better open it, then, hadn't I?'

'Go on, do it for me.'

Carefully Claire pulled the ribbons apart and tossed them to Bill and Ben, who had been eagerly watching the flailing ends.

The cats had been desexed, which had calmed them down considerably. They were now large, reformed characters who no longer tried to destroy furniture with their claws, nor linen with wayward toilet habits. Derek had helped Claire install a cat door, which meant they now spent their days lounging around inside or out fossicking in the garden, and their nights sprawled across the end of Claire's bed.

The silver wrap came off to reveal a plain purple unmarked box. Claire opened it to find a box about half the size and wrapped with equal care and precision. She rolled her eyes at Derek in mock exasperation. He shrugged again. Claire tore off the plain pink gloss wrap expecting the 'pass the parcel' theme to continue. Instead, she found a plain business-sized envelope. She blinked in slight surprise, picked it up, turned it over and pulled the seal apart. The contents were two plane tickets—one in her name, the other in Derek's—to Kangaroo Island. The date was today's. Shit! She couldn't just drop everything at a moment's notice. Or could she? *Of course I can*, she told herself.

'Wow, it's wonderful. Thank you,' she cried, reaching over and embracing Derek.

'Happy birthday, darling. Hope you don't mind sharing with me,' he murmured, rolling Claire over and beginning to kiss his way down her body.

'Mmm, not at all,' she murmured back, already aroused and responding to his gentle touch.

As if on cue, the phone started ringing moments after Claire had finished in the shower and Derek had stepped in. Jack rang, and then put Maddie on to wish her a good day, and then Bernadette called and Claire had to break the news she wouldn't be able to have dinner with them as planned. She felt dreadful and said so, but Bernie didn't seem to mind, and David sounded as if he hadn't even decided on what to cook.

Claire was packing her carry-on bag when Derek appeared and began snuggling her neck. 'Darling, we're only going for one weekend,' he purred.

Claire was excited and only the tiniest bit apprehensive. She was still only a beginner 'go with the flow' girl, but with Derek she felt safe enough to be spontaneous. He seemed to understand where her anxieties lay, always mapping everything out and encouraging her to keep pushing beyond her comfort zone. Today her only concern was for Bill and Ben, whom Derek had already sorted: Maddie had been charged with dropping by to care for them.

She'd never admit it aloud, but Claire McIntyre was beginning to like the idea of someone else making the decisions.

'What fun!' she said as they parked Derek's car in the long-term car park. Claire loved everything about flying, even the food. She hadn't been in a plane since she'd left her office job. It was one of the few things she missed.

As they unloaded the boot, she noticed Derek check his watch and bite his lip.

'Is there something wrong?'

'Sorry? Oh, no, just trying to remember if I packed my toothbrush.' Claire thought it odd—Derek was such a seasoned traveller, surely a toothbrush was the last thing he'd forget.

'If not, you can borrow mine,' she offered, cringing at the thought as she did. It was weird; they probably swapped all sorts of bacteria when they kissed, but the thought of sharing a toothbrush still made her feel uncomfortable.

They got to the terminal and Derek was still uneasy. For some reason he also seemed to be stalling. Claire could see the check-in line growing.

'Come on, quick,' she said, tugging at his hand. 'Before that tour group gets here.'

'There's plenty of time,' he said, standing his ground but still looking edgy.

'What are you waiting for?'

Just then Derek's phone chirped and he answered it. He looked relieved. Claire turned away to give him his privacy. She was a little annoyed—she wanted to make the most of the airline's lounge. She loved the free open bar and buffet of nibbles. Claire sighed. The little things were what she missed the most from her corporate life. But then, she hadn't been able to sleep in every second day, regularly indulge in long lunches or spend so much time in the garden. Life was full of compromises. And she wouldn't change what she had now for quids.

Shit! Claire stiffened. She wouldn't miss Paycheque's first full gallop, would she? No, Jack wouldn't let that happen. Actually, hadn't Will said he had something else on and couldn't make it that weekend? They'd been adamant to wait until Will was there in case anything went wrong. Claire shook her head at the memory of Paycheque that night after his accident. Thank God they hadn't taken the first vet's advice, and thank goodness David had known Will.

Ah, David. She'd certainly been wrong about him. When Bernadette had finally finished telling Claire the whole story only a few weeks ago, it all made sense. When some people lose someone they love, they pick themselves up, dust themselves off and get on with life.

And then there were those, like David, who made the decision to never get back on the bicycle again. David had lost his fiancée, Caroline, to cancer and had withdrawn from everything familiar. He'd sold the successful corporate gift basket business he and Caroline had run in the city and moved to the country. He'd let people believe he was gay so he wouldn't meet another woman and risk having to fully open himself up emotionally again. It had worked well until he'd been befriended by Bernadette and then Claire. Reverse psychology had worked its magic.

Trust Bernadette to sort him out, Claire thought, smiling to herself.

Claire was brought back to the reality of PA announcements and people bustling about her and by the snapping shut of Derek's mobile. He was looking around as if he were waiting for someone. Claire cringed, hoping he hadn't arranged to meet one of their old colleagues. That would be awkward.

Just then, Derek turned and gave her a peck on the lips, his big smile lighting up his full, handsome features. She was about to ask about the call when she heard familiar voices and turned around to see Bernadette running awkwardly, red hair fanning out behind her. She dragged a suitcase on wheels with one hand and David with the other.

'Sorry we're late—there was an accident on the freeway by the tunnel,' Bernie cried breathlessly.

Claire stared from her friends' faces down to their suitcases. 'What's going on?' she asked.

'Haven't you told her, Derek? Remember how Claire hates surprises,' she added with a knowing grin.

Claire rolled her eyes at her friend.

'She's getting used to them, aren't you, darling?'

Claire nodded dumbly. David regained his composure, and breath, and pecked her on the cheek.

'Happy birthday—again.'

'Thanks. So, are we all going to K.I. or is there some other surprise going on here?'

'Ooh, I see what you mean. You really are turning her into a "go with the flow" kind of girl,' Bernadette said, nudging Derek.

'I don't care what we're doing as long as we make the most of the free grog and nibblies in the lounge. Come on, I'm looking forward to a gin and tonic,' Claire said, making her way to the end of the queue, leaving her friends to exchange bemused smirks before bolting to catch up.

Claire sat back, buckled her seat belt and awaited the safety demonstrations. She was suddenly very weary. Their weekend had been jam-packed with trying to see as much as they could fit in.

They'd consulted the tourist brochure and decided to try to visit all the natural sites. But in the end they got sidetracked by wineries, art galleries, a honey farm and a sheep dairy. While she'd really enjoyed what they'd done, Claire was a little disappointed that they hadn't got to the other end of the island. Derek promised to bring her back for her next birthday, and David and Bernadette had joined in on the pact.

In the car on the way from the airport to the Adelaide Hills, she was glad they'd taken the extra day and come back on Monday morning. Jack had called to say Will was available that afternoon and they'd decided the time was right to put Paycheque through his paces. She was both excited and apprehensive.

Jack, Will, David, Bernie, Derek and Claire were standing at the fence down the long side of the paddock they used as a racetrack. Maddie warmed Paycheque up and then did a lap at a fast canter.

'Righto, open him up,' Jack called as she went past them to start her second lap. They watched as Maddie crouched low and then, as if he were a spring uncoiling slowly, Paycheque's stride lengthened and he shot forward. His stride went from three beats to four, where all four hooves left the ground for an instant. After three months, Paycheque was finally galloping again. Claire bit her trembling lip. She, Jack and Will watched through binoculars for the slightest sign his injury wasn't holding up, as he and Maddie made their way around the far side of the paddock. Claire let out a sigh of relief as they went past again. Everything was still looking good.

'Pretty good time, too,' Derek said, holding out a stopwatch for Claire to see.

'Look, Dad.'

'Not bad,' Jack said, nodding.

'Not bad? It's bloody brilliant!'

At the far side of the paddock Maddie brought the horse gradually back into a steady canter and then a trot. Will had warned her not to pull him up too quickly and risk jarring his tendon. Finally the bystanders had stopped leaping about hugging each other and crying out with excitement and delight, and were calmly chatting amongst themselves when Maddie came to a halt in front. They clambered around her, some patting the horse, others patting Maddie on the legs.

Back at the stable they all stood around while Will gave Paycheque a going-over. They all held their breath as he stood up, stretched his back and patted the horse on the neck before declaring him sound. They erupted into cheers, startling the poor little horse.

Jack grinned. 'Think it's time to break out the champagne.'

They were sitting, waiting for two batches of Claire's soup to defrost in the microwave, when Jack cleared his throat and began to speak.

'Derek, now you're almost part of the family, I was wondering if I could pick your brain.'

'Sure.'

'It's about the Spring Carnival.'

'Yes?'

'Well, have you entered for any of the spring races over in Melbourne?'

'Cavalcade is qualified for the Cox and I've got Humble entered in the Caulfield, but he's yet to qualify— you?'

'We've never gone before but I've been thinking about it—you only live once.'

'Really? You didn't tell me,' Claire said, pouting.

'Jeez, Claire, give a bloke a chance. I only opened the latest newsletter over the weekend and saw the reminder that nominations were due soon. You were away, remember?'

'But the cost, the logistics. Even if we could afford it, where would we stay?'

'That's what I wanted to discuss with Derek. Old Scrubber Fitzpatrick has been offering me his stables forever, but I've never had the talent worth taking. I reckon both Howie and Paycheque might just be the ones.'

'I agree,' Derek said.

'But the fees,' Claire said. 'Final declaration for the Caulfield Cup alone is over twenty grand. And then you've got all the other costs. We just don't have that sort of money, Dad.'

'I'd be happy to help out.'

'Derek, we can't...'

'Claire's right. Derek, it's very kind of you to offer but we couldn't.'

Claire got up to check the soup. As doubtful as she'd been, she couldn't help feeling disappointed.

'So, Derek, how long are you going for?' Jack asked.

'Probably the whole two months—that's how long Jackson, my trainer, is going for.'

'Two months?' Claire said, unable to hide her disappointment.

'Claire, I wouldn't dream of not asking you. I just wanted to know exactly what I was doing before discussing it.'

'I couldn't be away that long—wish we could go in our own right,' she said.

'Well, maybe you will. It's still a couple of months away. A lot can happen in that time. Why don't you nominate them—only costs five or six hundred—and then worry about them qualifying.'

'Derek, you're not listening—the final declaration fee for the Caulfield Cup is almost twenty thousand dollars. We just don't have the money for such a huge gamble.'

'It's only money.'

Fine for some, Claire thought, beginning to doubt whether two people with such clearly different attitudes to money could work long-term. She shook away the thought.

'Oh, Claire Bear, I almost forgot,' Jack said suddenly. 'Some mail came for you Friday—mustn't have caught up with your new address. It's over on the bench by the phone.'

Claire got up to retrieve the items. One was a clothing catalogue, another was an offer for a new credit card. 'Maybe we should sign up for this,' she said, tossing it onto the table.

The last item was a business-sized envelope with Sydney G.P.O. return address in the top left corner. She opened it thinking advertisers were getting craftier by the day. Inside was a letter on the letterhead of the insurance company Keith had dealt with. *Oh God*, Claire thought. *What now?* It had been months since they'd notified her of their 'final decision' not to pay out on his vehicle and life policies. That reminded her: she hadn't had a response since writing to the Insurance Ombudsman. That was ages ago. Should she follow it up?

As she unfolded the letter something fell to the table. Claire ignored it and read. The colour drained from her face and her hands began to shake.

'What is it?' Derek and Jack asked together.

'This fell out. Looks like a cheque,' Maddie said, holding it out to Claire.

'Oh! My! God!' Claire said, staring at the letter in one hand and the cheque now in the other. Her mind was swimming.

In stunned silence she reread the figure at the bottom of the letter, trying to keep track of the zeros. It said the accompanying cheque was for three hundred and seventy-eight thousand dollars.

Just when she'd finally managed to banish his memory to the far corner of her mind, Keith was effectively securing her future from the grave—her future with another man.

Thirty-Nine

Lying in bed that night, Claire was still surging with a heady mix of emotions. Derek held her tightly to him, not even hinting he wanted to make love.

'I'm here if you want to talk about it,' he whispered, kissing her on the forehead. Claire hugged him tighter and buried her face in his smooth, soft shoulder. She started to cry. He stroked her hair and offered soothing words of comfort, which made her cry harder for a few moments. She was annoyed with herself for being so ridiculous. Why should she feel guilty anyway? Keith *would* want her to be happy, wouldn't he?

Derek had said months ago that he thought you never *got over* the pain and loss, but rather *got through* it to the other side, where life went on but was different. It had taken him two years to even consider looking for a new partner. Was she callous to feel so much for someone so soon? Or was it different for Derek because he'd had a daughter to raise and protect?

The kittens, as if sensing the emotion in the room, made their way across the pillows behind Claire's and Derek's heads, pausing to sniff at the tears on Claire's cheek. She laughed at the playful paws patting away her troubles and reached up to stroke Bill, the gentler natured of the two.

Ben, sensing he was missing some fun, launched himself onto Derek's chest and tried to snuffle his way under Claire's hair. He put his wet nose in her ear. She and Derek erupted into a fit of giggles, sending the cats leaping about the bed, pouncing on imaginary mice they thought were moving under the quilt.

Slowly they quietened down and curled up at the end of the bed for a nap. *They really are the best medicine*, Claire thought with an inward sigh. She eased herself up onto an elbow and looked at Derek.

'Derek, I'm really sorry. It's just taken me by surprise, made me think about things I didn't want to—hadn't—for ages.'

'I know. You don't have to explain, and you certainly don't have to apologise. I've been through it, too, you know,' he said, pulling her back to him and kissing her tenderly on the lips. 'Just promise you won't bottle things up. I want you to feel that you can talk to me about anything.'

'I do,' Claire said, and genuinely meant it.

Claire was deep in thought as she slowly munched her way through her toasted muesli. Derek was reading the morning paper. She was glad he'd decided to wait until after the peak hour traffic before heading to the office.

'Derek?'

'Hmm?'

'Can I have your honest opinion?'

'Of course. On what?' he said, looking over his paper.

'Do you really think it's worth taking Howie and Paycheque to Melbourne? It's just, now I've got the money...'

Derek put his paper down. 'Absolutely. As you rightly said the other night, horseracing is a big gamble, but I certainly think their form is up there with the best of them.'

'But we're just small fry from the bush.'

'So are the majority of trainers out there—it's only the media who'll have you think it's just the big boys with all the money that do well. They figure so prominently because they have the numbers. But if you looked into the stats you'd find success is pretty evenly spread. You've seen how much it costs to enter the group ones. That's what excludes the smaller outfits—not the quality of their training, or their horses.'

Claire frowned and looked down at the bowl in front of her.

'Claire, I am not just saying it. Believe in yourself. Take a risk. Put your horses in with the best of the best and see where the chips fall. That's all you can do. Sorry, I don't mean to go on.' He laughed, blushed ever so slightly and picked up his paper again.

'Thank you, it was a lovely speech.' Claire laughed, leant over and kissed him. 'And I really do appreciate your faith in me.'

'You may be new at this training thing, but you're damn good at it.'

And right there Claire McIntyre decided she would do everything in her power to give the horses the chance they deserved. And Jack. The Cup Carnival in Victoria that had always been out of reach was going to be a reality—just being there would be an honour for him. With the fluttering of excited butterflies in her stomach, Claire wondered how Paycheque and Howie would cope with the atmosphere, people, noise. How would she? She was nervous just thinking about it.

'One step at a time,' she muttered. 'Nominate and then qualify.'

'That's my girl,' Derek said, leaning over and giving her a kiss. 'Though you'll have to beat my Humble first,' he said, leaping up and ducking just in time to avoid being hit in the head with the paper.

'You're on,' Claire said, gritting her teeth with determination.

Claire was at the café early. Neither Bernadette nor David were anywhere in sight. She grabbed an old copy of *New Idea* on the way to their usual table. Bernadette had never been very punctual, but was becoming less so the closer she got to the wedding date.

She and David had decided to wait until after the Melbourne Cup to get married, but were discussing having a pre-wedding honeymoon in Melbourne during the Carnival. Claire really hoped they would—she'd need Bernie on hand to keep her grounded.

But where would they stay? She, Derek, Maddie and Jack had arranged to put a borrowed caravan at the Fitzpatrick farm, where the horses would be. Not exactly the glamour the Carnival was renowned for, and a far cry from a five-star hotel and a corporate box. Claire felt a clenching in her stomach, the flutter of nerves. She'd been getting it almost hourly since Saturday's race at Morphettville—Howie had qualified for the Underwood Stakes.

Unfortunately, Paycheque had missed out, only picking up a fourth and a sixth for the day. They were outstanding results, given his catastrophic injury of only a few short months ago, but still she'd hoped for more. If he'd qualified, she'd be able to get that worry off her mind. She couldn't believe Jack was so matter-of-fact about it; for him it was the culmination of a lifetime's work. Claire was more nervous than excited; so much could go wrong.

'So sorry I'm late,' said Bernadette, plonking herself onto her usual chair and dumping her handbag on the floor. She tried to push some unruly tendrils from her flushed, damp face but they bounced back.

'What's going on?'

'Oh, you know, the usual stuff. Delivered half a truckload of cow poo to Tom Barnett but he reckons he ordered sheep poo,' she said, flapping a hand. 'So I'm in the shit—well, he is.' She grinned, rolling her eyes.

'So, what are you going to do?'

'He'll just have to get over it—Darren's got the paperwork clearly stating cow. End of story. So, what are we eating?' She turned around to consult the handwritten menu board behind them.

Claire stared in wonder at her friend. No matter what went wrong at the nursery, Bernadette sorted it with ease, yet the tiniest problem with the upcoming nuptials sent her over the edge.

She'd phoned the other night in tears because the Golf Club was already booked the night they wanted to hold their reception. She'd been nearly hysterical until Claire had recited back her own philosophy to her, saying it clearly wasn't meant to be and that there'd be somewhere much nicer available. Bernie had wailed that she'd wanted photos by the lovely big gum tree out front, and Claire had calmly pointed out that the land was a public reserve and she didn't need Golf Club permission to have her photos there.

Finally, Bernadette had let out a big sigh. 'I don't know what is wrong with me. This wedding is doing my head in.'

'They do that,' Claire had replied, thinking back to some of the ordeals she'd faced all those years ago. It was like some kind of test, a baptism of fire.

Derek had been married before, so he was unlikely to want a big wedding—*if* they decided to get married. Not that she and Derek had even discussed it. Nonetheless, she could picture a simple exchange of rings under the weeping willow out behind her cottage and a few select guests sipping champagne. Claire revelled in her daydream for a few moments before snapping her attention back to the menu.

'You're a little calmer than the other night—got the wedding under control, then?' she ventured.

'Wedding! I don't know what I was thinking. I've never been so stressed in my life.'

Claire offered a sympathetic expression. 'You can change your mind. It's probably not too late.'

'That's the thing. I know it'll be fabulous on the day. I just want it to be easier.'

'They don't call it the biggest day of your life for nothing.'

'Enough of my whingeing. How are my boys? Sorry I couldn't make it on Saturday—how did they go?'

'Howie qualified for the Underwood Stakes.'

'Wow, that's fantastic. Shit! That means he won sixty grand—drinks are on you, then.'

'Yeah, well, it sounds a lot but it isn't even enough to clear the farm's overdraft. I still can't get over how much money is tied up in the game.'

David appeared beside them holding two effervescing glasses of champagne. 'Here you are, girls,' he said, putting them down. 'On the house.'

'What are we celebrating?' Claire asked, looking from David to Bernadette. *Don't tell me you're pregnant*, she thought—though that might explain a few things.

David shrugged. 'Life, future happiness, Paycheque's return to health—take your pick,' he said, and laughed.

'Thanks. Care to join us?' Claire asked.

'Can't. Sorry.'

'He's so sweet,' Claire said, picking up her glass.

'Isn't he just the best?' Bernadette said, staring after her fiancé all doe-eyed.

'So, what are we drinking to?' Claire asked, breaking the spell.

'I don't know.'

'Okay, what about the good life? About sums it up.'

They clinked glasses and toasted, 'The good life.'

Claire took a deep, savouring sip of champagne as they waited for their chicken and avocado crêpes. She really did feel life was perfect. Except for one niggling issue. It had been bothering her since she and Derek started spending so much time together.

'Bernie, I need your opinion on something.'

'Yes, darling, anything. Madam Bernadette awaits you.'

Claire hesitated, looked away.

'Sorry, I was being silly. Seriously, what's up?'

'Well, do you and David... Do you ever get competitive?'

'In the bedroom?'

'No, life. Like earning more money, businesses doing better—that sort of thing?'

'Oh, he earns a tonne more money than me. I don't care. This place takes a lot more effort than my little patch,' Bernadette said, waving an arm around.

'But does it ever bother you? Like when he has heaps of customers and your business is quiet?'

'No, we're in two completely different industries—there is no competition. Ahh, I get it. You're worried about you and Derek both being in horseracing.'

'Exactly.'

'Well, for one thing, Claire, you're a highly competitive person—which I'm not—so you can't compare you and Derek to David and me.'

'But you want to do well.'

'I'm determined, passionate and strong-willed, but if I'm competitive, it's only with myself. If you compete with someone else, then essentially someone has to win and someone has to lose.'

'I hadn't thought of it like that. So what do I do?'

'About what, exactly?'

'I'm worried it means our relationship can't work long-term.'

'Why not? You adore each other!'

'I know, but I've kind of stopped telling him what I'm up to with the horses and I think he's noticing.'

'Claire, you can't compete with someone who isn't in the same race.'

'We might both have horses in the Caulfield yet, fingers crossed.'

'You're missing my point. You're a trainer, he's an owner—you can't compete directly.'

'But I'll want my horse to win, which—as you pointed out—will be at the expense of his. That's competition.'

'I don't think you've been truly tested. If your horse beat his I think you'd be genuinely disappointed for him.'

'Of course I would.'

'Oh God, I don't know.' Bernadette laughed, gave a shrug and downed the dregs in her glass. 'Talk to Derek, that's the best I can offer.'

Their meals arrived while Claire was still trying to sort out what Bernadette had said, and decide whether her advice was worth heeding.

'Eat while it's hot, Claire, and forget I said anything at all. My head's all over the place at the moment,' she said, waving her fork.

As she picked up her own fork, Claire couldn't help wondering if indeed Bernadette had been onto something. One thing that made sense was to talk it over with Derek. She felt a little guilty; not so long ago she'd promised him she could talk to him about anything, and would, no matter how difficult.

Claire was pleased Derek was at the cottage when she got home—she really wanted to get this off her chest. She made them a cup of tea and asked him to sit down. He looked worried, which made her feel terrible. She pushed on.

'Oh, you silly thing. Is that all?' he asked with obvious relief when she'd finally lowered her silencing hand indicating he was free to speak. 'You're worried we're too competitive?'

She was annoyed with herself for building it up into such a drama.

'Your drive and determination are what I love most about you. Just don't ever say, "Nah nah, beat you," or else I shall have to spank your pretty little arse.'

'Promises, promises.' She laughed.

He playfully tried to grab her behind. She squirmed and wriggled, pretending to resist, but was pinned down on the couch beneath him, her body already tingling in anticipation.

Forty

Three months later

'Oh, Derek, it's so exciting just to be here,' Claire said, clapping her hands before accepting a cup of tea from him.

'Yes, truly five-star,' Derek deadpanned, looking around him.

She slapped at his arm. 'Not *here*, silly, Melbourne. The Cup Carnival. I just can't believe we're actually taking part.'

Claire looked around the borrowed caravan that would be home for the next eight weeks. The brown, orange and cream floral curtains matched the bedspread and perfectly picked out the orange in the vinyl of the upholstered bench seat. It was dated, but clean and comfortable. More important, it was free: a loan from a friend of a friend of Derek's. It had seemed to take forever to get organised, make the trip and finally get the horses and themselves settled.

'Well, you've worked hard. You deserve it.'

'Had a bit of luck, too, don't forget.'

'Nothing wrong with using luck to get your way—
we've all done it more than once.'

'Yes, but…'

'I know, sweetheart,' he said tenderly, putting his arm
around her shoulders. 'But he's up there wishing us all
the best, just like Amy. It's meant to be.'

'But I still feel a little guilty.'

'We can't keep going over this. If you weren't meant
to be here, the money wouldn't have come through.'

'But what if I've wasted it? It's terribly self-indulgent.'

'No, it's not.'

'It will be if we don't win anything back.'

'Have you seen the joy on your father's face? This
is a dream come true for him. When you consider that,
how could it possibly be a waste—or self-indulgent, for
that matter? Just enjoy the opportunity.'

'You're so wise. I love you, Derek Anderson,' she
said, leaning over and kissing him.

'I should think so,' he said, kissing her back.

Claire sipped her tea. 'I'll never forget seeing how
excited Dad looked standing outside Paycheque's stall
earlier. Like a kid at Christmas.'

Claire stared into her cup. A big grin lit up her features as she thought what a great feeling it was to be
able to bring that sort of joy to someone. She felt a lump
forming in her throat and swallowed it back, offering a
silent thankyou to Keith as she did so.

'It's going to be interesting to see how they cope
with the crowds.'

'Howie's pretty relaxed—he'll be fine. Paycheque
will either freak out or revel in the attention.'

'I'm hoping for not freaking out, but he's always full
of surprises.' Claire laughed. 'I hope Todd Newman is

here to see the horse he sent to the knackery entered into the Caulfield.'

'He's here—tied up with Dick Hayworth's team.'

'Well, I hope we beat him.'

'Word of advice,' Derek said gently. 'Focus on your own race. Don't get caught up in worrying what anyone else is doing.'

'I know you're right. It's just that it still riles me when I think about what Paycheque went through. It's hard to believe he's even here, let alone entered in a big one. Sorry, darling, enough about me. When are you catching up with your team? How's Humble?'

'I'm only an owner, Claire. No need for me to get too involved. I've found it works best to stay out of the way—just be available for the odd comment, photo, acceptance of trophy. My main job is to keep you calm.'

'Thanks—I think I'm going to need it.'

'Claire McIntyre, I've got to say, you're particularly gorgeous when you're vulnerable.'

'Well, don't get used to it, mister.'

'Seriously, Claire, I'm so excited and proud of you. I really am,' Derek said, hugging her tightly.

'Same here, Derek. I just know Humble is going to do well. Maybe we can get first and second in the Caulfield.'

'Who first? You or me?'

'Doesn't matter.'

'That's my girl—not that I believe you,' he said, kissing her on the nose and then down her neck.

The caravan door opened and Maddie appeared. 'Sorry, am I interrupting something?' she asked with raised eyebrows.

Claire sat up and straightened her clothes.

'Don't be silly, come on in,' Derek mumbled, and put some distance between himself and Claire.

'Well, they're settled,' Maddie said, flopping onto the nearest bench seat. 'Jack will be here any second. He's just offering Paycheque a few extra words of advice.'

'Hopefully he's telling him to ease up on the food. That horse is such a greedy guts,' Claire said.

Maddie was bleary-eyed and snippy after her third night sleeping in a spare stall at the stables. She mumbled vague greetings and pretended to engross herself in her Weet-Bix. Ordinarily, she was chirpy and full of energy after taking the horses out for their morning exercise. Derek and Claire exchanged concerned frowns.

'How were they this morning?' Claire asked, feeling a little guilty for having slept in while the horses were just lightly exercised. Not that the average person would consider eight o'clock a sleep-in.

'Howie's fine, no different from being at home. I reckon he's up to a full workout tomorrow.'

'And Paycheque?'

'Pain in the arse. He's all over the place. Nutty one minute, sluggish the next.'

'Was he any better last night?'

'No. I don't think he slept a wink—neither did I. Again. I can't do another one. Sorry, but I'm going to have to cramp your style here tonight.'

'What do you think is wrong with him?' Derek asked Claire.

'I don't know. Maddie, any ideas?'

'I'm too bloody tired to think. I thought he might be scared of the dark or something—even left the light on for him last night. Don't tell old man Fitzpatrick, he'll have a fit.'

'Did it help?' Claire asked.

'Nope, not a scrap. He still paced and stomped about—sounded like he even started kicking out at the walls.'

'Well, let's just hope he gets his act together and doesn't embarrass us at Werribee,' Claire said.

Forty-One

'I wondered where you'd got to,' Claire said, looking up from her paperwork as Derek came into the van with both arms full of newspapers.

'Thought we should keep up with what's going on—know our competition, as they say.'

Claire snorted. 'Know our competition! We're hardly competitive thanks to Paycheque's little performance yesterday.'

'Howie's doing all right. Maybe Paycheque just needs longer to settle.'

'He's had a week. Little shit! At this rate we'll be the laughing-stock of the Carnival.'

'Least the journos will be too busy watching the big guns—they usually are.'

'Small mercies. Cup of tea?' she asked, getting up.

'Yes, thanks.' Derek opened *The Age* and went straight to the sports section. Claire stood by the kettle, waiting for it to boil.

'I just wish we could do something—I hate him being so unhappy,' she mused.

'Least he's still eating.'

'Like I said, small mercies.'

'Uh-oh.'

'What?'

'You wouldn't believe it, Claire, but you've made the paper.'

'Great,' she groaned. 'So much for Gai Waterhouse and David Hayes hogging the spotlight. Here, let me look—it can't be good.'

'It's only tiny, just on the side.'

'Give it here,' Claire growled.

'Well, okay, but you're right, it's not good.' He gave a sympathetic wince as he turned the paper towards her.

The small bold title read: 'Paycheque should be "canned", says former owner.' Claire's mouth dropped open. She read on:

South Australian horse Paycheque showed some of the form that saw him previously banished to the abattoir. Former trainer Todd Newman said, 'Difficult is an understatement. He was a bloody menace. Ate too much. Had a shocking temper. He deserves to be canned—literally.'

'Only because you don't know how to handle horses,' Claire growled before reading on.

Stewards at yesterday's meet at Werribee might possibly agree, after the horse put up a fierce battle at the barriers before finally relenting to run last by what could only be described as a country mile. One can only wonder at trainers Jack Mc-

Intyre and daughter Claire's logic in nominating the horse for the Caulfield Cup.

'Jesus. It's humiliating,' Claire said, pushing the paper aside and rubbing her hands over her face. 'And why would Newman care enough to comment anyway?'

'Because he was asked. You know what he's like—always looking for his five minutes of fame. Probably feeling threatened, too—heard around the traps how well the horse he'd condemned was doing.' Derek shrugged.

'What am I going to do? It's a bloody disaster.'

'Nothing you can do. You can't make a horse behave any more than you can control what these idiots write. You can only do your best to get the horse in a good frame of mind. Then it's up to him.'

'How, though? I don't even know what's upsetting him. It's not like he's on his own, and Howie seems fine.'

'But he hasn't been through what the little guy has. We all handle pressure differently. Could be he's just picking up on your stress.'

'I am stressed. What if all the progress we've made with him this year has been lost?'

'You need a different approach.'

'Like what? Seriously, Derek, if you've got any suggestions, I'm listening.'

'Take the pressure off him.'

'How do I do that?'

'By taking it off yourself for a start. You're already a success because you're here. He's qualified for the Caulfield Cup. Treat the rest as a bonus.'

'I can't put him in it like he is.'

'So don't. What does it matter?'

'Well, the money for a start— it cost us a bloody fortune.'

'See, there's my point—too much pressure. Claire, the money's spent, gone. Let it go.'

'But…'

'It's like people who insist on eating everything on their plate at a restaurant, even when they're so full they feel sick. What do they achieve?' He shrugged. 'The meal is the same price, regardless of how much is eaten.'

Claire threw her hands up. 'So, I'm meant to pretend none of this matters?'

'Yep. Just chill, enjoy the ride. Continue with your plans, but lose the high expectations.'

Claire thought about what Derek had said. It made perfect sense, if only she could do it. But she had to, didn't she, for Paycheque's sake. He'd come too far to become a nervous wreck again. If only she'd inherited more of her father's easygoing genes.

That night they went to the pub for tea, all keen to escape the unravelling of their dreams. But they'd been seated less than five minutes before Paycheque again became the main topic of discussion.

'So, what's different for him here than at home?' Derek asked.

'Everything, nothing.' Maddie shrugged. 'He's stayed in plenty of other stables and been fine. He's eating and drinking okay, so he can't be too distressed.'

'Unless he's eating for emotional security,' Claire offered.

'God, surely not,' Derek scoffed. 'Are they capable of that, like people?'

'Don't see why not,' Claire said.

'I don't know about you people, but it's driving me to drink. Anyone else?' Jack said, getting up.

'You stay put, Jack. I'll get them,' Derek said.

'Don't. You make me feel like an old man. What are we all having?'

'House red, whatever it is. Thanks, Dad,' said Claire.

'Just another water for me, thanks,' said Maddie, before continuing her conversation. 'He's better during the day—other than being a bit cranky, which could be lack of sleep.'

'So, what's different at night here than at home?'

'Well, it's no quieter, no noisier—except for the commotion he's creating. It's a bit on the chilly side but I don't think it's that. He's moving about enough to keep warm. I had to swap the thick under-rug for the lighter one. Oh, I don't know, it's doing my head in!'

'Mmm, me, too. Now, changing the subject, I'm ringing Bernie later to check on things. Any messages?'

'A cuddle for Terry and Sandy from me,' said Maddie.

'Suppose you're missing them keeping your feet warm at night?'

'No, they don't sleep with me. They chose early on to stay in the stables. Probably spend all night hunting mice.'

Derek slapped his leg. 'Oh, well, there's your problem! Your horse is missing all the night-time activity so he's creating some of his own,' he said with a laugh.

'I thought they slept with you,' Claire continued, ignoring Derek.

'You're kidding! They purred so loud that I turfed them out after the first night. And Sandy snores. It's quite cute but it's enough to keep a person awake,' Maddie said.

'Or put you to sleep, if you like that sort of thing,' Claire said thoughtfully, staring at the table.

Maddie noticed her father blush slightly. 'You a snorer, Dad?'

'Not that I was aware. Something you're trying to tell me, Claire, darling?'

'What? Sorry? No, not you—well, only sometimes. I was thinking about Paycheque. What if the cats' snoring and purring helps him sleep?'

'Utterly ridiculous,' Derek sneered. 'Whatever next?'

'Well, it is something he has at home and not here,' Maddie said.

'Should I scout about, see if I can borrow some cats so you can test your little theory?' Derek mocked.

There was silence. Claire chewed on her bottom lip in total concentration. Maddie watched her. It was a full minute before she spoke.

'I'm going to see if Bernadette can put them on the plane. What do you think, Maddie?'

'We don't have any other ideas, and quite frankly, I'm at the point where I'd do anything to get a decent night's sleep—and I'm sure Howie would agree.'

'Have you both gone completely mad? How are you going to keep them here? Tie them up with a miniature halter and lead-rope? They'll try to find their way home—it's what cats do.'

'We'll have to hope they don't. They settled at the farm okay. Maybe they're missing Paycheque as much as he is them,' Maddie said.

'Hopefully *that's* the problem,' Claire said.

'I feel it my duty to point out to you, Claire McIntyre, that I think you are totally insane.'

'Thank you, Derek. Your comment is duly noted,' Claire said.

'Well, I don't think it's so different to the group bringing that Shetland pony—Henry, I think his name was—out from England to keep Jardines Lookout company,' Maddie said, picking up her menu.

Jack put a tray of drinks on the table.

'Jack, you'll back me up, won't you? I'm being ganged up on here,' Derek said.

Jack held his hands up in surrender. 'Sorry, mate, not against these two—they're always right. What is it this time?'

'They're only going to fly in two cats to keep a horse company! Whatever next?!'

'Like Henry the pony? Good idea if it improves Paycheque's disposition—cantankerous bastard tried to take a piece out of me before I left. And old Fitzpatrick's getting worried his stable's going to be destroyed.'

'Jesus, I'm surrounded by nutters,' Derek groaned, putting his head in his hands.

'And that's why you love us so much,' Claire said, draping an arm around his shoulders.

'So, who's for a big juicy steak?' Jack asked, rubbing his hands together.

Maddie groaned. 'I have weights to make, remember? Maybe in a couple of months.'

'Sorry, didn't mean to tease you,' Jack said.

'The smell of steak is but a distant memory,' she said with a resigned sigh. 'I'll have the warm chicken salad—minus the dressing.'

Forty-Two

'I hope they'll be all right,' Maddie said, poking a finger into the carry box on her lap where the two cats huddled. 'I don't think they liked flying much. They look terrified.'

'Pity we didn't think to bring them in the car and save them the trauma. Not long now. You'll be all right,' Claire said, addressing the carry box. 'At least they have each other.'

'Look, we've got a surprise for you,' Maddie called to the horses. Paycheque's and Howie's heads appeared over their gates. Maddie and Claire each took a cat from the box and held the wriggling creatures up for the horses to see. The wide-eyed felines took in their surroundings and gradually calmed. Paycheque stretched his neck out and nickered as he sniffed the closest, Sandy. Howie blew a gentle puff of hot air at Terry, who threw out a paw and whacked the horse on the nose.

'No claws. That must have been a friendly wallop,' Maddie said, and laughed.

'Hey, Sandy's purring,' Claire said. She could feel the gentle vibrations through her rugby top.

'So is Terry,' Maddie said, holding the smaller of the two up so his stomach was at her ear. 'Think it's safe to put them down?'

'We'll have to do it sometime.' They squatted down and released the cats. Terry and Sandy looked about briefly before disappearing together into Paycheque's stall. Claire and Maddie leant over the gate to watch and laughed when the cats went to separate corners and dug holes in the sawdust. The cats stopped mid-dig to look back at them.

'Sorry, we'll give you some privacy,' Maddie said, turning her back to the stall. Claire followed suit.

When they turned around a few moments later, the cats were climbing into Paycheque's empty feed bin, the curious horse snuffling at them playfully.

'Let's set up their food and water out here. That way Howie will get a look-in. He seems just as pleased to see them,' Claire said.

'I could watch them for hours,' Maddie said with a contented sigh.

'Me, too—might just do that yet. Make sure they're not going to run away.'

Derek appeared behind Claire, putting his head over her shoulder. 'How's "Operation Feline" going?'

'So far, so good,' Claire said, turning her head and kissing him on the cheek.

'So, they've arrived safely, then,' Jack said, peering over Claire's other shoulder.

'Yep. Tonight will be the big test,' Claire said.

'So, how did we sleep?' Claire asked Maddie the next morning, when she came into the caravan for breakfast. Jack and Derek looked on.

'Like a baby,' Maddie said, beaming as she squeezed into the booth next to Jack.

'What, woke every four hours and cried?' Derek said.

'Dad, you're *so* hilarious. *Not*,' Maddie said, slapping at him across the table.

'So, you slept all right—the horses were quiet?' Claire asked.

'Yes and yes!'

'Mere coincidence,' Derek said.

'You wish, Dad. I'll have my twenty bucks now, thanks,' she said, holding out a hand.

'But there's actually no proof it was the cats.'

'And no proof it wasn't.' Maddie shrugged, snapping her fingers. Derek reluctantly pulled his wallet from his pocket and removed a twenty-dollar note. He slapped it on the table in front of his daughter.

'Pleasure doing business with you,' Maddie said with a treacle smile.

Claire laughed to herself at the similarities between father and daughter. 'So, I want the full report.'

'Well, when I last checked at around eleven-thirty, Paycheque was curled up with both cats wedged against his chest. I wish I'd had a camera. It was so cute. This morning Sandy and Terry were off roaming around, checking their new kingdom, and Paycheque was at his gate looking bright-eyed—like his old self. I'd better give him a decent workout on the lunge before I get on—looks too full of beans.'

'How's Howie?'

'Good, even calmer. His resting heart rate is back to what it is at home.'

'Great, so we're right back on track, then,' Jack said, clapping his hands together.

'I still don't believe it was the cats,' Derek said later, when he and Claire were again alone.

'You don't have to, darling. Remember,' she said, batting her eyelashes, 'the world's bigger than us—some things are beyond our control.'

'Yep, I deserved that,' he said with a wry laugh.

Claire reflected on the race with a great sense of relief as she made her way back to the stalls. Paycheque's introduction to the turf at Caulfield had been drama free. Although he'd finished mid-field in his race, it was more due to an unlucky start than anything else. *Team McIntyre was definitely back on track, so to speak.* She chuckled to herself as she strode on. Hopefully all would go well with Howie as well. Claire was at the gate marked 'Authorised Entry Only' when a voice called from behind her.

'Claire McIntyre?'

She stopped and turned. 'Yes?' A middle-aged man in a battered straw fedora waved an arm at her. He hurried to catch up with an uneven, almost skipping gait. A large stomach hung below his belt and wobbled back and forth with every step. A lanyard dangled from his neck, but whatever was on it was covered by the notepad he clutched to his chest. The heavy creasing of his short-sleeved lemon shirt stopped where his stomach strained against the buttons.

'Bill Holloway,' the man said, puffing and thrusting out his hand. The beginnings of sweat glistened in the stubble just below his dark grey sideburns. As Claire returned his rough handshake she wondered where she'd heard the name. '*The Age*, sports,' he added with a gasp.

'You want to interview me?'

'Yes, would you mind?'

'I think you've got the wrong person. I train the horse that came fifth.' She laughed and moved to push the gate open.

'Damn sight better than at Werribee.'

Claire stopped. Something clicked in her mind. 'Ah, you're the one who wrote that piece in the paper.'

'Yeah. Hey, quite the turnaround—what did you do?'

Claire shrugged. 'Just needed more time to settle after the trip. He's new to travelling.'

'No way. What I saw last week was nothing to do with post-travel nerves. He was a total fruitcake.'

'Gee, thanks—I imagine you got that from Todd Newman as well.'

'That's why I'm trying to talk to you.'

'Why, exactly?'

'To get the full story. That horse has true potential.'

'Really?' Claire said with unmistakeable sarcasm. 'Bet you didn't get *that* from Todd.'

'No. So come on, what did you do between then and now? He's like a different horse.'

'You wouldn't believe me if I told you.' Claire threw her head back and laughed.

'Try me.'

'Look, I really don't have time—I've got another horse to get ready.'

'Hazardous Waste. Yes, I know.'

'You've certainly done your homework, Mr Holloway. Sorry, but I really do have to go,' she said, checked her watch and made to move on.

'It's Bill, and I'm happy to wait.'

'Well, you're welcome to, but I'll be a while.' Claire offered an apologetic shrug. She held up her pass, got the nod from the security officer and pushed the gate open.

'Who's your friend?' Jack said, pausing from towelling down Paycheque to indicate towards the man still standing at the gate.

'Some journo. Wants to talk about Paycheque.'

'Why?'

'He wants to know what we've done to bring about such a miraculous change since Werribee—he's the one who wrote that small piece quoting Todd Newman.'

'So, what are you going to tell him?'

'Don't know if I'm going to tell him anything.'

'But aren't you going to at least talk to him?'

'Haven't decided. You can if you want. Toss you for it.'

'No, thanks. They don't want the ramblings of an old fart.'

'Maybe he'll find someone more interesting before I get a chance.'

Derek strode towards the gate where the journalist was still waiting.

'Bill Holloway, how the hell are you?'

'Derek, old mate!'

'Editor of the sports section yet?'

'Not exactly. I'm lucky to even get a by-line half the time.'

Claire stood listening, hidden by Paycheque.

'Hey, aren't you connected to Claire McIntyre?'

'We're involved. Why do you ask?'

'I wanted to talk to her about Paycheque's turnaround since Werribee last week—remarkable.'

'Yes, it certainly is remarkable,' Derek said, shaking his head.

'So, what have they done?'

'You wouldn't believe me if I told you.'

'That's what she said. What's going on?'

'Not for me to say.'

'Aw, come on, Derek. Give me something here.'

'Not without Claire's permission. Bill, you're a married man. Rule number one—don't piss the missus off, right?'

'Well, could you at least get her to talk to me? Here's my card. I'm heading back to the members'.'

'I'll pass it on. You know, you could always do something on me—I own Humble Beginnings.'

'Yeah, sorry, mate. No offence, but there's no angle in consistently average.'

'Well, worth a try.' Derek grinned. He turned and walked back to where Claire was doing up Paycheque's rugs.

'Saw you talking to that journalist,' Claire said.

'Bill Holloway? I've known him for ages—he's harmless enough.' He shrugged.

'So, did you say anything? About us, Paycheque?'

'Not my place.'

'Good, thanks.'

'But you probably should—give him his interview, that is. I think it would be a good idea.'

'Yeah, I've been thinking about it.'

'He left his card—he'll be at the members' bar for a while yet.'

'Oh, I'm nervous now. What do I say?'

'Whatever you want. Just be your gorgeous, charming self and you can't go wrong.'

'Hope he doesn't want a picture, I'm covered in horse snot and sweat.'

'So, how did your first big media conference go?'

'I had a drink with him—a ten-minute chat—hardly a big media conference, darling. But it was relatively painless. He's going to try to get something in for Monday, so we'll see then if we're the laughing-stock of the Spring Carnival.'

'You told him about the cats, then?'

'I had to. He was obsessed with Paycheque's suddenly reformed character. I didn't want him raising speculation we were into doping or anything.'

'Good point. I wonder if he'll do a serious piece or take the piss.'

'You know what? I don't care. People can laugh all they want, but the fact is, it worked.'

'That's my girl,' he said, hugging her tightly.

Claire had been both eagerly and apprehensively awaiting the article and was surprised by how disappointed she felt when it failed to appear in Monday's paper. She tried to pretend she hadn't noticed, but Derek knew her too well. He gave her hand a knowing squeeze and her forehead a sympathetic kiss. She tried to put it out of her mind by being annoyed at the journalist for letting her down.

But then she stopped. Why was she taking it personally? It was totally beyond her control. For all she knew the article had missed its deadline, or been too long for the allocated space. Even if they'd decided she wasn't interesting enough to cover, it wasn't her fault. She'd been pleased with how she'd conducted herself. She'd spoken honestly and openly, displaying a good mix of pride and humility, charm and determination. She expelled the tension with a slow outward breath, something she'd become very good at recently. Really, what good did worrying about things you couldn't change do? She smiled up at Derek.

Claire was startled when Jack burst into the caravan crying, 'Check this out!' He laid a newspaper open on the table in front of her. She stared—almost in disbelief—at the article stretching across two columns with a small photo of her standing next to Paycheque peering out of his stall: 'Cats Save Caulfield Cup Campaign'.

In a move not dissimilar to Jardines Lookout being accompanied by Henry the Shetland pony, part-owner/trainer Claire McIntyre's move to fly in two moggies has put her Caulfield Cup campaign back on track.

All indications point to success, with the unorthodox move seeming to have worked wonders on the cantankerous Paycheque. Just over a week ago the pint-sized bay kicked up a storm at the barriers at Werribee, leaving those in the industry to scratch their heads over the McIntyres' decision to nominate the horse for the Caulfield Cup. On Saturday he lined up in race four for his first run at Caulfield, and while his feisty nature could be seen bubbling just below the surface, he behaved every bit the perfect gentleman. He was un-

lucky, only managing fifth after a poor start and being pushed out wide on the first turn.

After the race I asked Claire McIntyre about the turnaround in his behaviour. 'Well, it seems he's no different to the rest of us,' Claire said. 'He gets cranky when he doesn't get enough sleep. I just underestimated how much influence the cats had.' Apparently Paycheque sleeps lying down with two cats, Sandy and Terry, curled up against his chest, and when he was here without them, he spent his nights fretting and pacing.

'Maddie, our jockey, was sleeping nearby and being kept awake. We had to do something and thank goodness it seems to have worked,' Claire said.

After thirty years as a trainer out at Mount Pleasant, this is Jack McIntyre's first Melbourne Spring Carnival. Look out for the McIntyres' other promising mount, Hazardous Waste, in the sixth at Sandown Wednesday.

'Not bad. Not bad at all,' Jack said with obvious pride.

'Wish I sounded more intelligent,' Claire said, blushing. 'I thought he'd paraphrase, make it up.'

'Be grateful he didn't or else we could have come across the freaks of the carnival.' Jack laughed.

'Nah, Bill's one of the good guys,' Derek said.

'Let's hope Howie lives up to the hype,' Claire said, closing the paper and pushing it aside.

Forty-Three

Claire began to eagerly await the Monday morning newspaper, which devoted a considerable space to the weekend's horseracing coverage. She'd scour the small print for references to them and their horses, filling with apprehensive excitement when she found one, and increasingly disappointed when she didn't.

It was like a drug of increasing dependence; after the first few articles she'd begun to expect coverage, and then crave it every week. She spent hours feeling disappointed if she hadn't featured. Even Derek commented that it wasn't healthy to let the media have so much power over her.

Claire had to admit he was right. She'd been doing so well at being chilled, had really eased the pressure off herself, the horses and Maddie. Until that first article appeared. Since then, she'd been on a gradual slide backwards. Why did she care anyway? It wasn't as if she'd change her training methods or what races she entered based on what was written. *Exactly! It really doesn't matter what they write.* She wished Bernadette was there to help keep her grounded. But she wasn't.

One Sunday afternoon, when Claire was alone, she wrote herself a note on a scrap of paper: 'I do not give a shit. The media has no power over me'. She folded it and put it in her pocket with the note Bernadette had given her almost exactly a year ago. Bernie's note was now so tattered it barely held together at the folds. She no longer needed to refer to it, but continued to keep it with her out of habit.

'It seems we've finally made the paper because of our form, rather than our ratty horses and weird training methods,' Jack said with a laugh the following morning. He slapped the open paper on the caravan table. 'You even rated a mention today, Derek,' he added. They all jostled for a view of the article: 'Favourites Trounced as South Aussies Clean Up at Sandown'.

Little-known South Australian horses Hazardous Waste (owner/trainers Jack and Claire McIntyre) and Humble Beginnings (owner Derek Anderson, trainer Blue Jackson) were convincing winners at Sandown on Wednesday, leaving connections of Melbourne Cup favourites Inferno and Mystery Girl scratching their heads and no doubt rethinking their Cup preparations.

The McIntyres enjoyed further success with Paycheque winning by a length in the fourth, proving he is certainly one to watch over the coming weeks. Claire McIntyre said she thought winning was more about luck than anything else, but was especially pleased to see Paycheque doing so well after such a bad year. Claire refused to elaborate further, except to say the horse had made a brave

*comeback after a training accident. 'He's really
special to us—not just a horse we're training, but
part of the family,' she said.*

*Recently we reported on Paycheque's pen-
chant for feline stablemates, but something tells
me this isn't the last we'll hear of this eccentric
little horse from Mount Pleasant.*

'Now, that's good coverage,' Jack said, puffing his
chest out.

'Yeah, nice to finally share the limelight with you
guys,' Derek said.

'Paycheque'll love being referred to as eccentric.'
Claire laughed.

'Not to mention "one to watch",' said Jack.

Claire was pleased to feel a healthy detachment from
the words. Her handwritten mantra was working, and
she was back on track, too.

Claire was enjoying a middle-of-the-afternoon lie-
down when there was a gentle double-knock on the
flimsy aluminium door: Derek's trademark warning
he was coming in, with company.

'Claire?' he called. 'You decent? We've got visitors.'

She got up and moved the length of the caravan while
smoothing her appearance and forcing herself from her
dozy state.

'There you are. Nice snooze?' Derek gave her a peck
on the cheek.

'Lovely, thanks,' she said, looking past him and wondering who was visiting.

'Surprise!' Bernadette yelled, leaping into view.
David and Will appeared behind her.

'Wow!' Claire cried. 'What are you doing here? It's so good to see you. Come in! Come in! How did you find us?'

'They were lurking around the horses,' Derek offered. 'Clearly up to no good.'

'We had enough trouble finding this place—just trying to make sure we had the right one,' David said.

'But we spotted Paycheque and his harem of cats. I can't believe they made that much difference,' Bernie said.

'Thank goodness they did—he's a different horse now.'

'So, the piece in the paper was accurate. Fancy that,' David said.

'You'd better add felines to your list of alternative treatments, Will,' Bernadette said, chuckling.

They all thumped up the steps into the van and crowded around the laminex table.

'This is cozy,' Bernadette said, looking around.

'It is. We're having a ball, aren't we, Derek?'

'We are, now that I've convinced her to calm down and just enjoy the ride,' he said, giving Claire a squeeze and Bernie a knowing expression.

'So, where are you all staying?' Claire asked. 'Sorry, no room here at the inn, I'm afraid.'

'Will's sister is away so we've got plenty of space. We're very lucky—it's just near Flemington,' Bernadette said.

'It's so good to see you. I was beginning to get homesick,' Claire said, putting her arm around her friend.

'Hey, what about me?' Derek asked.

'But Bernie's my bestest friend forever,' Claire whined.

'So, you're here to stay? Till the end of the Carnival?'

'Yep, day after the Cup. I hope that's all right—we'll try to keep out of your way.'

'God, of course it's all right. And don't you dare keep out of my way.'

Derek, David and Will began chatting amongst themselves while Bernadette fired questions at Claire about the famous trainers, horses and celebrities she'd seen.

'It's not nearly as exciting as you're thinking,' Claire said. 'Though you're welcome to hang out and see for yourself. Anyway, I could do with the moral support,' she said, hugging her friend.

'What about me?' Derek said, pouting. 'Aren't I moral support?'

'Of course you are, darling,' Claire said, grabbing his hand across the table. 'It's just that now it won't need to be twenty-four-seven.'

'And of course, Derek, we'll be relying on you for some good tips for the betting ring,' David said.

'So, all's well with Paycheque, then?' Will asked after a pause.

'Absolutely. Wouldn't know he'd even been injured, thanks to you. So, are you working with other trainers while you're here?'

'Not at this stage.'

'Good, we'll have you all to ourselves.'

'Well, I'm actually hoping to get amongst the action— try to drum up some business. You can put in a good word for me.'

'Absolutely, it goes without saying. Derek knows heaps of people. Darling, you'll put the word around, too, won't you?'

'Of course. How about you spend Saturday with me at Caulfield.'

'Thanks, appreciate it.'

'Okay, who's for a glass of red? Then we were planning on testing out the local Chinese restaurant. Who's game?' Claire said.

The following afternoon, Claire and Bernadette watched Maddie put Howie through his paces on the practice track.

'He's looking good, Claire.'

'Yeah, isn't he?'

'You must be really stoked about being here and everything. It's terribly exciting.'

'And nerve-racking.'

'But Derek said you were calm, enjoying the ride.'

'Yeah, got him fooled. I just wish I could fool myself.' Claire laughed.

'You seem okay to me.'

'I'm constantly telling myself to not give a shit—even wrote a note, see?' She pulled out the tightly folded piece of paper and handed it to her friend. 'Trouble is, it's not working.'

Bernadette read it, nodded, silently refolded it and handed it back.

'So what do I do? At this rate I'll have a nervous breakdown before we even get back to Caulfield. Won't the media have a field day then?'

'You're more worried about what people are going to say about you than about the horses doing badly?'

'Of course. The horses do their best with what they get on the day—a lot of it's down to luck. Anyway, after Paycheque's tantrum the other week, they probably couldn't embarrass me now if they tried—nothing to fear there.' She watched Howic through the binoculars for a few moments, rocking in time as if riding his stride.

'So what is it—the money?'

She lowered the binoculars. 'No, actually. It's like Derek said, it's already spent—even if they don't race.'

'Well, you've managed to chill out about that, Claire. And let's face it, money's always been your thing to worry about.'

'I know. So why am I feeling so out of control?'

'Because you are.'

'Sorry?'

'Darling,' Bernadette said, putting an arm around her friend. 'You're just being you—you want to be in control and you're not. You know you can't be so it's sending you crazy. It's an inherent part of who you are.'

'Great, the old control-freak chestnut again. Haven't we had this conversation before?'

'Exactly. After the big upheaval, you'd finally put your life back into a manageable box and learnt to cruise along. Now you're here, and it's a little too out of your new box.'

'I'm so glad you're here, you've no idea.'

'Not sure I'm helping much. It's all very well to point out the problem.'

'Well, they do say recognising the problem is half the solution.' Claire shrugged. She brought the binoculars back up to her eyes.

'Hmm,' Bernadette said thoughtfully, watching Howie way off in the distance. 'Can I borrow some paper?'

'Sure.' Claire handed over the small notebook and pencil she used to write down the horses' times, performances and any other observations.

'He's looking as good as any of the other horses I've seen,' Claire said, again peering through the binoculars. 'We'd better get back and see what Maddie has to say about his run. Come on.'

'Here, same deal as last time, as often as needed,' Bernadette said, handing over the folded piece of paper with all the solemnity of a doctor handing over a prescription.

Claire grinned, accepted the note and unfolded it. 'Enjoy the ride. There's nothing to prove', was written over two lines in Bernadette's large flowing script.

'Maybe it's the magic of my handwriting that does the trick,' Bernadette offered with a shrug.

'Thanks. I hope you're right.' Claire folded the note and tucked it into her jeans pocket. She gave her friend a hug. 'You're a lifesaver. I'm so glad you're here.'

'Permission to slap you about the head every time you're looking stressed?'

'Permission granted.' Claire laughed. 'Come on, time for the wash up.'

As they strode across the paddock, Claire patted the pocket where Bernadette's new note sat. She knew it was ridiculous, but as with the previous one, which had finally fallen apart only a few days before and had been left beside her bed, she felt certain she could actually feel its warmth. No matter how silly her mind told her it was, Claire really did feel Bernie's note held some kind of power. She shook her head at how nutty she'd be considered if she told a journalist *that*. But somehow it was like putting her worries into her pocket.

Forty-Four

Claire was sweating, having practically ridden Howie herself for the past five hundred metres. She lurched, nearly losing her balance in the stands, as he made a final lunge to finish first by a nose. She stared—eyes wide, mouth open—at Bernadette jumping up and down beside her.

'He won! He won!' Bernie cried, throwing her arms around her friend. Claire hugged her back, unable to speak because of a large lump lodged in her throat. Around her, Jack, David, Derek and a multitude of strangers hugged, slapped backs and offered congratulations.

But out of the corner of her eye she saw it, just as the race caller announced it. There was something wrong with Howie. Maddie had dismounted, was comforting him and checking him over.

Claire tried to keep them in sight as she pushed past the people in the stands and on the stairs. Sensing her urgency, they parted.

Will was already at the gate with his black bag, trying to convince security to let him through. Claire shoved him ahead, thrust her pass into the guard's face, and then followed Will onto the track.

Apart from the comments from the race caller trying to be upbeat, and keep the crowd from thinking too much about what was unfolding just beyond the finish line, the strained, collective silence was noticeable.

It felt like hours, but was only minutes later, when Jack, followed by Will, led a severely lame Howie from the track. The crowd seemed to collectively avert their eyes, as if embarrassed at being caught enjoying the spectacle.

Derek walked behind and tried to put his arm around Maddie. But she resisted and shrugged him off. She ran to catch up to the hobbling Howie.

'Jack, I've got to get to weigh-in!' she cried.

'There's no point, love,' Jack said, putting a hand gently on her shoulder. 'The win's not worth having now.'

Maddie pushed his hand away. She undid the girth, dragged the saddle from Howie's back and started walking back to the enclosure.

Back at the Fitzpatrick stables, Will diagnosed a badly strained near shoulder and called for volunteers to do stints of rigorous massage. The good news was that the injury was neither life-threatening nor career-ending.

For Claire, the relief was so immense she had to escape to the solitude of the caravan for a good weep. Curled up on the floral-covered bed, she thought about the irony of Bernadette's note tucked away safely in her pocket: 'Enjoy the ride'.

That night, entwined in a comforting embrace, Derek

and Claire dissected the rest of the day's events. Derek's Humble had been bullied to the line to win in the fifth, an important lead-up race to the Caulfield and Melbourne Cups. It was an exciting result overshadowed by Howie's injury. Claire felt a little guilty about it, but Derek didn't seem to mind.

'Can you believe Maddie thought to take Howie's gear and front up for correct weight with all that was going on?' Claire said.

'At first I couldn't understand what she was on about—she practically had to belt me to stop me dragging her off to the stalls.'

'I didn't even give it a thought. We would have been disqualified.'

'She's always been cool in a crisis. When she was nine her Pony Club mount—Duke—cut his leg on a fence. He probably would have bled to death if it'd been left to me. She rang the vet and applied pressure while I sat on a bucket with my head between my knees feeling faint.'

'Actually, I thought today you were looking a little green.'

'Why do you think I took care of the jockey and stayed away from the horse? Just seeing them in pain is enough for me.'

'Poor sensitive baby,' Claire crooned, hugging Derek tighter. 'Thank God Will was here. He really is a miracle worker, isn't he?'

'Without a doubt.'

'What a day! I'm exhausted.'

'Too exhausted to…?' he said, running a finger lightly across her breast.

'Sorry. Too exhausted even for that.'

* * *

'Darling, you'll be needing an agent soon,' Derek said, arriving at the caravan with two takeaway coffees and a newspaper tucked under his arm.

With raised eyebrows, Claire relieved him of the paper and a coffee, and settled down to read: 'Vet Works Miracle'.

When Hazardous Waste pulled up lame after winning the Underwood Stakes at Caulfield just over two weeks ago, it seemed this promising stayer's Cup campaign, possibly even his career, was over. But in what is becoming their trademark, the McIntyres have again chosen an unconventional approach.

Shunning course vets, the McIntyres turned to holistic vet Will Douglas, already at the course, to examine the horse, leaving racing traditionalists shaking their heads. Fellow racehorse owner Derek Anderson defended girlfriend Claire McIntyre's decision. 'I would have said the same a year ago, but what he did for Paycheque can only be described as miraculous. The normal vet who showed up told them to put the horse down after he tore a tendon in a training accident—most vets would have. But Will reckoned he could help and, well as you've seen, the rest is history.'

Claire confirmed the story, adding that Dr Douglas is a traditionally trained vet specialising in alternative therapies. 'He's not a quack like people are making out. We would never put the welfare of our horses at risk, but they do deserve the best chance of recovery we can give them. Too often vets are just reaching for the gun without looking at alternatives. As I've said before, we consider our horses part of the family, not just a business, so of course we're going to try anything for a good outcome. If other people have a problem with it, then so be it.'

When asked about Hazardous Waste's injury and prognosis, Claire said, 'It's not as serious as first thought. Just a strain to his near shoulder— probably when he lunged right at the finish.' She said the horse had responded well to massage, acupuncture and herbal supplements.

Asked about his name still being on the ballot for the Melbourne Cup, Claire said, 'He'll start back with a gentle workout next week. We'll see then how he is, but at this stage we're not ruling him out.'

With the McIntyre horses tucked away at Ian Fitzpatrick's stables, no one has seen Hazardous Waste in the flesh. But if he truly does recover for the Melbourne Cup in just over two weeks, then we really will have seen something of a miracle.

'I don't see why the concept of natural medicine is so hard to grasp,' Claire said with a sigh, closing the paper and pushing it aside.

'Come on, Claire. Even you were questioning it not so long ago,' Derek said.

'Well, not anymore. I hate the way he suggests we would have ignored Howie's welfare if Will hadn't been there. And not saying up front that he's a fully qualified vet.'

'You're reading too much into it. He's just doing his

job—trying to sensationalise. And it's not like he's misrepresented the facts or what we said.'

'No, you're right, I'm just being too sensitive. Hopefully the publicity will be good for Will.'

'And no one died, which is what really matters.'

'You're right—as usual,' she said, rolling her eyes.

'Yes, and don't you forget it.' He laughed and gave her a hug.

Forty-Five

An image of Claire, clad in jeans, R.M. Williams boots, chambray shirt and navy sleeveless microfleece vest, came into view on the large plasma screen.

'Oh my God,' she groaned, blushing and burying her head in her hands. 'The camera adds ten pounds, not five.'

'Shh, it's starting,' Bernadette scolded, slapping at her friend's leg.

They were assembled at Will's sister's house to watch Claire's interview, which had been filmed the week before. It was the only place where the whole of Team McIntyre—as they'd begun calling themselves—could comfortably be accommodated. David had insisted on working out how to record it, even though she'd told him the station was sending her a copy.

The opening was the quintessential racehorse training scene—fog of early morning, steamy breath issuing forth from nostrils and mouths and off the rumps of sweaty horses wandering past. Other than the fact she was all hips and arse, Claire thought it looked perfect. And so it should: it had taken almost half an hour to get right. They had just finished filming when the fog lifted to reveal the dilapidated corrugated iron stables with piles of rolled fencing wire and other discarded farm refuse rusting behind them.

They'd wanted to start at five-thirty to capture the atmosphere of early morning and the rising sun. Claire got them to agree to do their opening shots without her so she could turn up with the horses nearer six-thirty.

Even still, poor Paycheque had his nose puckered into a sneer of distaste, and the crew were lucky they hadn't got too close. Otherwise it might have ended in tears. Howie showed his objection to the early hour with a few pigroots—he impressed the television people but merely caused the sure-seated Maddie to laugh.

They'd asked Claire to yell orders but she'd refused, opting instead for their second choice: studying the stopwatch, nodding and muttering with approval before making notes in her pocket-sized spiral-bound notebook. Part of her had wanted so badly to giggle, but thankfully her nerves had suppressed it.

Now Maddie giggled.

'Oi, enough of that,' Claire said, trying to glare stonily but failing. 'They *made* me, all right,' she whined.

'Come on, you two,' Bernadette said.

The shot faded to reveal Claire seated on a canvas director's chair, mug in hand, backed by the wall of the caravan. The interviewer was out of sight.

With her lower half hidden, she didn't look too bad on camera. The shoot hadn't stretched to professional hair and makeup, but Claire had seen enough training videos at work to know she'd look ghostly pale if she didn't apply a stack of foundation and concealer. She'd felt self-conscious at appearing so obviously overdone, but was now relieved she'd made the effort.

Derek gave her shoulder a squeeze with the arm he had draped around it. 'You look great,' he whispered, before kissing her on the ear.

Claire hoped she didn't have one of those voices that sounded all right to its owner but like an alley cat being strangled to the rest of the world. But after the first question was answered, she gave a sigh of relief and settled back into the plush cream leather couch to watch:

> '*I have with me Claire McIntyre, who recently joined her father Jack's stables near Mount Pleasant in the Adelaide Hills. Jack has over thirty years' experience as an owner/trainer, but this is their first Spring Carnival. Their horses Hazardous Waste and Paycheque have treated us to some spectacular highs and lows over the past six weeks, and with both horses entered in the Melbourne Cup, the story isn't over yet.*
>
> '*Claire, I'm sure there is much the whole of Australia is dying to know, but first, what's the story with the long stirrups? Every other jockey as far back as we can remember has worn their stirrups short, but not yours. Why?*' He laughed.

Claire remembered how it had immediately put her at ease.

> '*Well, Mike, it really comes down to safety. They say the reason for short stirrups is that being directly over the withers improves the horse's balance. But if your weight is evenly distributed,*

what's the difference if your legs are down the horse's sides or up under you? My view is that if you have a lower centre of gravity you're more likely to stay on if the horse stumbles. Also, with more leg on the horse, you've got a better chance of steering them away from trouble. I guess we're just looking at things a little differently,' she added with a shrug.

'Speaking of which, you have a strong objection to the use of whips, too, don't you?'

'Absolutely. In my opinion they serve no useful purpose...'

'Doesn't it encourage the horse to run faster? And I'm told it doesn't hurt.'

'Well, that's the theory, but if you belted yourself with one, I'm not sure you'd agree...'

'You go, girl,' David said to the television, pumping a raised fist.

'...As to running faster, I can't see how. They're like any other athlete. If they've got the desire to win, they'll run as fast as they can. If not, no amount of whipping is going to help.'

'You're actually trying to get whips banned completely, aren't you?'

'Yes. When the Cup Carnival is over I'm going to start actively lobbying the various racing bodies. Currently most jockeys carry a whip, except ours, of course. So what would be the difference if nobody did? Everyone would have the same advantage or disadvantage.'

'*But don't jockeys also use the whip to keep the horse straight?*'

'*So I've heard. But I think there's a lot to be said for jockeys keeping both hands on the reins and not having the distraction of a whip, not to mention the disruption to balance. We've worked hard to train our horses to move away from the leg so Maddie, our jockey—a very talented and compassionate horsewoman—can put them where she wants on the track. Take Howie's— sorry, Hazardous Waste's—run in the Underwood Stakes. He ran wide and avoided being caught up in the kerfuffle on the turn...*'

'Hope we're all going to rate a mention,' Bernadette said.

'And what part have you played, my darling?' David asked.

'Um…'

'My point exactly! Be prepared to be disappointed, sweet pea.'

'Well, I did send the cats.'

'Shush, you two,' Claire said.

'Don't get your knickers in a knot,' David said, smiling sweetly. 'I'm recording it—on DVD—so it'll be available for all eternity.'

'*Speaking of Hazardous Waste, how is he doing?*'

'*Almost completely back to form.*'

'*That's amazing—only a month ago people were saying his career might be over.*'

'*Well, as we all know, Mike, the Spring Car-*'

*nival brings about all sorts of melodrama. But
seriously, it might have been, had it not been
for our vet, Will Douglas.'*

'There's your mention, Will. Only me and Bernie
left,' David said.

'Don't forget Sandy and Terry. They've played a part
in all this,' Will joined in.

'And the caravan,' David added.

'No, that's already covered—it's the backdrop,' Will
said.

'Ah, yes, so it is.'

'Would you lot just shut up and let me enjoy my fifteen minutes of fame,' Claire snapped.

They made a show of shooting each other pained
expressions of guilt before returning their silent attention to the screen.

*'...Yes, I've heard him described as a miracle
worker.'*

*'Well, to us he is. Paycheque's career—his
life, in fact—was considered over before he in-
tervened.'*

'Would you care to elaborate?'

*'Well, a traditional vet, who shall remain
nameless, advised euthanasia after Paycheque
tore a tendon during training. But we sought another opinion and were lucky to find Will.'*

*'And is it true you had saved Paycheque from
the slaughterhouse previously?'*

*'Yes. When Dad became ill last year the horses
were dispersed. Apparently Paycheque clashed
with a number of trainers and ended up there. I*

tracked him down and bought him back—it was terrible, I prefer not to think about it.'

'What inspired his name?'

'Well, it's a bit ironic, really. Dad called him Paycheque in the hope that the potential he saw would pay off. And when I found him again it was part of my redundancy payout—effectively my last paycheque—that paid for him.'

A collective sigh of 'ahh' reverberated around the room.

Claire shot them all a sharp glare. A couple of suppressed giggles escaped before silence was restored.

'Well, it's certainly paid off, so to speak, hasn't it?'

'Yes.'

'And no doubt there's more to come. Claire, can you give us an exclusive? Will he line up for the Cup on Tuesday? And what about Hazardous Waste?'

'Sorry, Mike. We've yet to make a decision ourselves. About either horse.'

'Will it be down to track conditions?'

'Of course, the track is a consideration, especially given their recent injuries, but it will more come down to how they feel on the day.'

'Sorry, I don't follow...'

'Well, we all have good and bad days.'

'You're saying it's somehow up to the horses themselves?'

'Yes.'

'So, you'd actually consider scratching one

or both horses when they're in form and have a chance of winning Australia's most prestigious race?'

'We've had a great run, really enjoyed the Carnival. For us, there really is nothing more to prove. If they want to run, we'll let them. If not, they won't.'

'But how will you know?'

'Intuition, gut feeling, the way the pieces of the puzzle of the day fall into place.'

'You're not serious, are you?'

'Well, Mike, hindsight tells us most things happen for a reason. By being more aware of the bigger picture, there's a chance of avoiding a lot of the things that can go wrong.'

'You mean God?'

'Not necessarily. Call it what you want, but there's a lot in life that's beyond our control. I've learnt the hard way that life becomes easier if you just let some things go...'

Derek squeezed Claire hard to him.

'There are viewers out there right now saying you're mad.'

'Only the narrow-minded, Mike.'

'Well, that's all we have time for. Thank you, Claire McIntyre, for taking time from your busy schedule. Now it's back to the studio for the latest racing results and other sports news...'

Claire smiled to herself. They made it sound like a live interview, which of course it wasn't. And there had been many more questions she'd answered. It seemed her ideas were a little much for the butch sports reporter, or the powers that be back in the editing suite. She wasn't surprised—a year ago she would probably have had the same reaction herself.

The group on the cream sofas began cheering and clapping.

'That's my girl. Claire, the enlightened spirit,' Bernie said with genuine pride.

Jack quickly brushed at the corner of his eye and swallowed deeply. He'd remained silent during the interview, and now Claire wondered with a stab of guilt whether he was feeling overshadowed, left out. She really should have insisted on including him. *What if his initial protests had just been out of politeness?* Her throat constricted. The whole trip was just one big roller-coaster of emotion.

'Coffee, tea, more wine, anyone?' Will asked, getting up and going to the open-plan kitchen behind the granite-topped bench.

Slowly David, Bernadette and Maddie unwrapped their legs and made their way over to assist Will.

'A tea would be great, thanks, after you've pointed me to the nearest loo,' Jack called, getting up.

'End of the hall,' Will called.

Claire cornered Jack in the bathroom while he was washing his hands. He seemed cheery enough, but Claire couldn't leave it unsaid.

'Dad, I'm really sorry you were left out…'

'Sorry?'

'Well, the television piece. I did say a whole lot about you—they must have cut it.'

'I thought it was great. If I'd wanted to be included I'd have agreed to be interviewed.'

'So you're not upset?'

'No. What makes you think I'd be upset?'

'Dad, I saw you right at the end. The… You seemed upset.'

'Oh, that. Well, don't tell anyone, can't have them thinking I'm a big old wuss.' He put his arm around Claire and held her tightly to him. 'Claire, the few tears, which I will never admit to again, were for you. I'm just so proud of how you've dealt with everything you've been through, especially this past year. You're a remarkable person, Claire McIntyre, and wonderful horsewoman. And just like Howie and Paycheque, you've got nothing to prove, to me or anyone else.'

Claire managed a lip-trembling nod before putting her head on her father's shoulder, and indulging in a few moments of unabated sobbing.

Jack McIntyre carefully turned his daughter away from him and said, 'Come on, time to pull yourself together. We've still got a little way to go yet.'

'Yeah, we have,' she said, smiling through her sodden lashes.

First Jack and then Claire returned to the spacious living area, where the goings-on had continued uninterrupted. One by one everyone returned to the sofas with their chosen beverages. Will put a mug in front of Jack. Claire noticed some odd looks and hushed words being exchanged between Bernadette and David, before Bernie disappeared and returned a few seconds later with a soft, squishy-looking package wrapped in gold.

Bernadette cleared her throat and spoke carefully. 'This is a gift from David, Will, Derek and I, to commemorate the first of hopefully many interstate trips, and to say how proud we are of your journey, whether it includes the Cup or not. Here you are, Jack, as the longest serving member of Team McIntyre.'

'Thank you, all of you,' Jack said, accepting the package and casting his eyes around the assembled group clutching their hands with childlike eagerness.

He spent a few perplexed moments trying to untie the gold ribbon before submitting to the cries of 'Just rip it open!' With the package on his lap, he tore the thin paper off to reveal carefully folded silk fabric displaying their bright racing colours.

'They're beautiful,' Claire whispered as Jack held up the first of two brand-new racing silks, tears clearly evident in his wise old eyes.

'We had your old ones copied,' David said.

'They're just perfect,' Claire said, getting up and hugging each of her friends in turn.

She couldn't believe how bright the gold and red shone: like shimmering flames. When they'd decided to make the journey, she'd wanted to suggest replacing the faded set, but hadn't been able to broach the subject with her father. Theirs were more than bits of shiny cloth worn by their jockey—the current set had been made by her mother just weeks before her death. The design, taken from the McIntyre family crest, was a silent reminder of their need to stick together.

Once, Claire had dismissed her father and his apparent contentment in rural mediocrity for a life of corporate excess in the city. What was worse, she knew he had seen her disappointment and shame whenever she'd visited with Keith. Even as adults, children could be so cruel.

But they were past all that now, she told herself as she accepted with a smile the silks being handed to her. Everyone in the room had played their part. But there was one absent person—Keith—without whom none of it would have happened. She studied the design of a red eagle with wings outstretched on gold background and black sleeves.

'Look inside,' Bernadette urged.

Claire frowned at the thin buttoned-up shirt. What was she looking for? What could be inside? After considerable searching, she finally found it. There was a black label sewn over the maker's tag, embroidered with gold cursive print, not unlike Bernadette's large sprawling hand. On it was their family motto in Latin: 'Per ardua'.

'Through difficulties,' Claire translated quietly.

Epilogue

They were in the Flemington enclosure on the first Tuesday in November. In less than half an hour, Australia and much of the world would stop for the three and a half minutes it took for the Melbourne Cup—The Race That Stops the Nation—to be run.

Claire was shaking with nerves as she struggled to hoist Maddie into the saddle, but for once Paycheque made it easy by standing still. Everyone had been relieved to find him in a good mood that morning. Claire had barely slept, and now she was beginning to feel headachey and wobbly on her feet, just as she'd felt every time she competed at Pony Club.

Back then it was pressure from her mother. Today, she tried to tell herself it was excitement, that they'd come so far they really couldn't fail. But she knew that wasn't true. The Cup had gone global. Practically the whole world was watching. This was their chance to prove themselves.

'Now, Maddie, you're totally sure about this?'

'Absolutely.'

'Really, it's not too late to back out.'

'Not a chance. I'm fine.'

'Honestly, we won't think less of you.'

'Claire, it'll be all right. We've talked about it. I'll take him easy—keep him out as far away from the others as I can. We'll be okay. But seriously, you need to calm down. You'll have a heart attack or something.'

'I can't. I…'

'And breathe! Claire, you've got to breathe!'

'I'm just nervous because of all the hype, the cameras. But please don't think that means there's pressure on you. Honestly, I just want you both back safe and sound.'

'I know.'

Paycheque stood with his head hung slightly. Claire was pleased he was calm, but he hardly looked like an athlete primed for the race of his life. He looked half-asleep. *Well, better that than naughty and bad-tempered*, she supposed.

'You look after her, won't you, mate?' She stroked his face. 'Maddie, whatever you do, steer clear of both Todd Newman's runners. Who knows what he's put his jockeys up to.'

'Claire, I know.'

'And remember. Don't let him get near the rail—either of them.'

'You already said that.'

'Right, yes, so I did—sorry.'

'Claire, it's time for me to go.'

'Yes, yes, but there's something else I have to tell you—I know there is—but I can't remember.'

'We've gone over everything a million times—what's going to happen is going to happen. Look, I've really gotta go.'

'Yes, go. Good luck and stay safe, Maddie.'

'I will. But we're not going anywhere if you don't let go of my reins,' Maddie said with a laugh.

'Shit! Sorry, I didn't realise.' Claire's hand was fused around the reins and she had to consciously tell herself to open it. 'Good luck,' she said, stepping back to let Maddie pass.

'Thanks. See ya.'

Claire stared after Maddie. She couldn't believe how calm the kid was. This was the Melbourne Cup and Maddie looked as if she was just going out for a casual stroll. She watched as Paycheque joined the queue and was swept out onto the lush green track. His small stature meant he was dwarfed by the bigger horses around him. Only when he was cantering up the straight towards the barriers did she turn back to the grandstand where the rest of Team McIntyre was waiting.

Derek appeared beside her as she left the enclosure. 'All well with them?' he asked.

'Yep. It's only me who's a mess of nerves,' she said, trying to laugh it off.

'Well, Maddie's always been pretty good under pressure. Come on, Bernie and the others have saved us a great spot.' Derek grabbed her hand and tugged.

They edged their way between the small groups of people sitting on chairs and lounging on picnic rugs on the grass, the effects of too much sun and alcohol apparent in their dishevelment and the litter around them.

'I really hope I didn't upset her with my rambling,' Claire said to Derek, speaking loudly to be heard over the roar of the goings-on around them.

'She knows what you're like. She won't have given

it a second thought, so stop beating yourself up!' he shouted back. 'Quick, come on.'

They fought their way in slow motion through the crowd standing shoulder to shoulder in the area below the stands. No one wanted to let them through and risk losing their position.

'Bet the crowd parts like the Red Sea for Gai and David,' she growled, but her voice was carried away by the noise of revellers.

Claire was exhausted by the time she got to the foot of the stairs. Looking up at the stands looming in front of them, she really didn't think she had the stamina to climb all those steps.

'Quick, come on,' Derek urged. 'We don't have long.'

'I don't think I can,' she said, clutching at the stitch now forming at her left side.

'Well, you won't see a thing from down here,' Derek growled, stopping and facing her.

'Might be a good idea, though. In case something happens and Maddie needs me.' They were being bumped by people all around them trying to get into the stands.

'There's nothing you can do now. It's out of your hands. I'm sure as hell not missing it, and neither are you. Come on!'

Claire allowed herself to be practically dragged up the steps and into the middle of the stand to where Bernie, David, Will and Jack were spread out, saving extra space for them. They were directly opposite the finish line and had a great view of the giant screen. But they were so far up, and the stand was so steep, that Claire felt dizzy when she looked down at the crowd they'd just made their way through.

'You okay?' Bernie shouted. 'You look terribly pale.'

'No. I want to throw up I'm so nervous,' she shouted back with a tight laugh.

'Well, focus on something else, like how well you've done to get here.'

Claire cast an eye across to where Jack stood beside Will. He was an awful grey colour, looked even worse than she felt. He gave her a thumbs-up sign and a broad smile. As he did, a little colour returned to his face. She grinned and gave a thumbs up in return, and let herself feel a tiny sense of relief.

'God, I hope he's going to be okay at the barriers. Maybe I should have stayed down...'

'Shut up, Claire!' Bernie, David and Derek said in unison.

She turned her attention to the screen beside the finish line, as one by one the horses were shown leaving the circling group behind the barriers and entering their stalls. She was just in time to watch Maddie turn and walk Paycheque forward into his allocated space.

'He's in,' she muttered, and let out a sigh of relief.

Within seconds the orange light atop the barriers was spinning, signalling that it was safe to start the race. A split second later the gates sprung open and the caller announced, 'And they're off and racing...' The horses leapt out in a mass of colour. They began making their way down the track before splitting into two groups and taking a side each.

Claire glanced at both groups but couldn't make out Maddie and Paycheque in either. She grabbed the binoculars from Bernie, put them to her eyes and looked for them coming up the straight. Paycheque suddenly appeared: behind the horses that had left the two groups to make a third in front.

Claire was pleased to see him out on his own, but she didn't like how fast he seemed to be travelling. They still had over three thousand metres to go. Going out too hard could be a fatal move in a race this long.

'Come on, steady now. Ease him back. Let him settle,' she whispered, barely able to hear her voice above her heart beating against her ribs, and the pounding of blood inside her ears.

And as she watched through the binoculars, he did settle slightly. Maddie was low over him and there was a nice curve to the reins along his neck. Claire nodded in time with his rhythm, trying to count the beats of his stride between hundred-metre markers, in an effort to both keep herself calm and calculate his speed.

But as the horses came in front, Claire pulled the binoculars away and let herself enjoy the deep, hollow thunder of nineteen sets of hooves on the turf, and the flap of leather as they whizzed by in a blur below the stands. She loved those sounds, savoured them every Cup Day.

She returned her eyes to the hard black sockets of the binoculars. Paycheque was holding his own now in the middle of the second pack. Despite his speed, he seemed to be in a great rhythm, calm. He was starting to darken with sweat but no more than all those around him. He was still on a nice long, low frame, but not too low to suggest he was tiring. With the pounding of blood in her ears, Claire could hardly hear the race caller or the crowd going wild around her. She was being bumped and shoved from all directions, but still she kept the binoculars to her eyes and her focus on the horses completing the first turn. Paycheque was now on the far side of the track and out of her line of sight.

Claire lowered the binoculars and looked around her. Bernadette was biting on her fingernails, David on his bottom lip. Both had their eyes glued to the big screen, barely blinking. Will's lips were moving as if he was saying a mantra over and over. She accidently bumped Derek as she looked across at Jack. He moved his binoculars away long enough to offer Claire a quick grin before returning to the action on the track.

Jack had his binoculars clamped hard against his face—the same set he'd carted everywhere for the past thirty-odd years. He, too, was nodding in time with the rhythm of the horses, his lips muttering encouragement and instructions to Maddie and Paycheque, and curses to those getting too close. Claire couldn't hear him but had stood beside him at enough races to know what was likely being said. She wondered if he was the mess of nerves inside that she was—he looked so damn calm. Then he mouthed the words, 'No! Maddie, watch out!'

Quickly Claire refocussed on the last group of horses making their way down the straight at the far side of the track. She was just in time to see a jockey in Todd Newman's colours come in close to Paycheque and elbow Maddie in the ribs.

'Leave her alone!' Claire growled. She searched the track for an escape route for Maddie, but other horses were closing in around her. Both of Todd's horses now flanked Paycheque, their sixteen-plus hands dwarfing his fifteen. Maddie was turning her head from side to side, no doubt giving each jockey a mouthful.

They were approaching the final long sweeping turn. As Claire watched, Paycheque moved across closer to the outside. They'd talked about Maddie staying out wide until halfway round and then cutting the corner as much as she could, depending on how balanced Paycheque felt and how tired he was. Then, once the corner was complete and they were heading up the final straight, Maddie was to take him as far away from the others as possible, to avoid the flurry of whips and flapping reins, and prevent him losing his focus and getting a fright.

If the majority then went wide she'd take Paycheque nearer the middle, but if they hugged the inside rail then she'd take him right to the outside. But the leading horses were still in two groups—against both the inside and outside rails. Behind them was a group coming up the middle and closing in fast. Paycheque was about to be swallowed up by the larger horses. *Shit, where was she going to go?*

Claire closed her watering eyes for a split second while she wondered what advice she'd give Maddie if she had the chance—not that it mattered; she didn't. She opened her eyes and refocussed on the race unfolding down below to her far left. About six horses were right on Paycheque's heels. His head was too low now, he was starting to fade.

'Hang on, mate. Hang on—nearly there,' she urged. There were now less than four hundred metres to go.

At that moment the group came alongside Paycheque, and Claire realised the colours on the bobbing helmets of the jockeys either side of him were those of Todd Newman.

'Maddie, get out of there,' she whispered.

But there was nowhere to go—they were stuck. She saw Maddie's head turn twice—taking note of who was alongside. Claire didn't want to watch, didn't want to think about the argy-bargy and intimidation that was going on. She hoped Derek wasn't watching but when she heard him shout, 'Bloody hell!' she knew he was seeing what she was. Her heart was in her mouth. They were well on their way down the straight now. The crowd was a deafening, screaming roar, and people were leaping up and down. The people on the grass surged towards the fence to urge on the horses they'd backed. There were three hundred metres to go.

The last group of horses had fallen way behind, joined by a couple who'd gone out too fast at the start. She couldn't see Paycheque, but he had to be between the large chestnut and the grey—he hadn't surged forward and he hadn't dropped back. The jockeys were flapping their whips furiously—Paycheque would be copping it on the shoulder and neck from both sides. *The poor thing must be terrified*, she thought, biting her lip.

'Just pull him up, Maddie,' she urged. 'It's not worth it.'

There were now only one hundred and fifty metres to go. The frontrunners seemed to be slowing slightly, despite the furious flapping of whips and pushing of hands up and down necks urging them on. Paycheque and Todd's two horses were now right behind them. Claire had been so worried about Paycheque being caught between the two horses that she hadn't taken notice of where the group was in relation to the rest of the field.

Claire's heart rate suddenly slowed. The pounding against her ribs seemed to be only every second beat. Her mouth was dry, and the inside of her ears was strangely quiet: the blood pounding through them had stopped. It seemed to grow still around her—she

could see the mouths of those all around her opening
and shutting, screaming out encouragement. Her eyes
were bruised from the binoculars being jammed against
them, but she couldn't pull them away. There were only
a few seconds to go.

She watched as the two big horses peeled away from
Paycheque, the chestnut on the inside and the grey ma-
noeuvring behind him slightly to join his stablemate at
the inside rail. Paycheque was now on his own at the
heels of the frontrunners, two from the outside. The
finish line was closing in fast.

'Come on! Go, go, go!' Claire shouted.

Maddie was crouched lower than she'd ever seen
her. Claire's mouth fell open and she just stared as Paycheque surged forward to join the frontrunners spread
most of the way across the track. She couldn't speak.
She watched the mirrored finish line swallowed up by
a mass of horseflesh and coloured silks. Her heart rate
quickened to a furious pounding again.

And then the horses were slowing and scattering as
they rounded the bend past the finish. Claire let out a
big sigh and lowered the binoculars. She stared at the
television screen, where the result was frozen but inde-
cipherable. She tried to hear what the commentator was
saying but the crowd below was too loud. She looked
around her at Bernadette, David, Will, Derek and Jack.
They were standing still, shrugging, and exchanging
questioning expressions. The crowd was subdued. No
one was tearing up betting slips or tossing them away.
There was a collective focus on the giant screen in front.

Out on the track, the horses were cooling down, the
jockeys chatting amongst themselves. A television reporter was making his way through the group on his

small bay horse, clearly identifiable by the station's logo on his saddle cloth and the microphone in his hand. He'd have his work cut out trying to interview the winning few horses when around six were caught up in a photo finish. Even the commentator hadn't deciphered the result yet.

'Jesus, this is excruciating,' Bernie said.

Damn right, thought Claire. All those times she'd watched footage of the winning connections instantly leaping about, hugging each other, celebrating their win. And here she was, finally participating, not swanning around a corporate box, and they had the most complicated result—the biggest photo finish—on record. But they'd done it—Paycheque and Maddie had got around safely. Though she'd better check for sure, she suddenly thought, putting the binoculars back to her bruised eyes.

Maddie and Paycheque were looking as relaxed as ever. They'd turned and were heading slowly back towards the finish line. Maddie's legs were out of the stirrups and hanging down Paycheque's sides. She held the reins by the buckle and Paycheque's head was stretched low. They looked as casual as if they had just finished a Pony Club lesson, not Australia's most famous horserace.

Claire let out a gasp as Paycheque gave a sudden jerk on the reins, lowered his head right to the ground and snatched up a chunk of Flemington turf. Maddie was caught unawares and was almost sent tumbling over his neck. Managing to save herself just in time, she gave the horse a light reproachful slap. Meanwhile Paycheque was trying to dislodge the clod of dirt that was attached to his mouthful of grass by tossing his head up and down furiously.

'Little monster,' Claire said, chuckling.

'What?' Bernadette asked.

Without a word Claire handed her the binoculars. There were chuckles all around as Derek and Jack took a look through theirs.

'Typical,' Bernie said.

'Better get down there,' Claire said, and they all made their way down the steps of the grandstand.

'Bit of an anticlimax, not knowing where you came,' Derek said from beside her. 'And there are bound to be some protests yet. Might be one from Maddie by the looks of what went on out there with Todd's boys.'

'No, we won't be protesting. I'm just glad they're both back safe and well.'

They were now at the rail watching Maddie and Paycheque make their way towards them. Claire looked for any signs his gait was uneven, that he was lame. But he looked fine. Tired, but fine. The horse that had twice been condemned to death had just run the Melbourne Cup—watched by the whole of Australia and much of the world.

'Bloody hell,' Claire said under her breath, the enormity of it just hitting her.

'What? What's wrong?' Derek asked.

'Shh,' she said, and tilted her head to listen to the commentator reading out the preliminary results.

'...fifth, Paycheque, sixth, Ragamuffin...'

She stared at Derek with big wide eyes. 'Derek, did you hear that? Oh! My! God! Paycheque's just run fifth in the Melbourne bloody Cup! I don't believe it!'

They grabbed each other and leapt up and down hugging, not caring what cameras were on them or who was watching.

Claire pulled away first and looked up at Derek. 'I'm sorry you didn't have a runner.'

'It was worth it to see you this happy, Claire. Anyway, I will next year when you're training my horses.'

'What?'

'You heard me. I want to bring my horses to Team McIntyre.'

'Even with our whacky training methods and weird ideas?'

'*Especially* with your whacky training methods and weird ideas.' Derek pulled her to him again and buried his face in her hair. 'Marry me, Claire McIntyre.'

'I thought you'd never ask,' Claire whispered back.

'So, is that a yes?'

'Yes, Derek Anderson. That is a yes.'

* * * * *

ACKNOWLEDGEMENTS

Thank you to Michelle Meade and the wonderful team at my publishers, and Sue Brockhoff, Annabel Blay, Cristina Lee, Michelle Laforest and the lovely people at Harlequin Australia for all the amazing support. Special thanks to Haylee Nash for seeing the potential in my original manuscript and for taking a chance on me, and to editor Lachlan Jobbins for bringing out the best in my writing. I am so truly grateful to everyone who has had a hand in turning my loose pages into such lovely books and played a part in making my dreams come true.

Thanks to my very dear friends Carole and Ken Wetherby, Mel Sabeeney and Arlene Somerville, who provide so much love, support and encouragement — you all mean the world to me.

Thanks to Andrew Holmes of the Victorian Racing Club (in Australia) and Marilyn Smith of TAFE South Australia for clarifying some of the technical details of horseracing. Special thanks to Dr Douglas Wilson of the Holistic Veterinary Clinic for being so very generous with his time in providing detailed information around the injury and recovery of my fictitious racehorse. If you'd like to know more about Dr Wilson's fantastic work, please go to www.holisticveton line.com. Any errors or inaccuracies are my own or due to taking creative liberties.

  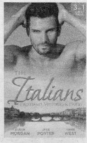

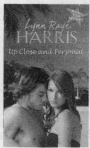

MILLS & BOON®

It's Got to be Perfect

IT'S GOT TO BE
Perfect

UNCORRECTED
PROOF COPY

HALEY HILL

* cover in development

When Ellie Rigby throws her three-carat engagement ring into the gutter, she is certain of only one thing. She has yet to know true love!

Fed up with disastrous internet dates and conflicting advice from her friends, Ellie decides to take matters into her own hands. Starting a dating agency, Ellie becomes an expert in love. Well, that is until a match with one of her clients, charming, infuriating Nick, has her questioning everything she's ever thought about love...

Order yours today at
www.millsandboon.co.uk

Don't miss Sarah Morgan's next Puffin Island story

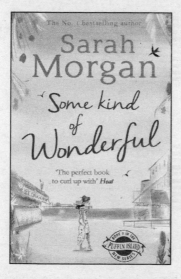

Brittany Forrest has stayed away from Puffin Island since her relationship with Zach Flynn went bad. They were married for ten days and only just managed not to kill each other by the end of the honeymoon.

But, when a broken arm means she must return, Brittany moves back to her Puffin Island home. Only to discover that Zach is there as well.

Will a summer together help two lovers reunite or will their stormy relationship crash on to the rocks of Puffin Island?

Some Kind of Wonderful
COMING JULY 2015
Pre-order your copy today